WHAT THE FUTURE HOLDS

CHOOSING TOMORROW, BOOK 3

Written by Diane Kann

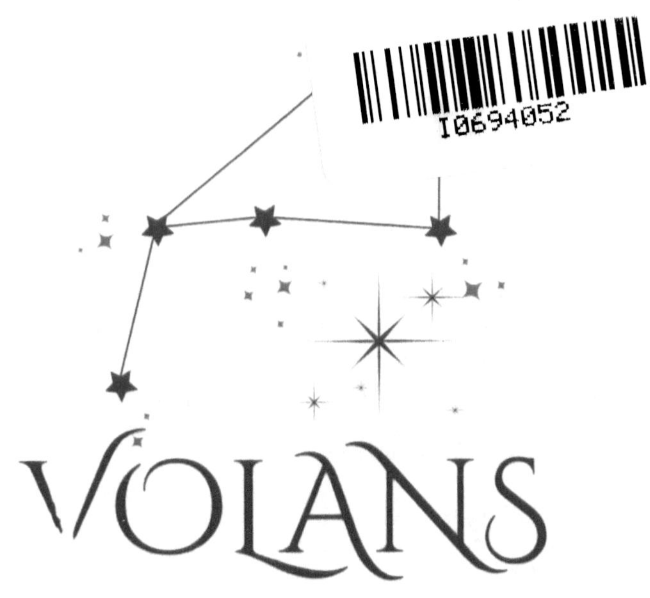

Brought to you by Volans Galaxy Press

Published by Kannceptual Creations LLC

An imprint of Volans Galaxy Press

ISBN: 978-1-971356-46-4

Printed in the United States of America

First Edition, January 2026

CONTENTS

AUTHOR'S BIOGRAPHY

Diane Kann writes sweet romance stories that celebrate love, second chances, and the quiet moments that change everything. Her stories focus on emotional connection, gentle healing, and relationships built on trust, hope, and heart.

When she's not writing, Diane enjoys spending time in nature with her family and dogs, finding inspiration in peaceful landscapes and everyday moments, and dreaming up tender stories rooted in compassion.

CHAPTER ONE

THE WHISPERS OF PERMANENCE

The scent of pine, sharp and clean, had always been a solace to Mara. But now, it felt different. It wasn't just the smell of survival, of the forest providing shelter after the storm had passed. It was the fragrance of permanence, of a future intentionally built, molecule by molecule, upon the scorched earth of their past. She stood beside Eli on the gentle rise overlooking Havenridge, the late afternoon sun casting long, benevolent shadows across the valley.

The buildings, once skeletal remains, now stood sturdy and whole, their windows reflecting the golden light like welcoming eyes. The air, usually alive with the frantic energy of those simply trying to endure, now vibrated with a quieter, more profound hum – the murmur of progress, of lives finding their rhythm.

This was the landscape of their hard-won stability. Gone were the days of scrambling for resources, of counting every salvaged nail, every rationed meal. The physical reconstruction, the monumental task that had consumed them for so long, was complete. The scars of the struggle remained, etched into the very soul of Havenridge, but they were no longer open wounds. They were a testament to resilience, a constant reminder of the collective spirit that had refused to be extinguished. Mara traced the line of the horizon with her gaze, the familiar ache of vulnerability momentarily lulling into a gentle curiosity. They were no longer just survivors. They were architects.

Eli stood beside her, his presence a familiar anchor. He didn't need words to communicate the shared sense of accomplishment that settled between them like a warm blanket. His quiet observation of the valley, the slight tilt of his head as he absorbed the scene, mirrored her own internal contemplation. He, too, had shed the skin of a man solely reacting to circumstances, emerging as someone who actively shaped them. His hands, calloused and strong from years of labor, now rested lightly on the weathered railing of the overlook, a gesture of quiet possession, not of ownership, but of profound investment.

"It's... quiet," Mara murmured, her voice soft, almost a whisper against the vastness of the sky.

Eli turned to her, his eyes, the color of a clear forest stream, holding a depth of understanding that needed no explanation. "It's the sound of building," he replied, his voice a low rumble. "Not just walls and roofs, but foundations. Of lives."

Mara nodded, a slow, thoughtful movement. The spirit of rebuilding, that raw, urgent drive that had propelled them through the darkest of times, was still present, woven into the very fabric of Havenridge. But it was evolving. It was no longer a desperate scramble against oblivion, but a deliberate cultivation, a nurturing of something that deserved to endure. The resilience that had once been a fierce shield was now a steady undercurrent, powering a quiet confidence. They had learned the hard lessons of interdependence, of relying on each other not out of desperation, but out of a deep-seated understanding of shared strength. Each salvaged beam, each repaired window, each community gathering had been a brushstroke in a larger masterpiece, a testament to their collective spirit.

She remembered the early days, the raw uncertainty that had hung heavy in the air, thicker than any smoke from the fires that had ravaged their home. The fear had been a constant companion, whispering doubts in the dead of night. But they had pushed through it, one sunrise at a time. They had learned to trust not just their own capabilities, but the capabilities of others, weaving a tapestry of support that was as strong as any woven from lumber and nails. The community's collective resilience wasn't just about surviving hardship; it was about learning from it, about transforming the ashes of their past into the fertile ground for a future.

Eli's gaze drifted back to the cluster of homes nestled in the valley. "Remember when we thought this view was just... land?" he mused aloud, a ghost of a smile playing on his lips. "Now, it's... ours. Not in ownership, but in shared responsibility."

Mara understood precisely what he meant. The land, once a resource to be defended, a battleground against the elements, had become something more profound. It was a living entity, a legacy they were entrusted to protect and nurture. The scent of pine, the rustle of leaves, the very earth beneath their feet – it all spoke of a deeper connection, a bond forged not just through shared struggle, but through a shared commitment to its well-being. The initial rebuilding had been an act of survival; this new phase was an act of stewardship, a conscious decision to honor the land that had sustained them.

She thought of the carefully planned agricultural plots, the sustainable forestry initiatives already in motion, the nascent efforts to protect the local watershed. These weren't just practical measures; they were expressions of gratitude, acknowledgments of their place within a larger ecosystem. The resilience that had seen them through the immediate crisis was now being channeled into foresight, into ensuring that the beauty and bounty of Havenridge would be there for generations to come. The lessons learned from scarcity had bred a deep appreciation for abundance, and a fierce determination to manage it wisely.

The physical reconstruction was, in many ways, the easier part. The rebuilding of structures, however complex, was a tangible task with a clear endpoint. The emotional landscape, however, was a far more intricate terrain, constantly shifting, evolving. The stability they had fought so hard to achieve was creating its own set of challenges, subtle but significant, that nudged at the edges of their hard-won peace. They had conquered the external threats, but now, the internal shifts, the quiet redefinitions of self and community, were beginning to demand their attention.

Mara felt a familiar stir, a faint tremor beneath the surface of her contentment. It was the whisper of that old fear, the one that always seemed to lie dormant, waiting for the opportune moment to resurface. The idea of permanence, of solidifying their lives, their community, their relationships, was a double-edged sword. It offered security, a bulwark against the chaos they had known, but it also carried the subtle threat of stagnation, of boundaries that could, if not carefully managed, become cages.

She looked at Eli, his profile etched against the vast expanse of the sky. He embodied a quiet strength, a groundedness that had been her constant support. But as they stood on the cusp of this new era, an era defined by formalization and enduring legacies, she wondered if the very stability they had built might also require them to confront aspects of themselves and their relationship that had previously been obscured by the urgency of survival.

The scent of pine, once a simple comfort, now carried the weight of their shared history, a reminder of the storms they had weathered together. But beneath the scent of pine, there was something else, too. The subtle fragrance of wild roses, just beginning to bloom along the edges of the path, a promise of sweetness, of enduring beauty, blooming from the resilience that had been their bedrock. It was the scent of a future not just rebuilt, but reimagined, and Mara, for the first time, felt a genuine curiosity about what that reimagining might hold.

The emotional landscape was indeed shifting, and while it brought with it its own set of uncertainties, it also felt like the fertile ground for a deeper, more profound kind of growth. The hard-won stability was not an end, but a beginning, and the quiet hum of progress was the prelude to a new, more complex, but ultimately more hopeful chapter.

The worn oak table, scarred by countless meals and urgent planning sessions, now bore a different kind of weight. It was no longer just a surface for survival; it was a foundation for permanence. Mara watched from her usual place at the periphery of these gatherings, a quiet observer amidst the focused energy of Havenridge's established leaders. The scent of woodsmoke, a comforting staple of their communal life, mingled with the crisp, clean aroma of the newly drafted documents spread across the polished surface. These were not mere blueprints for more buildings or revised rationing schedules. These were architectural plans for the very soul of Havenridge, designed to withstand the passage of time, to outlast the hands that had painstakingly built it.

The discussions were deliberate, nuanced. Words like 'stewardship,' 'succession,' and 'legacy', once abstract concepts whispered in moments of profound hope, were now concrete proposals, laid out with the careful precision of seasoned planners. It was a transition Mara had sensed was coming, a natural evolution from the fierce, immediate need to survive to the considered, long-term commitment to thrive. The very air in the room seemed to hum with a new kind of resolve, a collective understanding that their work had transcended mere physical reconstruction. They were now engaged in the profound act of embedding their spirit, their values, into the very fabric of this place, ensuring that Havenridge would not simply endure, but flourish.

Eli, his brow furrowed in concentration, his hand steady as he gestured towards a particularly dense section of legal text, was the anchor of these proceedings. His practicality, once focused on the immediate needs of rebuilding, now steered their collective vision toward the horizon. He had a way of distilling complex ideas into actionable steps, of translating hope into tangible plans. Mara felt a familiar warmth spread through her chest as she watched him, a quiet pride in the man who had, alongside her, navigated the treacherous currents of their past and was now, with unwavering resolve, charting their future.

"The land stewardship agreements," Eli's voice cut through the thoughtful silence, calm and assured, "outline our commitment to not just utilizing, but nurturing Havenridge's natural resources. It's a pact, not just with ourselves, but with the generations who will follow. We're defining how we harvest, how we replant, how we protect the watershed – not as a matter of immediate necessity, but as a matter of sacred trust." He tapped a finger on the parchment. "This ensures that the bounty we've fought so hard to reclaim is sustained, that the delicate balance we've come to understand remains intact."

Beside him, Elara, whose knowledge of the local flora and fauna was as deep as her commitment to Havenridge, nodded in agreement. Her role in shaping these agreements had been instrumental, her insights into the interconnectedness of the valley's ecosystem ensuring that practicality was balanced with reverence. "It's about more than just sustainability," she added, her voice soft but firm. "It's about honoring the resilience of this land, recognizing that it, too, has weathered storms and deserves our careful guardianship. These aren't just rules; they're promises."

Then came the discussion of leadership succession. This was the delicate heart of their endeavor, the acknowledgment that no single person, no matter how dedicated, could guarantee Havenridge's future indefinitely. The individuals gathered around the table represented the pillars of their community, the ones who had proven their mettle, their wisdom, their unwavering commitment. Now, they had to consider who would carry that torch forward, how knowledge would be passed on, and how the continuity of their shared vision would be secured.

"We've identified potential candidates for key roles," Eli continued, his gaze sweeping across the faces of his peers. "Individuals who have demonstrated not only competence but a deep understanding of Havenridge's ethos. The proposals include mentorship programs, cross-training initiatives, and a defined pathway for leadership transition that prioritizes collaboration and shared responsibility.

It's not about replacing individuals, but about ensuring a seamless continuation of purpose."

A thoughtful silence followed, each leader absorbing the implications. This was a step into unfamiliar territory, a deliberate move away from the ad-hoc, crisis-driven decision-making that had defined their early years. It was the embodiment of permanence, the construction of a framework designed to outlast the founding generation. Mara felt a complex blend of emotions – pride in the maturity and foresight of her community, and a subtle tremor of apprehension. The very act of formalizing their future felt both exhilarating and daunting.

"It's necessary," Anya, the community's wise elder and matriarch, stated simply, her voice resonating with quiet authority. "We built Havenridge with our hands and our hearts. Now, we must build it with our foresight. This ensures that the sacrifices made, the lives built here, are not subject to the whims of chance. It provides a stable structure, a guiding principle, for those who will come after us."

Mara's gaze drifted to the windows, where the late afternoon sun was beginning to paint the sky in hues of amber and rose. She saw not just the physical landscape of Havenridge, but the invisible architecture of trust, commitment, and shared purpose that was being meticulously constructed within these walls. The challenges they had faced had forged an unbreakable bond, a collective spirit that refused to be extinguished. Now, that spirit was being channeled into a new form of creation, one that promised not just survival, but a lasting, meaningful legacy.

The discussions continued, delving into the specifics of council appointments, conflict resolution protocols, and educational mandates designed to instill Havenridge's core values in the younger generations. Each point was debated, refined, and ultimately agreed upon with a quiet consensus that spoke volumes about their shared commitment. Eli, ever the steady hand, guided the conversation with a combination of firm logic and gentle encouragement, ensuring that every voice was heard and every perspective considered.

Mara found herself drawn to the tangible elements of the proposals – the detailed maps for land management, the organizational charts for leadership succession, the draft charters for community councils. These were not just papers; they were promises, etched in ink, of a future meticulously planned. They represented a profound shift from reacting to circumstances to proactively shaping them, from enduring hardship to cultivating prosperity.

The resilience that had once been their shield was now being transformed into a robust framework, a testament to their growth and their unwavering dedication to building something that would truly last. The scent of pine, though still present, was now overlaid with the crisp, distinct aroma of possibility, the subtle fragrance of a future being deliberately and thoughtfully designed.

The air in the communal hall, though thick with the murmur of collective decision-making, seemed to thin and clarify whenever Mara's gaze found Eli's. It was a silent language they had perfected in the crucible of their shared past, a glance that could convey reassurance, understanding, or a pang of longing. The gravity of the discussions around the oak table – the meticulous planning for Havenridge's enduring future, the careful establishment of leadership succession, the sacred promises being made to the land itself – it all swirled around them, a powerful current of purpose. Yet, amidst this grand design for permanence, an equally profound, albeit far more personal, question had begun to whisper between them.

It wasn't a question spoken aloud, not yet. It was a question held in the lingering touch of hands that had once held only the desperate need for survival, now exploring the contours of comfort and quiet companionship. It was in the way Eli's eyes, usually so focused on the larger picture, would soften when they met Mara's, a momentary softening that spoke of shared memories and a future they both, in their hearts, envisioned together. They had weathered storms that would have splintered lesser bonds, faced down dangers that would have broken weaker spirits. Their shared history was a tapestry woven with threads of fear, resilience, and an unwavering loyalty that had long since deepened into something far more profound.

Mara traced the rim of her worn ceramic mug, the lukewarm herbal tea within a pale imitation of the warmth that often flooded her when she observed Eli. He was a constant, a steady lighthouse in the often-turbulent seas of their existence. She remembered the early days, the sheer, unadulterated terror of their initial displacement, the gnawing hunger, the ever-present threat of the outside world. Eli had been her rock then, his quiet strength a bulwark against despair. He'd been the one to meticulously ration their meager supplies, to scout for safe havens, to offer a steady hand when the ground beneath them felt as if it might crumble. They had leaned on each other, not out of romantic inclination, but out of sheer, primal necessity. Survival had been their only shared language, their only common goal.

But Havenridge had grown, and so had they. The desperate scrabbling for existence had given way to the deliberate cultivation of life. The fear had receded, replaced by a quiet confidence, a burgeoning sense of belonging. And with that shift, the unspoken question had begun to emerge, tentative at first, like the first shoots of spring pushing through frozen earth. It was a question of permanence, not just for their community, but for their partnership. Was this shared existence, forged in fire, destined to remain a matter of shared responsibility, or could it bloom into something more?

She remembered a quiet evening, just a few moons prior, after a particularly grueling harvest. The community had gathered for a rare moment of respite, a shared meal under a sky ablaze with stars. Eli had sat beside her, not out of obligation, but by choice. Their shoulders had brushed, a small, insignificant contact that had nonetheless sent a jolt of something akin to anticipation through her.

He had spoken of the satisfaction of seeing the fruits of their labor, his voice low and content. And then, he had turned to her, his gaze holding hers for a beat longer than necessary. "We did good, Mara," he'd said, a quiet affirmation that had resonated deeper than any public praise. In that moment, she had seen it – not just the co-architect of Havenridge, but the man who had, thread by thread, woven himself into the very fabric of her being.

The irony was not lost on her. They were dedicating weeks, months, to crafting documents that would ensure Havenridge's future for generations to come. They were meticulously planning for leadership succession, ensuring that wisdom and responsibility would be passed down, that the core values of their community would endure. Yet, the most significant union, the one that felt as foundational as the very earth beneath their feet, remained unacknowledged, an unspoken pact held in the quiet spaces between their words.

Elara, usually so attuned to the nuances of human connection, had noticed. Mara saw it in the knowing glances Elara occasionally cast their way, a subtle smile playing on her lips. Elara, who had seen Mara through the darkest of times, who understood the depth of Mara's quiet resilience and Eli's steady competence, she understood the unspoken currents running beneath the surface of their days. Perhaps Elara, in her wisdom, recognized that some questions were too profound to be rushed, that some unions needed to ripen naturally, like the fruit they so carefully tended.

There were moments, stolen fragments of time, that felt like tiny oases in the desert of their communal duties. A shared walk to the western fields at dawn, the mist clinging to the valley floor, the world still hushed and expectant. Eli would often fall into step beside her, his presence a comforting weight. They wouldn't always speak, but the silence between them was charged, alive with an unspoken understanding. He might point out a particularly vibrant cluster of wildflowers, or remark on the dew-kissed spiderwebs glinting in the nascent sunlight. These small observations, insignificant to anyone else, felt like profound revelations to Mara, pieces of a puzzle she was slowly assembling in her heart.

She recalled one such walk, a few days after the initial drafting of the land stewardship agreements. The weight of responsibility, the sheer enormity of securing Havenridge's future, had settled upon her shoulders. She had felt a familiar prickle of anxiety, the echo of past uncertainties. Eli, sensing her mood without her needing to utter a single word, had reached out and gently clasped her forearm. His touch was firm, grounding. "We've faced worse, Mara," he'd said, his voice a low rumble. "We'll face this too. Together." The simple declaration, the unspoken acknowledgment of their shared journey, had been enough to quell the rising tide of her unease. It was in these quiet affirmations, these small gestures of unwavering support, that the unspoken question found its most eloquent expression.

The challenge, Mara mused, was that settling into a shared life, a life of partnership beyond the immediate demands of survival, felt like a different kind of undertaking altogether. Survival had been about immediate action, about instinct, about unwavering focus on the task at hand. Building a life together, a life of shared dreams and quiet companionship, felt more nuanced, more vulnerable. It required a different kind of courage, a willingness to expose the softer parts of oneself, to risk the potential for heartbreak in the pursuit of enduring happiness.

She remembered how, in the early days, their interactions had been defined by practicality. Eli would ask for her assessment of the water reserves, and she would provide it. She would bring him news of any new arrivals or concerns within the smaller settlements, and he would listen with grave consideration. Their conversations were efficient, focused on the well-being of the collective. But lately, the questions had begun to shift.

He would ask about her day, not just in terms of tasks completed, but in terms of how she *felt*. He'd inquire about her well-being, not as a health check, but as a genuine concern for her spirit. And she, in turn, found herself wanting to share the small joys, the fleeting moments of beauty she encountered, with him.

One evening, during a brief lull in the council meetings, Mara had found herself lingering near the entrance of the main hall, watching Eli engage with a group of younger settlers. He was explaining the principles of the new agricultural rotation schedule, his hands moving with practiced ease, his voice patient and clear.

A pang of something akin to possessiveness, a feeling entirely new and startling, had shot through her. It wasn't just that he was a leader; he was *her* Eli, the man who had seen her at her worst and had, through it all, shown her unwavering respect and a quiet kindness that had burrowed deep into her heart.

The very discussions happening around them, the meticulous planning for Havenridge's permanence, amplified the unspoken question. They were building a lasting legacy, a community that would stand the test of time. But what about the legacy they would build together, man and woman, partners not just in rebuilding a world, but in building a life? The thought was both exhilarating and terrifying. It required a vulnerability that felt almost alien after so many years of guarded self-reliance.

She thought back to a particularly difficult winter, years ago. A fever had swept through the community, a chilling reminder of their fragility. Mara had worked tirelessly, tending to the sick, her own exhaustion a constant companion. Eli, despite his own responsibilities, had always ensured she had a moment to rest, a warm meal, a quiet word of encouragement.

He'd never demanded anything from her, never imposed his needs, but his presence had been a constant, unwavering source of strength. She remembered one frigid night, after a particularly harrowing day, of collapsing onto her cot, tears of pure exhaustion streaming down her face. Eli had appeared, not with words of platitude, but with a simple, warm blanket and a silent nod. He'd sat with her for a while, his quiet presence a balm to her frayed nerves, before quietly leaving. That silent vigil, that unspoken understanding of her pain, had spoken volumes more than any declaration of affection. It had been a promise, as potent as any written in the land stewardship agreements.

Now, as they sat in this hall, surrounded by the tangible evidence of their collective foresight, Mara felt the weight of that unspoken question pressing in. The meticulously drafted documents, the carefully considered succession plans, they all pointed towards a future built on stability and enduring commitment. And as she glanced at Eli, his brow furrowed in concentration as he debated a point with Anya, she couldn't help but wonder if their own future, their personal narrative within the grand tapestry of Havenridge, was also poised to take a more permanent, more intimate form. The whispers of permanence were all around them, not just in the grand designs for their community, but in the quiet, hopeful yearning of their own hearts. It was a question that lingered, a sweet ache in the space between them, waiting for the courage to finally find its voice.

The scent of drying herbs and aged parchment filled Mara's small study, a familiar comfort that usually soothed her racing thoughts. Outside, the Havenridge valley lay bathed in the soft, diffused light of late afternoon, a landscape of gentle slopes and carefully tended fields that spoke of order, diligence, and a hard-won peace. Yet, today, the tranquility of the scene did little to quell the disquiet stirring within her. The discussions in the communal hall had been about permanence, about ensuring the survival and continuity of Havenridge for generations to come. They were laying foundations, drafting charters, weaving a future so robust it could withstand the tides of time. And in the midst of it all, a question, as insistent as a persistent spring rain, had begun to fall upon her own heart.

Permanence. The word itself had once been a distant, almost mythical concept, a luxury afforded to those who hadn't known the constant gnawing of uncertainty. For so long, Mara's life had been a relentless pursuit of control, a desperate attempt to impose order on the chaos that had threatened to swallow her whole. She'd built walls, not of stone and timber, but of vigilance, self-reliance, and a fierce determination to never again be at the mercy of forces beyond her command. Every decision had been weighed, every risk calculated, every emotion meticulously banked. There had been no room for vulnerability, no space for surrender, only the unwavering imperative to survive, to protect, to *control*.

She ran a hand over the smooth, worn surface of her writing desk, her gaze drifting to the meticulously organized stacks of documents. This space, her sanctuary, was a testament to that drive. Here, she had poured over maps, charted resources, devised strategies, and, in essence, held the reins of their nascent community with a grip that was both steady and absolute. She had learned to lead not through charismatic pronouncements, but through quiet competence, through the sheer force of her will and her unwavering commitment to the well-being of Havenridge. She had been the architect of its stability, the guardian of its fragile peace.

But the world outside these walls had changed, and with it, something within her had begun to shift, too. The constant state of alert had gradually, almost imperceptibly, receded. The sharp edges of her defenses had begun to soften, not through any conscious effort, but through the steady presence of Eli and the growing sense of belonging that Havenridge offered. She had found herself trusting others more, delegating tasks not out of necessity, but out of a growing understanding that true strength lay not in doing everything herself, but in fostering the strengths of those around her. She had learned to let go, a little at a time, of the suffocating need for absolute control. It was a slow, sometimes hesitant, evolution, a shedding of an old skin that had protected her for so long.

Now, as the community debated the very notion of permanence, it brought that old, familiar fear crashing back to the surface. Permanence for Havenridge was a noble pursuit, a testament to their collective vision. But permanence in her own life? A shared life, a deep and binding partnership, the idea of entwining her existence so completely with another... it stirred a primal anxiety deep within her. Would it mean a dilution of her own hard-won autonomy? Would the boundaries she had so carefully constructed begin to crumble, leaving her exposed and vulnerable once more?

She picked up a small, intricately carved wooden bird from her desk, its wings spread as if in mid-flight. It was a gift from Eli, a small token he'd found on one of his scouting expeditions and had insisted she keep. He'd said it reminded him of her, of her spirit that was both grounded and capable of soaring. At the time, it had filled her with a warmth that had surprised her. Now, she traced the smooth lines of its form, her fingers lingering on the delicate details. Was this the essence of the permanence they were all contemplating? Not a rigid, unyielding structure, but something more organic, more adaptable, something that could still retain its individual beauty while being part of a larger, more profound whole?

Her internal struggle was a quiet one, waged in the solitude of her study while the collective mind of Havenridge deliberated. She observed Eli's steady presence in the council meetings, his thoughtful contributions, his unwavering commitment to their shared future. He was a pillar of strength, a man whose actions spoke louder than any words. He had earned her trust, not through grand gestures, but through consistent, unwavering support and a deep, intuitive understanding that transcended their shared history of hardship. He saw her, not just as a fellow survivor or a capable leader, but as Mara, with all her complexities and quiet strengths.

Yet, the fear persisted, a phantom limb that still ached with the memory of past losses. She remembered the ache of isolation, the gnawing fear of being utterly alone in a world that offered no solace. That fear had been the fuel for her relentless drive for control. It had made her capable, resilient, and, at times, fiercely independent to a fault. To embrace a life of shared permanence felt like stepping into uncharted territory, a realm where her carefully honed instincts might no longer be enough. It required a different kind of strength, a willingness to relinquish some of the reins, to trust not just in her own abilities, but in the strength and sincerity of another.

She remembered a conversation with Elara a few weeks ago, after one of their late-night strategy sessions. Elara, with her uncanny ability to see beyond the surface, had paused as Mara was tidying her notes. "You've come so far, Mara," she'd said, her voice soft, laced with a familiar wisdom. "You used to hold onto every single detail, afraid that if you let go of even one, the whole structure would collapse. Now..." Elara had gestured vaguely towards Mara, a gentle smile playing on her lips. "Now you're starting to build structures that can stand on their own, and you're learning to trust that they will."

Mara had dismissed it then, a fleeting acknowledgement of Elara's perceptive observation. But now, the words echoed in her mind, resonating with a truth she had been avoiding. Her journey had been one of shedding layers, of learning that true strength wasn't about hoarding power or knowledge, but about sharing it, about fostering growth in others. She had learned that leadership wasn't about dictating, but about guiding, about empowering. This shift had been subtle, a slow blossoming from within, and it had profoundly altered her perception of herself and her capabilities.

The concept of permanence, as it applied to her personal life, was a particularly daunting one. She envisioned it not as a cage, but as a garden, one that required constant tending, a space where new blooms could emerge, and where established roots could deepen. But the gardener in her, the one who had spent so long tending only to herself, felt a tremor of apprehension. What if she planted seeds of dependence and they choked the very life out of her own growth? What if the shared soil nourished Eli's roots more than her own? These were the insidious whispers of doubt, the old anxieties resurfacing with a renewed, albeit quieter, intensity.

She stood and walked to the window, her reflection a faint ghost against the darkening pane. The community hall, where the crucial debates about Havenridge's future were unfolding, was a warm glow in the distance. She imagined Eli there, his steady presence a reassuring anchor. He had, in his own way, already offered a form of permanence – a steadfast commitment to their shared cause, a quiet loyalty that had become as reliable as the sunrise. He had never pressured her, never demanded anything more than what she was willing to give, and in that space of gentle respect, her own feelings had begun to unfurl.

The shift from a survival-driven existence to a life of community building had demanded a transformation of her very identity. She was no longer just the woman who had fought for her life; she was the woman who helped build a world. She was no longer defined solely by her resilience, but by her capacity for care, for leadership rooted in compassion. This evolving identity was a source of pride, a testament to her inner strength. But it also brought with it new questions, new vulnerabilities.

Was it possible to build a life with another, a life of deep intimacy and shared purpose, without sacrificing the self that had been so painstakingly forged? Could she, Mara, who had learned to rely solely on herself, now learn to lean, to share the burdens and the joys, to intertwine her future with Eli's without losing the essential core of who she was? The very idea of permanence, in this personal context, felt like a delicate balancing act. It wasn't about disappearing into another, but about becoming a stronger, more complete version of herself, a version that was capable of both independent strength and profound connection.

She closed her eyes, picturing the community's new charter. It spoke of shared responsibilities, of mutual respect, of a collective commitment to the common good. These were principles she championed, principles she had helped to enshrine. And yet, the personal application of such ideals felt infinitely more complex, more fraught with the potential for emotional entanglement. It was easier to draft a charter for a community than to write the intricate, deeply personal covenant of a shared life.

The setting sun cast long shadows across the valley, painting the landscape in hues of orange and gold. It was a beautiful, transient spectacle, a reminder that even in permanence, there was always an element of change, of flow. Perhaps that was the key. Permanence wasn't about stasis, about building something so rigid it could never be altered. It was about creating a foundation strong enough to allow for growth, for adaptation, for the unfolding of new possibilities.

Mara turned back to her desk, her gaze falling on a half-finished letter, a draft of a proposal for agricultural zoning. She had been so focused on the external structures of Havenridge that the internal landscape of her own heart had been, by necessity, deferred. But now, the whispers of permanence were growing louder, more insistent. They spoke not just of community survival, but of a personal future, a future that felt increasingly, wonderfully, terrifyingly possible.

The fear was still there, a low hum beneath the surface, but it was no longer the dominant note. It was being joined by a new melody, one of hope, of anticipation, and of a quiet, burgeoning courage. She understood, in that moment, that the greatest act of control was not to hold everything tightly, but to have the courage to let go, to trust, and to embrace the beautiful, unpredictable unfolding of a life shared. The journey of building Havenridge had, in its own profound way, been a journey of building herself, and now, it seemed, that self was ready for a new kind of permanence.

Eli watched Mara from across the communal hall, the flickering lamplight catching the thoughtful lines around her eyes. Her focus, as always, was a potent force, yet he sensed a subtle undercurrent of unrest, a familiar echo of the vigilance that had once been her sole companion. He understood it, of course. He had walked a similar path, from a place where mere survival dictated every decision, to a burgeoning understanding of what it meant to *build*, to take on the weight of responsibility not just for oneself, but for a community, for a future. His own journey had been one of shedding the instinct to simply *adapt* to circumstances, and embracing the active, often daunting, role of shaping them. It was a profound shift, and he recognized its parallel in Mara.

For so long, their lives had been a tapestry woven with threads of necessity. Every action was a response to an immediate need, every choice a calculated risk against the ever-present specter of scarcity. Eli remembered those days with a clarity that still sent a shiver down his spine – the constant gnawing hunger, the gnawing fear, the absolute reliance on his own wits and speed. He had learned to blend into the shadows, to read the subtle cues of danger, to extract what he needed without leaving a trace. It was a life of calculated movement, of constant assessment, a mastery of the art of being present yet unseen.

But Havenridge, and Mara, had changed all that. The slow, steady rhythm of community life had begun to seep into his bones, a balm to the raw edges of his past. He had found himself drawn to the tangible act of creation, to the satisfaction of seeing a seed sprout, a wall rise, a shared meal prepared. More than that, he had found a quiet pride in contributing, in knowing that his strength, once honed for solitary survival, could now serve a larger purpose. His adaptability hadn't vanished; it had transformed, evolving into a deeper, more deliberate sense of responsibility. He no longer just reacted; he anticipated. He no longer just survived; he thrived, and in doing so, he actively contributed to the thriving of others.

The discussions of permanence, of charters and enduring legacies, resonated deeply within him. It was no longer an abstract concept born of desperation, but a deliberate choice, a conscious weaving of a future that was stronger than the sum of its individual parts. And at the heart of that future, he saw Mara, her quiet competence a cornerstone of their shared world. His commitment to her, and to Havenridge, was as solid as the earth beneath their feet. It was an unwavering anchor, a truth he held close.

Yet, the idea of formalizing their bond, of stepping onto a path that felt both inevitable and monumental, gave him pause. It wasn't a hesitation born of doubt in his feelings, or in Mara's. It was a recognition of the weight of such a declaration, of the profound implications of intertwining their lives in a way that transcended their current, deeply connected existence. It required more than just shared affection and mutual respect.

It demanded a conscious, intentional act of choosing, of declaring, of stepping into a future that was both his and hers, inextricably linked. He understood that for Mara, who had built her world on such careful foundations of self-reliance, such a step might feel like stepping off a precipice. He saw the subtle tightening of her jaw when the conversation veered too close to personal futures, the way her gaze would momentarily unfocus as if wrestling with an unseen adversary.

He had watched her navigate the complexities of leadership, her strength a quiet, formidable presence. She had learned to trust, slowly and deliberately, but the scars of her past ran deep. He knew that for her, permanence wasn't just about building a strong community; it was about building a life where her own hard-won autonomy wouldn't be eroded, where her vulnerabilities wouldn't become weaknesses. He admired her strength, her resilience, but he also recognized the quiet battle she waged, the constant reevaluation of boundaries she had so meticulously erected.

Eli's approach, honed by years of observing the subtle dynamics of nature and human interaction, was one of quiet observation and deliberate action. He wouldn't rush her. He wouldn't impose his will. Instead, he would create the space for her to make that choice, to feel secure in it. He would show her, through his own actions, what true commitment meant in this new era of Havenridge.

He began by subtly weaving their shared future into the fabric of his daily contributions. When discussing plans for the new irrigation system, he spoke not just of community needs, but of ensuring the land would be fertile for generations to come, land that they would tend together. When helping to reinforce the outer palisade, he mentioned the importance of a secure home, a place where they could build a life without fear. He made his intentions clear, not through grand pronouncements, but through consistent, understated integration of their personal future into the communal vision.

He also made a point of spending more time with her in their shared quiet moments. After council meetings, when the energy of the day began to wane, he would seek her out. He wouldn't pry, wouldn't demand answers to questions she wasn't ready to voice. Instead, he would simply be present. He would listen to the rustle of parchment as she organized her notes, offer a steadying hand as they walked back to their respective dwellings, or share a cup of herbal tea, the silence between them comfortable and understanding. He wanted her to feel his presence not as a pressure, but as a gentle, unwavering support.

One evening, as they sat by the dying embers of the communal hearth, he found himself speaking more directly, yet still with his characteristic quietude. "Mara," he began, his voice low and steady, "I know the word 'permanence' carries a heavy weight. For a long time, it was a luxury none of us could afford. But we've built something here. Something real." He looked at her, his gaze earnest. "And I've built something, too. A life. A future. And in that future, I see you. Clearly. Steadily."

He paused, allowing his words to settle. "I don't expect you to leap. I only want you to know that I'm not asking you to give up what you've fought so hard for. I'm asking you to share it. To build upon it. With me." He picked up a fallen twig and traced patterns in the warm ash. "Responsibility... it's not just about holding things together, Mara. It's about creating something that *can* hold. Something that can grow, and endure. And for me, that means building that foundation with you."

He felt a subtle tension ease from her shoulders, a small sigh escaping her lips. He saw a flicker of something in her eyes – not fear, not entirely, but perhaps a dawning understanding, a recognition of his intention. He knew that for her, the greatest fear wasn't of him, but of losing herself. And he was determined to show her that commitment, true commitment, wasn't about erasure, but about expansion.

He began to conceptualize his own steps towards formalizing their union, not as a demand, but as an offering. He thought about the traditions of the old world, the simple ceremonies that spoke of partnership and mutual pledge. He didn't want a grand spectacle; that wasn't their way. He wanted something that reflected the essence of Havenridge, something grounded, sincere, and deeply meaningful.

He started sketching designs for a small, sturdy ring, not of precious metal, but of carved wood, perhaps inlaid with a polished stone he'd found on his travels. A symbol of their shared journey, of the earth that sustained them, of the enduring strength he saw in their bond. He considered the practicalities, too. He wanted to ensure that any formal step they took would not only solidify their personal commitment but also strengthen their standing within the community, reinforcing the idea of stability and continuity that was so vital.

He found himself reflecting on his own transformation. He had arrived in Havenridge as a man adrift, a survivor defined by his ability to adapt. Now, he was a man rooted, a man who understood the power of deliberate action, of chosen responsibility. He had learned that true strength wasn't in solitary endurance, but in the shared effort of building something that would last. His commitment to Mara was the embodiment of that understanding. It was a commitment to more than just her; it was a commitment to the future they could forge together, a future that was both permanent and vibrant, a testament to the enduring power of love and shared purpose.

He continued to observe Mara, to sense the subtle shifts in her demeanor. He saw the way her gaze would linger on him during council meetings, the way her hand would instinctively reach for the wooden bird he had given her when she thought she was unobserved. These were small signs, but they were enough. They spoke of a heart that was slowly, deliberately, opening.

His plan was simple, and it was rooted in the very principles of Havenridge: honesty, sincerity, and a deep respect for the journey each individual undertook. He would continue to be her steadfast support, her quiet anchor. He would speak his truth, not with urgency, but with unwavering conviction. And he would trust that Mara, the woman who had learned to build a community from the ground up, would also find the strength and the courage to build a life, a permanent life, with him. His path to responsibility had led him here, to this place of quiet certainty, and he was ready to walk it, hand in hand with her, into whatever the future held.

He understood that true permanence wasn't about sealing something away, but about cultivating a fertile ground for continued growth, a space where love, like the ancient trees of the valley, could deepen its roots and reach for the sky, together. He knew that this next step, this formalizing of their bond, was not about a conclusion, but about a profound and beautiful beginning, a testament to the enduring strength that came not from isolation, but from a deeply chosen, shared existence. His journey had been about finding his place in the world, and now, his deepest desire was to build that world, brick by brick, with Mara by his side.

CHAPTER TWO

SHADOWS OF AUTONOMY

Mara's fingers traced the faded ink of the land stewardship agreement, the parchment cool beneath her touch. The communal hall was hushed, the only sounds the occasional rustle of paper and the distant chirping of crickets from the open windows. Lamplight cast long, dancing shadows, but her focus remained resolutely on the meticulous clauses laid out before her.

These were the bedrock of Havenridge's future, the legal frameworks designed to ensure its prosperity and survival for generations to come. Each word was chosen with deliberate precision, each stipulation a safeguard against the uncertainties that had once plagued their existence. She found a grim satisfaction in this very act of meticulous planning, in imposing order and foresight onto the wild, untamed expanse of what lay ahead.

Yet, as her eyes scanned the detailed descriptions of crop rotation, water rights, and resource allocation, a familiar disquiet began to stir within her. It was a subtle undertow beneath the calm surface of her professional concentration, a counterpoint to the solid, immutable nature of the documents she held. These agreements, so vital for the community's enduring stability, felt... heavy.

They spoke of permanence, of unyielding commitments, of futures meticulously charted and bound by law. And in that, Mara saw a reflection of her own burgeoning personal future, a path that, while undeniably appealing, also whispered of constraints, of doors closing as others swung open.

She recalled the early days, when survival had been a moment-to-moment proposition. The concept of 'long-term' was a luxury, an abstract notion for those not constantly scanning the horizon for threats or opportunities. Now, Havenridge was a testament to the power of sustained effort, of collective will. They had built not just a settlement, but a legacy.

The land stewardship agreements were tangible proof of that, evidence that their endeavors were not ephemeral, but rooted and destined to grow. She believed in this, fiercely. She had poured her very being into creating this haven, into ensuring its resilience.

But the very permanence she had so diligently championed for Havenridge now felt like a subtle, almost imperceptible, tightening around her own spirit. The meticulous planning for the future, the laying of foundations that would withstand the test of time, also meant delineating boundaries. It meant making choices that would shape not just the community, but the lives within it, including her own. The freedom she had so fiercely guarded, the autonomy that had been her shield and her sword, now seemed to be facing a new kind of challenge. It wasn't the external threats of scarcity or conflict, but the internal calculus of shared responsibility and intertwined destinies.

She took a deep breath, trying to compartmentalize. Her role as a steward of Havenridge demanded this clear-eyed assessment of its future. These agreements were not just about land; they were about commitment. They were about ensuring that the hard-won peace and prosperity would not be squandered by shortsightedness or negligence. She imagined the leaders of tomorrow, reading these same parchments, benefiting from the foresight she and the council were now exercising. There was a profound satisfaction in that, a sense of contributing to something truly lasting.

Still, the echo of Eli's words resonated in the quiet of the hall. He spoke of permanence with a quiet conviction that mirrored her own, but his perspective was tinged with a different kind of longing. He saw permanence as an opportunity for shared growth, for building a life together. And while a part of her yearned for that same shared future, another part felt a tremor of apprehension. The idea of irrevocably intertwining her life with another's, even with someone as steadfast and understanding as Eli, felt like a significant crossing.

She reread a section concerning water rights, specifically the provisions for its equitable distribution during prolonged dry spells. It was a testament to their collective responsibility, a guarantee that no one would be left to suffer unduly. This was the essence of Havenridge: mutual support, shared burden. But the act of formalizing such an arrangement, of drawing lines in the sand that would dictate behavior for generations, was a powerful reminder of the permanence she was now contemplating on a personal level.

Her mind drifted to the concept of individual autonomy. She had spent so long forging her own path, relying on her own judgment, her own strength. It was a hard-won independence, a core element of her identity. The thought of willingly entering into a bond that would, by its very nature, alter that independence, even in the most loving and consensual way, brought a subtle tension to her jaw. It wasn't a fear of losing herself entirely, but a deep-seated need to ensure that her core self, the self that had weathered so much, would remain intact, even amplified, within the context of a shared life.

She remembered the initial resistance she had felt when the council first proposed the idea of formal land charters. It had felt too definitive, too binding, too much like the restrictive rules of the world they had left behind. But she had come to understand that such structures were essential for growth, for stability, for the very survival of the community they had built. They were the fences that protected the garden, allowing the plants within to flourish. Now, she was applying the same logic to her own life, to the potential of her relationship with Eli.

Could she, Mara, who had always been the architect of her own destiny, willingly step into a future where decisions were made, not just by her, but *with* another? Where her autonomy was not a solitary pursuit, but a shared endeavor, subject to the ebb and flow of a partnership? It was a question that gnawed at her, a complex interplay of desire and ingrained self-reliance.

She shifted her gaze from the documents to the fire, its flames dancing with an untamed energy that felt akin to her own spirit. The agreements were about managing that wildness, channeling it for the common good. And perhaps, she mused, her own personal future was much the same. Perhaps true strength lay not in maintaining an absolute, unyielding independence, but in finding a way to harmonize that fierce autonomy with the deep connection she felt with Eli, with the profound desire to build something enduring *together*.

The weight of these future pacts, both communal and personal, settled upon her. It was the weight of responsibility, yes, but also the weight of possibility. The land stewardship agreements represented a promise to Havenridge, a commitment to its future. And the unspoken pacts forming between her and Eli represented a promise to each other, a commitment to a shared future. She understood that the meticulous planning for Havenridge's land was not about limiting its potential, but about ensuring its capacity for growth and endurance. In the same way, a commitment to Eli would not be about diminishing her spirit, but about creating a space where it could deepen, expand, and truly thrive, grounded by a love that was as strong and as enduring as the land itself.

She picked up a quill, dipping it into the inkwell. Her hand felt steady as she began to make notes in the margins of the agreement, not just legal observations, but reflections. She was mapping out the future of Havenridge, and in doing so, she was also mapping the terrain of her own heart, charting a course towards a future that promised both security and the thrilling, terrifying prospect of a shared permanence. The permanence of these agreements, she realized, was not a cage, but a foundation. And she was beginning to understand that a foundation, when built with love and trust, could support the most magnificent structures. Her own spirit, she hoped, could be one such structure, built not in isolation, but in steadfast partnership.

The autonomy she cherished would not be extinguished, but transformed, evolving into a shared strength, a richer, more resonant expression of who she was, and who they could become, together. She was learning to reconcile the fierce independence that had kept her alive with the burgeoning desire for a connection that promised to enrich her life beyond measure. It was a delicate balance, a continuous negotiation, but one she was increasingly willing to undertake. The weight of these future pacts was significant, but it was no longer a burden; it was the solid, reassuring ground upon which a new chapter of her life, and Havenridge's, would be built.

The scent of damp earth and blooming night jasmine filled the air as Mara and Eli ambled along the winding path that meandered through Havenridge's communal gardens. Dusk had begun to paint the sky in hues of lavender and rose, casting a soft, ethereal glow over the carefully tended plots. Fireflies, like scattered embers, began to prick the deepening twilight, their silent flashes mirroring the quiet thoughts that flickered between the two figures. The air was alive with the gentle murmur of crickets, a natural symphony that underscored the profound peace of the evening. Mara's hand brushed against Eli's as they walked, a familiar, comforting contact that spoke volumes without a single word exchanged.

Eli, ever observant, sensed a subtle shift in Mara's usual composed demeanor. Her gaze, usually sharp and focused, was softened, more distant, as if she were gazing at something beyond the visible rows of ripening vegetables and flowering herbs. He didn't press her, didn't break the spell of their shared quietude with an intrusive question. Instead, he tightened his grip on her hand almost imperceptibly, a silent offering of support, a gentle anchor in whatever sea of contemplation she might be navigating. His presence was a constant, a steady rhythm against the sometimes-unpredictable currents of her thoughts.

"The tomatoes are really thriving this year," Mara finally murmured, her voice a low, melodic sound that seemed to blend with the rustling leaves. She gestured towards a sprawling vine laden with plump, crimson fruits. "The new compost mix the gardeners devised is making a remarkable difference."

Eli followed her gaze, a genuine smile touching his lips. "It's a testament to their hard work, and to your guidance, Mara. You have a way of making things grow, both in the soil and in the spirit of this place."

His words, so simple, so sincere, landed in Mara's heart with a warmth that surprised her. It was a warmth that had nothing to do with the fading heat of the day and everything to do with the unspoken acknowledgment of their shared journey. He saw her, truly saw her, not just as the architect of Havenridge's stability, but as someone who nurtured life in all its forms. This understanding, this quiet appreciation, was a language they had developed over months, a dialect of shared glances, knowing smiles, and the gentle pressure of hands.

"It's not just me," Mara replied, her fingers now tracing the intricate veins of a broad basil leaf. "It's all of us. This garden, like Havenridge itself, is a tapestry woven from many hands, many hearts. Each thread, no matter how small, is essential." She paused, her eyes drifting towards the distant, softly lit windows of the communal hall, where the lingering scent of parchment and council deliberations still seemed to cling to her memory. "And sometimes," she added, her voice barely a whisper, "it feels like we're weaving a future so intricate, so vast, that it's hard to see where one thread ends and another begins."

Eli stopped, turning to face her fully. The deepening twilight cast his features in a soft shadow, but his eyes, even in the dim light, held a depth of understanding that always unnerved and soothed her in equal measure. He didn't need her to articulate the internal struggle she'd been grappling with, the quiet tug-of-war between her fiercely guarded autonomy and the burgeoning desire for a shared permanence. He felt it, she suspected, in the subtle shift of her weight, the almost imperceptible tension in her shoulders.

"It's a good tapestry, Mara," he said, his voice low and steady. "Strong. Beautiful. And if it feels intricate, that's because it's built to last. Built to adapt. Not all structures meant to endure are rigid, you know. Some are designed to flex, to bend with the wind, yet remain standing."

His analogy resonated deeply. He was speaking, she knew, not just of the community's physical structures, but of the intangible bonds that held them together, the evolving nature of their collective life. He was speaking, too, of the unspoken framework of *their* lives, a structure that was taking shape organically, yet with an undeniable gravity.

They continued their walk, the silence between them now a comfortable, companionable one. Mara pointed out a patch of wild strawberries, their tiny, sweet fruits a hidden treasure among the greenery. Eli, in turn, showed her a fledgling bird's nest tucked away in the crook of an apple tree, a delicate masterpiece of twigs and moss. Each shared observation was a small affirmation, a quiet beat in the rhythm of their shared existence. These were the moments that formed the bedrock of their connection, the subtle, everyday exchanges that built a love as sturdy and as vital as the earth beneath their feet.

"Remember when we first started clearing this section?" Mara mused, her gaze sweeping over the orderly rows of kale and chard. "It was all overgrown. Brambles and weeds, choking out any hope of growth. It felt... insurmountable."

"But you didn't let it," Eli said, his voice laced with admiration. "You saw the potential, even beneath the chaos. You had a vision, and you brought it to life, piece by painstaking piece."

His words painted a vivid picture of her past, a past she had often tried to distance herself from, a past where survival had been the only guiding principle. Now, looking at the flourishing garden, she saw not just a triumph of effort, but a symbol of something more profound. It was a testament to the power of directed intention, the quiet strength of building something with care and foresight. And it was in this very act of cultivating growth and order that she found herself grappling with the notion of cultivated intimacy, of tending to a relationship with the same diligence and care.

"I suppose I've always been drawn to shaping things," Mara admitted, her voice tinged with a touch of weariness. "To imposing a kind of order on the wildness. Whether it's land, or... or lives." The unspoken addition hung in the air between them, heavy with unspoken questions.

Eli squeezed her hand gently. "And there's nothing wrong with that. Order brings stability. It brings peace. But sometimes, Mara, the most beautiful things bloom not from rigid control, but from allowing space. From trust. From letting the natural currents guide you." He stopped again, and this time, his gaze held hers directly. The question in his eyes was not demanding, but open, inviting. "Are you afraid of that space, Mara? Of the currents?"

His directness, delivered with such tenderness, disarmed her. She had been so adept at guarding her inner world, at building walls around her vulnerabilities. Yet, with Eli, those walls seemed to melt away, not under duress, but under the sheer force of his unwavering acceptance. She saw her own internal conflict reflected in his understanding eyes – the ingrained habit of self-reliance warring with the undeniable pull towards shared vulnerability.

"It's not about fear, exactly," she confessed, choosing her words carefully. "It's more about... learning to trust the currents. My whole life has been about navigating the storms, about charting my own course, often alone. The idea of sharing that helm, even with someone I trust implicitly... it's a new kind of uncharted territory." She gestured vaguely towards the expanse of the gardens, the neat rows stretching out into the twilight. "These agreements, the charters we're drafting for the land – they're about creating certainty. About defining boundaries so that growth can happen safely. But what about the boundaries of the heart? How do you draft those with the same precision?"

Eli smiled, a slow, gentle unfolding that warmed her. "You don't draft them, Mara. You discover them. You feel them. They aren't etched in parchment; they're written in shared experiences, in laughter, in quiet understanding. They're the spaces between your breaths when you're together, the unspoken acknowledgments that you're not alone." He paused, his thumb stroking the back of her hand. "And sometimes, they're the brave admissions of uncertainty. Like this one."

His words were a balm to her restless spirit. He wasn't asking her to abandon her hard-won independence, but to integrate it, to allow it to evolve within the context of a shared life. He was suggesting that true strength lay not in absolute autonomy, but in the harmonious interplay of individuality and connection.

"This garden," Mara said, her voice softer now, more contemplative, "it has its own rhythm. The planting, the tending, the harvest. It's a cycle. And each stage requires a different kind of attention, a different kind of trust in the process." She looked at him, a newfound clarity dawning within her. "Perhaps... perhaps relationships are much the same. There are seasons for growth, seasons for quiet waiting, seasons for sharing the bounty. And each season demands a different kind of courage. The courage to plant, the courage to nurture, and the courage to... to simply be, together."

Eli's gaze softened, his eyes reflecting the nascent stars that were beginning to emerge in the darkening sky. "And you, Mara," he said, his voice a low rumble, "you have the courage for all of them. I see it every day. In how you lead, in how you care, in how you face down challenges with unwavering resolve. And I also see it in the way you're looking at me now, a flicker of something vulnerable, something that wants to bloom."

The directness of his observation sent a tremor through her, a mixture of apprehension and a burgeoning sense of release. He saw through her carefully constructed defenses, not to exploit them, but to acknowledge the tender shoots of hope that were pushing through. He understood that her meticulous planning for Havenridge, the rigorous structuring of their communal future, was a reflection of her own deep-seated need for security, a need that extended to her personal life, to the very core of her being.

"It's just... the permanence," Mara admitted, the word feeling heavy on her tongue. "The idea of a future that is so firmly established, so defined. It feels both incredibly reassuring and... a little daunting." She looked at him, her heart laid bare in the twilight. "My autonomy has always been my refuge, Eli. My shield. The thought of willingly sharing that space, of allowing another's needs and desires to become as integral as my own... it requires a different kind of strength."

Eli's hand found hers again, his grip firm and reassuring. "And it's a strength you possess, Mara. You've shown it time and again. Havenridge needs your strength, your vision. And I..." He hesitated, his gaze deepening, "I need *you*. Not just the leader, but the woman who finds beauty in a wild strawberry, who understands the language of growing things, who is brave enough to question the very foundations she herself has laid."

He stepped closer, his presence a warm, grounding force. The scent of the earth, the jasmine, the distant woodsmoke from a hearth – it all mingled with the unique scent of Eli, a subtle aroma of leather and the outdoors. In that moment, surrounded by the quiet hum of their burgeoning community, Mara felt a profound sense of peace settle over her. The anxieties that had been swirling within her for weeks began to recede, replaced by a quiet certainty.

"You see the tapestry," Mara whispered, her voice thick with emotion, "but you also see the individual threads. You understand that weaving them together doesn't diminish their own beauty, but enhances it."

Eli's eyes, dark and luminous in the fading light, held hers. "Precisely. And I wouldn't have it any other way. Your autonomy isn't something to be surrendered, Mara. It's something to be celebrated, to be woven into the fabric of our shared life. It's what makes you, you. And it's what makes our future, *our* future."

He gently lifted her hand, pressing a soft kiss to her knuckles. The simple gesture, imbued with profound sincerity, spoke volumes. It was a silent promise, an unspoken commitment that transcended any formal agreement. It was the language of hearts, speaking to each other in the quiet spaces, in the shared glances, in the comfortable silences that were, in truth, the loudest conversations of all.

The unspoken held a power, a depth, that words could rarely capture. And in that moment, under the vast, star-dusted sky, Mara understood that the most enduring foundations were not built on rigid certainty, but on the quiet, unwavering strength of shared trust and mutual understanding. The autonomy she cherished would not be lost; it would be amplified, transformed, and woven into something richer, something stronger, something that could truly weather any storm. The intricate tapestry of Havenridge, and the equally intricate tapestry of their lives, were destined to be beautiful, enduring works of art, created not in isolation, but in the profound and comforting embrace of a shared future.

The familiar rough bark of the ancient oak pressed against Mara's back, a comforting anchor as she gazed out over the sleeping village. Havenridge, bathed in the soft glow of moonlight, looked like a constellation of scattered embers against the dark velvet of the land. The wind, a gentle caress, whispered through the leaves, carrying with it the faint, mingled scents of woodsmoke, pine, and the distant, calming presence of the sea. It was here, in this quiet sanctuary, that the tendrils of her deepest anxieties often uncoiled, drawing her back to the precipice of her oldest fears.

She remembered, with a vividness that was both a comfort and a torment, the years when survival had been her sole compass. The gnawing hunger, the biting cold, the constant, exhausting vigilance against unseen threats – those were the crucible that had forged her fierce independence. She had learned, through bitter experience, that relying on others was a gamble, a luxury she could rarely afford. Each act of dependence had felt like a chip taken from the bedrock of her self-sufficiency, leaving her feeling exposed, vulnerable, and terrifyingly adrift.

There was the winter of the Blight, when the crops had withered on the vine, and despair had threatened to consume Havenridge. Mara, barely out of her teens, had found herself shouldering a burden far heavier than her young frame could bear. The whispers of surrender had been seductive, the comfort of giving up the fight a siren's call. But something within her, a stubborn, unyielding core, had refused to yield.

She had rallied the dwindling stores, organized rationing with an iron fist, and driven her own exhausted body to the brink, all to ensure that no one in Havenridge succumbed to the encroaching darkness. In those desperate days, she had felt her individuality fragmenting, her own needs and desires dissolving into the collective struggle. The self she knew had been subsumed by the urgent, pressing needs of the community. It was a necessary sacrifice, she'd told herself then, a pragmatic compromise. Yet, the echo of that dissolution, the sensation of her own identity being absorbed and diluted, had never truly faded.

Then there was the time she'd been forced to leave Havenridge, to seek aid in the distant cities, a journey fraught with peril and uncertainty. She had travelled with a small, hand-picked group, her resolve a shield against the gnawing fear of the unknown. Every decision, every risk taken, had been hers alone. The weight of responsibility had pressed down on her, a constant companion. She had learned to anticipate dangers, to read the subtle cues of a hostile world, to trust her own instincts above all else. In those solitary months, her sense of self had been honed to a razor's edge.

She was Mara, the survivor, the strategist, the one who could navigate the treacherous currents of the outside world. Her autonomy had been her lifeblood, her freedom to act and react on her own terms an absolute necessity. To compromise that, to cede even an inch of that hard-won independence, felt like a betrayal of the very person she had fought so desperately to become.

And now, here, in the quiet embrace of Havenridge, with Eli's steady presence a constant, gentle force in her life, that old fear began to stir. The thought of fully merging her life with his, of weaving her existence so tightly into the fabric of his, and by extension, into the intricate tapestry of Havenridge, felt like walking back into that suffocating fog of anonymity. It wasn't that she doubted Eli's love, or his respect for her. It was far more primal than that. It was the deep-seated terror of being erased, of her own unique spark being extinguished by the sheer force of shared identity.

She remembered the days after her parents had disappeared, lost to the unforgiving sea. She had been adrift, a small boat with a tattered sail, tossed about by the indifferent waves of grief and uncertainty. For a time, she had felt utterly lost, a ghost in her own life. It had taken years, years of painstaking effort, of deliberate self-creation, to rebuild herself, to forge a new identity from the ashes of her loss. She had poured every ounce of her energy into establishing Havenridge, into creating a place where such losses, such dissolutions, could be prevented.

The community, with its shared responsibilities and collective strengths, was her bulwark against the crushing solitude she had once known. And yet, the very act of building it, of defining its boundaries and structures, had been a way of asserting her own will, her own presence, in a world that had tried to make her disappear.

The notion of surrendering that control, even in the most loving and consensual way, felt like dismantling the very walls she had so carefully constructed around her heart. She envisioned her individual threads of self – the sharp intellect, the unyielding pragmatism, the quiet yearning for solitude – being rewoven into a larger pattern, a pattern that might not fully accommodate her own unique colours and textures. What if her edges, so carefully defined by years of self-reliance, became blurred? What if the quiet hum of her inner world was drowned out by the symphony of shared lives?

She traced a pattern on the rough bark with her fingertip, the movement a silent manifestation of her internal turmoil. She saw herself, in her mind's eye, as a solitary flame, fiercely burning, illuminating her own path. Now, the prospect was of joining that flame with another, creating a larger, warmer fire. But what if, in that joining, the original flame was diminished, its singular brilliance lost in the collective glow? The thought sent a shiver down her spine, a stark contrast to the gentle night air.

Her past self, the one who had clawed her way back from the brink, the one who had learned to trust only her own resilience, was a formidable entity. This past self viewed the present proposal of deep, committed partnership with a wariness born of hard-won experience. It saw the potential for compromise, for the subtle erosion of self that often accompanied deep connection. It whispered cautionary tales of lost identities, of individuals who had faded into the background, their own dreams and aspirations sacrificed on the altar of companionship.

Yet, another part of her, the part that had been awakened by Eli's unwavering presence, the part that had begun to blossom in the fertile soil of Havenridge, yearned for that very merging. It was a nascent desire, tentative and shy, but potent nonetheless. It longed to share the burdens, to celebrate the triumphs, to experience the quiet comfort of a hand reaching for hers in the darkness. This present self recognized the profound loneliness that still sometimes stalked the edges of her carefully constructed life, a loneliness that even the vibrant community of Havenridge couldn't entirely dispel.

The conflict was a silent war waged within her soul. The fierce protector of her autonomy, honed by years of solitary struggle, stood guard against the growing vulnerability that Eli's love had coaxed into existence. She found herself replaying moments from her past, not just the triumphs, but the instances where she had felt her own essence threatened. There was the time she had been forced to relinquish leadership of a critical project to a more politically connected, but less capable, individual. The humiliation had been sharp, the feeling of being sidelined and disregarded, deeply wounding. She had channeled that anger, that sense of injustice, into a renewed commitment to her own path, a silent vow to never again allow her agency to be so easily undermined.

Then there was the period when she had been desperately trying to secure Havenridge's charter, navigating a labyrinth of bureaucratic hurdles and political machinations. She had felt her own voice, her own needs, relegated to the background as she worked tirelessly to ensure the survival of the community. It had been an all-consuming effort, and in its intensity, she had felt her personal identity recede, her sole focus being the external goal. The victory had been sweet, but the memory of that self-negation lingered, a cautionary reminder of the price of single-minded devotion.

These memories, fragments of a life lived on the edge, fueled her current apprehension. They were the bedrock of her fear of dissolution. They whispered that commitment, that deep entanglement with another, was inherently a pathway to losing oneself. The idea of her meticulously crafted identity, her carefully guarded independence, being diluted or subsumed was a prospect that sent a cold dread through her. It felt like risking the very foundations of her being, the hard-won sense of self that had been her sole companion for so long.

She leaned her head back against the rough bark, closing her eyes, allowing the night sounds to wash over her. The crickets chirped their incessant song, the wind rustled through the leaves, and somewhere, a nightingale poured out its mournful, beautiful melody. These were the sounds of nature, of life unfolding organically, without conscious design or imposed structure. And in their untamed beauty, she found a flicker of reassurance. Perhaps her fear was not entirely founded.

Perhaps the blending of lives, like the blending of natural elements, didn't have to result in erasure, but in a new, richer form. Perhaps, just as the oak tree stood strong and independent, yet was sustained by the very earth that nourished it, she too could find a way to be fully herself, while also being deeply connected to another. The challenge, she realized, was not to retreat from the prospect of union, but to find a way to embrace it without sacrificing the core of who she was. It was a delicate dance, a tightrope walk between vulnerability and self-preservation, and it was a dance she was only just beginning to learn.

The shadows of her past clung to her, a familiar weight, but for the first time, she felt a nascent stir of hope, a quiet belief that perhaps, even in the deepest of connections, her own flame could continue to burn, bright and undimmed.

The scent of freshly planed wood, a comforting balm to Mara's frayed nerves, often drew Eli to the communal workshop. It was his sanctuary, a place where the clamor of his thoughts could be silenced by the rhythmic rasp of his tools and the satisfying thud of hammer against chisel. Tonight, the air was thick with the rich aroma of cedar, a testament to the intricate rocking chair taking shape under his skilled hands.

Each curve of the armrest, each precisely fitted joint, was a testament to his patience, his unwavering focus. His movements were fluid, economical, born of years of practice and an innate understanding of the material. He worked by the soft glow of a single lantern, its light casting long, dancing shadows across the workshop floor, mirroring the subtle shifts in his own contemplation.

His mind, however, was not solely occupied with the task at hand. It was a constant, gentle current, always flowing towards Mara. He watched her, not with possessive eyes, but with a quiet understanding that had deepened with every shared sunrise and whispered conversation. He saw the flicker of apprehension that sometimes crossed her face when the conversation turned to their future, the subtle tightening of her jaw when the idea of complete union was broached. He understood, with a clarity that surprised even himself, that her fierce independence was not a barrier to their love, but a testament to the strength of the woman he adored.

He had witnessed, firsthand, the arduous journey she had undertaken to reclaim herself, to build a life, and indeed, a community, from the very foundations of her being. He remembered the stories she had shared, the hushed accounts of her solitary struggles, the harrowing fight for survival that had forged her into the resilient, self-possessed individual she was today. He knew that for Mara, autonomy was not a choice; it was an intrinsic part of her identity, as essential as her heartbeat.

He ran a calloused thumb along the smooth, polished wood of the rocking chair, the subtle grain a map of its history, much like Mara's own life was a testament to her experiences. He understood her fear, not as a rejection of him, but as a natural consequence of her past. She had learned to rely on herself because, for so long, she had had no other choice. She had built her world brick by painstaking brick, each decision, each sacrifice, a deliberate act of self-preservation. To suggest she simply dismantle those walls, even for the sake of love, was to ask her to betray the very essence of what had made her strong.

Eli's own journey had been different. He had grown up in Havenridge, a place where interdependence was woven into the very fabric of daily life. While he possessed his own quiet strengths and skills, he had never known the gnawing terror of absolute solitude. He had always been part of something larger, a collective that offered a sense of belonging, a shared responsibility. This understanding of community, of shared strength, was what he now sought to offer Mara, not as a replacement for her hard-won autonomy, but as an addition to it.

He knew that his role in her life, and in their burgeoning partnership, was not to demand or to absorb, but to be a steadfast presence. He needed to demonstrate, through his actions, that commitment did not equate to confinement. He had to be the quiet assurance in the storm, the unwavering hand that offered support without seeking to control. He envisioned their future not as a merging that diluted her light, but as a partnership where their individual flames could burn even brighter, their combined warmth a comforting hearth for them both.

He picked up a fine-grit sandpaper, its gentle friction smoothing the wood to a silken finish. This, he thought, was akin to how he needed to approach Mara. Not with force, but with a persistent gentleness. Not by erasing her edges, but by refining them, by showing her that vulnerability, when met with unwavering love and respect, could be a source of profound strength. He understood that her fears were deeply rooted, a tangle of past traumas and ingrained survival instincts. To simply dismiss them would be to dismiss a part of her that had shaped her into the woman he loved.

He remembered a conversation they'd had weeks ago, under the canopy of the whispering pines. Mara had been tracing the constellations, her voice a low murmur as she spoke of feeling like a lone star, destined to orbit in solitary splendor. He had listened, his heart aching with a desire to reassure her, but also with a profound respect for the fierce beauty of her individuality. He hadn't offered platitudes or easy answers. Instead, he had simply taken her hand, his grip firm and warm, and said, "Even the brightest star shines alongside others, Mara. And sometimes, the light of two stars together can illuminate a path that neither could find alone." It was a simple statement, born of his own quiet wisdom, but he saw the flicker of hope it ignited in her eyes.

He continued to work on the rocking chair, the rhythm of his sanding a meditation. He imagined Mara sitting in it, the gentle sway a mirror of the steady rhythm of their life together. He pictured her reading, the lamplight catching the strands of her hair, her brow unfurrowed by worry. He saw himself nearby, perhaps tending to the hearth, his presence a silent, comforting constant. It wasn't about possession; it was about belonging. It was about creating a space where she could be her truest self, without fear of judgment or erasure.

He understood that for Mara, autonomy was akin to breathing. To ask her to relinquish it entirely would be to suffocate her. His promise, his commitment, needed to be that he would always champion her right to breathe, to be her own unique, extraordinary self. He wouldn't build a cage of love; he would build a sanctuary, a place where her wings could spread, not be clipped. He would be the steady ground beneath her feet, allowing her the freedom to soar.

He carefully fitted the final piece of the rocking chair, a small, intricately carved bird that perched on the armrest. It was a symbol, he mused, of freedom, of the spirit taking flight. This was what he wanted for Mara. He wanted her to feel free, to feel liberated by their union, not bound by it. He wanted her to know, without a shadow of a doubt, that his love was a force that amplified her own spirit, not one that sought to diminish it.

The workshop was quiet, save for the soft rasp of his tools and the steady beat of his heart. He felt a profound sense of peace, a quiet certainty settling over him. He couldn't erase Mara's past, nor could he force her to forget the lessons it had taught her. But he could offer her a different narrative, a story of love where two individuals, each fiercely unique, could weave their lives together without losing the essential threads of who they were. He could be her constant, her steadfast presence, a living testament to the fact that permanence, in the right embrace, could be the most liberating force of all.

It wasn't about claiming her; it was about cherishing her, about creating a space where her autonomy could flourish, nurtured by a love that understood and celebrated its profound importance. He would be the silent guardian of her spirit, the unwavering anchor that allowed her to explore the boundless seas of her own being, always knowing that a safe harbor awaited her return. He understood that trust, in this context, was not a passive gift, but an active, ongoing demonstration of respect and unwavering devotion. He would earn that trust, day by day, by being the kind of partner who saw her strength, celebrated her independence, and offered a love that was as vast and as deep as the ocean she so feared, yet was drawn to.

His commitment was not a chain, but a sturdy, well-crafted vessel, designed to carry them both through any storm, with her always at the helm of her own destiny, and his unwavering support a constant force at her back.

The last rays of sunlight, softened and diffused by the gathering twilight, painted the communal dining hall in hues of lavender and rose. The simple meal of roasted root vegetables and freshly baked bread was a familiar comfort, its earthy aromas mingling with the faint scent of woodsmoke that always seemed to cling to Havenridge. Eli watched Mara across the rough-hewn table, the gentle curve of her cheek illuminated by the flickering candlelight. Tonight, the usual vibrant spark in her eyes seemed to hold a deeper, more contemplative glow, as if she were observing not just the present moment, but the intricate tapestry of possibilities that lay beyond it.

A comfortable silence had settled between them, a testament to the many unspoken conversations they'd already shared. But as Eli reached for his water, he sensed a shift in the air, a subtle prelude to a revelation. Mara's gaze, which had been fixed on the gentle dance of the flames, now met his, her expression earnest and open.

"Eli," she began, her voice a soft murmur that carried across the hushed room, "I've been thinking a lot, about... us. About what we want." She paused, her fingers tracing the rim of her wooden bowl, a familiar gesture of introspection. "Not just for ourselves, but for Havenridge. For the future we're building."

Eli nodded, his own thoughts aligning with hers. He had seen this introspection in her before, a quiet contemplation that preceded moments of profound clarity. "I've been thinking too," he replied, his voice gentle. "About the kind of community we want to foster. About how we can ensure it remains a place that nurtures growth, for everyone."

Mara's gaze lifted again, meeting his directly. "That's just it," she said, her voice gaining a touch more conviction. "Growth. For me, it's always been about growth. About pushing outward, building myself up. And sometimes," she confessed, a hint of vulnerability coloring her tone, "I worry that 'building ourselves up' together might feel like... shrinking. Like losing the space I fought so hard to create."

The words hung in the air, not as an accusation, but as a quiet confession of an inner landscape she was just beginning to map out. Eli felt a familiar ache of understanding, a deep resonance with the courage it took for her to voice these fears. He reached across the table, his hand covering hers. Her skin was warm, the calluses on her fingertips a testament to her hard work, her resilience.

"I understand, Mara," he said, his voice low and steady. "And I want you to know that I see it. I see the strength it took to carve out that space for yourself. It's not something I want to diminish, or to fill. It's something I want to honor."

Her thumb brushed lightly against his, a silent acknowledgment. "It's just... Havenridge, as a concept, as a community, it's built on us. On shared purpose. And when I think about a shared purpose between us, between you and me, my mind sometimes goes to the old ways. To being absorbed. To losing myself in the 'we'." A faint tremor ran through her voice. "I know that's not what you want, not what this is about. But the echoes are still there, you know? The ingrained fear that autonomy, once relinquished, is gone forever."

Eli squeezed her hand gently. "Those echoes are understandable, Mara. They're part of your story, and your story is one of incredible strength. But the 'we' I envision, the 'we' that Havenridge represents, isn't about absorption. It's about augmentation. It's about two distinct lights shining together, creating a larger, brighter illumination. It's about creating a space where you can be even *more* yourself, not less."

He paused, letting his words settle, observing the subtle shift in her expression. The tension in her shoulders seemed to ease almost imperceptibly. "When I think about our dreams, Mara, I don't see myself taking over your landscape. I see myself building a sturdy, welcoming structure alongside it. A place where you can retreat, or from which you can launch even greater explorations. A place where you feel seen, and supported, in every facet of who you are."

"But how?" she asked, her voice barely above a whisper, the vulnerability laid bare. "How do we ensure that structure doesn't become a boundary? That the support doesn't feel like a leash?"

Eli met her gaze, his own clear and unwavering. "Through constant, open communication. Through listening, truly listening, to each other's needs and fears. Through respecting each other's boundaries, and actively working to understand them, not just to observe them. For me, it means recognizing that your need for independence is as vital as my need for connection. And for you," he continued, his voice soft but firm, "it means allowing yourself to believe that connection doesn't have to erase independence. It can, in fact, strengthen it."

He saw a flicker of something in her eyes – not quite conviction yet, but a spark of hope, a willingness to consider the possibility. "I dream of a Havenridge where individuals are empowered to pursue their passions, to hone their skills, to contribute their unique talents without feeling the pressure to conform. And within that larger vision, I dream of a partnership with you that allows for both our individual growth and our shared journey. I dream of a future where your autonomy is not just tolerated, but celebrated. Where your independence is seen as a vital asset to our partnership, not a potential threat."

Mara looked down at their hands, her fingers now intertwined with his. The candlelight cast dancing shadows, making the familiar room feel both intimate and vast. "It's... a lot to consider," she admitted. "The idea that my strength, my self-reliance, can be a foundation for something more, rather than a reason to stand alone."

"Exactly," Eli affirmed, his heart swelling with a quiet sense of purpose. "It's not about you needing me, Mara. It's about us choosing to walk together. It's about building a life where we can both be fiercely independent individuals, and yet, in our shared moments, find an even deeper strength, a richer experience, than we could ever find alone. Imagine the possibilities, Mara, if the resilience you've cultivated within yourself could be mirrored by a resilient connection with another. A connection built not on dependence, but on mutual respect and a shared desire for each other's well-being."

He leaned forward slightly, his gaze earnest. "I don't want you to doubt your own strength, Mara. Ever. I want to be the person who stands beside you, not behind you, not in front of you. Someone who offers a steady presence, a listening ear, a hand to hold when you need it, but who also trusts you implicitly to navigate your own path. Our shared dreams for Havenridge are born from our individual dreams, and I believe that our individual dreams can flourish even more vibrantly when they are shared and supported by someone who truly sees and values them."

"I've always felt like I was on a solitary journey," Mara confessed, her voice softer now, the fear receding, replaced by a hesitant curiosity. "Even when I was building this community, it felt like I was laying down individual stones, each one placed with immense care, but each one separate. The idea of weaving those stones together with yours, of creating a pattern that is uniquely ours, is... compelling. But also, terrifying."

"Terrifying because it's new, and because it involves vulnerability," Eli acknowledged. "And that's okay. Vulnerability is not weakness, Mara. It's the space where genuine connection is born. It's the courage to be seen, flaws and all, and to trust that you will be met with love and acceptance. My promise to you, my dream for us, is to create that space. A space where you can be fully, unapologetically yourself, and know that my love for you will only deepen, not diminish, your brilliance."

He watched her as she absorbed his words, the candlelight reflecting in her eyes. It was a small shift, a subtle opening, but it felt like a monumental step forward. The landscape of their shared dreams was beginning to take shape, not as a pre-drawn map, but as a living, breathing entity, co-created with each honest conversation, each shared vulnerability, each quiet moment of understanding.

"You see the community as a garden," Mara mused, her gaze distant for a moment, as if seeing their shared vision unfold. "And I've always seen it as a fortress. Built to protect the fragile seeds of autonomy within. But maybe," she conceded, a hint of wonder in her voice, "a garden needs both fertile soil for growth and strong walls to protect it from harsh winds. And perhaps, in a garden, the strongest growth happens when different plants are allowed to intertwine, drawing strength from each other's roots."

Eli smiled, his heart full. "That's it, Mara. That's exactly it. The fortress was necessary for you, for a time. To protect yourself. But now, we can begin to cultivate the garden. Together. Where your autonomy is the most vibrant, resilient bloom, and my presence is the steady sunlight and the nourishing rain that helps it thrive."

He rose and moved around the table, taking the seat beside her. He placed his arm around her shoulders, drawing her gently against his side. She leaned into him, a sigh escaping her lips, a sound of both exhaustion and relief.

"I want to believe in that garden, Eli," she whispered, her voice muffled against his tunic. "I want to believe that two people can build something profound without losing themselves in the process."

"You don't have to believe it all at once," he murmured, pressing a kiss to her temple. "We have time. We have each other. And we have these shared dreams, these nascent hopes, that we can nurture, like the most precious seeds. We'll water them with honesty, tend to them with patience, and watch them grow, side by side."

As the last embers of twilight faded, leaving the dining hall bathed in the warm glow of lanterns and candlelight, Mara and Eli sat in comfortable silence, their bodies pressed together. The conversation had been a turning point, a hesitant exploration of fears that had long resided in the shadows of their individual histories. Now, those fears were brought into the light, examined, and understood. The ground was being laid, not for a merger that erased their distinct identities, but for a partnership that embraced and amplified them.

The landscape of their shared dreams was vast and inviting, and for the first time, Mara felt a genuine sense of anticipation, not dread, for the journey ahead. The fortress of her autonomy was not being dismantled, but rather, its gates were being opened, inviting a gentle, respectful presence to share its grounds and cultivate something beautiful together. The subtle opening of her heart, mirroring the quiet opening of the community's own path, was a testament to the power of honest vulnerability and the unwavering strength of a love that sought not to possess, but to uplift. The shared meal had concluded, but the feast of possibility had just begun.

CHAPTER THREE

LOVE, A DELIBERATE CHOICE

The gentle hum of Havenridge settled around them like a familiar blanket as Mara and Eli walked hand-in-hand, the embers of their earlier conversation still glowing in the twilight. The shared vision of a flourishing garden, a space where individual blooms could thrive while drawing strength from interconnected roots, had softened the edges of Mara's long-held anxieties. Eli's steady presence beside her felt like a grounding force, a quiet testament to the deliberate choice they were both beginning to embrace.

"It's a beautiful metaphor, Eli," Mara murmured, her voice laced with a newfound softness. "The garden. It's so unlike the fortress I've always felt compelled to build. A fortress, by its very nature, is about defense, about keeping things out. A garden, though... a garden is about invitation. About nurturing what's within and encouraging growth, even when the world outside is harsh."

Eli squeezed her hand, his thumb tracing absentminded circles on her skin. "And a garden requires constant tending," he added, his gaze sweeping across the rolling hills that would soon be their shared canvas. "It's not a one-time act of creation. It's a daily commitment. To weeding, to watering, to ensuring the soil is rich and the sunlight reaches every corner. It's work, Mara, but it's a purposeful work. A work that yields abundance."

"That's what I've been pondering," Mara confessed, her gaze drifting towards the distant, star-dusted horizon. "The difference between the feeling of love, the deep affection we clearly share, and the *act* of loving. The feeling, it's a gift. It washes over you, unexpected and beautiful. It's the warmth of the sun on your face, the comfort of a familiar melody. It's what drew us together, what makes every moment with you feel so... right."

She paused, a thoughtful frown creasing her brow. "But you're right, Eli. It's not enough, is it? Not for building something that lasts. Not for Havenridge, and certainly not for us, in the long run. The feeling can ebb and flow, like the tides. It can be influenced by external storms, by moments of doubt or fatigue. If our love were solely reliant on that feeling, it would be as fragile as a wildflower in a gale."

Eli turned to face her, his expression earnest. "And that's where the choice comes in, isn't it? Love, the deliberate choice, is the sturdy oak that withstands the gale. It's the decision, made anew each day, to show up for each other. To listen, even when it's difficult. To forgive, even when the hurt feels raw. To prioritize the well-being of the relationship, and by extension, our shared future, above our immediate impulses or our individual comfort."

"It's about recognizing that the 'we' we are building is a living entity, a third being, if you will, that needs to be nurtured and protected," Mara mused aloud. "It requires more than just shared affection. It requires shared responsibility. It demands that we actively choose to invest in our connection, to feed it with understanding, with empathy, with patience. It's the conscious effort to remain in dialogue, even when silence feels easier."

"Exactly," Eli affirmed, his voice resonating with conviction. "It's the willingness to see our partner's perspective, to try and walk a mile in their shoes, even when their path feels entirely foreign to our own. It's the commitment to seeing the best in each other, even when we're faced with our flaws. Because we all have them, Mara. We all stumble. And a love that is only present in the sunshine will wither and die when the storms inevitably arrive."

He gestured towards the budding trees that lined the path. "Think of these saplings. They're beautiful now, full of youthful promise. But they won't grow into strong, majestic trees without care. They need pruning, to shape them and remove weaknesses. They need fertile soil, to nourish them. They need protection from harsh weather. And all of that requires deliberate action. It requires the gardener's choice to invest time and energy, even when their back aches or the sun beats down relentlessly."

Mara's gaze softened as she looked at him. "And that gardener, in our analogy, is us. We are the conscious architects of this relationship. We are the ones who decide whether to let the weeds of resentment choke the delicate blossoms of joy, or whether to diligently pull them out, one by one. We decide whether to let the drought of indifference dry up the roots of our connection, or whether to actively seek out the springs of shared experience and pour them forth."

"It's a powerful realization, isn't it?" Eli said, his voice low. "That the magic we often seek in love, the enduring, unwavering quality, isn't some external force bestowed upon us, but an internal commitment that we cultivate. It's the willingness to do the unglamorous work, the consistent, often invisible labor, that truly builds a love that can weather any season."

"I've always equated love with a certain effortless grace," Mara confessed. "A feeling of being swept away. And while there is certainly an element of that, a beautiful, exhilarating surrender, I'm beginning to see that the truly profound love, the kind that builds legacies and shelters communities, is built on a bedrock of deliberate, conscious choice. It's the steady, unwavering commitment that allows the moments of effortless grace to flourish."

"It's the understanding that 'happily ever after' isn't a destination we arrive at, but a path we actively walk, day by day, moment by moment," Eli added. "It's the quiet resolve that says, 'Even when I'm tired, even when I'm frustrated, I choose you. I choose us. I choose to invest in this.' That choice, repeated over and over, is what transforms a fleeting infatuation into a deep, abiding, and resilient love."

"And that choice, for me, feels intrinsically linked to Havenridge," Mara said, her voice gaining a new strength. "This community we are building, it's a reflection of our values, our aspirations. If we want Havenridge to be a place of enduring strength, of continuous growth, then our own relationship must embody those same principles. It must be a living testament to the power of deliberate commitment, of choosing to nurture and sustain, even when it requires sacrifice or effort."

Eli nodded, his gaze meeting hers, a shared understanding passing between them. "It's not about extinguishing our individual desires or dreams, Mara. It's about integrating them. It's about recognizing that our individual quests for fulfillment are often amplified, not diminished, when they are shared and supported by a chosen partner. It's about seeing the relationship not as a constraint, but as an accelerant. A partnership that allows us to reach heights we might never have attained alone."

"The idea of sacrifice," Mara continued, her voice thoughtful, "it's often painted as a negative, as a loss. But when the sacrifice is made consciously, for the good of something we deeply value – for our partner, for our shared future, for the community – it transforms. It becomes an act of profound love, a testament to our priorities. It's not a giving up, but a choosing. A choosing of what truly matters."

"And that choice is a powerful thing," Eli agreed. "It's the foundation upon which trust is built. When we consistently choose our partner, when we demonstrate through our actions that their well-being and the health of our bond are paramount, we create an unshakeable sense of security. It's a knowing that no matter what life throws at us, we have each other, and we have committed to navigating it together."

"So, the feeling of love is the spark, the initial light," Mara summarized, weaving together their thoughts. "But the deliberate choice, the ongoing commitment, that's the steady flame. It's what keeps the hearth warm when the initial spark has settled into a glowing ember. It's the sustained energy that fuels the garden, that allows it to bloom year after year, even through the harshest winters."

"And that flame is fueled by intention," Eli added. "By consciously deciding to tend to the relationship, to invest in its growth. It's about those small, everyday acts of kindness, of understanding, of appreciation. It's about making our partner feel seen, heard, and valued, not just when it's convenient, but consistently. It's about actively working to understand their needs, their fears, their aspirations, and aligning our actions with supporting them."

"It's about moving beyond the passive acceptance of affection and stepping into the active cultivation of a profound, enduring partnership," Mara concluded, a sense of peace settling over her. "It's about understanding that love, in its deepest, most meaningful form, is not just something that happens to us, but something we actively create, day by day, choice by choice."

As they continued their walk, the moon rose, casting a silvery glow over Havenridge. The quiet affirmation of their conversation had laid a new groundwork, a philosophical underpinning for the commitment they were slowly, deliberately forging. The affection they shared was a precious gift, but it was the conscious, ongoing choice to nurture that gift, to build upon it with intention and care, that promised to be the true foundation of their lasting love. It was the understanding that love, in its most robust form, was a deliberate act, a continuous weaving of two souls into a tapestry far richer and more resilient than either could create alone.

Eli's gaze met Mara's, a quiet understanding passing between them, a silent agreement that their burgeoning love was not merely a fleeting emotion but a conscious, ongoing construction. The previous conversations had laid the fertile ground for a deeper understanding of commitment, but now, Eli felt a gentle, insistent pull to translate those profound realizations into tangible actions.

He wasn't thinking of grand pronouncements or dramatic declarations; instead, his mind began to map out a series of quiet, deliberate steps, each one a carefully placed stone in the foundation of their shared future. These weren't grand gestures designed for applause, but rather the steady, consistent affirmations that spoke volumes about the depth and sincerity of his feelings.

He recognized that within the fabric of Havenridge, where community and shared life were woven so tightly, commitment often had a visible, almost tangible quality. It wasn't simply an internal feeling; it was an outward expression, a declaration of belonging and shared purpose. Eli's thoughts turned to how he could, in his own way, begin to articulate this partnership. He didn't want to rush or force anything, but he felt a growing need to acknowledge, both to himself and to the community that was becoming their shared home, that Mara was no longer just a cherished companion, but an integral part of his life's design. He envisioned a series of acts, small in scale but significant in their intent, that would serve as quiet milestones on their journey together.

The idea of a shared dwelling, for instance, began to solidify in his mind, not as a mere practical necessity, but as a profound symbol of their intertwined lives. He began to mentally sketch out how he might approach the idea with Mara, ensuring it felt like a natural progression, a mutual desire rather than a unilateral decision. It wasn't about possession or obligation, but about creating a sanctuary, a shared space where their individual lives could seamlessly merge. He pictured the comfortable clutter of two lives becoming one, the shared meals, the quiet evenings, the mornings where waking up meant reaching for each other.

He considered the practicalities, of course – the logistics of merging households, the financial considerations – but these were secondary to the emotional weight of the decision. It was about forging a physical manifestation of their emotional union, a place that would bear witness to their growing love and commitment.

Beyond the immediate prospect of a shared home, Eli's thoughts drifted to the more symbolic gestures that would resonate within Havenridge. He considered how they might publicly acknowledge their partnership. It wasn't about a formal wedding, not yet, but about something that signaled their intention to build a life together, a declaration of a shared future that would be recognized and respected by their neighbors.

He thought about the simple act of introducing Mara not just as a friend or a guest, but as his partner, his chosen confidante, the woman with whom he envisioned his life unfolding. The weight of those words, spoken with genuine intention, felt significant. It was a subtle shift in language, perhaps, but one that carried immense meaning.

He also began to contemplate the idea of shared responsibilities and future planning. This wasn't about burdening Mara, but about openly discussing their aspirations and dreams, and how they could work towards them together. He imagined sitting down with her, not with a formal agenda, but with an open heart, to discuss their financial futures, their long-term goals, and their roles within the Havenridge community.

It was about creating a shared vision, a roadmap for their life together that they had both helped to draw. He saw these conversations as acts of profound trust, opportunities to deepen their understanding of each other and to solidify their commitment to supporting one another's individual growth within the context of their shared journey.

Eli felt a particular pull towards the community garden, the very place that had become a symbol of their budding relationship. He envisioned them planting something together, a tree perhaps, or a special patch of flowers that would represent their shared commitment. It wouldn't be a grand ceremony, but a quiet, meaningful act. He imagined the soil beneath their hands, the shared effort of digging and planting, the quiet satisfaction of knowing they were creating something beautiful and lasting, a living testament to their bond. This, he felt, would be a way for Havenridge to witness their commitment, not through a formal declaration, but through a shared act of creation and nurturing. It was about planting roots, both literally and figuratively, in the soil of their shared life.

He also considered the idea of sharing more of his personal history and vulnerabilities with Mara, not as a burden, but as an offering of trust. He realized that true commitment involved opening oneself up, allowing the other person to see not just the strengths and joys, but also the doubts and fears. He began to think about specific stories he wanted to share, moments from his past that had shaped him, insights into his fears and aspirations. He saw this as a crucial step in building a deep and resilient bond, a way of saying, "This is who I am, fully and completely, and I choose to share that with you." It was about creating a space where both of them could feel safe to be their authentic selves, knowing that they would be met with understanding and acceptance.

Furthermore, Eli contemplated the practicalities of integrating their lives more fully within Havenridge. He imagined them attending community events together, not as individuals, but as a couple. He pictured them volunteering for projects side-by-side, their shared efforts contributing to the betterment of their community. These were not grand gestures, but the consistent, daily acts of partnership that would weave them more tightly into the fabric of their shared life.

It was about demonstrating, through their actions, that they were a team, a unit, committed to supporting each other and contributing to the well-being of Havenridge. He saw these shared endeavors as opportunities to build shared memories and a shared history, strengthening their bond with each passing experience.

He also reflected on the importance of consistent communication, not just about important decisions, but about the everyday ebb and flow of their lives. He imagined establishing a routine of checking in with each other, sharing their thoughts and feelings, listening with undivided attention. This wasn't about constant dialogue, but about creating dedicated moments of connection, spaces where they could truly hear and be heard. He understood that true intimacy was built on open and honest communication, and he was committed to cultivating that within their relationship. He saw these daily interactions as the vital nutrients that would nourish their love and allow it to flourish.

Eli's mind was a whirlwind of quiet intentions, each one a delicate thread woven into the larger tapestry of their shared future. He understood that commitment wasn't a single event, but a continuous process of choosing, of nurturing, of investing. It was about the small, everyday acts of kindness, of understanding, of appreciation. It was about making Mara feel seen, heard, and valued, not just when it was convenient, but consistently.

It was about actively working to understand her needs, her fears, her aspirations, and aligning his actions with supporting them. He realized that the true art of intentional commitment lay not in grand pronouncements, but in the steady, unwavering dedication to building a love that was as resilient and enduring as the ancient oaks of Havenridge itself. It was a commitment to the 'us', a conscious and deliberate choice that would guide their every step forward.

He considered how he might subtly shift his language, incorporating Mara into his narrative in a way that reflected their deepening bond. Instead of speaking of his plans in isolation, he began to mentally frame them as "our plans," or "what Mara and I are thinking." This wasn't about erasing his individuality, but about acknowledging that his future was now intrinsically linked to hers. He saw this as a quiet but powerful way to solidify their partnership, both in his own mind and in the eyes of those around them. It was a subtle recalibration of his internal compass, pointing firmly towards their shared horizon.

The idea of a shared project, beyond the garden, also began to take root. Perhaps it was something that would benefit Havenridge directly, something they could build together, pouring their collective energy and talents into a common goal. This could be anything from restoring an old building to developing a new community initiative. The specifics were less important than the shared purpose and the collaborative effort. He imagined the late nights spent working together, the problem-solving, the shared triumphs, and the quiet understanding that they could achieve anything when they worked as a team. This, he felt, would be a powerful testament to their partnership, a tangible symbol of their ability to create and contribute together.

Eli also mused on the idea of creating rituals together, small traditions that would mark their journey and provide a sense of continuity and comfort. It could be a weekly date night, a special way of celebrating milestones, or even a simple shared cup of tea at the end of a long day. These rituals, he knew, were the threads that would weave their individual lives into a rich and vibrant tapestry of shared experience. They were the anchors that would keep them grounded amidst the inevitable storms of life, providing a constant reminder of their connection and their shared commitment.

He understood that this deliberate commitment wasn't about sacrificing his own dreams or desires, but about integrating them into a shared vision. It was about recognizing that their individual quests for fulfillment were often amplified, not diminished, when they were shared and supported by a chosen partner. He saw their relationship not as a constraint, but as an accelerant, a partnership that would allow them to reach heights they might never have attained alone. This perspective shift, from seeing love as a potential limitation to viewing it as a powerful catalyst for growth, was a crucial element of his evolving understanding.

Finally, Eli felt a growing desire to express his gratitude to Mara, not just for her presence in his life, but for her willingness to embrace this journey with him. He considered how he might articulate this gratitude, perhaps through a heartfelt letter, or simply through consistent, genuine appreciation in their daily interactions. He understood that acknowledging and celebrating the gifts of their relationship was as important as actively working to build and sustain it. This, he believed, was the essence of intentional commitment – a constant, conscious effort to nurture and cherish the love they were building, day by day, choice by choice.

Mara watched Eli, not with the anxious scrutiny of before, but with a quiet, unfolding appreciation. The subtle shifts in his demeanor, the way he'd begun to weave "we" into his conversations about Havenridge's future, the shared glances that spoke of unspoken plans

– these weren't the actions of someone seeking to possess or define her. Instead, they were the deliberate strokes of an artist painting a canvas, a canvas that now included her in every intentional hue.

Her initial anxieties, those tendrils of fear that whispered of losing herself in the powerful current of Eli's presence, began to loosen their grip. She had entered this relationship with a cautious heart, a survivor who had learned to guard her own space with fierce protectiveness. The idea of merging, of building a life so intertwined, had felt like a potential erasure of her own hard-won identity. But Eli's approach was different. It was not about absorption; it was about augmentation.

She saw it in the way he discussed the expansion of the community's irrigation system. Before, his thoughts would have been his alone, meticulously planned and then presented for her consideration. Now, he'd pause, look at her, and ask, "Mara, how do you think this would affect the south-facing plots? You have a better sense of the microclimates there." Or, when discussing the upcoming harvest festival, he wouldn't just outline his ideas for the stalls; he'd ask, "What kind of music do you think would best capture the spirit of this year's bounty? Something lively, or more reflective?" These weren't perfunctory questions; they were invitations to co-create, to share the vision and the labor. It was a subtle but profound distinction, one that resonated deeply within Mara. He wasn't asking for her approval of his plans; he was inviting her to help shape them.

This sense of shared purpose, that grand, almost daunting ambition to not just live in Havenridge, but to actively build and nurture it into something even more vibrant, was becoming the bedrock of their connection. Mara had always been drawn to the idea of community, of belonging to something larger than herself. But her previous experiences had taught her that such belonging often came at a cost, demanding a sacrifice of individuality.

Eli, however, seemed to understand that true strength, both in a relationship and in a community, lay in the synergy of diverse contributions. He saw Havenridge not as a monolithic entity to be molded, but as a living organism, its health dependent on the vibrant health of each of its parts. And he was, in his quiet, steadfast way, inviting her to be not just a part, but a vital organ, contributing to its very lifeblood.

Her own contribution to Havenridge, her quiet expertise in the medicinal herb gardens, had always felt like a separate, cherished project. She poured her heart into it, finding solace and purpose in the earthy scents and the silent growth of life beneath her hands. She had imagined that eventually, she would have to choose between the deep satisfaction of her solitary work and the demands of a shared life.

But Eli had surprised her by actively seeking to understand and even integrate her passion into his vision for Havenridge. He'd spoken of creating a dedicated space within the community center for a small apothecary, a place where she could continue her work, perhaps even share her knowledge with others. He hadn't proposed it as a duty or an obligation, but as an enhancement, a recognition of the unique gifts she brought to their shared world.

"Your knowledge of these plants, Mara," he had said one evening, his voice warm with genuine admiration, "it's a kind of magic. It heals, it soothes, it sustains. And it's a part of Havenridge, a part of what makes this place truly special. We need to make sure that part is nurtured, too."

Mara had felt a lump form in her throat, a mixture of gratitude and surprise. It was as if he had seen a hidden part of her, a part she had kept tucked away, and had not only acknowledged its worth but had made it clear that it was valued, that it was essential to the tapestry he was weaving. This wasn't about Eli dictating what her role should be; it was about him recognizing and supporting the role she was already carving out for herself. It was about him seeing her not as a supporting character in his life, but as a co-author of their shared narrative.

The fear of permanence, the one that had once held her captive, was slowly being replaced by a different kind of understanding, a redefinition of what permanence truly meant. For so long, permanence had conjured images of being trapped, of being fixed in place with no room for growth or change. But with Eli, permanence was beginning to feel like deep roots, anchoring them to a fertile ground that allowed for soaring growth. It wasn't about being static; it was about having a stable foundation from which to explore, to expand, to become even more fully themselves.

She observed how Eli handled disagreements within the community council. He was never confrontational, but he was firm in his convictions, always seeking to find common ground, to understand the underlying needs of each person involved. He would listen intently, his brow furrowed in concentration, and then he would offer a perspective that often diffused tension and opened up new possibilities.

Mara realized that this wasn't just a skill; it was a reflection of his character, a commitment to building, not to conquering. And this same approach, she saw, was being applied to their relationship. He wasn't trying to force her into a pre-defined mold; he was patiently working with her, allowing their shared life to take shape organically, guided by mutual respect and shared aspirations.

One afternoon, as they were walking through the newly planted community orchard, Eli stopped and gestured to a young sapling, its slender branches reaching towards the sun. "This one," he said, his eyes alight with a quiet joy, "this one feels like us, Mara. Still growing, still finding its way, but with the promise of bearing fruit for years to come. We'll need to tend to it, protect it from the harsh weather, make sure it gets enough water, but imagine, in a few years, the shade it will provide, the sweetness it will offer."

Mara reached out and brushed her fingers against his arm. The touch was light, but it conveyed a wealth of unspoken emotion – her growing trust, her burgeoning love, her profound relief. She was no longer just observing Eli's deliberate actions; she was experiencing their impact. She was beginning to understand that his commitment was not a cage, but a carefully constructed trellis, designed to support their shared growth, allowing them to reach new heights together.

The concept of shared purpose was evolving in her mind. It wasn't a monolithic obligation that overshadowed their individual needs. Instead, it was a dynamic force, a shared energy that propelled them both forward. Havenridge, with its inherent challenges and its boundless potential, was becoming the crucible in which their individual strengths were being refined and their shared vision was taking flight. She saw how Eli's dedication to the community mirrored her own dedication to her herb gardens; both were acts of nurturing, of building something that would endure and enrich.

She found herself sharing more freely with him, not just her thoughts on gardening or community matters, but her deeper reflections, her dreams, and even her lingering fears. The protective walls she had built around her heart were gradually being dismantled, not by force, but by the gentle, persistent warmth of Eli's understanding. He listened without judgment, offered support without presumption, and celebrated her triumphs as if they were his own. This was the essence of true partnership, she realized – not the absence of individual identity, but the amplification of it, supported and encouraged by a loving connection.

The idea of permanence, once a source of dread, was now being reimagined as a promise. It was the promise of shared mornings, of quiet evenings, of weathered storms faced together, and of abundant harvests reaped side by side. It was the promise that even when life presented its inevitable challenges, there would be a constant, unwavering presence beside her, a hand to hold, a heart to share. This wasn't a passive acceptance of fate; it was an active, deliberate choice, a choice she was increasingly making every day, alongside Eli.

She understood now that Eli's deliberate actions were not about control, but about creation. He was not building a life *for* her, but a life *with* her. The shared purpose of Havenridge, far from being a constraint, was the fertile soil in which their individual identities could not only survive but flourish. It was the foundation upon which they were building a future that was both secure and expansive, a testament to the power of love, deliberately chosen and continuously nurtured.

Her trust in him, and in their shared journey, was no longer a fragile sprout, but a deep-rooted certainty, one that promised shade, sustenance, and enduring beauty for years to come. She felt a profound sense of belonging, not just to Eli, but to the vision he was so carefully cultivating, a vision that now included her in every vibrant, hopeful stroke. This was the sweet, quiet revolution of trust, the realization that in building something together, they were each becoming more fully themselves.

The fire in the hearth crackled, casting dancing shadows across the familiar comfort of their shared living space. It was a quiet evening, the kind that settled deep into the bones after a long day, a silence not of emptiness, but of contentment. Mara sat curled in her favorite armchair, a book resting unread in her lap, her gaze drifting towards Eli. He was across the room, meticulously cleaning a carving tool, his brow furrowed in concentration, a picture of quiet dedication. It was in these unscripted moments, bathed in the warm glow of their home, that the most profound conversations often began.

"Eli," Mara began softly, her voice a gentle ripple in the peaceful atmosphere, "we talk a lot about Havenridge, about its future, about what we're building here. But I've been thinking... what does 'legacy' truly mean to us?"

Eli paused his work, the small piece of wood held steady in his hand. He looked up, his eyes meeting hers, and a slow smile spread across his face. He set the tool down and rose, crossing the room to sit on the hearth rug, facing her. He reached out, taking her hand, his thumb stroking the back of her palm.

"That's a big question, Mara," he said, his voice a low rumble. "And I think it's one that's been growing between us, hasn't it? Not just about Havenridge, but about... us."

Mara nodded, her fingers lacing with his. "Exactly. I mean, we're talking about land stewardship, about irrigation systems, about ensuring the community thrives for generations. Those are tangible things, important things. But I feel like there's something more. Something less... concrete."

"The values," Eli said, his gaze thoughtful. "The way we choose to live. Not just the structures we build, but the foundation upon which those structures are built. What does that look like for us, for Havenridge?"

He pulled her gently from the armchair, guiding her to sit beside him on the rug, their shoulders touching. The firelight illuminated the sincerity in his expression. "For me, it's about the integrity we bring to our work, the respect we cultivate, not just for the land, but for each other. It's about demonstrating that a community can be built on collaboration and genuine care, not just on contracts and agreements. It's about showing that even in challenging times, there's a way to approach problems with kindness and a willingness to understand."

Mara leaned her head against his shoulder, breathing in the subtle scent of wood and earth that always clung to him. "Yes," she murmured. "It's about the kindness. I see it in how you lead the council, how you listen even when you disagree. It's about fostering that spirit. And for me," she continued, turning to look at him, her eyes earnest, "it's about nurturing. Not just the plants in my gardens, but nurturing relationships, nurturing understanding. It's about the quiet persistence of growth, the belief that even from a small seed, something beautiful and life-sustaining can emerge."

"And that's where our personal journey becomes intertwined with Havenridge's story, isn't it?" Eli mused, his gaze softening as he looked at her. "The way we choose to love each other, the way we choose to build our life together – that's a powerful message in itself.

It's a testament to what's possible when two people are committed to building something strong, something real."

He tightened his grip on her hand. "I don't want our legacy to be just about fertile fields and well-maintained buildings, Mara. I want it to be about the resilience of the human spirit, about the enduring power of connection. I want it to be about showing people that love, true, deliberate love, can be the most powerful force for good. That it can heal, and build, and transform."

"It's about the 'how' as much as the 'what'," Mara added, her mind making connections. "How we tend the land, how we treat our neighbors, how we handle conflict. Those are the echoes that will remain long after we're gone. If we lead with empathy, with a genuine desire for collective well-being, that's the kind of legacy that truly matters. It's not just what we leave behind, but the example we set."

Eli's thumb traced a gentle pattern on her skin. "And our commitment to each other, Mara, is at the heart of that. It's not just about our personal happiness, though that's certainly a cherished outcome. It's about demonstrating that a partnership, built on mutual respect, trust, and a shared vision, can be a bedrock of strength for the entire community. When people see us working together, supporting each other, facing challenges side-by-side, it validates their own hopes for connection. It makes the idea of building something lasting seem not just possible, but attainable."

"I used to think of legacy as something grand and external," Mara confessed, her voice hushed. "Something to be achieved, like a monument. But you're right. It's internal, too. It's the inner architecture of our lives, the way we choose to be, day in and day out. It's in the quiet moments of understanding, the shared laughter, the comfort we find in each other's presence. Those are the invisible threads that weave the tapestry of our lives, and ultimately, the legacy we leave."

"And this home, this hearth," Eli said, gesturing around the room with his free hand, "this is where that internal legacy is forged. It's where we choose our values, where we practice our empathy, where we learn to forgive and to grow. It's where our personal commitment to each other becomes a model, however small, for the larger community. When Havenridge sees us living out our love, not as a fleeting emotion, but as a deliberate, daily choice, it plants a seed of hope."

Mara felt a surge of warmth, not just from the fire, but from within. The idea of their personal relationship being a vital part of Havenridge's enduring story was both humbling and exhilarating. It elevated their love from a private affair to a public testament, a quiet sermon preached through their actions.

"It's about cultivating a spirit of generosity, isn't it?" she continued, exploring the idea further. "A spirit of giving without expecting immediate return, of investing in the well-being of others, of the land, of the future. That's what our land stewardship agreements are, in a way. They're promises to the future, made tangible. But the spirit behind them, that's what truly defines our legacy."

Eli squeezed her hand. "Exactly. And that spirit starts here, with us. It starts with the way we treat each other, the way we communicate, the way we support each other's dreams. When we are strong and united, that strength radiates outwards. When we are kind to each other, it encourages kindness in the community. Our personal legacy isn't separate from Havenridge's legacy; it's woven into its very fabric.

Our love story is becoming a part of the soil, a part of the water, a part of the air that sustains this place."

The thought settled deep within Mara, a comforting weight. She had always felt a profound connection to Havenridge, a sense of belonging that transcended mere residency. Now, she understood that her deepest connection was being forged not just with the land, but with Eli, and through him, with the very soul of the community. Their shared purpose, the deliberate choice to build a life together, was becoming the bedrock upon which Havenridge's enduring narrative was being written.

"So, our legacy isn't just about what we leave behind," Mara summarized, her voice filled with newfound clarity. "It's about the values we embody, the way we choose to live. It's about demonstrating that love, integrity, and a deep respect for life – all life – are the foundations of a truly thriving community. And that our commitment to each other is the living proof of that belief."

Eli turned to face her fully, his eyes alight with a shared understanding. He gently cupped her cheek, his touch tender. "Precisely. It's about defining what we stand for, not just for ourselves, but for those who will come after us. It's about creating ripples of positivity that extend far beyond our own lifetimes. And it's about knowing that in choosing each other, we are also choosing to contribute to something larger and more meaningful than ourselves. We are choosing to define a legacy, together."

The fire crackled, a silent witness to their profound realization. The legacy they were building was not a grand pronouncement etched in stone, but a quiet, persistent unfolding of love, integrity, and shared purpose, a legacy that would resonate in the heart of Havenridge for generations to come. It was in the warmth of their shared hearth, in the steady rhythm of their breathing, in the quiet strength of their clasped hands, that the truest meaning of their enduring legacy was being defined. It was a legacy born of deliberate choice, nurtured by unwavering commitment, and destined to bloom in the fertile soil of a community built on love.

The quiet hum of the evening had shifted, the comfortable silence now charged with an unspoken gravity. Mara had spoken of legacy, of the tangible and the intangible, of the imprint they were leaving on Havenridge. Eli had echoed her sentiments, weaving their personal commitment into the fabric of the community. But as the fire's embers glowed lower, a different kind of conversation began to stir within Mara, a conversation that had been a subtle undercurrent for a while, now surfacing with an insistent tug. She turned on the rug, not quite facing Eli, but angled towards the hearth, her gaze fixed on the dancing flames. The subject of permanence, of leaving a mark that would endure, had brought her to a precipice she hadn't anticipated.

"Eli," she began, her voice softer than before, almost hesitant, the words carefully chosen. "We've talked about what we're building here, about the future of Havenridge. And it's... it's all so real, so solid. The land, the community, the agreements we're making. It feels like we're etching our names into the very stone of this place." She paused, gathering her thoughts, the vulnerability in her tone a stark contrast to the usual strength she projected. "But lately, I've been wrestling with a different kind of permanence. The kind that's... fragile."

Eli remained still beside her, his presence a steady anchor. He didn't press her, allowing the silence to hold her words, to give them space to breathe. When he finally spoke, his voice was a low, comforting murmur. "Fragile permanence? Tell me, Mara. What does that feel like?"

She turned her head slightly, her eyes meeting his, and in their depths, he could see a flicker of something akin to fear. "It feels like... like it could all disappear. Like the very foundations we're laying could crumble. Not because of anything external, not a blight or a drought or a market crash. But from within. From us." The admission hung in the air, raw and exposed. "I worry about our strength, Eli. Not our strength to build, or to lead, or to steward. But our strength as *us*. As Mara and Eli. What if the bonds that hold us together, the ones that feel so unbreakable now, what if they weaken? What if *I* falter? What if *you* falter?"

Her voice cracked on the last word, a small, involuntary tremor that spoke volumes. She looked away again, her gaze returning to the fire, her shoulders tensing. "It's not a lack of faith in you, Eli. Please, never think that. It's... it's the opposite. It's because I have so much faith in you, and in us, that the thought of losing that, of tarnishing what we have, feels so terrifying. It's admitting that even something as beautiful and strong as what we share, can be... impermanent. That I can be the weak link."

Eli's hand found hers, his fingers gently interlacing with her own. His touch was warm, grounding, a silent assurance. He didn't immediately offer platitudes or dismiss her fears. Instead, he acknowledged the depth of her confession. "Mara," he began, his voice laced with a profound tenderness, "what you're feeling... it's not weakness. It's courage. It's the profound honesty of someone who truly understands what's at stake."

He shifted closer, his arm wrapping around her shoulders, drawing her gently against his side. She leaned into him, the familiar comfort of his embrace a balm to her exposed nerves. "You're not the weak link, Mara," he continued, his voice a low rumble against her hair. "You are the heart of this. And if your heart harbors doubts, then it's my job, our job, to understand them, to hold them, and to show you that they don't diminish what we are. They simply make us more human."

"But the idea of leaving a legacy," she whispered, her voice muffled against his chest, "it feels like it requires an unwavering strength, a certainty that transcends the everyday. And I'm just... I'm afraid of the 'everyday' eroding that. Afraid that the challenges, the disagreements, the sheer weight of living, might chip away at the foundation of our love, and in doing so, compromise the legacy we're trying to build for Havenridge."

Eli held her a little tighter, his thumb stroking her arm. "Let's reframe 'strength,' then," he suggested softly. "Is strength only about resilience, about never bending? Or is it also about the ability to be vulnerable, to admit when we're afraid, and to trust that our partner will be there to catch us? Is strength not also found in the courage to be imperfect, to be human, and to still choose love, day after day?"

He pulled back just enough to look into her eyes, his gaze steady and unwavering. "You see permanence in the land, in the structures, in the systems we create. And I see that too. But I also see permanence in the choices we make, Mara. In the choice to be honest, even when it's difficult. In the choice to extend grace, even when we're hurt. In the choice to forgive, not just others, but ourselves. That's where the real, enduring strength lies. It's not in an impenetrable shield, but in the willingness to be open, to be seen, and to be loved despite our flaws."

"But what if my flaws, my fears, are too much?" she asked, her voice barely audible. "What if the weight of my own doubts is too heavy for you to carry, in addition to all the other responsibilities we have?"

Eli's smile was gentle, reassuring. "Mara, my love," he said, his voice brimming with an earnest sincerity that always managed to quiet her anxieties. "You are not a burden. You are my partner. My equal. The fears you carry are not yours alone to bear. They become ours. And the strength you question? I see it every single day. I see it in the way you nurture your gardens, coaxing life from the soil with patience and unwavering dedication. I see it in the way you advocate for the most vulnerable in our community, your voice firm and clear even when facing opposition. And I see it most profoundly, right now, in this very moment. The courage it takes for you to voice these deepest anxieties, to lay bare your most vulnerable self to me... that is a strength that can move mountains."

He paused, his thumb gently tracing the curve of her cheekbone. "Your vulnerability is not a threat to our legacy, Mara. It is its foundation. It's the living, breathing testament to the depth of our connection. When people see that we can weather storms, not by pretending they don't exist, but by holding onto each other, by supporting each other through them, that's a far more powerful lesson than any edifice we could ever build. It shows them that love is not just a feeling, but a deliberate act of unwavering commitment, even in the face of fear."

A wave of emotion washed over Mara. It was the relief of being understood, the profound comfort of acceptance, and the quiet exhilaration of realizing that her deepest fears, when shared, could be transformed into something beautiful. She had always prided herself on her strength, on her ability to stand tall and face challenges head-on. The idea that admitting her own fragility could be a source of strength, rather than a weakness, was a revelation. It was a paradigm shift, a gentle recalibration of her own internal compass.

"I always thought of vulnerability as a chink in the armor," she admitted, her voice gaining a newfound steadiness. "A place where doubt could creep in and undermine everything. But you're right. It's not the absence of armor, but the decision to take it off, to trust that someone else will stand guard with you. That's where the real intimacy lies, isn't it? In the shared vulnerability."

Eli nodded, his gaze never leaving hers. "Precisely. It's the knowledge that you can be fully seen, fully known, with all your imperfections and insecurities, and still be cherished. That's the safety net that allows us to be bold, to take risks, to build something as ambitious as Havenridge. Your willingness to share your fears with me doesn't make you less capable; it makes our partnership more profound. It means that when challenges arise, we face them not as two separate individuals trying to maintain a facade of invincibility, but as a united front, drawing strength from our shared understanding and mutual support."

He laced their fingers together again, squeezing her hand. "Think about it, Mara. If we were to project an image of flawless strength, what would that tell the people of Havenridge? That perfection is the goal? That struggle is a sign of failure? That's not the message we want to send. We want to show them that life is messy, that challenges are inevitable, but that through connection, through honesty, and through a deliberate choice to love and support each other, anything is possible. Our journey, with all its moments of doubt and fear, is a crucial part of the story we're telling."

Mara let out a breath she hadn't realized she was holding. The weight on her chest had lightened, replaced by a quiet sense of resolve. The fear hadn't vanished entirely, but it had been transmuted, its sharp edges softened by Eli's unwavering acceptance. She understood now that true intimacy wasn't about presenting a perfect front, but about the courage to be imperfect, to be transparent, and to find solace and strength in the unwavering presence of a partner who truly saw her, and loved her, all the same.

"So, our legacy," she mused, the concept taking on a new dimension, "it's not just about the tangible achievements, or the flawless facade of strength. It's also about the testament to our own human experience. It's about showing that love can endure, not by avoiding the difficult conversations, but by embracing them. By choosing each other, even when it's hard. Even when doubt creeps in."

Eli brought her hand to his lips, kissing her knuckles gently. "Exactly. It's about demonstrating that vulnerability is not a failing, but a gateway to deeper connection. It's about creating a space within our partnership where fears can be shared without judgment, where insecurities can be met with compassion, and where the act of leaning on each other becomes the ultimate expression of strength. That is the legacy of our love, Mara. A legacy built not on the absence of storms, but on the unwavering commitment to navigate them together."

The fire had dwindled to a soft, pulsing glow, casting long shadows that no longer seemed ominous, but intimate. The air in the room felt different now, cleaner, lighter. Mara rested her head against Eli's shoulder, a profound sense of peace settling over her. She had shared her deepest anxieties, her fear of impermanence, and in doing so, had found not weakness, but a new, unshakeable foundation for their shared future.

The courage to be vulnerable, met with the unwavering strength of Eli's love and acceptance, had forged a connection more profound than she had ever imagined. Their story, their legacy, would be one not of flawless perfection, but of enduring love, nurtured by the very human act of trusting each other with their deepest fears, and finding solace in their shared embrace. This was the emotional climax, the quiet, powerful realization that true strength lay not in never falling, but in always choosing to rise, together.

Chapter Four

WEAVING THE THREADS OF LEGACY

The weighty oak doors of Havenridge's Great Hall swung open, admitting the warm, late afternoon sun and a palpable buzz of anticipation. Dust motes, caught in the golden shafts of light, danced like tiny, industrious spirits above the long, polished tables. This was where decisions were made, where the collective heartbeat of Havenridge found its rhythm, and tonight, the very foundations of its future were being solidified.

The Community Council was in session, a gathering of faces known and respected, each a stakeholder in the unfolding narrative of this unique settlement. The air was alive with the murmur of voices, the rustle of parchment, and the clinking of mugs as villagers settled into their places, a shared purpose drawing them together.

Mara surveyed the scene, a sense of quiet satisfaction blooming within her. The hall, once a space she'd approached with a hesitant reverence, now felt like an extension of her own home, a testament to the deep roots they were all cultivating. The anxieties that had surfaced in the quiet intimacy of her conversation with Eli had not vanished entirely, but they had been reframed, their sharp edges smoothed by understanding and a newfound resolve.

The tapestry of Havenridge, she realized, was not just woven with threads of intention and aspiration, but with the very fabric of their daily lives, the tangible manifestations of their commitment. Tonight's council meeting was a crucial stitch in that ongoing creation.

Eli, his presence a grounding force beside her, offered a subtle nod, his eyes conveying a quiet pride that warmed her more than any spoken praise. He had witnessed her transformation, from the woman wrestling with the fragility of legacy to the leader now poised to shape its practical implementation. His unwavering belief had been the soil in which her confidence had taken root, and now, she felt it ready to blossom. She returned his gaze, a silent acknowledgment of their shared journey, their intertwined destinies now inextricably linked to the fate of this valley.

The agenda was focused, the discourse direct. Elder Maeve, her silver hair pulled back in its customary neat bun, stood at the head of the main table, her voice resonating with calm authority. "Welcome, all," she began, her gaze sweeping across the assembled faces. "Tonight, we finalize the Long-Term Land Stewardship Plan. This is a document born from months of careful deliberation, countless hours of research, and a shared vision for the enduring health of Havenridge." She gestured to a detailed map unfurled before her, marked with intricate lines and notations. "We are not merely allocating parcels; we are charting a course for generations to come. We are defining how we will coexist with this land, not as its masters, but as its careful custodians."

Mara felt a surge of engagement as Maeve spoke. The initial draft of the plan had been a comprehensive yet somewhat impersonal document. But through subsequent workshops and smaller group discussions, it had evolved, infused with the collective wisdom and specific needs of the community. Mara's own contributions, once hesitant suggestions, had now become integral parts of the plan, particularly in areas concerning soil regeneration and biodiversity preservation. She had spent weeks poring over agricultural studies, consulting with botanists and geologists, her earlier fears about the potential for external factors to impact their endeavors fueling a meticulous approach to anticipating and mitigating such risks.

"As we've discussed," Maeve continued, her finger tracing a section of the map depicting the northern farmlands, "this sector will see a phased implementation of crop rotation and cover cropping. The aim is to restore nutrient levels and improve soil structure, ensuring its fertility for decades. The initial investment in specialized seed mixes and consultation with soil scientists is significant, but the long-term returns, both ecological and economic, are undeniable."

A farmer named Silas, his hands calloused and his face weathered by years under the sun, raised a hand. "Maeve, Mara," he said, his voice a rumble that commanded attention. "I've seen the preliminary reports. The figures for yield reduction in the first two years of transition are... concerning. It's a risk, no doubt. My family's livelihood depends on these fields."

Mara met Silas's gaze directly, her voice clear and steady. "Silas, I understand your concern, truly. The initial dip in yield is a factor we've accounted for. However, the soil health assessments, conducted over the past eighteen months, show a significant depletion in organic matter. If we continue with current practices, we risk a far steeper decline, and potentially, irreversible damage. The cover crops we've identified, like crimson clover and hairy vetch, are not just about adding nitrogen; they break up compacted soil, improve water infiltration, and provide a habitat for beneficial insects.

We've also factored in a community-supported loan program to help offset immediate income disparities for those adopting the new methods. The sustainability of our farmlands is not just an ecological imperative; it's an economic one. We are investing in the future productivity of your land, and by extension, the future of Havenridge."

Her explanation wasn't just a recitation of facts; it was a narrative, a story of cause and effect, of short-term sacrifice for long-term prosperity. She spoke of the symbiotic relationships within the ecosystem, of how beneficial insects, nurtured by the cover crops, would naturally reduce the need for pesticides, saving costs and safeguarding the health of the land and its inhabitants. She painted a picture of thriving fields, of richer harvests, of a Havenridge that could feed itself sustainably, even in the face of changing climates. Eli watched her, a silent testament to her growth, her ability to translate complex ecological principles into practical, community-focused solutions.

"And what about the water usage?" another council member, Elara, a former botanist who now managed the community's arboretum, inquired. "The revised plan allocates more water to irrigation in the transition phase for these new crops. Havenridge is fortunate to have reliable water sources, but we must remain prudent."

"Elara, your point is well taken," Mara replied, gesturing towards another section of the map. "We've integrated a multi-pronged approach to water management. Firstly, the improved soil structure from the cover cropping will significantly enhance water retention, meaning less water is needed over time. Secondly, we are implementing drip irrigation systems in all new long-term cultivation zones. This technology delivers water directly to the root zone, minimizing evaporation and reducing water consumption by up to 60% compared to traditional overhead sprinklers.

Furthermore, we are investing in rainwater harvesting infrastructure, with cisterns strategically placed to capture runoff from the Great Hall and other communal buildings. The aim is not just to meet the demands of the transition period, but to establish a water-wise culture for the future. This plan ensures we are using every drop as efficiently as possible, protecting this precious resource for all."

She elaborated on the types of crops being prioritized – hardy, drought-resistant varieties that could thrive with minimal intervention once the soil had been revitalized. She spoke of the potential for diversifying Havenridge's agricultural output, reducing reliance on a few staple crops and creating a more resilient food system. Her words painted a picture of a community not just surviving, but flourishing, a testament to their collective foresight and their willingness to adapt. The council members listened, their initial skepticism giving way to a thoughtful consideration of the proposed strategies.

Elder Maeve then turned her attention to the forested areas bordering the settlement. "The plan also addresses our forest stewardship," she announced. "We've outlined a sustainable forestry management program, focusing on selective harvesting of mature trees for timber, while ensuring the replanting and protection of younger growth. This will not only provide a renewable resource for our building needs but also maintain the ecological balance of the surrounding woodlands."

A younger man, Finn, a carpenter who had been instrumental in the recent expansion of the community's workshops, voiced his thoughts. "I've been looking at the projections for timber availability, Maeve. With the increased demand for building materials as we grow, are we certain that selective harvesting will be enough to meet our needs without over-taxing the forest? I'd hate to see us cut down our future for immediate use."

Mara stepped forward again, her understanding of the interplay between community needs and environmental limits evident. "Finn, your pragmatism is vital. The plan accounts for this. We've projected our needs for the next fifty years, factoring in anticipated growth. The selective harvesting strategy prioritizes older, less vigorous trees, which often contain diseases or pests that could spread. By removing them, we not only gain usable timber but also create space and light for younger trees to flourish.

Furthermore, we've allocated a significant portion of the community's investment in sustainable forestry to a dedicated replanting initiative. For every mature tree harvested, we will be planting at least five new saplings of native species, chosen for their resilience and suitability to our climate. We are also exploring alternative building materials, like bamboo cultivation in specific microclimates, and advanced techniques in wood preservation to extend the lifespan of our timber. This isn't about simply cutting trees; it's about actively managing and nurturing our forest as a living, renewable resource."

She spoke of the importance of the forest not just as a source of timber, but as a crucial element in Havenridge's water cycle, its role in preventing soil erosion on the slopes, and its contribution to the overall biodiversity of the region. She described how the undergrowth, carefully managed, would provide crucial habitat for various species, supporting the delicate ecosystem that benefited them all. The council members nodded, recognizing the thoroughness of her approach.

The conversation then shifted to the community's energy infrastructure. "The plan proposes a transition towards a more diversified energy portfolio," Maeve explained, pointing to a section of the map detailing potential sites for renewable energy installations. "While our hydroelectric turbine has served us well, relying solely on one source carries its own risks. We are exploring the feasibility of solar arrays on south-facing slopes and smaller wind turbines in higher elevations."

A woman named Clara, who ran the local apothecary and was deeply concerned with the air quality and environmental impact of their operations, spoke up. "The solar array proposal is promising. I've been reading about advancements in photovoltaic technology that make them increasingly efficient, even in less than ideal sunlight conditions. What are the projected energy yields, and what is the plan for energy storage?"

"Clara, I'm glad you brought that up," Mara responded, her voice filled with enthusiasm for the technological advancements. "The solar feasibility studies have been quite encouraging. We've identified several locations that receive excellent solar irradiance throughout the year. The projected yield from the proposed array, when combined with our existing hydroelectric power, is more than sufficient to meet our current and projected energy needs.

Crucially, the plan includes a significant investment in battery storage technology. We're looking at cutting-edge lithium-ion systems, capable of storing excess energy generated during peak sunlight hours for use during the night or on cloudy days. This ensures a consistent and reliable power supply, minimizing our reliance on any single energy source. Furthermore, the transition to renewables will significantly reduce our carbon footprint, contributing to cleaner air for everyone in Havenridge."

She went on to describe how the solar panels would be integrated into the roofs of new community buildings, minimizing their visual impact and maximizing their efficiency. She spoke of the potential for individual households to adopt smaller-scale solar solutions in the future, fostering a sense of energy independence and collective responsibility. The plan, as presented, was not just about meeting immediate needs; it was about building a resilient and sustainable energy future for Havenridge, a future powered by the very elements that surrounded them.

The discussion then moved to waste management and recycling. "Our current approach to waste management is adequate for our present size," Maeve stated, "but as Havenridge grows, so will our waste. The plan outlines a comprehensive strategy for reducing, reusing, and recycling, with the ultimate goal of achieving near-zero waste."

"Near-zero waste is an ambitious goal," commented Silas, the farmer. "What does that entail in practical terms? How do we ensure compliance and manage the logistics?"

Mara addressed the challenge head-on. "It requires a multi-faceted approach, Silas. Firstly, we're implementing a community-wide composting program for all organic waste, which will significantly reduce the volume of material going to landfill. This compost will then be used to enrich our agricultural lands, closing the loop. Secondly, we are establishing a dedicated recycling center, equipped to sort and process a wide range of materials, from glass and metal to plastics and paper. We're also exploring partnerships with external recycling facilities for specialized materials.

Thirdly, and perhaps most importantly, we are launching an education campaign to foster a culture of waste reduction. This will involve workshops on repairing and repurposing items, encouraging the use of reusable containers, and educating residents on proper sorting and disposal practices. We're also looking into innovative waste-to-energy technologies for any residual, non-recyclable waste, ensuring that even the remaining fraction is managed responsibly."

She spoke of the economic benefits of a robust recycling program, of how salvaged materials could be used in local crafts and manufacturing, creating new opportunities within Havenridge. She emphasized that near-zero waste wasn't just about environmental responsibility; it was about resourcefulness, about maximizing the value of everything they consumed. The council members seemed impressed by the thoroughness of the plan, the consideration given to every aspect of waste management.

As the evening wore on, the detailed proposals for land stewardship, resource management, and sustainable infrastructure were met with thoughtful questions and constructive feedback. Mara, standing beside Eli, found herself increasingly at ease, her earlier hesitations replaced by a quiet confidence. The anxieties that had once loomed large – the fear of her own limitations, the possibility of compromise – had been met and, in many ways, transmuted through the process of shared creation. She had seen how her personal growth, her willingness to confront her own vulnerabilities, had directly translated into a more robust and visionary approach to building Havenridge.

Eli's hand found hers under the table, his grip firm and reassuring. His quiet presence was a constant affirmation, a silent acknowledgment of her strength and her dedication. He had seen her pour over reports, had witnessed her late-night research sessions, and had listened patiently as she articulated complex ecological principles. Now, seeing her articulate these ideas with such clarity and conviction to the entire council, his pride was evident in the subtle softening of his gaze, the almost imperceptible smile that touched his lips.

The tangible aspects of their legacy were coming into sharp focus, not as abstract ideals, but as concrete plans and achievable goals. The land stewardship plan was more than just a document; it was a promise to the earth, a commitment to ensure that Havenridge would thrive in harmony with its environment. The sustainable infrastructure proposals were not just about building structures; they were about creating a resilient and self-sufficient community. The carefully outlined waste management strategies were not just about tidiness; they were about fostering a culture of responsibility and resourcefulness.

Elder Maeve, after facilitating a particularly productive discussion on water conservation, addressed the council. "We have before us a comprehensive and forward-thinking plan for the long-term stewardship of our land and resources," she declared, her voice resonating with a deep sense of accomplishment. "It reflects the collective wisdom of this community, and it is a testament to the dedication and insight of individuals like Mara, whose hard work has been instrumental in shaping these proposals."

A ripple of applause spread through the hall, genuine and heartfelt. Mara felt a warmth spread through her, not of ego, but of deep satisfaction. She met Eli's eyes, and in that shared glance, she saw the culmination of their journey thus far. The legacy they were weaving was not merely in the structures they built or the land they tended, but in the very fabric of their community, a community that was learning to live in balance, to innovate with purpose, and to face the future with a shared sense of responsibility and hope.

The tapestry of Havenridge was growing richer, more vibrant, each thread a testament to their collective effort, their enduring commitment, and the profound strength found in unity. The council meeting concluded not with finality, but with a renewed sense of purpose, a shared understanding that the work of building a lasting legacy was an ongoing, beautiful endeavor, one that would continue to unfold with each sunrise over the valley.

The murmurs of the council meeting had subsided, leaving a gentle hum of shared accomplishment in the Great Hall. Yet, for Mara and Eli, the work was far from over. As the last villagers filed out, their faces alight with the prospect of a future secured by sound planning, Mara turned to Eli, a thoughtful expression softening her features. "It's a remarkable feeling, isn't it?" she said, her voice low. "To see months of deliberation coalesce into tangible action. The land stewardship, the infrastructure... it's all so concrete."

Eli nodded, his gaze meeting hers with that familiar warmth. "It is. But as you said, Mara, a legacy isn't just built from stone and soil. It's built from people. And our work has just begun in earnest." He gestured towards the setting sun, painting the sky in hues of amber and rose. "There's a particular kind of growth that can't be charted on a map or measured by yield reports. The growth of a leader."

Their conversations, particularly in the weeks and months that followed the adoption of the Long-Term Land Stewardship Plan, began to take on a new dimension. While the practicalities of implementing the plan occupied much of their days, their private discussions often drifted to the future of leadership within Havenridge. They found themselves drawn to the ancient oak tree that stood sentinel at the edge of the communal gardens, its gnarled branches reaching towards the heavens like wizened arms. It was here, in the dappled shade of its enduring presence, that they would often pause, the symbolic weight of the tree grounding their contemplation of Havenridge's future.

"We've laid the groundwork," Mara mused, tracing a pattern on the rough bark of the oak. "We've created systems, established practices that will ensure the land flourishes and our community thrives. But what happens when the stewards themselves are no longer here to guide them? A well-built bridge needs strong foundations, but it also needs skilled engineers to maintain it, to adapt it, to guide others across it."

Eli sat beside her, the silence between them comfortable, filled with a shared understanding. "Exactly. We've focused so much on the 'what' of our legacy – the sustainable farming, the renewable energy, the resource management. Now, we must focus on the 'who'. Who will inherit these responsibilities? Who possesses the vision, the integrity, and the dedication to carry Havenridge forward?"

Their conversations were not about identifying a single heir apparent, but about fostering a culture of leadership that was as resilient and diverse as Havenridge itself. They recognized that the complexities of their evolving community demanded a multifaceted approach to governance, one that could draw on a variety of strengths and perspectives. This meant looking beyond the obvious, beyond those who already held positions of authority, and actively seeking out those who demonstrated a quiet competence, a genuine concern for the collective good, and a hunger to learn.

Mara recalled the early days of the Long-Term Land Stewardship Plan, the initial hesitancy of some, the insightful questions of others. Silas, the farmer, had voiced his very real concerns about yield reduction, not out of resistance, but out of a deep-seated responsibility to his family and the community. His pragmatism, she realized, was not a hindrance but a vital component of responsible leadership. And Elara, with her botanist's keen eye for detail and her unwavering commitment to ecological balance, had been instrumental in shaping the water management strategies. These were not individuals seeking power, but individuals dedicated to the well-being of Havenridge.

"Silas," Mara said, her gaze distant, as if seeing him across the sprawling fields. "His understanding of the land, his direct experience with its challenges. He's not just a farmer; he's a steward in his own right. We need leaders who understand the practical realities on the ground, who can translate our long-term vision into tangible actions that resonate with everyone."

Eli's brow furrowed in thought. "And Elara. Her scientific rigor, her ability to see the interconnectedness of things. Her focus on sustainability isn't abstract; it's rooted in a deep respect for the natural world. We need that analytical mind, that commitment to evidence-based decision-making."

Their discussions under the ancient oak weren't formal meetings; they were organic exchanges, born from shared observation and a genuine desire to see Havenridge flourish beyond their own lifetimes. They would speak of Finn, the young carpenter, whose practical skills were matched by an almost innate understanding of sustainable building practices. He had a way of seeing how materials could be used efficiently, how structures could be designed to minimize their environmental impact, and how they could be built to last. His willingness to experiment, to learn new techniques, and to share his knowledge with younger apprentices marked him as someone with a future in leadership.

"Finn's contribution to the workshop expansion was remarkable," Mara recalled. "He didn't just follow instructions; he improved upon them. He's thinking about the lifespan of what he builds, about the resources he uses. That's a leader's mindset."

"And his patience," Eli added. "He takes the time to explain things, to guide the apprentices. He understands that building capacity isn't just about physical construction; it's about transferring knowledge and fostering confidence."

They also spoke of Clara, the apothecary, whose deep understanding of natural remedies and her commitment to community health were undeniable. Her meticulous research into plant cultivation and her dedication to ensuring that Havenridge's medicinal needs were met sustainably made her a natural leader in her domain. Her quiet diligence, her ability to foster trust within the community, and her unwavering ethical compass were qualities that extended far beyond the realm of healing.

"Clara's efforts to establish the herbal gardens have been invaluable," Mara said. "She's not only ensuring access to natural medicines but also teaching us about the power of local biodiversity. Her understanding of symbiotic relationships, both in nature and in the community, is profound."

"She embodies the spirit of careful stewardship," Eli agreed. "She nurtures what she cultivates, and she nurtures the well-being of those around her. Those are essential qualities for anyone who will one day have a hand in guiding Havenridge."

Identifying these individuals was only the first step. The true challenge, they knew, lay in nurturing their potential, in providing them with the opportunities to grow and to learn. This wasn't about assigning them roles; it was about creating pathways for development, about offering guidance without dictating outcomes, and about empowering them to forge their own leadership styles.

"We need to actively mentor them," Mara stated, her voice firm with conviction. "Not just by giving them tasks, but by sharing our experiences, our lessons learned, both the successes and the failures. They need to see that leadership is a journey, not a destination, and that mistakes are opportunities for growth."

Eli picked up a fallen leaf, examining its intricate veins. "Precisely. It's about creating a space where they feel safe to experiment, to take calculated risks. We can offer them advisory roles on specific projects, invite them to participate in community planning discussions, not as passive observers, but as active contributors. They need to feel the weight of responsibility, but also the support that underpins it."

The ancient oak, with its deep roots and its branches that had weathered countless storms, became a silent witness to their growing commitment to this aspect of their legacy. They would often find themselves under its shade, discussing how to delegate certain aspects of the land stewardship to Silas, or how to involve Elara in the ongoing refinement of resource management strategies. They envisioned creating a more formal mentorship program, where experienced members of the community could guide and support emerging leaders.

"Imagine a council of advisors," Eli suggested, his eyes reflecting the dappled sunlight filtering through the leaves. "Not a formal governing body, but a group of individuals, chosen for their diverse expertise and their proven commitment, who can offer counsel and perspective to whomever is leading Havenridge in the future. It would provide continuity, a safeguard against impulsive decisions, and a repository of collective wisdom."

Mara's heart swelled at the idea. "That's brilliant, Eli. It formalizes the informal mentorship we've been practicing. It creates a structure that supports the very essence of our legacy – enduring values, shared responsibility, and a commitment to the future."

The process was not without its nuances. They understood that leadership was not a one-size-fits-all model. Silas's grounded, practical approach was as vital as Elara's analytical foresight or Finn's innovative craftsmanship. Clara's deep understanding of community well-being and her ability to foster trust were equally indispensable. Mara and Eli dedicated themselves to understanding and nurturing these individual strengths, encouraging each potential leader to embrace their unique contributions rather than trying to emulate others.

"We must also be careful not to impose our own visions too rigidly," Mara cautioned, her gaze meeting Eli's. "Our role is to provide the framework, the foundational principles, but they must be allowed to shape the future in ways that reflect their own understanding and the evolving needs of Havenridge. True legacy is about empowerment, not replication."

Eli reached out and gently squeezed her hand. "And that's where true strength lies, Mara. In cultivating a community that is capable of adapting, of innovating, of growing organically. The oak doesn't dictate how the saplings grow, but it provides the environment for them to thrive. That's our role."

Their conversations under the oak tree were a testament to their evolving understanding of leadership and legacy. It was a recognition that building a lasting future wasn't just about the structures they erected or the plans they meticulously crafted. It was about the careful, intentional cultivation of individuals who would carry the spirit of Havenridge forward, who would embody its values, and who would continue to weave its story with threads of wisdom, integrity, and unwavering commitment.

The ancient oak stood as a silent promise – that just as it had endured for centuries, so too could the legacy they were so diligently building, a legacy rooted in the present, but reaching for an ever-brighter tomorrow. They understood that the success of Havenridge wouldn't be measured solely by its present achievements, but by the continued flourishing of its people, guided by a new generation empowered to lead.

The quiet hum of the Great Hall had long since faded, replaced by the soft rustle of pages and the gentle crackling of the hearth. Mara found herself returning to her study, not out of obligation, but out of a newfound sense of purpose that seemed to emanate from the very stones of Havenridge. In the days and weeks following the council's resounding approval of the land stewardship plan, a subtle yet profound shift had occurred within her. The initial apprehension, the lingering shadow of a fear that entwining her life so deeply with Eli, with Havenridge, might somehow diminish her own essence, had begun to recede like a morning mist.

She had once believed that love, especially the profound, anchoring love she felt for Eli, was a force that demanded compromise, a surrender of parts of oneself to create a harmonious whole. It was a romantic notion, perhaps, born from a lifetime of solitary pursuits and the quiet independence she had cultivated. But now, she understood that this was a misconception, a narrow view of the boundless nature of genuine connection. Her relationship with Eli wasn't a dilution of her identity; it was an expansion. It was like discovering a hidden chamber within a familiar dwelling, revealing not emptiness, but an unexpected abundance of space and light.

This realization had blossomed not in a single, dramatic revelation, but in a series of quiet moments. It was in the shared glance across the council table when a particularly complex issue was resolved, a silent acknowledgment of their combined strength. It was in the late-night conversations, where Eli, with his steady presence, encouraged her to explore nascent ideas, not just about Havenridge's future, but about her own. He saw the spark of innovation in her, the strategic mind that had always been there, and instead of extinguishing it with the demands of their shared life, he fanned its flames.

She remembered a particular afternoon, a few weeks after the land stewardship plan was ratified. They had been walking through the newly designated communal orchards, the air thick with the scent of blossoms. Mara had been sketching designs for a small, decentralized apiary, a project she had been contemplating for months but had hesitated to fully commit to. It felt... frivolous, somehow, in the face of the monumental task of securing Havenridge's future.

"What are you dreaming up there?" Eli had asked, his voice a warm rumble beside her.

Mara had gestured to her sketchbook. "Just a small idea. A few hives. For pollination, of course, and honey, but also... I don't know, a different kind of quiet harmony. A connection to the rhythms of the land."

Eli had taken the sketchbook, his brow furrowed in concentration as he studied her drawings. He hadn't dismissed it, hadn't suggested she focus on more pressing matters. Instead, he had asked insightful questions, probing the feasibility, the potential benefits, the practicalities. He had engaged with her vision, not as a distraction, but as a valuable facet of her multifaceted nature.

"This is wonderful, Mara," he had said, his eyes meeting hers with genuine admiration. "It's exactly the kind of forward-thinking, sustainable integration we need. It's not just about large-scale agriculture; it's about understanding the smaller, intricate webs of life that support it. And you, with your keen eye for detail and your intuitive understanding of natural systems, you're perfectly suited to see this through."

His words had resonated deeply, like a perfectly struck chord. He wasn't just accepting her passions; he was celebrating them. He was recognizing that these seemingly smaller pursuits, these diversions that had once felt like indulgent detours, were in fact integral to the larger landscape of who she was. They were not distractions from her leadership; they were extensions of it. Her capacity for love, for partnership, had not shrunk her world; it had made it infinitely larger, more vibrant, and more deeply resonant.

This expanded horizon was evident in her approach to her advisory roles. Where once she might have felt the pressure to present a singular, unified vision, she now felt empowered to explore multiple avenues, to champion diverse initiatives. The establishment of a community-run seed bank, an idea she had initially shelved due to its perceived complexity, now seemed not only feasible but essential. She saw it as a natural extension of the land stewardship plan, a vital safeguard for Havenridge's agricultural future, and a project that would allow her to delve into the intricate science of plant genetics, a field that had always held a quiet fascination for her.

Eli's unwavering support was the bedrock upon which this newfound confidence was built. He never questioned her dedication; he amplified it. When she spoke of the hours she intended to spend researching heirloom varieties or collaborating with Silas on the best methods for seed preservation, he simply nodded, a knowing smile playing on his lips. "Go," he would say, "and sow the seeds of knowledge. I'll be here, tending to the soil of our present, ensuring the ground is fertile for all your endeavors."

It was this beautiful symbiosis that Mara had come to cherish. She was not merely a partner in building Havenridge; she was a partner in cultivating herself. Her leadership, once a carefully constructed edifice, now felt more organic, more fluid. It was informed by her experiences, yes, but also by the richness of her personal life, the depth of her connection with Eli. The fears that had once whispered doubts in her mind were silenced by the undeniable reality of her own growth.

She found herself embracing opportunities that previously might have seemed daunting. When the council suggested creating a dedicated artisan's guild to foster traditional crafts and encourage new forms of artistic expression, Mara was not only willing to lend her organizational skills but also eager to contribute her own burgeoning interest in textile arts. She envisioned a space where the natural fibers harvested from Havenridge's lands could be transformed into beautiful, functional works, a testament to the community's self-sufficiency and creative spirit. This was not a deviation from her duties; it was a manifestation of the very principles of sustainability and resourcefulness that underpinned the land stewardship plan.

The joy she found in these pursuits was not a solitary pleasure; it was a shared experience. Eli would often join her in the evenings, perhaps not to delve into the technicalities of seed viability or the intricate patterns of weaving, but simply to be present. He would read by the fire while she worked, his quiet presence a comforting anchor, a reminder of the solid foundation upon which her expanding world was built. He would ask about her progress, his interest genuine, his encouragement unwavering.

"You have a gift for seeing the potential in everything, Mara," he remarked one evening, watching her meticulously sort dried lavender buds for a new herbal blend. "Not just in the land, or in the people, but in the very essence of what Havenridge can become. And you have the courage to bring that potential to life."

His words were more than just praise; they were an acknowledgment of her evolving identity. She was not the Mara who had arrived in Havenridge, carrying the weight of her past and the uncertainty of her future. She was a Mara who had been embraced, nurtured, and empowered. Her love for Eli had not been a cage; it had been a trellis, upon which her spirit had climbed, reaching for new heights, bearing fruit she had never imagined possible.

She began to see leadership not as a mantle to be worn, but as a dance to be performed, a fluid exchange of energy and ideas. Her role in fostering the development of younger leaders, a topic she and Eli had often discussed under the ancient oak, now felt less like a duty and more like a privilege. She found immense satisfaction in guiding Finn's innovative carpentry ideas, in encouraging Elara's research into sustainable pest control, and in supporting Clara's vision for expanding the community's medicinal garden. She saw in them echoes of her own journey – the initial hesitations, the burgeoning confidence, the quiet drive to contribute.

"It's not about making them duplicates of ourselves," she explained to Eli one crisp autumn evening, as they watched the leaves fall in a gentle cascade. "It's about helping them discover their own unique strengths, their own ways of contributing to Havenridge. We provide the framework, the foundational principles, but they must be allowed to build their own towers of innovation, their own gardens of wisdom."

Eli smiled, his gaze soft. "And you, Mara, you have become the master gardener. You cultivate not just plants and ideas, but the very spirit of growth within this community. Your horizon has expanded, and in doing so, you have expanded ours."

His words were a balm to her soul, a confirmation of the truth she had come to embrace. Her life with Eli, her commitment to Havenridge, had not diminished her; it had multiplied her. She was more than she had ever been, a richer, more complex tapestry woven with threads of love, leadership, and an unwavering dedication to the flourishing future they were building together. The fear of losing herself had vanished, replaced by the exhilarating joy of discovering that in giving, in loving, and in leading, she had found herself, more fully and vibrantly, than ever before.

She was a testament to the enduring power of connection, a living embodiment of how embracing permanence could, paradoxically, set one free to soar. The expansive sky above Havenridge seemed to mirror the boundless possibilities that now unfurled before her, a future she was eager to explore, with Eli by her side, and the wisdom of her own expanded self as her guide.

The days that followed Mara's profound realization of their shared future were marked by a deepening of purpose, not just for her, but for Eli as well. He, too, seemed to be shedding old reservations, embracing the weight of his responsibilities with a renewed clarity. It was during one of their quiet evenings, the scent of woodsmoke mingling with the lingering aroma of Mara's experiments in the apothecary, that Eli first articulated this evolution in his own thinking. He had been unusually pensive, tracing the rim of his mug with a thoughtful finger, his gaze fixed on the dancing flames in the hearth.

"You know," he began, his voice low and measured, "for a long time, I equated freedom with the absence of any discernible boundaries. I thought that true autonomy meant being able to go where the wind took you, unburdened by obligation, unanchored to any particular place or person." He met Mara's eyes, a flicker of that old restlessness present, but now tempered with a profound understanding. "It's a romantic notion, isn't it? The lone wolf, the independent spirit. And there's a certain beauty in that, I suppose, but it's a fragile beauty. It's the beauty of a wild flower, lovely for a season, but ultimately vulnerable to the slightest storm."

He paused, gathering his thoughts. "What I'm beginning to see, what your own journey here has helped me understand, is that true strength, true lasting freedom, comes not from the absence of structure, but from its presence. Not from the lack of commitment, but from its intentional embrace. Havenridge... it's not just a collection of buildings and land. It's a community, and a community needs roots. It needs a shared understanding, a commitment to each other, a framework that allows us all to grow, but grow together, in a way that's sustainable and supportive."

Mara leaned forward, captivated. His words echoed her own recent discoveries, yet they came from a different perspective, a testament to the way their individual journeys were converging. "You're talking about the agreements," she murmured, thinking of the meticulously crafted documents that had been debated and refined over weeks, outlining land use, resource sharing, and community governance. "The bylaws, the charters..."

"Yes," Eli confirmed, a faint smile touching his lips. "Those things. But it's more than just parchment and ink. It's about a shared vision, solidified. It's about us, as individuals, making a conscious, deliberate choice to bind ourselves to something larger than ourselves. It's about saying, 'This is what we stand for. This is how we will operate. This is the foundation upon which we will build.'"

He gestured with his mug, a sweeping motion that encompassed their cozy study, and by extension, Havenridge itself. "Think of a mighty oak. It's powerful, enduring, its branches reaching towards the heavens. But what makes it so resilient? It's not just its size; it's its deep, anchoring roots, its strong, well-defined trunk. Without that structure, it would be at the mercy of every gust of wind."

He shifted, turning more fully towards her, his expression earnest. "And in my own life, Mara... this applies to us, too. My commitment to you, our shared life here, the future we are building... I used to see it, perhaps subconsciously, as a constraint. Another anchor, another tether. But now, I see it as the very thing that allows me to soar. Because I know, with absolute certainty, that no matter what happens, no matter how turbulent the winds of change may blow, I have a stable center. I have you. And you have me. That certainty, that shared structure, is not a cage; it is the launchpad."

His words resonated deeply, painting a vivid picture of a philosophy he had clearly been wrestling with. It was a subtle shift in perspective, but a profound one. He was moving from a view of commitment as a surrender to a view of commitment as an empowerment.

"It's about intentionality, isn't it?" Mara said, the concept crystallizing in her mind. "We're not just passively falling into a way of life; we are actively choosing it, shaping it, and dedicating ourselves to it. We're not just letting the community happen; we're building it with deliberate care."

"Exactly," Eli agreed, his eyes shining with a shared understanding. "And that intentionality extends to everything. The way we manage our resources, the way we resolve disputes, the way we educate our children, the way we care for our elders. It all requires a framework. Without clear principles, without agreed-upon structures, even the most well-intentioned efforts can become chaotic. We'd be like sailors without a compass, adrift on a sea of good intentions."

He leaned back, a sense of contentment settling over him. "I've been thinking a lot about the land stewardship plan, and how we're implementing it. It's not just a set of rules. It's a testament to our collective understanding of our responsibility to this place. It's a promise we've made to future generations. And that promise requires structure. It requires us to formalize our commitment, to create systems that ensure its longevity. It's not about limiting what we can do with the land, but about ensuring that what we *do*, is done with wisdom and foresight."

Mara nodded, picturing the intricate web of responsibilities and guidelines they were weaving. It wasn't about restriction; it was about responsibility. It was about creating a legacy that would outlast them, a legacy built on a solid foundation of shared values and structured action.

"I see it like this," Eli continued, his voice gaining a quiet momentum. "Imagine building a magnificent tapestry. You could try to weave it freestyle, letting the threads fall wherever they may. You might create something interesting, perhaps even beautiful in its randomness. But if you want to create a masterpiece, something with intricate patterns, enduring beauty, and profound meaning, you need a loom. You need a warp, a framework that holds everything in place, guiding your every movement, ensuring that each thread contributes to the overall design."

He looked at Mara, his gaze steady and reassuring. "Our community agreements, our shared vision, my commitment to you and yours to me – these are our looms. They provide the structure. And within that structure, within that intentional framework, there is infinite space for creativity, for growth, for individual expression. You can weave the most exquisite designs, knowing that the integrity of the tapestry will hold. You are free to explore, to innovate, to flourish, precisely *because* of the strength of the underlying structure."

This was a significant evolution for Eli. He had always been a man of action, a doer, but he had also possessed an undercurrent of independence that had sometimes made him wary of entanglements. Now, he was embracing the power of those entanglements, not as limitations, but as the very source of their collective strength.

"It's about trust, too, isn't it?" Mara added. "Trusting that the structure will hold, and trusting that the people within it will act with integrity. It's a reciprocal relationship. The structure supports us, and our commitment to it, in turn, strengthens the structure."

"Precisely," Eli affirmed. "It's a feedback loop of stability and growth. When people know where they stand, when they understand the rules of engagement, and when they feel secure in their commitments, they are liberated. They can focus their energy on building, on creating, on contributing, rather than on navigating uncertainty or defending against potential pitfalls. It frees up mental and emotional space for innovation and collaboration."

He thought of the new apprentice program they were planning, a structured mentorship initiative designed to pass down skills and knowledge from the older generation to the younger. "That apprentice program, for instance," he mused. "It's not just about teaching someone a trade. It's about creating a formal pathway for knowledge transfer, for building relationships, for fostering a sense of belonging. It's a structure that supports individual development while simultaneously reinforcing the community's collective expertise. Without that structure, it might just be ad hoc learning, valuable but ultimately less impactful and less sustainable."

Mara found herself nodding in agreement, picturing the possibilities. Eli's vision wasn't about rigidity; it was about intentionality. It was about understanding that freedom and commitment, stability and growth, were not mutually exclusive. In fact, they were intrinsically linked.

"And for us, personally," Eli continued, his voice softening, "my commitment to you. I used to worry that it would tether me, that it would somehow diminish my capacity for decisive action, for leadership. But now, I see it as the opposite. Knowing that we are a united front, that we are building this together, that our futures are intertwined... it gives me a clarity and a resolve I never possessed before. It's like having a trusted co-pilot. You can navigate far more complex skies with someone by your side, someone who shares your destination and your understanding of the journey."

He reached across the small table, his hand covering hers. His touch was warm, firm, and filled with a quiet conviction. "Your own journey, Mara, has illuminated this for me. You arrived here, carrying your own independence, your own formidable strengths. And instead of seeing my own commitment as a threat to that, you've embraced it, woven it into the fabric of your own life here. And in doing so, you haven't lost yourself. You've become more. You've expanded. And that expansion, that willingness to embrace a shared structure, has made you an even more powerful force for good here."

The sincerity in his gaze was palpable. It was a rare and beautiful thing to witness Eli articulate such a profound shift in his worldview. He had always been a man of integrity, but this was a deeper, more nuanced understanding of what that integrity meant in the context of a shared life and a shared community.

"It's about creating a resilient ecosystem," Mara said, picking up on his analogy. "Whether it's an ecological system or a community system, it thrives when there are clear structures that support its components, allowing them to interact and contribute effectively. It's not about control; it's about cultivation. It's about creating the right conditions for things to flourish."

"Precisely," Eli echoed, his thumb gently stroking the back of her hand. "And what I'm committed to cultivating here, with you, is a Havenridge that is not just prosperous, but enduring. A place where people feel safe to take risks, to innovate, to be vulnerable, because they know there's a strong, supportive framework beneath them. A framework built on trust, on mutual respect, and on a shared understanding of our purpose."

He squeezed her hand. "It's a different kind of freedom than I once imagined. It's not the freedom of the unbound wanderer, but the freedom of the master craftsman, who, through skill and dedication to his tools and his craft, can create wonders. It's the freedom that comes from mastery, from intentionality, from a deep and unwavering commitment. And that, Mara, is the kind of freedom I want to build here, with you, for all of us."

The quiet strength of his words settled over Mara like a comforting embrace. She saw now, with absolute clarity, the parallel in their journeys. Her own burgeoning understanding of how love and commitment could expand, rather than diminish, her own identity had mirrored Eli's dawning realization about the power of structure and intentionality in community building and personal relationships. They were not two separate visions, but two facets of the same evolving truth. Havenridge was not just a place they were building; it was a way of being they were actively choosing, a commitment they were consciously and joyfully forging, thread by intentional thread, within the sturdy loom of their shared lives.

The days that followed Mara's profound realization of their shared future were marked by a deepening of purpose, not just for her, but for Eli as well. He, too, seemed to be shedding old reservations, embracing the weight of his responsibilities with a renewed clarity. It was during one of their quiet evenings, the scent of woodsmoke mingling with the lingering aroma of Mara's experiments in the apothecary, that Eli first articulated this evolution in his own thinking. He had been unusually pensive, tracing the rim of his mug with a thoughtful finger, his gaze fixed on the dancing flames in the hearth.

"You know," he began, his voice low and measured, "for a long time, I equated freedom with the absence of any discernible boundaries. I thought that true autonomy meant being able to go where the wind took you, unburdened by obligation, unanchored to any particular place or person." He met Mara's eyes, a flicker of that old restlessness present, but now tempered with a profound understanding. "It's a romantic notion, isn't it? The lone wolf, the independent spirit. And there's a certain beauty in that, I suppose, but it's a fragile beauty.

It's the beauty of a wild flower, lovely for a season, but ultimately vulnerable to the slightest storm."

He paused, gathering his thoughts. "What I'm beginning to see, what your own journey here has helped me understand, is that true strength, true lasting freedom, comes not from the absence of structure, but from its presence. Not from the lack of commitment, but from its intentional embrace. Havenridge... it's not just a collection of buildings and land. It's a community, and a community needs roots. It needs a shared understanding, a commitment to each other, a framework that allows us all to grow, but grow together, in a way that's sustainable and supportive."

Mara leaned forward, captivated. His words echoed her own recent discoveries, yet they came from a different perspective, a testament to the way their individual journeys were converging. "You're talking about the agreements," she murmured, thinking of the meticulously crafted documents that had been debated and refined over weeks, outlining land use, resource sharing, and community governance. "The bylaws, the charters..."

"Yes," Eli confirmed, a faint smile touching his lips. "Those things. But it's more than just parchment and ink. It's about a shared vision, solidified. It's about us, as individuals, making a conscious, deliberate choice to bind ourselves to something larger than ourselves. It's about saying, 'This is what we stand for. This is how we will operate. This is the foundation upon which we will build.'" He gestured with his mug, a sweeping motion that encompassed their cozy study, and by extension, Havenridge itself. "Think of a mighty oak. It's powerful, enduring, its branches reaching towards the heavens. But what makes it so resilient? It's not just its size; it's its deep, anchoring roots, its strong, well-defined trunk. Without that structure, it would be at the mercy of every gust of wind."

He shifted, turning more fully towards her, his expression earnest. "And in my own life, Mara... this applies to us, too. My commitment to you, our shared life here, the future we are building... I used to see it, perhaps subconsciously, as a constraint. Another anchor, another tether. But now, I see it as the very thing that allows me to soar. Because I know, with absolute certainty, that no matter what happens, no matter how turbulent the winds of change may blow, I have a stable center. I have you. And you have me. That certainty, that shared structure, is not a cage; it is the launchpad."

His words resonated deeply, painting a vivid picture of a philosophy he had clearly been wrestling with. It was a subtle shift in perspective, but a profound one. He was moving from a view of commitment as a surrender to a view of commitment as an empowerment.

"It's about intentionality, isn't it?" Mara said, the concept crystallizing in her mind. "We're not just passively falling into a way of life; we are actively choosing it, shaping it, and dedicating ourselves to it. We're not just letting the community happen; we're building it with deliberate care."

"Exactly," Eli agreed, his eyes shining with a shared understanding. "And that intentionality extends to everything. The way we manage our resources, the way we resolve disputes, the way we educate our children, the way we care for our elders. It all requires a framework. Without clear principles, without agreed-upon structures, even the most well-intentioned efforts can become chaotic. We'd be like sailors without a compass, adrift on a sea of good intentions."

He thought of the tangible manifestation of this intentionality, the community gardens that were being meticulously planned, each plot assigned with consideration for crop rotation and water access. It wasn't merely about growing food; it was about cultivating a shared responsibility, a system designed for mutual benefit and sustainability. Similarly, the nascent education council was already grappling with how to impart not just knowledge, but also the values and principles that underpinned Havenridge, ensuring a continuity of purpose. These weren't arbitrary rules; they were the scaffolding upon which a thriving community would be built, each element interconnected and reinforcing the others.

He leaned back, a sense of contentment settling over him. "I've been thinking a lot about the land stewardship plan, and how we're implementing it. It's not just a set of rules. It's a testament to our collective understanding of our responsibility to this place. It's a promise we've made to future generations. And that promise requires structure. It requires us to formalize our commitment, to create systems that ensure its longevity. It's not about limiting what we can do with the land, but about ensuring that what we do, is done with wisdom and foresight."

Mara nodded, picturing the intricate web of responsibilities and guidelines they were weaving. It wasn't about restriction; it was about responsibility. It was about creating a legacy that would outlast them, a legacy built on a solid foundation of shared values and structured action. She saw it extending beyond mere practicalities. The weekly council meetings, the open forums for discussion, even the established protocols for conflict resolution – these were all threads in the larger tapestry, designed to ensure that Havenridge remained a place of growth and harmony, rather than discord.

"I see it like this," Eli continued, his voice gaining a quiet momentum. "Imagine building a magnificent tapestry. You could try to weave it freestyle, letting the threads fall wherever they may. You might create something interesting, perhaps even beautiful in its randomness. But if you want to create a masterpiece, something with intricate patterns, enduring beauty, and profound meaning, you need a loom. You need a warp, a framework that holds everything in place, guiding your every movement, ensuring that each thread contributes to the overall design."

He looked at Mara, his gaze steady and reassuring. "Our community agreements, our shared vision, my commitment to you and yours to me – these are our looms. They provide the structure. And within that structure, within that intentional framework, there is infinite space for creativity, for growth, for individual expression. You can weave the most exquisite designs, knowing that the integrity of the tapestry will hold. You are free to explore, to innovate, to flourish, precisely *because* of the strength of the underlying structure."

This was a significant evolution for Eli. He had always been a man of action, a doer, but he had also possessed an undercurrent of independence that had sometimes made him wary of entanglements. Now, he was embracing the power of those entanglements, not as limitations, but as the very source of their collective strength. He saw how his personal journey, his deepening love for Mara, had become an integral part of this broader philosophy.

Their commitment to each other wasn't a private affair confined to their hearth; it was a public declaration, a foundational pillar upon which their leadership and their vision for Havenridge rested. Their strength as individuals was amplified by their strength as a couple, and that unified strength was what the community needed.

"It's about trust, too, isn't it?" Mara added. "Trusting that the structure will hold, and trusting that the people within it will act with integrity. It's a reciprocal relationship. The structure supports us, and our commitment to it, in turn, strengthens the structure."

"Precisely," Eli affirmed. "It's a feedback loop of stability and growth. When people know where they stand, when they understand the rules of engagement, and when they feel secure in their commitments, they are liberated. They can focus their energy on building, on creating, on contributing, rather than on navigating uncertainty or defending against potential pitfalls. It frees up mental and emotional space for innovation and collaboration."

He thought of the new apprentice program they were planning, a structured mentorship initiative designed to pass down skills and knowledge from the older generation to the younger. This program, a clear embodiment of their structured approach, was not merely about skill acquisition; it was about fostering intergenerational bonds, ensuring that the wisdom of experience was passed on with intention and care.

"That apprentice program, for instance," he mused. "It's not just about teaching someone a trade. It's about creating a formal pathway for knowledge transfer, for building relationships, for fostering a sense of belonging. It's a structure that supports individual development while simultaneously reinforcing the community's collective expertise. Without that structure, it might just be ad hoc learning, valuable but ultimately less impactful and less sustainable." He felt a surge of pride in the foresight of their planning, a tangible result of their evolving understanding of intentional community building.

Mara found herself nodding in agreement, picturing the possibilities. Eli's vision wasn't about rigidity; it was about intentionality. It was about understanding that freedom and commitment, stability and growth, were not mutually exclusive. In fact, they were intrinsically linked. She saw how their personal relationship had become a crucible for these ideas, a testing ground where the abstract concepts of governance and sustainability were being forged into practical application. Their love for each other wasn't a distraction from their public duties; it was the very engine that powered them.

"And for us, personally," Eli continued, his voice softening, "my commitment to you. I used to worry that it would tether me, that it would somehow diminish my capacity for decisive action, for leadership. But now, I see it as the opposite. Knowing that we are a united front, that we are building this together, that our futures are intertwined... it gives me a clarity and a resolve I never possessed before. It's like having a trusted co-pilot. You can navigate far more complex skies with someone by your side, someone who shares your destination and your understanding of the journey."

He reached across the small table, his hand covering hers. His touch was warm, firm, and filled with a quiet conviction. "Your own journey, Mara, has illuminated this for me. You arrived here, carrying your own independence, your own formidable strengths. And instead of seeing my own commitment as a threat to that, you've embraced it, woven it into the fabric of your own life here. And in doing so, you haven't lost yourself. You've become more. You've expanded. And that expansion, that willingness to embrace a shared structure, has made you an even more powerful force for good here."

The sincerity in his gaze was palpable. It was a rare and beautiful thing to witness Eli articulate such a profound shift in his worldview.

He had always been a man of integrity, but this was a deeper, more nuanced understanding of what that integrity meant in the context of a shared life and a shared community. Their personal bond was no longer a private sanctuary, but a public beacon, reflecting the values they espoused for Havenridge. When they presented a united front, their words carried more weight, their intentions seemed purer, and their vision for the future felt more attainable. This synergy was not a coincidence; it was the direct result of their conscious effort to integrate their private lives with their public responsibilities.

"It's about creating a resilient ecosystem," Mara said, picking up on his analogy. "Whether it's an ecological system or a community system, it thrives when there are clear structures that support its components, allowing them to interact and contribute effectively. It's not about control; it's about cultivation. It's about creating the right conditions for things to flourish." She thought of the delicate balance of their own apothecary experiments, where precise conditions were necessary for potent growth. It was the same principle applied to human community.

"Precisely," Eli echoed, his thumb gently stroking the back of her hand. "And what I'm committed to cultivating here, with you, is a Havenridge that is not just prosperous, but enduring. A place where people feel safe to take risks, to innovate, to be vulnerable, because they know there's a strong, supportive framework beneath them. A framework built on trust, on mutual respect, and on a shared understanding of our purpose."

He squeezed her hand. "It's a different kind of freedom than I once imagined. It's not the freedom of the unbound wanderer, but the freedom of the master craftsman, who, through skill and dedication to his tools and his craft, can create wonders. It's the freedom that comes from mastery, from intentionality, from a deep and unwavering commitment. And that, Mara, is the kind of freedom I want to build here, with you, for all of us."

The quiet strength of his words settled over Mara like a comforting embrace. She saw now, with absolute clarity, the parallel in their journeys. Her own burgeoning understanding of how love and commitment could expand, rather than diminish, her own identity had mirrored Eli's dawning realization about the power of structure and intentionality in community building and personal relationships.

They were not two separate visions, but two facets of the same evolving truth. Havenridge was not just a place they were building; it was a way of being they were actively choosing, a commitment they were consciously and joyfully forging, thread by intentional thread, within the sturdy loom of their shared lives. Their personal strength, rooted in their commitment to each other, was the bedrock upon which their leadership in Havenridge would be built, ensuring not just survival, but a flourishing legacy for generations to come. It was a testament to the profound truth that the most enduring legacies are woven from both the inner strength of personal connection and the outward commitment to a shared vision.

CHAPTER FIVE

THE CROSSROADS OF COMMITMENT

The soft glow of the setting sun cast long shadows across Havenridge, painting the familiar landscape in hues of amethyst and rose. Eli found himself drawn to the edge of the lake, a place he often sought when the weight of his thoughts pressed a little too heavily. The water's surface, usually a mirror to the sky's mood, was today a placid expanse, disturbed only by the gentle ripple of a fish breaking the surface. It was in this quietude, this ephemeral pause between the day's labors and the night's embrace, that a realization, as profound as it was simple, settled upon him.

He had spoken, in their shared study, of the freedom found not in the absence of boundaries, but in their intentional embrace. He had articulated how commitment, to Mara, to Havenridge, was not a tether but a launchpad. Yet, in the solitary contemplation of this tranquil evening, those eloquent words distilled into a singular, undeniable truth: it was no longer enough to simply *love* Mara. He had to *choose* her, formally, unequivocally.

The journey from adaptability to intentionality had been a winding path, marked by moments of doubt and introspection. He had learned to be resilient, to adapt to the unpredictable currents of life, to flow with the needs of Havenridge as they arose. But this newfound understanding, this profound shift in perspective, demanded more than mere adaptation. It demanded a deliberate act of will, a conscious declaration of partnership that would resonate not only with Mara but with the very foundations of the community they were building.

He watched as a lone swan glided across the water, its movements effortless and graceful. It was a creature of instinct and elegance, but also one that, in its own way, committed to its path, to its mate, to its territory. Eli's own path had been one of constant navigation, of adjusting sails to the prevailing winds. He had prided himself on his ability to be resourceful, to find solutions as challenges presented themselves. But the prospect of a future with Mara, a future that had become not just a possibility but a deep, resonant certainty, called for a different kind of strength – the strength of steadfastness.

It wasn't just about the continuation of their shared life, though that was paramount. It was about the legacy they were creating, not just for themselves, but for all of Havenridge. He understood now that true partnership, the kind that weathered storms and celebrated sunlit days, was built not on a foundation of passive affection, but on the bedrock of active, unwavering choice. It was in the deliberate act of choosing, again and again, that the depth of commitment was revealed, and its strength was forged.

He thought back to their early days, to the hesitant steps they had taken towards each other. There had been a natural inclination, a mutual attraction that had felt as inevitable as the turning of the seasons. But love, he was discovering, was a dynamic force, capable of evolving and deepening, and in its evolution, it demanded a conscious affirmation.

To simply love Mara was to acknowledge the current state of their bond. To *choose* her was to declare that bond as the unshakeable cornerstone of his future, a future he was not merely willing to share, but actively, passionately, and irrevocably building with her.

The quiet revelation wasn't a sudden storm of emotion, but a slow, steady dawning. It was the quiet certainty of knowing, deep in his soul, that he wanted to walk beside Mara not just for a season, but for all seasons to come. He wanted to stand before their community, before the world, and declare his dedication. It was a desire that had been simmering beneath the surface, a natural consequence of the profound respect and love he held for her, a respect that had blossomed into admiration for her strength, her wisdom, and her unwavering spirit.

This wasn't a matter of obligation or societal expectation. It was an internal imperative, a soul-deep yearning to solidify their union in a way that reflected its profound significance. He envisioned a ceremony, not necessarily grand, but meaningful, a public testament to their shared vision and their mutual devotion. It would be a declaration that their partnership was not a transient arrangement, but a deliberate, enduring commitment, a promise etched not just in their hearts, but in the fabric of Havenridge itself.

He realized that his own growth, his own journey from adaptability to intentionality, had led him to this precipice. He had learned that true leadership, true strength, lay in making conscious choices, in building frameworks that fostered stability and growth. And in the realm of his personal life, the most significant choice he could make was to formalize his commitment to Mara. It was the ultimate act of partnership, of building a shared future not just on shared dreams, but on a shared, unwavering promise.

The tranquil lake, reflecting the deepening twilight, seemed to hold a silent understanding of his epiphany. The world around him was preparing for rest, for the quietude of the night, but within Eli, a new clarity had bloomed. He understood that this desire for formal commitment was not a surrender of his independence, but an expansion of it. It was the ultimate expression of trust, of faith in the strength of their bond, and in the enduring power of their shared purpose. He no longer saw commitment as a boundary, but as the very space within which true freedom – the freedom to love, to build, to grow, together – could flourish.

He wanted to etch their union into the very soul of Havenridge, to create a visible symbol of the strength that came from their unwavering connection. It would be a beacon, not just for them, but for others, a testament to the power of intentional partnership, of choosing to build a life, a community, together, with unwavering purpose and profound love.

The decision settled upon him, not with the fanfare of a storm, but with the gentle, irrefutable certainty of dawn. He would ask Mara to be his wife. He would choose her, not just today, but every day, for the rest of his life. This quiet revelation by the lake was the prelude to a new chapter, one he was eager to begin, hand in hand with the woman who had become the very heart of his world.

The air, cool and crisp with the coming of evening, carried the scent of pine and damp earth, a familiar perfume that always settled Mara's spirit. She walked alongside Eli, their hands brushing occasionally, each touch a subtle current that sent a jolt of awareness through her. Havenridge, in its twilight dress, was a symphony of soft grays and muted greens, a peaceful backdrop to the swirling emotions within her. She felt it, the palpable shift in Eli, a quiet hum of purpose that radiated from him like a gentle heat. It wasn't a boisterous declaration, but a deep, resonant certainty that settled around him, a subtle but undeniable aura of intent.

For weeks now, she had sensed this evolution in him, this gradual unfurling of a desire that had been simmering beneath the surface. It had begun as a new attentiveness, a way he looked at her, a certain quality in his voice when he spoke her name. Then came the deeper conversations, the sharing of his evolving perspectives on commitment, on the very fabric of building a life together. He had spoken of intention, not as a constraint, but as the fertile ground from which true freedom could bloom. And Mara, who had once flinched at the word 'permanence', found herself breathing it in, letting it settle into her being without the old, familiar prickle of fear.

Her heart, a creature of habit and caution, still held a faint echo of that apprehension. It was a whisper now, a phantom limb of an old wound, a reminder of a time when the idea of being irrevocably tied to someone had felt like a cage. But that whisper was so easily drowned out by the overwhelming symphony of trust that Eli had painstakingly built within her. She had seen his actions, his unwavering dedication to Havenridge, his gentle strength, his profound respect for her. He had not just spoken of love; he had woven it into the very tapestry of their shared existence, stitch by careful, deliberate stitch.

She stole a glance at him, the way the fading light caught the strong line of his jaw, the thoughtful crease between his brows. He was not rushing. There was a quiet deliberation in his steps, a sense of purpose that was both exhilarating and a little nerve-wracking. He was approaching something, and Mara knew, with a certainty that both thrilled and terrified her, that it was about them. It was about the future.

The path they followed was one of their favourites, a gentle incline that led to a small, secluded clearing overlooking the valley. The trees here were ancient, their branches reaching out like welcoming arms, their leaves rustling secrets in the breeze. It was a place of peace, a sanctuary where the noise of the world faded away, leaving only the quiet thrum of their shared existence. This was their Havenridge, not just the land and the buildings, but the space they had carved out for themselves, a space defined by mutual understanding and burgeoning affection.

As they reached the clearing, Eli paused, turning to face her. The last rays of sunlight painted his face in warm gold, illuminating the earnestness in his eyes. He took her hands, his touch firm and reassuring, sending a shiver of anticipation through her. The old fears, the ingrained skepticism that had once guarded her heart so fiercely, seemed to recede further into the shadows, like mist burning off in the morning sun. They were still there, a faint, almost imperceptible tremor, but they no longer held the power to dictate her response.

"Mara," he began, his voice a low, resonant melody that vibrated deep within her chest. "I've been doing a lot of thinking."

Her breath hitched. This was it. The moment she had both yearned for and subtly dreaded. She met his gaze, her own heart pounding a frantic rhythm against her ribs. "I know," she managed, her voice a little shaky. "I've felt it too."

He smiled, a slow, tender unfolding of his lips that eased some of the tension coiling in her stomach. "It's not just about... adapting anymore, is it?" he asked, his thumb tracing circles on the back of her hand. "It's about choosing. Deliberately. Unconditionally."

Mara nodded, her eyes welling with a sudden rush of emotion. How had he put into words the very essence of what she had been grappling with, and what she had finally begun to embrace? "I used to think that freedom was about having no ties," she confessed, her voice barely a whisper. "But you've shown me... that true freedom is in the strength of those ties, when they're chosen with intention, with love."

Eli's grip tightened, a silent affirmation of her words. "Exactly," he breathed. "And I want to choose you, Mara. Not just for today, or for this season. I want to choose you for all of them." He paused, his gaze deepening, searching hers. "I want to build a life with you, a partnership that is as strong and as enduring as the foundations of Havenridge itself. A life where we face everything, together."

The apprehension that had been a faint echo now seemed to dissipate entirely, replaced by a wave of overwhelming emotion. Hope, pure and unadulterated, surged through her, washing away the last vestiges of her doubt. She saw it then, not just in his words, but in the absolute conviction radiating from him. He wasn't asking out of obligation or convenience. He was asking from the deepest part of his soul, from a place of profound love and unwavering commitment.

"Eli," she whispered, the name a prayer on her lips. Tears pricked at her eyes, blurring the edges of his beloved face. "I... I'm ready."

The words hung in the air between them, charged with unspoken promises and shared dreams. The setting sun cast a warm, benevolent glow over them, as if Nature herself was blessing this nascent moment. Mara felt a profound sense of peace settle over her, a peace born not of complacency, but of a hard-won victory over her own internal battles. She had wrestled with her fear of permanence, with the ghosts of past hurts that had whispered cautionary tales. But in the steady, unwavering light of Eli's love, those ghosts had finally been silenced.

She had learned to trust the resilience of her own heart, to believe that love, true love, was not about fragility, but about strength. It was about finding an anchor in another soul, a companion with whom to navigate the inevitable storms, and a partner to celebrate the sun-drenched days. And Eli was that anchor, that partner, that steadfast presence she had unknowingly yearned for.

He drew her closer, his arms wrapping around her, holding her as if she were the most precious thing in the world. Mara leaned into his embrace, her head resting against his chest, listening to the steady, reassuring beat of his heart. It was a rhythm that had become as familiar and as comforting as her own.

"You have no idea," he murmured into her hair, his voice thick with emotion, "how much that means to me."

She smiled against his shirt. "I think," she said, pulling back just enough to look him in the eye, her own filled with a newfound boldness, "I'm starting to."

The journey to this crossroads had been long and winding for both of them. Eli's evolution from a man who prided himself on adaptability to one who understood the profound strength of intentionality had been a revelation, not just for him, but for her. She had witnessed it, felt it, and in turn, it had helped her to confront her own deeply ingrained reservations. The landscape of Havenridge, with its quiet beauty and its enduring spirit, had become a metaphor for their own growth, a testament to the fact that even the most seemingly immutable things could evolve, deepen, and transform.

As the last vestiges of daylight painted the sky in hues of deep purple and fiery orange, Mara felt a profound sense of readiness. The old anxieties were still shadows, faint and distant, but they no longer held her captive. Her trust in Eli, painstakingly nurtured and deeply earned, had become the solid ground beneath her feet. She was standing at the precipice of a new beginning, not with trepidation, but with an eager anticipation that fluttered like a bird in her chest. She was ready to embrace permanence, not as an ending, but as the most beautiful, most profound kind of beginning. She was ready to choose. And she knew, with every fiber of her being, that her choice would be him. Eli. Her Havenridge. Her future.

The twilight deepened, the air growing cooler, and with it, a subtle shift in Eli's demeanor. He hadn't rushed their conversation at the clearing, allowing Mara's own emotions to surface and settle. Now, as they walked back towards the main house, a new quiet settled between them, one of profound understanding and shared anticipation. Mara watched him, her heart still thrumming with the aftershocks of his declaration, and saw a different kind of intensity in his eyes, a focused thoughtfulness that spoke of future plans. He wasn't a man given to impulsive gestures or ostentatious displays. His strength lay in his deliberate nature, in the careful consideration he gave to every decision, especially those that touched their shared life at Havenridge.

He had spoken of building a life, of choosing her unconditionally, and now, Mara sensed, he was translating those powerful words into action. She saw it in the way he'd subtly steered their conversation away from any discussion of immediate, grand pronouncements. He hadn't mentioned a public proposal, a dazzling ring presented before an audience, or any of the conventional milestones that society often dictated. Instead, there was a quiet hum of intention about him, a sense that his mind was already working on the intricacies of how best to solidify the beautiful, nascent reality they were creating together.

Eli believed in the substance of commitment, in its quiet power rather than its outward fanfare. He understood that the true testament to their bond wouldn't be found in a public spectacle, but in the intimate, unwavering foundation they built, day by day, within the sanctuary of Havenridge. His love for her, Mara knew, was not a performance; it was an intrinsic part of his being, as deeply rooted as the ancient oaks surrounding their home. And the way he intended to ask her to formalize their commitment would undoubtedly reflect this core truth about him. It would be personal, heartfelt, and profoundly meaningful, an echo of the sincerity that had drawn her to him in the first place.

He stopped as they reached the porch, turning to her again, his expression earnest. "Mara," he said, his voice carrying the quiet weight of conviction. "What we've spoken about... it's not something to be rushed, but it's also not something to leave hanging in the air. It needs... grounding. A certainty that can be felt, not just heard."

Mara nodded, her gaze meeting his. She trusted his process, his innate understanding of what truly mattered. He wouldn't compromise the depth of the moment with superficiality. "I understand," she replied softly, her hand finding his, her fingers lacing through his. "Whatever you have in mind, Eli, I trust it."

A small, grateful smile touched his lips. "I've been thinking a lot about this," he continued, his thumb stroking the back of her hand. "About how to truly ask you to share this life with me. Not just in words, but in a way that feels... us. That honors where we've come from, and where we're going."

He paused, his eyes scanning the darkening landscape, as if drawing inspiration from the very land they were making their own. "I don't want a big production, Mara. No grand announcements in the town square. That's not us. Our story is woven into the fabric of Havenridge, into the quiet mornings, the shared meals, the challenges we've overcome together. It's in the simple, everyday acts of love and support."

He squeezed her hand gently. "I want to ask you, to make it official, in a place that means something to us. A place that symbolizes our journey. And the way I ask... it needs to be a reflection of the commitment I feel. Deep and true, not fleeting or for show."

Mara's heart swelled. This was precisely the Eli she had come to love – thoughtful, authentic, and utterly devoted. He saw their relationship not as a series of romantic clichés, but as a living, breathing entity that deserved to be nurtured with intention and sincerity. He wasn't interested in impressing others; he was focused on solidifying their bond in a way that resonated with their shared history and their private world.

"So, what have you been thinking?" she prompted, her curiosity piqued. She knew, with absolute certainty, that whatever he planned, it would be perfect for them.

Eli's eyes sparkled with a quiet excitement. "I've been thinking about the old oak grove," he said, a gentle smile playing on his lips. "Remember how we sat there, the first few times, when things were still so uncertain? It felt like a place where we could be honest, where the truth could unfurl without judgment."

Mara's breath hitched. She remembered. The dappled sunlight, the scent of earth, the tentative conversations that had laid the groundwork for everything that followed. It was a place of vulnerability and burgeoning hope.

"And I've been thinking about the fire pit," he continued, his gaze returning to hers, a newfound determination hardening his features. "Not just for warmth on a cold night, but for what it represents. For the way it brings people together, for the stories shared around its glow. It's a symbol of hearth and home, of community and belonging. And that's what I want to build with you, Mara. A home, a community, a shared life, grounded in the warmth of our love."

He pulled her gently closer, his voice dropping to a low, earnest tone. "I'm not going to get down on one knee in front of a crowd. I don't want a staged photo opportunity. I want to stand with you, under that old oak, with the fire lit beside us, and ask you, from the very bottom of my heart, to be my wife. To be my partner, my confidante, my forever."

He looked directly into her eyes, and Mara saw a profound depth of emotion there. It wasn't the flashy grandeur of a typical proposal, but something far more resonant: a quiet, unwavering promise, rooted in the shared history and the intimate landscape of their lives. This was Eli's way – deliberate, heartfelt, and perfectly tailored to them.

"I've been gathering some of the special stones from around Havenridge," he confessed, a shy smile gracing his features. "The ones that have a particular shimmer, or a unique shape. I'm going to arrange them around the fire pit, to mark the space. And within that circle, I'll ask you to commit your future to me. It will be our space, Mara. A place where our commitment is born, not of obligation, but of pure, unadulterated love and shared intention."

He paused, letting his words sink in. "It won't be a surprise in the sense of a sudden, unexpected event. I want you to know it's coming. I want you to be prepared for the depth of what I'm asking, and to be able to answer from that same place of certainty that you showed me tonight. But the *moment* itself... that will be ours. Private, sacred, and deeply meaningful. A testament to the journey we've taken to get here."

Mara felt a warmth spread through her, a profound sense of being seen and understood. This was not a man who understood love through the lens of societal expectations. He understood it through shared experiences, through mutual respect, and through the quiet, persistent building of a shared life. He had taken the abstract concept of 'commitment' that they had discussed and was now translating it into a tangible, deeply personal ritual.

"Eli," she whispered, her voice thick with emotion. "It's... it's perfect. It's more than perfect. It's us." She squeezed his hand, her thumb tracing the strong lines of his palm. "You've thought about this so deeply. It means everything to me that you want it to be a reflection of our journey, of what we've built together."

He pulled her closer still, his arms enfolding her in a comforting embrace. "Because that's what matters, Mara. Not the spectacle, but the substance. Not the fleeting attention, but the enduring bond. I want to build a future with you that is as strong and as beautiful as the land we inhabit. A future where every stone, every ember, every shared breath is a testament to our love."

He leaned back slightly, his eyes searching hers. "I've always admired your strength, your resilience, your capacity for truth. And you, in turn, have helped me understand the profound beauty of intentionality. You've shown me that true freedom isn't in avoiding commitment, but in choosing it, consciously and wholeheartedly. And I want to choose you, Mara. Every single day. I want to build our Havenridge, together, as partners, as lovers, as a family."

He continued, his voice a steady, comforting rhythm. "I've spoken to the elders, discreetly. They understand the significance of what I'm planning. They're supportive, of course. They've seen how we are, how we fit. They'll help with the preparations for the fire, with ensuring the grove is ready. But the words, the question, the promise... that will be between us."

Mara listened, absorbing every word. She knew that Eli's approach, while unconventional to some, was the epitome of his character. He was a man of quiet strength, of deep feeling, and of unwavering integrity. He wasn't interested in a fleeting moment of grandiosity; he was focused on creating a foundational experience, one that would forever be etched into the heart of their shared life at Havenridge.

"The stones," she mused, a soft smile gracing her lips. "Tell me more about the stones."

Eli's eyes lit up at her interest. "Well," he began, his voice filled with a gentle enthusiasm, "I've been collecting them for a while, without you knowing, of course. There are the smooth, grey river stones, which speak of the steady flow of time and the enduring nature of our bond. Then there are the quartz-flecked ones, catching the firelight, representing the sparkle of joy and the clarity of our connection. I've even found a few pieces of obsidian, dark and reflective, symbolizing the depths of our shared understanding, the willingness to face even the shadows together."

He gestured with his free hand, as if painting a picture in the air. "I'll place them in a rough circle, not too perfect, because our lives aren't perfect, but intentional. A boundary for our sacred space. And within that circle, with the fire casting its warm, golden light, I'll ask you. It will be a moment of pure authenticity, Mara. A testament to the fact that our love is not a grand, performative gesture, but a quiet, steady flame that burns brightly from within."

He then explained how he envisioned the evening unfolding, focusing on the intimacy of the experience. "I want it to be just us, initially. Perhaps the elders could join us afterwards, to share in our joy, but the proposal itself will be entirely private. A moment where we can truly focus on each other, on the magnitude of the decision we are making. There will be no distractions, no expectations from the outside world. Just the two of us, the fire, the grove, and our hearts."

He described the careful selection of the fire wood, the kind that would burn with a clean, steady flame, ensuring that the focus remained on their conversation and the profound moment of their commitment, rather than on the spectacle of the fire itself. He spoke of the subtle preparations, the gentle clearing of the undergrowth in the grove, the thoughtful placement of logs for a comfortable seat. Every detail, he explained, was designed to enhance the intimacy and significance of the occasion.

"I've also been thinking about a small, simple token," Eli confided, his gaze softening as he looked at her. "Not a diamond, perhaps. Something more... meaningful to us. I was considering a piece of polished petrified wood, found near the old creek bed. It's a symbol of time and transformation, of something natural and enduring becoming beautiful through the ages. It feels like a perfect representation of our own journey, and the commitment I'm asking you to make."

Mara was moved to tears, not of sadness, but of overwhelming joy and gratitude. This was not just a proposal; it was a carefully crafted declaration of love, a testament to their shared journey, and a vision for their future. Eli's approach was a powerful reflection of his character – grounded, sincere, and deeply rooted in the values they both cherished. He was not trying to fit their love into a predefined mold; he was creating a mold that was uniquely theirs, shaped by their shared experiences and their profound connection.

"Eli," she managed, her voice a soft whisper, "you are truly remarkable. This is... this is everything I could have ever dreamed of, and more. It's not about grand gestures; it's about the depth of your understanding, the sincerity of your heart. To have our commitment born in the same place where we first found solace and honesty with each other... it's incredibly profound."

He held her closer, his voice a low rumble against her temple. "Because that's where our strength lies, Mara. In the truth of our connection. In the quiet moments, the shared understanding, the unwavering support. I don't need a crowd to witness my love for you. I need you to witness it. I need you to feel it, deeply and truly, so that you can answer from that same place of certainty and love."

He continued to outline his plans, his voice calm and steady, weaving a tapestry of anticipation. He spoke of inviting Mara's closest friends and family, those who had been a part of her journey, to join them for a simple, celebratory meal *after* he had asked the question. This way, the sacredness of the proposal would remain between them, while still allowing for the shared joy and blessing of their loved ones to follow. It was a delicate balance, and Eli had struck it with his characteristic thoughtfulness.

"I want to give you something tangible, something real, to hold onto," he explained. "A symbol of this moment, of this promise. And then, once we've shared that deeply personal exchange, we can open our hearts to those who have supported us, and celebrate the beginning of our new chapter together."

He described the specific time of day he had chosen, just as the sun began its descent, casting long shadows across the grove, painting the sky in hues of orange and pink. "The light will be soft, magical," he murmured, his breath ghosting her ear. "It will be a natural kind of beauty, reflecting the beauty of the commitment we're about to make. No artificiality, just the raw, honest beauty of nature, mirroring the raw, honest beauty of our love."

Mara closed her eyes, envisioning the scene. Eli, standing before her, his eyes filled with love, the gentle glow of the fire illuminating his face, the ancient oaks bearing silent witness. It wasn't the fairy tale of glittering ballrooms and elaborate pronouncements, but it was something far more real, far more profound: a love story rooted in authenticity, nurtured by sincerity, and poised to blossom into an enduring legacy.

Eli's deliberate approach was not a compromise; it was an elevation, a testament to the fact that the most meaningful moments are often the most intimately held. And in that moment, Mara knew, with a certainty that resonated deep within her soul, that she would answer him with a resounding, joyful, "Yes."

The stillness of the night, once a comforting blanket, now held a subtle tension for Mara. Eli's proposal, a promise whispered beneath the ancient oaks and sealed by the flickering firelight, had shifted everything. It wasn't the question itself that unsettled her – that, she had embraced with every fiber of her being. It was the precipice of "forever" that lay beyond it, a vast, uncharted territory that, despite its allure, stirred a familiar tremor of apprehension deep within her.

The fear, a shadow that had long accompanied her through life, whispered insidious doubts: what if forever meant losing the essence of Mara? What if the fierce independence she had cultivated, the hard-won autonomy that defined her, became a casualty of shared destiny?

She found herself standing at the threshold of her own mind, not merely observing her thoughts, but actively wrestling with them. The image of a future with Eli, so vibrant and promising, was constantly being overlaid by a spectral vision of herself dissolving into him, her individuality a faint echo in the grand symphony of their shared life.

It was a fear born of past experiences, of relationships where love had felt like a cage, where compromise had slowly eroded the edges of her personality until she was barely recognizable, even to herself. She had fought so hard to reclaim that lost self, to rebuild the woman she was meant to be, and the thought of even a sliver of that being diminished by her commitment to Eli was a daunting prospect.

Yet, as she sat by the window, watching the moon cast its silvery light over Havenridge, she began to actively dismantle the fear, piece by painstaking piece. It wasn't enough to simply acknowledge the fear; she had to confront it, to dissect its roots and challenge its validity in the context of her relationship with Eli. She closed her eyes, deliberately pushing away the shadowy specter of a diminished self and conjuring a new vision, a different narrative. She imagined her future with Eli not as a surrender of her identity, but as an expansion of it.

She saw herself standing beside him, not behind him, not lost in his shadow, but as an equal partner, her own light shining brightly. She pictured their triumphs, not as individual victories, but as shared celebrations, each success amplified by the presence of the other. When Mara achieved something remarkable, perhaps a breakthrough in her art or a successful venture at Havenridge, she envisioned Eli's proud smile, his genuine admiration, not as a validation that eclipsed her own, but as an affirmation that deepened her joy.

He wouldn't simply witness her success; he would have been a part of the journey, a steadfast support, a sounding board, a source of encouragement that had helped her reach that pinnacle.

She saw their challenges, too. Not as moments of potential conflict that could fray their bond, but as shared battles to be fought side-by-side. When a difficult situation arose, whether it was a financial setback for Havenridge, a personal struggle for Eli, or a creative block for her, she imagined them facing it together. Eli wouldn't offer solutions that erased her agency, nor would she expect him to bear the burden alone. Instead, they would pool their strengths, their perspectives, their resilience.

She saw herself offering him her unwavering support, her keen insights, her emotional fortitude, just as he would offer her his calm wisdom, his steady presence, his unwavering belief in her capabilities. This wasn't about surrendering her will; it was about the profound strength that came from knowing she didn't have to carry every burden alone, that there was a partner whose presence made the weight lighter, not by taking it, but by sharing it.

She thought of the quiet moments, the everyday rhythm of their lives together. The early mornings, sipping coffee on the porch, the comfortable silence punctuated by the chirping of birds. The shared meals, where conversations flowed easily, ranging from the mundane to the profound. The evenings spent reading by the fire, or tending to the gardens, or simply existing in each other's presence. In these moments, she realized, her identity wasn't erased; it was affirmed.

Eli's presence was not a distraction from her own thoughts or pursuits, but a comforting backdrop that allowed them to flourish. He didn't demand her constant attention; he allowed her space to be herself, to pursue her passions, to simply *be*. And in turn, she offered him the same respect, the same freedom to be his authentic self.

Mara visualized a future where her own voice remained strong, where her opinions were valued, where her dreams were encouraged. She saw herself continuing to paint, to create, to explore new artistic avenues, and Eli would be her most ardent supporter, perhaps even her first critic, offering constructive feedback born of love and understanding, not of control or judgment. She imagined him celebrating her exhibitions, not with possessiveness, but with genuine pride in her accomplishments. She saw herself still taking on challenges, still pushing her own boundaries, and knowing that his belief in her was an inexhaustible wellspring of courage.

This active visualization was crucial. It was a conscious act of rewiring her ingrained fears, of replacing the old, worn-out narratives with new ones, richer and more accurate. She wasn't just hoping for a future where she wouldn't lose herself; she was actively building that future in her mind, brick by mental brick. She understood that commitment wasn't a contract that bound and restricted, but a sanctuary that sheltered and nurtured. It was a conscious choice, made daily, to invest in a shared life, to weave two individual threads into a tapestry that was stronger and more beautiful than either thread could be alone.

The fear of "forever" began to lose its sharp edges, softening into a sense of profound anticipation. She saw that her autonomy wasn't a fragile possession to be guarded, but an intrinsic part of who she was, a part that would, in fact, enrich her partnership with Eli. Her independence would bring new perspectives, her unique experiences would add depth to their shared journey, and her strong sense of self would ensure that their union was one of equals, two whole individuals choosing to build a life together, rather than two halves searching for completion.

She imagined the subtle ways their lives would intertwine, not by subsuming, but by enriching. Her love for gardening might inspire Eli to create new spaces for her to cultivate her passion. His appreciation for history might lead her to research the origins of Havenridge, breathing new life into her art through historical context. These weren't compromises; they were invitations to explore new facets of themselves and their shared world, guided by mutual curiosity and love.

The fear of losing herself was, in essence, the fear of the unknown. But by actively exploring the possibilities, by visualizing the expansion rather than the contraction of her world, she was charting that unknown territory. She was creating a mental map, and on that map, "forever" wasn't a void, but a landscape rich with shared experiences, mutual respect, and the unwavering presence of a love that celebrated, rather than diminished, the individual.

She realized that Eli's proposal, his thoughtful planning, was a testament to his understanding of this very principle. He hadn't asked her to surrender her life; he had asked her to share it, to build upon it, to create something new and lasting together. His own strong sense of self was evident in his deliberate approach, in his deep connection to Havenridge, and in his unwavering devotion to her. He wasn't looking for a reflection of himself; he was looking for a partner who would bring her own unique light to their shared existence.

This internal work was a deliberate, conscious decision to embrace permanence not as an end, but as a beginning. It was the understanding that true commitment wasn't about the absence of personal identity, but its fullest expression, shared within the safe harbor of a loving partnership. She was choosing to believe in a future where her dreams and Eli's dreams could coexist, complement each other, and perhaps even merge into something greater than either could have achieved alone. The fear of forever was slowly, steadily, giving way to the radiant possibility of a shared forever, a tapestry woven with the vibrant threads of two individual lives, creating a masterpiece of enduring love.

The gentle rustle of leaves, a symphony he knew by heart, guided Eli's steps. He found Mara not in the quiet solitude of her studio, nor amidst the familiar warmth of the inn's common room, but out where the land breathed its deepest secrets – at the overlook, their sentinel perch above the sleeping valley. The late afternoon sun, a painter itself, brushed the rolling hills with strokes of gold and amber, a scene so intrinsically them, so steeped in their shared history, that it felt like stepping back into a cherished memory. She stood by the weathered stone wall, her silhouette etched against the vast expanse, a quiet contemplation radiating from her. The breeze toyed with strands of her hair, and for a moment, Eli simply watched, absorbing the serene beauty of the woman who had become the compass of his world.

He approached slowly, his footsteps soft on the packed earth, not wanting to startle her, but eager to bridge the small distance between them. When she turned, her eyes, the color of a sun-drenched meadow, held a question, a quiet awareness that he had sought her out. He offered a small, reassuring smile, a silent acknowledgment of the unspoken dialogue that often passed between them.

"I thought I might find you here," he began, his voice a low rumble against the backdrop of nature's murmur. He gestured to the vista, the panorama of Havenridge unfolding below them, a testament to generations of stewardship and, now, to their burgeoning shared future. "It's always felt like the heart of this place. And lately," he paused, his gaze meeting hers, a depth of emotion swirling in his eyes, "it feels like the heart of everything."

He stepped closer, not invading her space, but settling into the shared silence that had always been a comfort. He could feel the subtle shift in the air, the unspoken weight of his proposal, of the future that now lay before them, shimmering and vast. It was a future he had not stumbled into, but one he had actively, deliberately, yearned for, and now, stood ready to embrace.

"Mara," he said, his voice softening, laced with a profound tenderness. "The other night, when I asked you... when I asked you to share your forever with me, it wasn't just a question born of love, though there is more love for you than I ever thought possible." He reached out, his fingers lightly brushing her arm, a touch that sent a familiar warmth through her. "It was a choice. A conscious, deliberate choice to build a life, a true partnership, with you. Not just for the sake of convenience, or comfort, or even just happiness, though I know those things will be abundant with you. But a choice for permanence. For a shared path, right here, within the heart of Havenridge."

He turned to face her more fully, the setting sun painting their profiles in warm hues. "This land, this inn, this community... they're not just a place to me, Mara. They're a legacy. A responsibility. And for a long time, I thought I could manage it alone, that my path was solitary. But then you came, and you brought your light, your strength, your unique way of seeing the world, and you showed me how much richer a path can be when it's walked with someone else. Someone who challenges you, who inspires you, who sees the potential not just in the land, but in *us*."

He looked out at the valley, his expression earnest. "I don't want just to be with you, Mara. I want to build *with* you. I want Havenridge to be a testament not just to my family's history, but to our shared story. I envision us, side by side, making decisions, nurturing this place, facing whatever challenges come our way, together. I want to hear your ideas for the inn, your vision for its future, your dreams for its evolution. I want to see you bring your art, your spirit, your passion to every corner of this estate. I want your touch to be as evident here as mine is."

He took a breath, his gaze returning to her, unwavering. "This commitment, this marriage... it's not about obligation. It's about a profound desire to weave our lives together, to create something lasting, something beautiful, that neither of us could achieve on our own. It's about choosing, every single day, to stand by your side, to support you, to encourage you, and to love you, through all the seasons of life. It's about creating a foundation here, at Havenridge, that will anchor us, that will be a sanctuary for us, and a place of warmth and welcome for others."

He moved closer, his hands gently finding hers, their fingers interlacing. "I want to wake up next to you every morning, Mara. I want to share quiet mornings with coffee on the porch, just like we have now, but as husband and wife. I want to face the inevitable storms, both literal and metaphorical, with you beside me, knowing that we can weather them together. I want our laughter to echo through these halls, our shared dreams to take root and flourish, and our love to be the very bedrock of Havenridge."

His thumb caressed the back of her hand, a tender gesture that spoke volumes. "I see a future where our individual strengths complement each other, where your creativity inspires new ventures, and my steady hand guides them to fruition. I see a future where our children, if we are blessed with them, will grow up knowing the love and stability that we build together. I see a future where we continue to grow, not just as individuals, but as a couple, our bond deepening with each passing year, our understanding of each other becoming more profound."

He stepped back slightly, his gaze sweeping over her again, as if imprinting this moment onto his soul. "This is not a hurried decision, Mara. This is a heartfelt invitation to a shared journey. It's about choosing the adventure of 'us,' of a permanent partnership, of building a legacy together, right here. It's about committing to a life, a shared path, that will be rich with love, respect, and a deep, abiding partnership. It's about you and me, building a forever, at Havenridge."

The silence that followed was not empty, but filled with the unspoken resonance of his words, of the future he so clearly envisioned. The valley, bathed in the fading light, seemed to hold its breath, waiting for her response, for the blossoming of a shared destiny that had been nurtured in the quiet corners of their hearts and now stood ready to unfurl in the grand embrace of Havenridge.

He waited patiently, his gaze soft, his heart laid bare, offering her not just a proposal, but the promise of a shared path, deliberately chosen and eternally cherished. He knew the weight of his words, the significance of this moment, and he offered it to her with all the sincerity and hope that resided within him, rooted deeply in the love he held for her, and the future he so passionately desired to build with her.

CHAPTER SIX

THE AFFIRMATION OF UNION

The air, though still carrying the scent of damp earth and late-blooming jasmine, felt charged with an anticipation that had been building for weeks, perhaps even months. Eli found Mara not at their usual spot by the overlook, bathed in the dramatic hues of sunset, but beneath the sprawling branches of the old willow tree that stood sentinel near the community center. Its gnarled limbs, heavy with the weight of years and stories, bowed towards the ground, creating a secluded, verdant chamber. The breeze, a playful whisper, rustled its leaves, weaving a soft, murmuring soundtrack to the moment that was, he felt with a certainty that settled deep in his bones, about to become etched into the fabric of their lives.

She was leaning against the rough bark, her gaze lost somewhere in the dappled sunlight that filtered through the canopy. A faint smile played on her lips, as if she were privy to some quiet, beautiful secret of the natural world. Eli approached with a gentleness born of deep respect and an even deeper love, his footsteps barely disturbing the fallen leaves. He didn't have a velvet box, no perfectly cut diamond glinting under the light. He didn't need them. His proposal, his heart's earnest plea, was woven into the very essence of their shared journey, into the land they both loved, into the future they had been unknowingly, and then knowingly, constructing together.

He stopped a few feet away, simply drinking her in. The way the light caught the subtle auburn in her hair, the serene tilt of her head, the quiet strength that emanated from her, even in repose. This was the woman who had, with a grace he still marveled at, woven herself into the tapestry of his life, transforming its muted threads into a vibrant, breathtaking masterpiece. He could feel the nervous flutter in his chest, a familiar companion to his love for her, but it was tempered by a profound sense of rightness, of inevitability.

"Mara," he said softly, his voice a low resonance that seemed to vibrate with the very air around them.

She turned, her meadow-green eyes meeting his, and the faint smile on her lips deepened, a silent acknowledgment of his presence, of the unspoken anticipation that had been a constant undercurrent between them. There was no surprise, only a gentle curiosity, a quiet readiness.

He walked the remaining distance, closing the small space that separated them, not with haste, but with a deliberate, measured pace. He didn't reach for a ring. Instead, his hands, strong and calloused from years of work, reached out and gently took hers. Her fingers, slender and artistic, fit perfectly into his, a tactile affirmation of their connection. He held her hands, not possessively, but as if anchoring himself to the most precious thing he had ever known.

"We've walked a lot of paths together, haven't we?" he began, his gaze locked on hers, pouring every ounce of his sincerity into his words. "From the first awkward conversations over dusty ledgers, to late-night talks under the stars, to facing down challenges that felt insurmountable. We've stumbled, we've learned, and we've grown. And through it all," he squeezed her hands gently, "you've been my constant. My north star."

He took a deep, steadying breath, the scent of the willow and the earth filling his lungs. "Remember when we first talked about Havenridge? Not just as a business, or a place to live, but as something more? Something that needed tending, that deserved our best efforts? I saw it as a legacy, a responsibility I was tasked with. And for a long time, I thought that meant carrying it alone, carving out my own solitary path within its embrace."

His thumb brushed softly over the back of her hand, a small gesture that spoke volumes of unspoken affection. "But then you came. And you didn't just see the stone walls and the fertile land. You saw the stories held within them. You saw the potential, not just for a thriving business, but for a vibrant community. You saw the art in the everyday, the beauty in the ordinary. You taught me that a legacy isn't just about what you inherit or what you build alone; it's about what you nurture, what you share, and what you create *together*."

He looked out beyond her, towards the gentle rise of the hills that cradled Havenridge, their familiar contours a testament to time and perseverance. "I've seen the way you pour your heart into everything you do, Mara. The way you bring life and color to everything you touch. Your art is a reflection of your soul, and your soul is something truly extraordinary. You have a vision, a passion, a spirit that this place, that *my* life, has been yearning for, even when I didn't know it."

He brought his gaze back to her, his eyes reflecting the earnestness of his purpose. "We've spent countless hours dreaming about the future of Havenridge. I've talked about renovating the west wing, about expanding the orchards, about restoring the old gristmill. But you... you've talked about the heart of it. About making the inn a place where people feel truly welcomed, truly at home. About creating spaces where creativity can flourish, where artists can find inspiration. About weaving this community together, stronger and more connected than ever before."

He paused, letting his words settle, allowing the weight of their shared aspirations to hang in the air between them. "And as I've listened to you, as I've watched you bring your unique magic to this place, something has become profoundly clear. My dreams for Havenridge, my vision for its future, are incomplete without you as my partner, not just in spirit, but in every sense of the word."

He leaned in slightly, his voice dropping to a more intimate, heartfelt tone. "Mara, I don't just want to build a future *at* Havenridge. I want to build our future *together*, with Havenridge as our foundation. I want us to be the architects of our own destiny, hand in hand, heart to heart. I want to make it official. Not just for the sake of tradition, though I understand its importance, but because I believe in the power of a formal union, a recognized partnership, to solidify what we already feel, to give it a deeper resonance, a clearer voice within this community we both cherish."

His grip on her hands tightened infinitesimally, a silent plea. "I want to ask you, Mara, not just for your love, which I feel so deeply and cherish so completely, but for your hand in marriage. I want to ask you to be my wife. To formalize this incredible journey we've embarked on, to stand by my side and build a life, a legacy, a family, here, in the heart of Havenridge. I want our partnership to be a beacon, a testament to the fact that love and dedication can create something enduring, something beautiful, something that will stand the test of time."

He searched her face, looking for any flicker, any sign. "I want to wake up every morning knowing that you are beside me, that we are facing the day together. I want to share the quiet joys and the inevitable challenges, knowing that we are a team, united in our purpose and in our love. I want our home here to be filled with laughter, with creativity, with the warmth of our shared lives. I want our names, Eli and Mara, to be synonymous with the best of Havenridge, with its enduring spirit and its forward-looking vision."

He took another breath, his gaze unwavering, his heart laid bare. "This isn't just about me wanting you, Mara. It's about wanting us. It's about choosing to intertwine our lives so completely that we become stronger, wiser, and more loving because of it. It's about a deliberate, conscious choice to commit to a shared existence, to a permanent union, built on the foundation of respect, trust, and a love that has grown deeper and more profound with every passing day."

He gently lifted her hands, bringing them to his lips, pressing a tender kiss to each of her knuckles. "I am asking you to be my partner in everything. My wife. To build with me, to dream with me, to live with me, here, at Havenridge. To make our love story an integral part of this place, a narrative that will be told for generations to come." The willow leaves rustled above them, as if whispering their agreement, their blessing.

The moment hung suspended, pregnant with possibility, a quiet symphony of love and commitment played out beneath the ancient tree, awaiting its final, perfect cadence. He waited, his heart in his eyes, his hands still holding hers, a silent testament to the depth and sincerity of his question. He had laid his soul bare, offering her not just a ring or a proposal, but the entirety of his future, woven inextricably with hers.

The gentle breeze, once a mere whisper, now seemed to carry the weight of unspoken emotions, rustling the willow leaves like a hushed applause. Mara's gaze, which had been fixed on some distant point in the dappled sunlight, now met Eli's with an intensity that held him captive. The question, so earnest and heartfelt, hung in the air between them, not as a demand, but as an offering – an offering of a future, a life, a partnership. And in that suspended moment, beneath the sheltering boughs of the ancient willow, something profound shifted within Mara.

The echoes of her earlier anxieties, the fleeting shadows of self-doubt that had sometimes clouded her vision of a shared future, receded with astonishing speed. They were not vanquished by force, but simply dissolved, like mist under the morning sun, in the face of Eli's unwavering sincerity and the sheer, undeniable truth of his love. What had once seemed like a potential surrender of her own identity now presented itself as a glorious expansion, a merging of her spirit with his, creating something infinitely richer and more complete than she could have ever envisioned alone.

A single tear, warm and shimmering, traced a path down her cheek. It wasn't a tear of sadness or apprehension, but of an overwhelming, almost breathtaking joy. It was the kind of tear that wells up when a long-held dream finally unfurls, when the impossible suddenly becomes gloriously, beautifully real. She looked at Eli, at the raw vulnerability etched on his face, at the hope that shimmered in his eyes, and she knew, with a certainty that resonated through every fiber of her being, that this was not just a proposal, but a homecoming.

His hands, still holding hers gently, felt like an anchor, grounding her in the present while simultaneously pulling her towards a future brimming with promise. She felt the steady beat of his heart through the pressure of his fingers, a rhythm that seemed to sync perfectly with her own. This was not about losing herself; it was about finding a deeper, truer self in his presence, in their shared journey. Havenridge, once a symbol of her own artistic aspirations and a place of healing, now felt like the embodiment of their collective dream, a testament to what two souls, united by love and purpose, could create.

"Eli," she began, her voice a little husky, a testament to the emotions swirling within her. The sound of his name on her lips felt different now, imbued with a new depth, a new significance. It was the name of her future, the name of her partner, the name of the man who had seen not just her art, but her soul.

She took a slow, steadying breath, the scent of damp earth and willow blossoms filling her lungs. The fear, the whisper of "what if?" that had occasionally accompanied her deepest desires, was gone. Replaced by a quiet, unwavering confidence. "Yes," she said, her voice gaining strength, becoming clearer, more resonant with each syllable. "Oh, Eli, yes."

The words, so simple, yet so potent, seemed to hang in the air, weaving themselves into the fabric of the moment. She saw his eyes widen, a flicker of disbelief quickly replaced by an explosion of relief and pure, unadulterated happiness. It was a look that mirrored the joy erupting in her own heart.

"Yes," she repeated, a soft smile blooming on her face, mirroring the one that was now transforming Eli's features. "A thousand times, yes." She squeezed his hands, her grip firm and reassuring. "I accept, Eli. I accept your proposal. I accept you. I accept us."

Her gaze swept over him, taking in the earnestness of his expression, the love that radiated from him like warmth from a hearth fire. She saw not just the man who had asked her to marry him, but the man who had patiently understood her creative spirit, who had celebrated her successes, and who had been a steady presence through her uncertainties. He had seen the potential in Havenridge, and more importantly, he had seen the potential in *them*.

"You asked if we've walked a lot of paths together," she continued, her voice now imbued with a lyrical quality that was distinctly her own. "And we have. But the path that led me here, to this moment, to you... it feels like the most important one. The one that was always meant to be." She chuckled softly, a sound of pure delight. "I remember thinking, in the early days, that Havenridge was my canvas, my sanctuary. And in a way, it still is. But now... now it's our canvas. Our sanctuary. Our home."

She shifted slightly, her hands still clasped in his, feeling the comforting strength of their connection. "You spoke of legacies, Eli, of building something that would last. And I've always believed that art, in its purest form, is a legacy. But you've shown me that a shared life, a partnership built on love and mutual respect, is the most enduring legacy of all. You haven't just built a business here; you've cultivated a place of belonging, a place where dreams can take root. And you've invited me to be a part of that cultivation, not just as an artist, but as your partner."

Her eyes met his again, a silent conversation passing between them. "When you talked about my art reflecting my soul, you saw something I sometimes struggled to articulate even to myself. You saw the passion, the vision, the desire to bring beauty and meaning into the world. And you didn't just appreciate it; you embraced it. You understood that my creativity is not separate from who I am, but an integral part of it. And you want that part of me to be woven into the very fabric of our life together. That is... everything."

She leaned her forehead against his, the rough bark of the willow a gentle reminder of the steadfastness of nature, a silent witness to their vows. "My fears," she admitted softly, "they were about losing that spark, about becoming someone I wasn't. But with you, Eli, I feel more myself than I ever have. You don't diminish me; you amplify me. You give me the space to bloom, the courage to soar, and the certainty that I will always have a safe harbor to return to."

"You spoke of me bringing color and life to everything I touch. And you, Eli, you bring a quiet strength, a profound integrity, and a depth of love that I had only ever dreamt of. You are the steady hand, the unwavering heart, the wise counsel. You are the calm in my storms, the joy in my quiet moments." She pulled back slightly, her gaze full of adoration. "You make me want to be better, to strive higher, to love deeper. And that, my dearest Eli, is a gift beyond measure."

"When you looked at Havenridge, you saw a responsibility, a task to be undertaken. And I saw a place to pour my heart into, a place to create. But together," she gestured around them, encompassing the ancient willow, the rolling hills, the very air that seemed to hum with their happiness, "together, we see a home. A life. A future so much richer and more vibrant than either of us could have imagined alone."

"You asked me to be your wife. To formalize this incredible journey. And I don't just accept that formalization; I embrace it with every fiber of my being. I want our names to be synonymous with Havenridge, yes, but more importantly, I want our names to be synonymous with a love that endures, a partnership that inspires, a life built on shared dreams and unwavering devotion."

She traced the line of his jaw with a gentle finger, marveling at the strong, kind features that she had come to love so dearly. "I want to wake up next to you every morning, Eli. I want to share the quiet sunrise with you, the aroma of coffee brewing, the gentle murmur of the day beginning. I want to face whatever challenges come our way, knowing that we face them together, as a team. I want our home to be filled with laughter, with the scent of drying paint and the murmur of shared stories. I want our lives to be an ongoing testament to the power of love, of commitment, of two souls finding their truest home in each other."

"You've given me so much already, Eli. You've given me your trust, your respect, your unwavering support. You've given me a vision of a future that is more beautiful than I could have ever conceived. And now you're asking me to give you my hand, my heart, my life. And I give them freely, with all the joy and certainty in my soul."

Her voice, though soft, carried an undeniable strength. "I want to be your wife. I want to build this life with you, here, at Havenridge. I want our love story to be the heart of this place, a melody that resonates through the years. I want to be your partner in everything, Eli. Your wife. Forever."

As she spoke the last word, a profound sense of peace settled over her. The world, which had seemed so vast and sometimes daunting, now felt intimate and secure, centered around the man whose hands still held hers so tenderly. The anxieties that had once threatened to overshadow her deepest desires had been replaced by a profound sense of belonging, a certainty that she was exactly where she was meant to be, with exactly the person she was meant to be with.

Eli's eyes, filled with an emotion that mirrored her own, searched hers for a moment longer, as if to reassure himself that this was real. Then, slowly, a broad, radiant smile spread across his face, a smile that reached his eyes and lit them with an almost incandescent joy. He brought her hands to his lips, not in a gesture of possession, but of reverence, pressing a kiss to each of her knuckles, a silent affirmation of their shared commitment.

"Mara," he breathed, his voice thick with emotion, "you have made me the happiest man in the world." He tightened his hold on her hands, his gaze unwavering. "This isn't just a formal union; it's the beautiful culmination of everything we are, and everything we will become. It's our promise to each other, etched not just in vows, but in the very spirit of Havenridge."

He looked out towards the gently rolling hills, the familiar landscape now imbued with a new significance. "We will nurture this place together, Mara. We will fill it with art, with life, with the echo of our laughter. We will make it a beacon for others, a testament to the fact that love, when built on a foundation of shared dreams and unwavering devotion, can create something truly extraordinary, something that will stand the test of time."

He turned his attention back to her, his eyes a deep, warm pool of affection. "You spoke of my steadiness, my integrity. And I will strive to embody those qualities in every aspect of our married life, to be the rock you can always lean on, the partner you can always trust. And you, my love, will continue to bring the color, the passion, the vibrant spirit that has transformed my life and this place. Together, we are a masterpiece in progress."

He caressed her cheek with the back of his hand, his touch sending a shiver of pure bliss through her. "This is not an end, Mara, but a glorious beginning. The beginning of our shared future, of our forever. The beginning of our family, our legacy, our life together. And I cannot imagine a more perfect way to start than right here, beneath this ancient willow, with your heart beating in time with mine, your hand in mine, your 'yes' echoing in my soul."

He drew her closer, enveloping her in a warm embrace. The scent of him, familiar and comforting, filled her senses. This was not just the embrace of a lover, but the embrace of a partner, of a future husband, of the man who would walk beside her through every season of life. She rested her head against his chest, listening to the steady rhythm of his heart, a rhythm that now felt like the very pulse of her own existence.

"I love you, Eli," she whispered, the words a soft benediction against his shirt. "More than words can say."

"And I love you, Mara," he replied, his voice a deep rumble of contentment. "With all my heart and soul. Today, tomorrow, and always."

The willow leaves above them seemed to shimmer, catching the late afternoon sun and casting a dappled, golden light upon the scene. The breeze, once a hesitant whisper, now sang a gentle, harmonious melody, a serenade of love and commitment. In that moment, under the watchful eyes of the ancient tree, their union was not just affirmed, but celebrated. It was a moment etched in time, a promise whispered on the wind, a heartfelt acceptance that marked the true beginning of their forever. The path ahead, though yet unwritten, felt certain and bright, illuminated by the unwavering glow of their shared love.

The news, as it often did in Havenridge, began as a gentle ripple and then spread like sunlight across a meadow. Eli and Mara's decision to formalize their partnership, their commitment to a shared future, didn't arrive with fanfare or grand pronouncements. Instead, it unfurled organically, a quiet understanding that settled over the community like the soft dew of a summer morning. It was the kind of news that prompted knowing smiles, a subtle nod of heads, and a pervasive sense of warmth that seemed to emanate from the very heart of Havenridge itself.

The initial whispers, carried on the breeze that rustled through the ancient oaks and whispered secrets through the newly painted studios, were met not with surprise, but with a profound sense of affirmation. For those who had witnessed the slow, beautiful bloom of Mara and Eli's connection, who had seen the way their lives had begun to intertwine as naturally as ivy climbing a sturdy trellis, their engagement felt less like a sudden revelation and more like the inevitable blossoming of a deeply rooted love. It was a confirmation of what many had already felt in their hearts – that these two souls were meant to walk this path together, weaving their lives into the very fabric of Havenridge.

Eleanor, her hands dusted with flour from her morning baking, was one of the first to hear. She'd been chatting with Old Man Fitzwilliam by the general store, discussing the late spring bloom of the roses, when young Finn, his face alight with a mixture of excitement and a touch of childhood earnestness, had delivered the news. "Mara and Mr. Thorne are getting married!" he'd announced, his voice clear and bright, as if he were sharing the most wonderful secret in the world.

Eleanor's smile widened, crinkling the corners of her eyes. "Well, isn't that just the most wonderful news, Finn?" she'd replied, her voice soft and full of genuine delight. "I always had a feeling those two were meant for each other." Old Man Fitzwilliam, his weathered face breaking into a rare, broad grin, had simply nodded in agreement, his eyes twinkling with the same quiet joy. "Aye," he'd rasped, his voice a low rumble. "It's about time. They're good for each other, those two."

Across town, in the bustling workshop where the scent of freshly cut lumber mingled with the promise of new creations, Thomas, Eli's most trusted craftsman, had also received the news. He'd been engrossed in the intricate work of carving a new banister for the main house when Eli, his usual stoic demeanor softened by an almost palpable joy, had stopped by. A simple, yet deeply meaningful, announcement. Thomas had put down his chisel, his eyes meeting Eli's with a look of profound understanding and unspoken pride. "That's wonderful, Eli," he'd said, his voice laced with warmth.

"Truly wonderful. Mara's a special woman. She brings a light to everything she touches, and she certainly brought one to you." He'd then clapped Eli on the shoulder, a gesture of camaraderie and hearty congratulations. "You've both built something beautiful here, together. This is just the next step, isn't it? A step that will only make Havenridge stronger."

The sentiment echoed throughout the community. The artists, the farmers, the shopkeepers, the families who called Havenridge home – they saw Mara and Eli's union not merely as a personal milestone, but as a strengthening of the very foundations of their shared existence. Havenridge wasn't just a place; it was a living, breathing entity, built on the collective spirit of its inhabitants, on shared dreams and a mutual respect for the land and for each other. Mara, with her vibrant artistry and her unwavering passion, had breathed new life into the old estate, transforming it into a sanctuary for creativity and a haven for those seeking solace and inspiration. Eli, with his quiet integrity and his deep-seated commitment to preserving the legacy of Havenridge, had provided the steady hand, the grounded vision that allowed those dreams to flourish.

Their union, therefore, felt like a natural and powerful affirmation of everything Havenridge stood for. It was a promise that the spirit of creativity and community would not only endure but would deepen, intertwined with the enduring strength of a love built on mutual admiration and respect. The artists, in particular, felt a surge of inspiration. Mara's journey, from finding her footing in this new landscape to finding her soulmate within it, was a testament to the transformative power of Havenridge. They saw in her engagement a validation of their own aspirations, a tangible example of how art and life, passion and partnership, could seamlessly merge into a beautiful, harmonious whole.

Isabelle, her easel set up overlooking the serene lake, her brushes poised, felt a particular resonance. She'd often spoken with Mara about the delicate balance between artistic solitude and the joys of shared companionship. Seeing Mara and Eli embrace their future together, knowing the depth of their mutual understanding and support, brought a sense of profound peace and encouragement. "It's like seeing a perfectly composed landscape," she mused to herself, a gentle smile gracing her lips. "All the elements are in place, harmonizing beautifully. Mara's brilliance, Eli's strength, and their shared vision for Havenridge. It's a masterpiece in the making, and their union is the vital brushstroke that brings it all into perfect focus."

Even the children, who possessed an uncanny ability to sense the prevailing mood of their surroundings, seemed to absorb the quiet joy. They'd noticed the smiles that lingered longer on the faces of their parents, the softer tone of conversations, the palpable sense of contentedness that seemed to permeate the air. For them, it meant more shared stories, more laughter echoing through the gardens, and the unspoken promise of a community that was not just growing, but deepening its roots, becoming even more of a family. Little Lily, who had taken a particular liking to Mara's vibrant paintings that adorned the walls of the community hall, declared with childish certainty, "Mara and Eli are going to build a castle of love for all of us!" And in its own way, her innocent declaration captured the essence of what their union represented to the heart of Havenridge.

The decision to formalize their partnership also brought a renewed sense of purpose to the ongoing projects and developments within Havenridge. Eli and Mara, now with an even stronger shared vision, began to discuss their plans with a renewed fervor. There were ideas for expanding the artist residency programs, for creating new communal spaces that would foster even greater connection among the residents, and for establishing a long-term legacy that would ensure Havenridge continued to be a source of inspiration and beauty for generations to come. These weren't just business plans; they were the tangible expressions of a shared commitment, a promise to nurture and grow the haven they had both come to cherish.

Mara, in particular, felt a profound sense of liberation and empowerment. The anxieties that had once whispered at the edges of her consciousness, the fear of losing herself in the embrace of a partnership, had completely dissipated. Eli's unwavering support of her artistic endeavors, his genuine admiration for her spirit, had not only allowed her to flourish but had also given her the courage to embrace a future that was richer and more expansive than she had ever imagined. She saw their upcoming marriage not as a compromise, but as an amplification – a way to bring the full spectrum of her creativity and her love into the shared life they were building. She envisioned her art not just as a personal expression, but as an integral thread woven into the tapestry of their life together, adding color, depth, and meaning to their shared existence.

Eli, too, felt the transformative impact. He saw in Mara not just a partner, but a muse, a confidante, and the embodiment of the very beauty and spirit he wished to cultivate within Havenridge. Her passion ignited his own, her insights broadened his perspective, and her love filled him with a profound sense of contentment and purpose. He realized that his own journey of building and preserving Havenridge had found its truest fulfillment in the act of sharing it with her. Their union was not just about solidifying their personal bond; it was about weaving their individual legacies into a shared narrative, creating a story that would resonate with the very soul of the place.

As the days turned into weeks, the gentle acceptance of the community solidified into a shared anticipation. There was a quiet excitement about the wedding, about the formalization of a bond that felt so intrinsically right. The preparations, undertaken with the collective spirit of Havenridge, were not just about planning an event, but about celebrating the union of two souls who had become an indispensable part of the community's heart. It was a testament to the fact that in Havenridge, personal milestones were not just celebrated individually, but embraced collectively, strengthening the threads that bound them all together. Their shared future, now publicly acknowledged, was not just their own; it was a promise to the very spirit of Havenridge, a beacon of love, creativity, and enduring community.

The morning sun, filtering through the ancient oaks, painted dancing patterns on the polished wood floor of the library. Mara traced the grain with a fingertip, a quiet contentment settling over her. Eli, his presence a comforting warmth beside her, watched her, a gentle smile playing on his lips. They had spent hours discussing the future, their voices low and earnest, the weight of their decision settling upon them not as a burden, but as a foundation.

"It's still sinking in, you know," Mara confessed, her gaze drifting to the shelves lined with stories of lives lived and loves enduring. "The idea of 'forever.' For so long, it felt like this unreachable peak, something you could only glimpse from a distance. And sometimes, I'll admit, it felt a little... daunting."

Eli's hand found hers, his thumb stroking the back of her palm. "Daunting? I understand. It's a grand word, isn't it? 'Forever.' It can conjure images of grand pronouncements, of an ending point, a definitive statement carved in stone." He paused, his eyes, the colour of warm earth, meeting hers. "But I've come to see it differently, Mara. Especially with you. It's not a static place we arrive at, is it? It's a journey. A continuous act of choosing."

Mara leaned into him, the scent of aged paper and Eli's subtle, clean fragrance a familiar comfort. "Choosing," she echoed softly. "Yes. It's the choice we make each morning, when we wake up and decide to build this life, together. It's the choice to listen, truly listen, even when we're tired or disagree. It's the choice to see the best in each other, even when the world feels challenging."

"Exactly," Eli affirmed, his voice deepening with conviction. "And it's not about erasing who we were as individuals. It's about weaving those individual threads into something richer, more vibrant. Havenridge has shown me that. It thrives on the unique contributions of everyone, and our partnership, our 'forever,' will be no different. It will be stronger precisely because we are still ourselves, but amplified by each other's presence."

He gestured around the library, a room that held so many stories, so many echoes of past lives. "Think of the stories within these walls. They aren't just tales of people who existed. They are testaments to choices made, to love that persevered, to resilience in the face of hardship. 'Forever' isn't about avoiding change; it's about navigating it together. It's about the courage to adapt, to grow, to become more than we were, side by side."

Mara smiled, a genuine, heartfelt smile that reached her eyes. "That's it, isn't it? It's the evolution. The understanding that 'forever' isn't a finished painting, but a canvas we continually add to. Our love isn't a finished sculpture, but a living, breathing thing that we nurture and allow to change and deepen." She thought of her art, how it had evolved since arriving in Havenridge, how her perspective had broadened. Her commitment to Eli felt like the most natural extension of that growth.

"I used to fear that commitment would somehow stifle my creativity, that it would demand a certain sameness," she admitted, her voice barely a whisper. "That the spark would dim. But with you, Eli, it's the opposite. You see the fire in my work, and you gently tend it, ensuring it burns brighter, not less. You don't ask me to be less me; you encourage me to be *more* me, and then you stand right there with me, celebrating it."

Eli squeezed her hand. "And you do the same for me, Mara. You see the quiet strength in my work, in my commitment to Havenridge, and you infuse it with a colour, a passion, that I might have otherwise overlooked. You remind me why I do what I do, and you inspire me to build something even more meaningful. Our 'forever' isn't about settling into a comfortable routine; it's about constantly finding new horizons to explore, together."

He tilted her chin up gently, his gaze steady and full of affection. "It's about building a shared purpose that transcends our individual dreams. Havenridge is a testament to that. It was built on a vision, a collective commitment to beauty, to community, to legacy. And now, our union is another layer of that. It's a promise that the spirit of this place, the spirit of love and creativity, will continue to flourish, guided by a love that understands its own enduring power."

"And it's a powerful thing, isn't it?" Mara mused, looking out at the sun-drenched gardens. "To know that our commitment isn't just about us, but about contributing to something larger. Havenridge feels like a living organism, and our decision to bind ourselves together is like a vital, strengthening root. It makes the whole system more robust, more resilient."

"Precisely," Eli agreed. "The fear I once associated with permanence, with being tied down, has completely transformed. It's been replaced by a profound sense of security and exhilaration. Knowing that I have your unwavering support, your love, your partnership, doesn't limit me; it liberates me. It gives me the confidence to take on greater challenges, to dream bigger for Havenridge, because I know I won't be facing them alone. Our 'forever' is the bedrock upon which we can build anything."

Mara leaned her head against his shoulder, a deep sigh of pure contentment escaping her lips. "I feel it too. It's like... like the world has opened up, rather than closed in. The possibilities feel endless because they are *shared* possibilities. We are not just two individuals living parallel lives; we are two hearts beating in rhythm, creating a symphony. And that symphony, I believe, will be our 'forever.'"

"And it's a symphony that will resonate throughout Havenridge," Eli said, his voice filled with pride. "The community has embraced us, believed in us, and now, our commitment is a tangible affirmation of that belief. It's a promise that the values they cherish – of dedication, of collaboration, of enduring love – will continue to be at the heart of this place. Our 'forever' becomes a beacon."

He stood, pulling her gently to her feet. "Come," he said, his eyes alight with a shared enthusiasm. "There are plans to be made, canvases to be filled, and a future to be built, one beautiful, chosen moment at a time." Mara's heart swelled, not with trepidation, but with an exhilarating sense of purpose. Their 'forever' was not a destination, but a magnificent, unfolding adventure, and she couldn't wait to embark on every single step of it with him. The notion of permanence, once a whisper of fear, had transformed into a thunderous declaration of strength and an endless wellspring of inspiration. It was a new definition of forever, one that was as vibrant and alive as the blossoming world around them.

The weight of their shared decision, a delicate yet powerful thing, settled not just between Mara and Eli, but seemed to ripple outward, embracing the very essence of Havenridge. It was more than a personal vow; it was the laying of a cornerstone for the community's enduring spirit. For so long, Havenridge had been a testament to resilience, a place where broken pieces had been meticulously gathered and reassembled with love and determination. The rebuilding phase, a period of intense effort and unwavering hope, had been paramount. But now, with their union, a new chapter was dawning—one of establishment, of weaving a future that was not just strong, but deeply rooted and lasting. Their commitment was the quiet affirmation that the rebuilding was complete, and the era of legacy had begun.

Mara understood this implicitly. Her art had always been about evolution, about adding layers and depth, and her life with Eli was no different. She saw their marriage not as an endpoint, but as the most significant brushstroke yet on the canvas of Havenridge. It was the bold, defining line that would shape the composition of the years to come, imbuing it with a sense of permanence and purpose. This wasn't just about their happiness, though that was an undeniable and beautiful outcome; it was about the very fabric of the community, about instilling a sense of stability and growth that would sustain Havenridge long after they were gone. Their personal joy was inextricably linked to the flourishing of the place they had both come to cherish.

Eli, with his inherent understanding of structure and sustainability, echoed her sentiments. He saw their union as the vital architectural element that would support Havenridge's continued ascent. The individual efforts of the community members had been magnificent, a testament to their collective will. But a truly enduring legacy required more than individual acts of brilliance; it demanded a foundational commitment, a visible symbol of shared purpose and unwavering dedication. Their marriage, he realized, served precisely this function. It was a public declaration that Havenridge was not just a project in progress, but a home, a sanctuary, a place built on bonds that would withstand the tests of time.

The community, too, seemed to sense this shift. There was a palpable sense of gratitude, a quiet approval that suffused the air. The residents had witnessed the transformation of Havenridge, from its fragile beginnings to its current vibrant state. They had seen Mara and Eli's love blossom, a steady flame that had brought warmth and light to the estate. Their decision to formalize their union felt like a collective sigh of relief, a shared understanding that the foundation was now truly secure. It was an affirmation that the values of commitment, of love, and of building a future together were not just ideals, but the very lifeblood of Havenridge.

Mara found herself reflecting on the individuals who had been instrumental in Havenridge's rebirth. Old Mr. Abernathy, with his steady hands and encyclopedic knowledge of the estate's history, had been a constant source of wisdom. The families who had returned, their faces etched with the scars of past hardship but shining with renewed hope, represented the soul of the community. Each of them had contributed to the rebuilding, laying their own bricks, planting their own seeds. Now, her and Eli's commitment felt like the mortar that would bind all those individual efforts together, creating a structure of unparalleled strength and beauty.

"It's almost as if our decision," Mara mused aloud one evening, as they watched the sunset paint the sky in hues of orange and violet from the veranda, "is a promise to all of them, too. A promise that their hard work, their sacrifices, haven't been in vain. That Havenridge will continue to be a place of stability and opportunity for generations to come."

Eli wrapped an arm around her, drawing her close. "Exactly. It's about more than just us, isn't it? It's about being stewards of something precious. We've inherited a legacy, and now we have the opportunity to add to it, to ensure its continuation. Our union is a tangible representation of that stewardship. It's a signal to everyone, both within Havenridge and beyond, that this place is built on a foundation of enduring love and commitment."

He paused, his gaze sweeping across the manicured gardens, the tranquil lake, the sturdy stone buildings that stood as testaments to a vision. "Think about the whispers of doubt we sometimes heard, the voices that said such a place could never truly recover. Our ability to not only rebuild but to thrive, and now to solidify our future through commitment, is the most powerful rebuttal to those doubts. It's proof that love, dedication, and community can overcome even the deepest of wounds."

Mara leaned her head against his shoulder, the familiar comfort of his presence a grounding force. "And it's a beautiful thing to be a part of, Eli. To know that our personal happiness is a thread woven into the larger tapestry of this community. When I look at the children playing in the fields, their laughter echoing through the valley, I see the future of Havenridge. And I feel so grateful that we are building that future together, with them, and for them."

Their decision to marry was not born out of a sudden impulse, but from a deep, resonant understanding that had grown between them over months of shared experience, of navigating challenges, and of celebrating small victories. It was the culmination of their individual journeys converging into a single, powerful stream, destined to nourish the landscape of Havenridge. The estate, once a symbol of loss and decay, had become a beacon of hope and renewal, and their union was the bright, unwavering light that would guide its future.

The transition from rebuilding to legacy was a subtle but profound one, marked by a shift in focus. Instead of solely concentrating on repairing what was broken, their attention was now directed towards cultivating what would endure. This meant investing in the community's infrastructure, not just physically, but also in its social and emotional well-being. It meant fostering traditions, creating opportunities for shared experiences, and ensuring that the spirit of collaboration that had defined the rebuilding phase would continue to flourish.

Mara envisioned a Havenridge where families felt secure, where artists found inspiration, and where the elderly were cherished. Eli saw a Havenridge that was a model of sustainable living, of community governance, and of artistic patronage. These were not separate visions, but complementary aspects of a singular, holistic future, a future that their commitment now made concrete and achievable. Their personal happiness was not a distraction from this larger purpose, but the very engine that propelled it forward, fueled by a love that sought to create something meaningful and lasting.

The legal and ceremonial aspects of their union, while important, felt almost secondary to the deeper significance of their decision. It was the internal affirmation, the profound realization of their shared destiny, that truly mattered. The wedding itself would be a celebration of this foundation, a joyous public acknowledgement of the enduring legacy they were building, brick by loving brick, heart by devoted heart.

There was a certain quiet confidence that settled upon Havenridge in the wake of their decision. It was the confidence of a community that knew its leadership was united, its purpose clear, and its future secure. The efforts of individuals were no longer isolated acts of hope, but integrated components of a grand, collective endeavor. Mara and Eli's love story had become a central narrative within Havenridge's larger story, a testament to the transformative power of commitment and the enduring strength of shared dreams.

As they walked through the grounds, hand in hand, Mara felt a deep sense of peace. The scent of blooming jasmine, the gentle rustle of leaves, the distant sound of children's laughter – it all spoke of life, of continuity, of a future being actively and lovingly shaped. Their union was not just the affirmation of their love; it was the affirmation of Havenridge's enduring spirit, a promise whispered on the wind, carried through the ancient trees, and etched into the very soil of this beloved place. It was the foundation of a shared legacy, solid, beautiful, and built to last.

Chapter Seven

BUILDING BRIDGES, NOT WALLS

The decision had been made, and now, the gentle hum of preparation filled Havenridge. It wasn't the frantic, opulent flurry that often accompanied grand unions, but a quiet, purposeful rhythm, imbued with the estate's characteristic grace. Mara and Eli wanted their commitment to be a reflection of what they had built together – something solid, authentic, and deeply connected to the heart of their community.

The idea of a large, ostentatious ceremony felt discordant with the values that had guided their journey, the shared understanding that true richness lay not in material excess, but in genuine connection and shared purpose. Instead, they envisioned a gathering that would be intimate in spirit, if not in precise numbers, a collective embrace of their shared future.

Mara found herself drawn to the idea of simplicity, of letting the natural beauty of Havenridge provide the backdrop. The old oak grove, with its ancient, sprawling branches, seemed to whisper promises of endurance, a perfect setting for an affirmation of lasting love. It was a place where so many quiet conversations had taken place, where plans had been hatched and dreams nurtured. It felt like a sanctuary, a place where their vows would be not just heard by those present, but echoed by the very spirit of the land.

Eli, ever the pragmatist, focused on the practicalities, ensuring that everything would be comfortable and welcoming for their guests. He organized the simple wooden benches, weathered and sturdy, to be arranged in a semi-circle beneath the grandest oak. He worked with the groundskeepers to ensure the pathways were clear and the area around the grove was tidied, not manicured into an unnatural perfection, but subtly enhanced, allowing the wild beauty to remain. His touch was always about strengthening what was already there, about revealing the inherent beauty rather than imposing a new one.

The invitations were not elaborate scrolls, but rather simple, hand-written notes, delivered by messengers who were themselves friends and neighbors. Each note carried a personal touch, a warm invitation to share in a moment of profound significance. There was no need for extensive guest lists or complex seating arrangements. The community of Havenridge was already a tightly knit family, and everyone understood the unspoken invitation extended to them. It was a gathering of kindred spirits, those who had weathered the storms alongside Mara and Eli, and who now rejoiced in their steadfast resolve.

Mara spent hours in her studio, not painting, but crafting small tokens of appreciation for the core group who had been instrumental in Havenridge's resurgence. These weren't extravagant gifts, but small, handmade ceramic pieces, each unique, reflecting the individuality of the recipient and the shared journey they had undertaken. She felt a deep sense of gratitude for each person – for Mr. Abernathy's unwavering guidance, for the resilience of the families who had returned, for the quiet strength of the artisans and laborers who had poured their hearts into rebuilding. These tokens were a tangible expression of that deep-seated appreciation, a way of saying, "You are a part of this."

The culinary preparations were a reflection of the same philosophy. Instead of a formal banquet, there would be a communal feast, a potluck of sorts, where each family contributed a dish that held meaning for them. It was a way of weaving the individual threads of their lives into a shared tapestry of abundance. Mara envisioned tables laden with hearty stews, freshly baked breads, vibrant salads, and sweet treats, each dish telling a story, a testament to the diverse skills and traditions of Havenridge. The air would be filled with the mingled aromas of home-cooked meals, a scent far more comforting and meaningful than any professionally catered affair.

As the days leading up to the ceremony passed, a palpable sense of anticipation settled over Havenridge. It wasn't the anxious buzz of performance, but the gentle thrum of shared joy. Neighbors stopped by Mara and Eli's cottage, not to offer unsolicited advice, but to share their own memories of the estate's transformation, to express their heartfelt wishes for the couple's happiness, and to offer their assistance in any small way. Children, with their uninhibited excitement, would present Mara with wildflowers they had gathered, their faces alight with the innocent understanding that something truly special was about to unfold.

One afternoon, Mara found herself sitting with Elara, Eli's aunt, under the shade of a cherry tree. Elara, a woman whose life had been a testament to quiet strength and unwavering love, held Mara's hand, her gaze steady and knowing. "You have chosen a path, my dear," she said softly, her voice like the rustle of leaves, "that honors not just your own hearts, but the heart of this place. This ceremony, it's not about a grand pronouncement, but about a deep, resonant echo. It's about the quiet certainty of knowing you are where you belong, with the one you are meant to be with, in the place you are meant to build a life."

Mara felt a warmth spread through her chest, a confirmation of the rightness of their decision. Elara's words resonated with her own deep-seated feelings. This wasn't about an exchange of vows dictated by tradition; it was about an internal alignment, a profound understanding that had blossomed between them and solidified with the very land they inhabited. The ceremony would be a public acknowledgement of this internal truth, a way of sharing their joy and their commitment with the people who had become their extended family.

Eli, too, found solace and strength in the community's embrace. He saw in their shared enthusiasm a reflection of his own dedication. Each smile, each offer of help, each shared memory was a reinforcement of the bonds that held Havenridge together. He understood that their marriage was not just a personal milestone, but a symbol of stability and continuity for the entire estate. The collective joy of the community was a powerful affirmation of this, a silent testament to the enduring strength of their shared endeavor.

The evening before the ceremony, a gentle rain fell, a soft patter on the roofs that seemed to cleanse the air and prepare the land. Mara stood by her window, watching the raindrops trace paths down the glass, each one a fleeting moment, yet collectively contributing to the nourishing flow of life. She thought of all the people who would gather the next day, each bringing their own unique perspective, their own hopes and dreams, all converging to celebrate a union that felt, to her, like the anchor of a new beginning.

The next morning dawned with a clear, crisp sky, the sun casting a warm, golden light across Havenridge. The air was alive with the scent of dew-kissed earth and the subtle perfume of early blooming roses. There was a palpable sense of quiet anticipation, a feeling that the world, for this one special day, had paused to witness something beautiful and true. The preparations continued, unhurried and filled with a profound sense of purpose. The benches beneath the ancient oak were already in place, simple and inviting. The path leading to the grove was adorned with sprigs of rosemary and lavender, their fragrant presence a testament to remembrance and devotion.

Mara, dressed in a simple, elegant gown of soft linen, felt a sense of profound peace wash over her. Her reflection in the antique mirror showed a woman grounded, radiant, and deeply content. Her hair was loosely braided, interwoven with a few delicate wildflowers, echoing the natural beauty of the setting. She wore no ostentatious jewelry, only a delicate silver locket that Eli had given her on their first anniversary, a quiet reminder of the journey they had already shared.

Eli, standing at the edge of the oak grove, looked equally at ease. He wore a suit of a subtle, earth-toned fabric, its simplicity mirroring the ceremony's understated elegance. His gaze was clear and steady, his smile warm as he greeted the arriving guests, his hand often finding the reassuring clasp of his aunt Elara's. He greeted each person with a genuine warmth, a quiet acknowledgement of their presence and their shared joy.

As the community began to gather, a gentle murmur of conversation filled the air, punctuated by laughter and soft greetings. It wasn't the boisterous din of a formal wedding, but a harmonious blend of voices, each one a note in the symphony of their shared experience. Children, their eyes wide with wonder, ran between the legs of the adults, their excitement a pure, unadulterated expression of the day's significance. They recognized the happiness radiating from Mara and Eli, a happiness that was infectious and reassuring.

Mr. Abernathy, his steps a little slower now but his eyes brighter than ever, was one of the first to arrive. He carried a small, worn leather-bound book, its pages filled with the history of Havenridge. He found a seat near the front, his presence a quiet anchor, a reminder of the deep roots from which their present had grown. He nodded approvingly at the arrangements, his heart filled with a profound satisfaction at seeing the estate flourishing, and its guiding lights so clearly defined.

The families who had returned to Havenridge, their faces etched with the stories of hardship but now alight with hope, clustered together, their conversations a tapestry of shared memories and future aspirations. They saw in Mara and Eli's union not just a personal commitment, but a promise of continued stability and growth for their own families. Their presence was a powerful affirmation of the community's collective strength, a testament to the enduring spirit of resilience and hope.

As Mara walked towards the grove, with her father's arm supporting her, she felt a deep sense of belonging. The path ahead, lined with smiling faces, felt like a path illuminated by a thousand shared dreams. She met Eli's gaze, and in that instant, the world around them seemed to fade away. It was just the two of them, standing on the precipice of their shared future, surrounded by the love and support of the community they had helped to forge.

The ceremony itself was beautifully understated. There were no elaborate readings or lengthy pronouncements. Instead, Mara and Eli spoke from the heart, their words simple, honest, and infused with a profound love. They spoke of their journey, of the challenges they had overcome, and of the unwavering strength they found in each other. They spoke of their commitment to Havenridge, to its people, and to the future they envisioned together.

Eli's voice, steady and clear, resonated through the quiet grove. "Mara," he began, his eyes locked with hers, "from the moment our paths first truly crossed, I knew I had found my home, not just in this place, but in you. You have shown me the power of resilience, the beauty of compassion, and the unwavering strength of a heart that dares to love fiercely. My commitment to you is as deep and as enduring as the roots of these ancient oaks. I promise to walk beside you, to support you, to cherish you, and to build a life with you, here, in this place we have made our own."

Mara's voice, though softer, carried an equal measure of conviction. "Eli," she replied, her voice catching slightly with emotion, "you have been my rock, my inspiration, my truest confidant. You saw the potential, not just in this estate, but in me, and you encouraged me to bloom. My love for you is woven into the very fabric of my being, as inextricably as the threads that bind this community. I promise to stand with you, to grow with you, to face whatever the future may hold with courage and unwavering devotion. Together, we will continue to nurture this haven, this home, this legacy."

Their words, spoken with such raw sincerity, brought a quiet tear to many an eye. It wasn't the performative emotion of a grand occasion, but the genuine outpouring of hearts touched by true love and shared purpose. The exchange of simple rings, crafted from a local wood and inlaid with a small, polished stone found on the estate grounds, felt more significant than any diamond. They were symbols of their unbroken circle, their commitment to each other and to the land.

Following their vows, the community members were invited to come forward, not to sign a formal document, but to offer their own blessings and well wishes. One by one, they approached, their faces alight with sincerity. Old Mr. Abernathy, his hand resting on the worn leather-bound book, simply said, "May your union be as steadfast as the foundations of Havenridge, and your love as enduring as its history." A young mother, holding her child's hand, offered a prayer for joy and laughter to fill their home. A craftsman, his hands rough from years of work, simply clasped Eli's hand firmly and said, "May your future be as strong and well-built as the walls you've helped raise."

These weren't grand pronouncements or empty platitudes. They were heartfelt expressions of support, of shared hopes, and of the deep sense of connection that bound them all together. Each blessing was a small, precious stone added to the foundation of Mara and Eli's commitment, reinforcing its strength and beauty. The air hummed with a quiet, powerful energy, a collective affirmation of love, community, and enduring promise.

After the blessings, the celebration shifted to a more relaxed, communal gathering. Tables, laden with the contributions from each family, were arranged in a long, welcoming line. The aroma of home-cooked food filled the air, a delicious testament to the diverse culinary talents of Havenridge. Laughter bubbled, conversations flowed easily, and the children, their energy seemingly boundless, chased each other through the dappled sunlight, their joyful shouts a soundtrack to the afternoon's festivities. Mara and Eli moved through the crowd, their hands often clasped, accepting hugs, sharing smiles, and engaging in quiet conversations. They were not the distant figures at the head of a banquet, but an integral part of the tapestry, their joy shared and amplified by the community's embrace.

Mara found herself drawn to a group of the elder residents, their faces etched with the wisdom of years. They spoke of past celebrations, of traditions long held dear, and of the evolving spirit of Havenridge. Their reminiscences were not tinged with nostalgia for a lost past, but rather with a gentle appreciation for the continuity of life and love. They saw in Mara and Eli's union a bridge between generations, a vital link in the ongoing narrative of Havenridge.

Eli, meanwhile, found himself in earnest conversation with some of the younger residents, discussing plans for the future – the expansion of the community gardens, the potential for new artistic workshops, and the ongoing efforts to ensure Havenridge remained a sustainable and vibrant place for years to come. Their discussions were filled with a shared sense of purpose, a collective vision for the estate's continued growth and prosperity. Their union had, in essence, solidified their roles as stewards, and the community was eager to continue working alongside them.

As the afternoon sun began to cast long shadows across the grounds, a sense of profound contentment settled over the gathering. It wasn't the end of a celebration, but the quiet acknowledgement of a new beginning, a reinforced commitment to the values that had brought them all together. The simple ceremony, born from a deep respect for authenticity and community, had served its purpose beautifully. It had not been about building walls of exclusivity, but about building bridges of connection, strengthening the very heart of Havenridge.

Mara and Eli, hand in hand, walked away from the lingering revelers, towards their cottage, the scent of blooming jasmine a sweet farewell on the evening breeze. The day had been a perfect embodiment of their love – genuine, grounded, and deeply rooted in the community they cherished. The simple ceremony had been more than just an affirmation of their union; it had been a testament to the enduring power of love, commitment, and the profound strength found in building a future together, not in isolation, but as one united heart.

The words that would bind Mara and Eli in their union were not elaborate pronouncements dictated by ancient texts or societal expectation, but rather the simple, profound truths that had been forged in the crucible of their shared experiences. They had chosen this path, not as a destination, but as a continuous journey, an active choice made anew each day. As they stood beneath the benevolent gaze of the ancient oak, the gathered community held its breath, not in anxious anticipation, but in a shared reverence for the power of spoken commitment.

Mara's father, his hand a comforting weight on her arm, had led her to the designated spot where Eli waited, his eyes holding hers with a depth of love that needed no embellishment. The silence that descended was not an emptiness, but a pregnant pause, filled with the rustling leaves, the distant birdsong, and the unspoken affection of every soul present. It was a silence that amplified the significance of the words to come, imbuing them with a weight that transcended mere sound.

Eli was the first to speak, his voice steady, yet carrying a tremor of deep emotion. "Mara," he began, his gaze never wavering, "we have built so much together. Not just structures of wood and stone, but a life woven from shared dreams, weathered storms, and the quiet strength of mutual understanding. Today, I choose you again. I choose the laughter we've shared, the tears we've comforted, the silent knowing glances that speak volumes. I choose the future we will continue to build, brick by brick, day by day, here, in this place that holds our hearts.

My commitment to you is not a chain, but an open hand, a willing heart, a steadfast presence, now and always." The simplicity of his words, the directness of his gaze, spoke of a love that was not performative, but deeply, undeniably real. Each phrase was a testament to their journey, acknowledging the realities of their lives rather than glossing over them with platitudes. He spoke of choice, of active participation, of a love that was a verb, not a noun.

Mara's response was a gentle echo, a mirror reflecting the same profound depth of feeling. She stepped forward, her hand reaching for his, her fingers intertwining with his, a silent affirmation before she spoke. "Eli," she began, her voice clear and resonant, though tinged with the sweetness of unshed tears, "you have seen me, truly seen me, in all my complexities. You have encouraged my spirit to soar, grounded me when I faltered, and celebrated every small victory as if it were your own. Today, I choose you. I choose the comfort of your presence, the wisdom of your counsel, the unwavering belief you have in us.

I choose the quiet mornings and the vibrant evenings, the shared silence and the joyful conversations. My commitment to you is a promise of an unfolding story, a continuous discovery, a constant nurturing of the beautiful garden we have planted together. I pledge my heart, my strength, and my unwavering devotion to you, as we continue to grow, here, in the heart of Havenridge." Her words painted a picture of their relationship as a living, breathing entity, one that required constant care and attention, a dynamic force rather than a static state. The metaphor of a garden spoke to the nurturing and growth that defined their connection.

The exchange of rings followed, not with grand pronouncements of ownership, but with a quiet acknowledgment of their shared journey. The simple bands of polished local oak, inlaid with a single, smooth river stone, felt weighty in their hands. As Eli slid the ring onto Mara's finger, he murmured, "A circle of enduring strength, mirroring the love we share." And Mara, as she placed his ring, whispered, "A reminder of our roots, and the future we will grow." These were not just symbols of possession, but of connection, of shared history, and of the enduring bond that tied them to each other and to the land. They were tactile representations of the intangible essence of their love.

Following their personal vows, the elders of Havenridge, those whose lives were interwoven with the very fabric of the estate, were invited to offer their blessings. Mr. Abernathy, his eyes twinkling with a deep, abiding affection for the couple, stepped forward first. He held a small, worn wooden cross, a relic from the estate's earliest days. "Mara, Eli," he said, his voice raspy with age but clear with conviction, "I have seen many seasons come and go in Havenridge. I have seen hope flicker and passion ignite. Your journey together has been a testament to the enduring power of resilience and the quiet strength of chosen love.

May your trust in each other be as unshakable as the bedrock of this land, and may your days be filled with the gentle blessings of peace and shared purpose. You are the new custodians of this legacy, and we, the old, give you our heartfelt approval and our enduring support." His words resonated with the weight of history, imbuing their union with a sense of continuity and deep-seated belonging. He spoke of chosen love, highlighting that their bond was not an accident of fate, but a deliberate and conscious decision.

Next, Elara, Eli's aunt, her presence a calming balm, approached. She had known both Mara and Eli since they were children, watching their individual paths converge. She placed a gentle hand on Mara's shoulder and then on Eli's. "My dear ones," she said softly, her voice a melodious whisper, "love is not merely found; it is cultivated. It is the quiet tending of a garden, the patient mending of a torn seam, the unwavering belief in the other's inherent goodness. You have shown us all what it means to build something true, not out of obligation, but out of a deep and abiding love.

May your home always be a sanctuary, filled with warmth, understanding, and the joyful echoes of your shared lives. May you always find strength in each other's embrace, and may your journey together be a testament to the enduring beauty of a love that chooses to grow, day after day." Her words emphasized the active nature of their commitment, the daily effort required to maintain and deepen their bond, much like tending a garden.

A young woman named Anya, a skilled weaver whose family had recently returned to Havenridge, her own story mirroring the estate's resurgence, stepped forward next. She held a length of intricately woven fabric, a symbol of their community. "Mara, Eli," she began, her voice filled with a youthful sincerity, "when I look at you, I see the spirit of Havenridge reborn. You have faced challenges with courage, and you have built bridges where walls once stood.

My blessing to you is one of continued connection. May your lives be like this tapestry, woven with threads of joy, resilience, and unwavering support from all of us who call this place home. May you always find strength in the weave of our community, and may your love inspire us all to keep building, together." Her offering was a tangible representation of their interconnectedness, a reminder that their union was not an isolated event, but a vital thread in the larger tapestry of Havenridge.

Others followed, each offering a unique perspective, a personal sentiment. A farmer, his hands rough from years of working the land, spoke of patience and fertile ground. A craftsman, his gaze steady and sure, wished them strength and enduring structure. A baker, her smile warm and inviting, blessed their home with sweetness and abundance. Children, their voices clear and bright, chimed in with simple, heartfelt wishes for happiness and fun.

There were no grand pronouncements, no sweeping declarations, only sincere affirmations of support, woven from the fabric of their shared lives. Each word, each gesture, was a building block, adding to the foundation of Mara and Eli's commitment, reinforcing its strength and beauty. The air vibrated with a quiet, yet powerful, energy, a collective testament to the enduring power of love, community, and the unwavering promise of a shared future. It was a mosaic of well wishes, each piece unique, yet contributing to a harmonious whole, reflecting the diverse yet united spirit of Havenridge.

This was not just an endorsement of their marriage; it was an embrace of their journey, a recognition of their role as pillars of the community, and an affirmation of the shared vision they embodied. The gathered souls, young and old, each played their part in this sacred ritual, their voices blending into a chorus of hope and encouragement. Their words were not just sounds, but intentions, prayers, and promises, imbued with the spirit of Havenridge itself. They spoke of resilience, a quality they had all demonstrated in their own ways, and of trust, the bedrock upon which any strong community, and indeed any strong relationship, must be built.

The power of "chosen love" was a recurring theme, acknowledging that their union was not merely a matter of circumstance, but a deliberate and cherished decision, a path they actively walked together. Their vows were a declaration of this active choice, a commitment to continue choosing each other, day after day, through all the seasons of their lives. The simplicity of their vows was their strength, cutting through the superficial and reaching the heart of what it meant to be truly united. They spoke not of an ending, but of a beginning, a continuous unfolding of their shared story.

The very act of gathering, of sharing these words, solidified the bonds that already existed, creating a tangible sense of unity and shared purpose. This moment was a bridge, connecting the past, present, and future of Havenridge, with Mara and Eli as its sturdy, hopeful anchors. The symbolic exchange was a profound moment, a silent dialogue between two souls who had found their truest home in each other. The rings, humble yet significant, became tangible anchors for their spoken promises, a constant reminder of the vows exchanged and the life they were building together. The act of speaking their truth, of articulating their deepest feelings, was a powerful catharsis, a release of pent-up emotion and a testament to their vulnerability and courage.

The community's participation was not merely an audience, but an active chorus, their blessings an integral part of the ceremony, weaving their own stories and hopes into the fabric of Mara and Eli's union. This collective endorsement transformed a personal commitment into a communal celebration, a testament to the strength derived from unity and shared values. The essence of the subsection lay not just in the words spoken, but in the resonating silence that followed, in the shared glances, and in the profound sense of peace that settled over the grove, a silent promise of a future built on love, trust, and an unwavering commitment to each other and to the heart of Havenridge.

The lingering warmth of Eli's hand in hers was a comforting anchor, a tangible connection that pulsed with the steady rhythm of their shared heartbeat. As the last of the well-wishes faded into the gentle rustle of leaves, a profound stillness settled over Mara, a quietude that resonated deeper than any spoken word. It was a peace that had been elusive for so long, a constant hum of anxiety that had always accompanied her thoughts of commitment, of forever. The fear of erasure, of a self dissolving into another, had been a shadow she'd wrestled with for years. But here, now, standing beside Eli under the benevolent canopy of the ancient oak, that shadow had not just receded; it had vanished, utterly and completely.

In its place was a sensation of expansion, a feeling of being more herself than she had ever been. It was as if the act of choosing Eli, of weaving her life with his so inextricably, had not diminished her, but magnified her. The boundaries of her individual self had not blurred into an indistinct haze, but rather had become defined with a clarity she'd never experienced. This wasn't about losing herself in him, but about finding new territories within herself that had been waiting, dormant, for the right catalyst to awaken. Committing to Eli hadn't meant relinquishing her autonomy; it had, paradoxically, granted her a deeper, more expansive sense of it. The fear of losing her identity had been rooted in a misunderstanding of what true union entailed. It wasn't a merging into one, but a harmonious co-existence, a delicate dance where each partner held their space while intrinsically connected to the other.

She looked at Eli, truly looked at him, and saw not a force that would absorb her, but a foundation upon which she could build even higher. His unwavering gaze, the gentle curve of his lips, the quiet strength that radiated from him – these were not chains, but the very elements that allowed her own spirit to unfurl. He saw her, not just the woman she was, but the woman she was capable of becoming, and his love was the fertile ground in which those possibilities could take root and flourish. The thought of leadership, of stepping into roles that had once seemed daunting, now felt not only achievable but exhilarating.

The responsibilities that came with their shared life in Havenridge, the stewardship of this beautiful, resilient place, no longer felt like burdens to be shouldered alone. They felt like opportunities, avenues for growth that she could now explore with Eli by her side, a constant source of encouragement and unwavering support.

This was not the end of her journey, she understood, but a significant and beautiful milestone. The words spoken, the rings exchanged, the blessings offered – these were not static pronouncements, but the opening lines of a new chapter, a chapter she was eager to write. The feeling of wholeness that pervaded her was a testament to the intricate tapestry of their lives, each thread vibrant and distinct, yet interwoven to create a pattern of unparalleled beauty and strength. She felt the collective energy of the gathered community, their unspoken hopes and affirmations, not as an external pressure, but as a gentle current carrying them forward. Their belief in her and Eli, their shared vision for Havenridge, was a powerful affirmation, a reminder that their love was not an isolated entity, but a vital part of something larger, something enduring.

The quiet understanding that passed between her and Eli was a language all their own, a silent conversation that acknowledged the profound shift that had just occurred. It was a shared breath, a mutual recognition of the sacred space they had created, not just between themselves, but within the heart of their community. She felt a profound sense of gratitude, a deep well of thankfulness for the journey that had brought them to this moment, for the lessons learned, and for the love that had guided them.

The fear that had once clung to her like a shroud had been replaced by a radiant, almost luminous joy, a lightness of being that made her feel as if she could float. This was the peace of permanence, not a static stillness, but a dynamic, vibrant tranquility, the kind that comes from knowing, with absolute certainty, that one is exactly where one is meant to be, with the one with whom one is meant to be.

The realization settled upon her with the gentle force of a sunbeam – this was not about compromise, but about enhancement. Her dreams had not been put on hold; they had been given new wings. The ambition that had always simmered beneath the surface, the desire to lead, to create, to make a meaningful impact, was now being met with a reciprocal energy from Eli and from Havenridge itself. He didn't just tolerate her aspirations; he celebrated them. He saw her strength, her intellect, her vision, and encouraged her to embrace them fully, not as separate from their union, but as integral to it. It was as if the very act of becoming his wife had unlocked a new level of confidence, a permission she hadn't realized she'd been withholding from herself.

She thought back to the times she had hesitated, the moments she had second-guessed her own capabilities, the ingrained belief that a woman's ambitions had to be somehow subdued to fit within the framework of a committed relationship. Those beliefs, like withered leaves, now detached and drifted away on the gentle breeze. Eli's love was not a constraint; it was a boundless horizon. He was her partner, her equal, and her greatest advocate. He had a way of seeing the best in her, even when she struggled to see it herself, and his belief in her was a powerful force that propelled her forward. This sense of shared purpose, this mutual nurturing of each other's dreams, was the bedrock of their foundation.

The responsibilities of leading Havenridge, of working to restore and revitalize the estate and its community, no longer felt like an overwhelming solo endeavor. With Eli, it felt like a shared quest, a collaborative effort where their strengths complemented each other perfectly. He had a deep understanding of the land, a grounded practicality that balanced her more visionary aspirations. Together, they were a formidable force, capable of tackling any challenge that lay ahead. She felt a surge of pride, not just in herself, but in them, in the partnership they had forged. It was a testament to their shared values, their mutual respect, and their unwavering commitment to the well-being of their home.

The fear of losing her individuality had been a self-imposed cage, built from the echoes of past societal expectations and personal insecurities. But the reality of her connection with Eli had shattered that cage. She could be a leader, a partner, a visionary, and deeply, profoundly loved, all at once. Her identity wasn't a fragile thing to be guarded, but a dynamic, evolving entity that was enriched by her relationships. The love she shared with Eli was not a surrender of self, but an amplification of it. It was a symbiotic relationship, where his presence allowed her to bloom more fully, and her growth, in turn, enriched their shared life.

As she stood there, the sunlight dappling through the leaves, illuminating the serene landscape of Havenridge, she felt a profound sense of belonging. Not just to Eli, but to this place, to this community, to this moment. The path ahead was not a predefined route, but an open expanse, inviting exploration and discovery. And for the first time, the prospect of that journey filled her not with trepidation, but with an unadulterated, unshakeable joy. The peace she felt was not passive; it was an active, vibrant sense of being fully alive, fully herself, and deeply, irrevocably loved. It was the peace of permanence, found not in static immobility, but in the vibrant, ever-unfolding beauty of a life lived in conscious, loving commitment.

The weight of the ring on her finger was a gentle reminder, not of a bond that restricted, but of a connection that empowered. It was a symbol of her expanded self, her newfound confidence, and the limitless potential that lay before her, hand in hand with Eli, in the heart of Havenridge. The world around her seemed to hum with a quiet energy, a resonance that mirrored the deep peace within her soul. Each rustle of leaves, each distant birdsong, was a note in the symphony of her contentment.

This was more than just happiness; it was a profound sense of rightness, a deep-seated affirmation that she was precisely where she was meant to be, living the life she was meant to live. The lingering echoes of the ceremony, the voices of blessing, settled into her like a warm embrace, reinforcing the certainty of her conviction. She had not lost herself; she had, in fact, found a richer, more expansive version of who she was always meant to be. The fear had been a phantom, a figment of her own making, now banished by the radiant light of truth and love.

Eli's gaze traced the graceful curve of Mara's jaw, the subtle flush that still lingered on her cheeks, a testament to the joy of their shared vows. It wasn't just the beauty of the moment, the golden light filtering through the ancient oaks, or the hushed reverence of their gathered loved ones that stirred his soul. It was Mara. It was the woman he had fallen in love with, the woman who had become his partner, his confidante, his north star. In her eyes, he saw not just the reflection of their union, but a universe of unspoken understanding, a quiet acknowledgment of the profound journey that had led them to this sacred precipice. A deep, resonant pride swelled within him, a quiet triumph that had nothing to do with possession and everything to do with witnessing the blossoming of a soul he cherished.

His journey towards this moment had been one of deliberate intention, of shedding old skins and embracing a vulnerability he hadn't known he possessed. He had learned that true strength wasn't in stoic independence, but in the courageous act of opening one's heart, of allowing another to see the raw, untamed landscape within. And Mara, with her fierce intellect and compassionate spirit, had not only seen it but had embraced it, weaving it into the tapestry of their shared existence. He had watched her navigate challenges with an unyielding grace, her resilience a constant source of inspiration.

He had witnessed her quiet determination to heal Havenridge, to breathe life back into its aging bones, and his admiration had only deepened with each passing day.

Now, as his wife, she was more radiant than ever. The fear that had once flickered in her eyes, the vestiges of past hurts and self-doubt, had been replaced by a luminous confidence. He saw it in the way she held herself, the steady set of her shoulders, the unwavering gaze that met his own. It was a testament to her own inner strength, yes, but it was also a reflection of the secure space they had built together, a sanctuary where her true self could unfurl without reservation. He felt a profound sense of fulfillment, not merely as a groom, but as a man who had found his purpose in supporting and cherishing the woman who ignited his every aspiration.

His devotion to Mara was no longer a nascent spark but a deep, steady flame, fueled by the knowledge of their shared future. It was a commitment that extended far beyond the intimate confines of their personal lives. It was a dedication to the life they were actively constructing, a life that was inextricably intertwined with the fate of Havenridge. He saw their union not as an isolated event, but as a vital thread in the larger fabric of this land and its community. Mara's vision for Havenridge, her passionate desire to see it thrive, resonated deeply within him. He understood that her leadership, her innate ability to inspire and to nurture, was precisely what this place needed. And his role, as she had so beautifully articulated, was to stand beside her, to offer his unwavering support, his practical grounding, and his boundless love.

He remembered the early days of their courtship, the cautious dance of two souls tentative about exposing their vulnerabilities. He had been drawn to her fire, her fierce independence, but he had also recognized the walls she had, perhaps unknowingly, erected around her heart. It had taken patience, a gentle persistence, and a willingness to meet her where she was, to earn her trust. And when she had finally allowed him into the deeper chambers of her soul, he had found a landscape of immense beauty and quiet strength, a place he felt privileged to call home. Her commitment to him, just as his was to her, was not a surrender, but an elevation.

The responsibility of leadership that Mara now embraced with such conviction was something he had always known she was capable of. He had seen it in the way she approached problems, dissecting them with logic and compassion, always seeking the most equitable and sustainable solutions. He had seen it in her interactions with the people of Havenridge, her genuine care for their well-being, her innate ability to make them feel heard and valued. It was a gift, a rare and precious talent, and he felt a deep responsibility to ensure that she had the freedom and the support to exercise it to its fullest potential. His pride in her was not possessive; it was protective. It was the fierce protectiveness of a lion guarding its mate, but also the quiet admiration of an artist observing a masterpiece.

He felt a renewed sense of purpose, a surge of energy that promised to carry them through whatever lay ahead. The challenges facing Havenridge were significant, the work of restoration and revitalization demanding. But with Mara by his side, their hands clasped, their hearts aligned, he felt an unshakeable optimism. Their partnership was not about dividing the burdens, but about multiplying their strengths. Her visionary leadership, combined with his grounded pragmatism, created a synergy that felt divinely ordained. He was not just her husband; he was her partner in every sense of the word, a steadfast ally in their shared endeavor.

His devotion was not a passive state, but an active, daily choice. It was in the quiet moments of shared laughter, in the late-night conversations where they mapped out their dreams, in the simple act of holding her hand as they walked through the orchards. It was in his unwavering belief in her, even when she might falter, and in his commitment to celebrating her triumphs, no matter how small. He understood that their love was the bedrock upon which they would build not only their personal happiness but the future of Havenridge itself.

He watched as Mara turned to address a small group of villagers who had lingered, her words flowing with a natural eloquence, a promise of shared effort and a brighter future. A profound sense of gratitude washed over him. He was not just marrying a woman; he was partnering with a force of nature, a beacon of hope, and a true leader. His heart swelled with a quiet, unyielding pride. He had found his life's greatest joy, his deepest purpose, in loving and supporting Mara. And together, hand in hand, they would build a future for Havenridge that was as enduring and as beautiful as their love. His commitment was a silent vow, an unbroken promise whispered to the wind and etched into the very soil of their shared home. He was devoted, not just to the woman, but to the legacy they would create together. This was more than a wedding; it was a reawakening, a testament to the power of love to forge not just a union, but a future.

The air in Havenridge seemed to hum with a renewed vibrancy, a palpable shift that settled over the land like a soft, warm blanket. It wasn't just the lingering scent of the wedding feast, the echo of laughter, or the undeniable glow that emanated from Mara and Eli. It was something deeper, a subtle yet profound affirmation that had rippled through the very soul of their community. The commitment they had so openly declared, the sacred vows exchanged beneath the ancient oaks, had resonated with a power that extended far beyond the personal. It was a testament to the enduring strength of chosen bonds, a quiet beacon illuminating the path towards a more connected and resilient future for Havenridge.

In the days that followed their union, a sense of calm settled over the estate, a tranquil stillness that encouraged reflection and fostered a deeper appreciation for the present. The whirlwind of wedding preparations had given way to a gentle rhythm, allowing the significance of Mara and Eli's commitment to truly sink in. The villagers, who had watched with bated breath as their beloved Mara stepped into this new chapter, now carried a quiet sense of optimism within them. The uncertainty that had sometimes shadowed their days seemed to recede, replaced by a collective understanding that stability had found a firm footing in Havenridge. Eli's presence, no longer that of a visitor or a suitor, but as Mara's devoted husband and an integral part of the Havenridge family, solidified this feeling of permanence. He was a steady hand, a voice of reason, and a staunch advocate for the shared vision that Mara championed. His integration into the community was not merely a social formality; it was a living embodiment of the bridges being built, the walls that were slowly but surely dissolving.

The impact of their union was most evident in the subtle shifts within the community's interactions. Conversations that had once been tinged with a degree of guardedness now flowed with an easy camaraderie. The shared celebration had served as a powerful reminder of what truly mattered – the strength found in unity, the comfort of mutual support, and the unwavering belief in a shared purpose. Neighbors who had previously kept to themselves began to seek each other out, their conversations often turning to the future of

Havenridge and the promising path laid out by Mara and Eli. There was a newfound willingness to contribute, to lend a hand, to share ideas and aspirations. It was as if the very act of witnessing Mara and Eli's unwavering devotion had unlocked a reservoir of goodwill and a collective desire to nurture the land and its people. This wasn't just about happiness; it was about building something lasting, something that would weather any storm.

Mara, in her characteristic way, embraced this shift with open arms and a grateful heart. She saw the burgeoning energy, the quiet enthusiasm that was spreading like wildfire through Havenridge, and she knew it was a direct consequence of the strength and security that her partnership with Eli now represented. Their union was more than just a personal triumph; it was a symbol, a powerful affirmation that love and commitment could indeed forge a brighter future. She often found herself reflecting on the journey that had brought them to this point, the challenges they had overcome, and the unwavering support they had found in each other. It was this shared resilience, this deep-seated trust, that now served as an inspiration to those around them. Eli, by her side, was not just a husband but a living testament to the power of partnership, a man who understood that true strength was not found in isolation, but in the courageous act of weaving one's life with another's.

The impact was also visible in the younger generations. Children, who had witnessed the palpable joy and the sense of renewed hope that had enveloped Havenridge, seemed to absorb it like sunshine. Their games in the fields took on a new exuberance, their laughter echoing with a lightness that hadn't been as prevalent before. They saw in Mara and Eli a model of dedication and love, a living example of how two people could come together to create something beautiful and enduring. This was crucial for Havenridge, a place that had seen its share of hardship and had, at times, struggled to maintain its vibrant spirit. The affirmation of Mara and Eli's bond acted as a powerful antidote to any lingering shadows of doubt or despair. It reinforced the idea that Havenridge was a place of belonging, a place where hearts could find solace and where futures could be built with unwavering optimism.

Eli, observing these subtle yet significant changes, felt a profound sense of satisfaction. He had always believed in the potential of Havenridge, in the spirit of its people, but he had also recognized the need for a unifying force, a symbol of hope and stability. He saw how his commitment to Mara had, in turn, strengthened the community's belief in itself. Their love story, once a deeply personal journey, had become a shared narrative, a source of collective pride and inspiration. He understood that the work of rebuilding and revitalizing Havenridge was a long and often arduous one, but he also knew that with Mara leading the way, supported by a community that now felt re-energized and united, anything was possible. The ripple effect of their union was not a fleeting wave; it was a steady, life-giving current that promised to nourish Havenridge for generations to come.

The spirit of mutual support, so crucial to the well-being of any community, was being rekindled with an intensity that warmed the hearts of all. Neighbors were once again looking out for one another, offering assistance without being asked, and sharing in the small victories that marked their daily lives. The orchards, once tended with a sense of individual effort, now saw groups of villagers working together, their shared labor imbued with a new sense of purpose and camaraderie. Eli, often working alongside them, found immense joy in this collaborative spirit, seeing it as a direct manifestation of the positive energy that Mara and he had helped to ignite. It was a beautiful synergy, a testament to the fact that when individuals felt secure and inspired, their capacity for collective action was boundless.

Mara, with her keen understanding of people, recognized that the true strength of Havenridge lay not just in its land or its history, but in the bonds that connected its inhabitants. Her marriage to Eli had, in a way, provided a focal point for these connections, a clear demonstration of what could be achieved when hearts and minds were aligned. She saw how their shared vision, now solidified by their union, had empowered others to believe in their own aspirations for Havenridge. The hesitant whispers of change had grown into confident pronouncements, and the quiet hopes had begun to blossom into tangible plans. This was the ripple effect in action, a beautiful unfolding of potential, nurtured by the unwavering affirmation of love and partnership.

The impact was not limited to grand gestures; it was woven into the fabric of everyday life. The local market, once a place of quiet transactions, now buzzed with a livelier energy. Conversations flowed more freely, laughter was more readily shared, and a sense of shared ownership of Havenridge's future was evident in every interaction. Eli and Mara, by simply being together, by embodying the values of commitment and shared purpose, had become living symbols of what was possible. They hadn't imposed their will; they had simply demonstrated the power of genuine connection, and in doing so, had inspired a community to embrace its own inherent strengths.

The affirmation of Mara and Eli's union had indeed sent positive ripples throughout Havenridge, reinforcing the community's commitment to stability, connection, and mutual support. Their solidified partnership served as a quiet inspiration, demonstrating that true strength lies in chosen bonds and shared purpose, enriching the collective spirit of their home. It was a profound reminder that in a world that often felt fragmented and uncertain, the power of love, commitment, and community could create an enduring legacy, a sanctuary of hope that would continue to ripple outwards, touching every corner of their beloved Havenridge.

The subtle shifts, the renewed sense of optimism, the deepening of connections – all were testament to the profound impact of a love that had not only united two souls but had also breathed new life into the heart of their home. This was the beginning of a new era, one built on the solid foundation of shared dreams and the unwavering belief in the power of togetherness. The land seemed to breathe easier, the trees whispered tales of renewed hope, and the hearts of the people of Havenridge beat with a stronger, more unified rhythm, a direct echo of the love that had bloomed so beautifully between Mara and Eli. It was a testament to the idea that sometimes, the greatest strength is found not in building walls to protect oneself, but in building bridges that connect us all.

CHAPTER EIGHT

THE LEGACY TAKES ROOT

The days following their wedding unfurled with a gentle cadence, each sunrise painting Havenridge in hues of peaceful continuity. For Mara and Eli, the vows exchanged beneath the ancient oaks were not merely words spoken, but a new architecture for their lives, a framework that subtly reshaped their routines and deepened the roots of their connection. The air itself seemed to hold a different quality, infused with a quiet certainty that settled into the very marrow of their beings. It was the feeling of embarking on a shared journey, not as individuals who had chosen to walk side-by-side, but as two souls intricately woven into a singular tapestry.

Mara found her days unfolding with a familiar rhythm, yet infused with a profound sense of intentionality. Her responsibilities as the heart of Havenridge remained, yet they were now undertaken with a new weight, a deeper purpose. When she walked through the orchards, overseeing the pruning and the careful nurturing of the young saplings, her movements were imbued with a quiet authority that was both instinctual and newly consecrated.

The gentle touch of her hands on the bark of a fruit-laden tree, the discerning eye that assessed the health of the leaves – these were acts she had performed countless times before, but now they felt like offerings, sacrifices made willingly on the altar of their shared future. Eli's presence, often a silent observer as he worked on the estate's infrastructure, or a gentle participant in their discussions, lent an unspoken strength to her endeavors. He was no longer an outsider looking in, but an integral part of the very soil she tended. His quiet nods of approval, the subtle insights he offered on crop rotation or the irrigation systems, were not just practical advice; they were affirmations of their unified vision.

Eli, too, discovered a subtle shift in his own engagement with Havenridge. His initial role as a protector and advisor had seamlessly transitioned into something far more intrinsic. The land, which he had come to love and respect through Mara, now felt like his own to steward. He found himself spending more time examining the structural integrity of the barns, mapping out new pathways through the woodlands, and engaging with the villagers about the upkeep of their homes and communal spaces.

His engineering mind, once focused on the mechanics of machinery, now turned its meticulous attention to the harmonious functioning of the entire estate. He saw the subtle inefficiencies, the potential for improvement, not with the detachment of an observer, but with the earnest desire of one who was building a permanent home. Mara's trust in his judgment was evident in the way she would often defer to his expertise on matters of construction and land management, a gesture that spoke volumes about their partnership.

Their conversations, once filled with the tentative exploration of feelings, now often revolved around practical matters – the best time to plant the winter wheat, the allocation of resources for repairing the mill, the planning of the upcoming harvest festival. These were not mundane exchanges; they were the building blocks of a shared life, conversations filled with the quiet understanding that their decisions today would shape the Havenridge of tomorrow.

The practicalities of their union were woven into the fabric of their daily lives with an ease that belied the significance of the change. Their shared meals, once intimate moments of burgeoning romance, now felt like strategic planning sessions, filled with laughter and the easy camaraderie of two people who understood each other implicitly. Mara would recount the concerns of the village elders regarding the spring thaw, and Eli would offer practical solutions, drawing diagrams on the back of parchment with a piece of charcoal, his brow furrowed in concentration. They would discuss the needs of the younger generation, Mara sharing her ideas for educational initiatives, Eli offering insights into how the estate's resources could support such endeavors. It was a constant dialogue, a dance of shared responsibility and mutual respect.

The evenings brought a different kind of intimacy. After the day's work was done, and the soft glow of lanterns filled their home, they would often find themselves in the library, not necessarily reading, but simply *being* together. Mara might be mending a torn tapestry, her needlework a testament to her patient hands, while Eli would sketch out designs for a new community garden, the lines on his paper reflecting the careful planning of his mind.

Sometimes, they would simply talk, their voices low and warm, recounting the day's events, sharing their hopes, and occasionally, delving into the deeper currents of their hearts. These quiet moments, free from the demands of the day, were where their connection deepened most profoundly. It was in the shared silence, the comfortable presence of each other, that they reaffirmed their commitment, not with grand pronouncements, but with the gentle, unwavering certainty of two souls who had found their home in one another.

The subtle shifts were also apparent in their interactions with the wider community. The villagers, who had witnessed the strength of their bond and the sincerity of their commitment, now approached Mara and Eli with an even greater sense of trust and openness. When Mara discussed plans for expanding the local schoolhouse, the villagers responded not with apprehension, but with eager offers of assistance, their hands ready to help with labor and resources. Eli, in turn, found the tradespeople more willing to share their expertise, to collaborate on projects that would benefit the entire community. The blacksmith, old Silas, who had always been a man of few words, would now readily engage Eli in discussions about reinforcing the bridge across the Willow Creek, his tone respectful and his suggestions valued.

Mara, ever attuned to the pulse of Havenridge, noticed how her leadership style had evolved. She still possessed her inherent warmth and empathy, but her decisions were now underpinned by a quiet confidence that came from knowing she had a steadfast partner by her side. She was more decisive, her vision for Havenridge clearer and more firmly rooted. When addressing the village council, her words carried an amplified resonance, a testament to the stability that her union with Eli represented. She saw the reflection of her own newfound assurance in the eyes of the villagers, a shared sense of purpose that solidified the foundation of their community.

Eli's integration was no longer an ongoing process; it was a settled reality. He was no longer the newcomer, but a respected member of the Havenridge family, his counsel sought, his presence valued. He moved through the village with an easy familiarity, his greetings warm and genuine. The children, who had once watched him with a mixture of curiosity and apprehension, now ran to him, their faces alight with recognition, eager to show him their latest drawings or share tales of their adventures. He would stoop to their level, his large hands gentle as he ruffled their hair, his eyes crinkling with a paternal warmth. This acceptance, this genuine affection, was a testament to the profound impact of his commitment to Mara and, by extension, to Havenridge itself.

Their shared responsibilities extended beyond the practicalities of estate management. They became the arbiters of community disputes, their impartiality and fairness unquestioned. When two neighbors found themselves at odds over a boundary fence, it was to Mara and Eli that they turned, their faith in the couple's wisdom and compassion unwavering. Mara would listen with her characteristic empathy, seeking to understand the root of the disagreement, while Eli would offer practical solutions, drawing on his understanding of land and property. Their approach was always one of reconciliation, of finding common ground, ensuring that harmony was restored.

The very rhythm of their lives had adapted to this new partnership. Their mornings began with a shared cup of tea on the veranda, a moment of quiet reflection before the day's demands began. They would discuss their priorities, delegate tasks where necessary, and simply enjoy the stillness of the dawn together. It was a ritual that grounded them, a quiet affirmation of their unity before they stepped out into the world. Lunches were often working meals, taken with groundskeepers or villagers involved in specific projects, allowing for spontaneous discussions and immediate problem-solving. And their evenings, as mentioned, were a sanctuary, a time for shared decompression and a deepening of their emotional bond.

This adjusted dynamic was not about a rigid division of labor, but about a fluid exchange of strengths. If Mara was occupied with a delicate negotiation with a neighboring merchant, Eli would step in to oversee the distribution of supplies to the outlying farms. If Eli was engrossed in a complex engineering project for the mill, Mara would take on the responsibility of mediating a dispute between two tenant farmers. There was an unspoken understanding, a trust that allowed them to seamlessly fill each other's roles when needed, their shared goal always paramount. This flexibility and mutual reliance were the cornerstones of their deeply connected partnership.

The legacy they were building was not just in the tangible improvements to Havenridge – the strengthened bridges, the revitalized orchards, the improved irrigation systems. It was in the intangible shift in the community's spirit, a collective consciousness that now recognized the power of unity and shared purpose. Mara and Eli, through their steadfast commitment and their harmonious partnership, had become the living embodiment of that ideal. Their actions, their words, and their very presence radiated a quiet strength that inspired those around them to believe in the possibility of a brighter, more connected future for Havenridge. They were not merely living *in* Havenridge; they were actively, consciously, and lovingly building *with* it, their roles as leaders and partners seamlessly merging into a single, powerful force for good.

The gentle hum of Havenridge, once a symphony solely conducted by Mara and Eli's shared vision, began to resonate with new, youthful harmonies. Their personal sanctuary had been solidified, not just in the stone and timber of their home, but in the interwoven certainty of their souls. With this profound bedrock of their shared existence firmly established, their gaze naturally broadened, encompassing the future custodians of the land they so deeply cherished. The legacy they were meticulously cultivating was not solely for themselves, but for the generations who would walk these paths, tend these fields, and hold the well-being of Havenridge in their hands. This burgeoning sense of responsibility, a natural extension of their commitment to each other, led them to a profound and purposeful endeavor: mentoring the future stewards of their community.

Mara, with her inherent understanding of the land's subtle language and the people's quiet hopes, felt a particular pull towards the younger members of Havenridge. She observed the earnestness in the eyes of the farmhands who were beginning to take on more responsibility, the budding curiosity of the children who asked insightful questions about crop yields and weather patterns, and the quiet determination of those who expressed a desire to contribute more actively to the community's governance. Eli, with his keen intellect and practical approach to problem-solving, saw the immense value in imparting his knowledge of sustainable practices, infrastructure development, and the intricate balance of resource management. Together, they recognized that a thriving legacy was not merely about maintaining the present, but about actively cultivating the future.

Their initial approach was organic, woven into the fabric of their daily lives. During communal gatherings, Mara would often draw young women into conversations, not just about the harvest, but about the history of their land, the stories behind the ancient oaks, and the importance of preserving these traditions. She would share anecdotes from her own upbringing, lessons learned from her predecessors, and the profound satisfaction that came from nurturing something that would outlive her. She spoke of the land as a living entity, deserving of respect, care, and a deep, abiding love.

Her words were never lectures, but gentle invitations to understand the interconnectedness of all things within Havenridge. She encouraged them to observe, to question, and to feel the pulse of the earth beneath their feet. She would often take them on walks through the orchards, pointing out the subtle signs of a healthy tree, the delicate dance of pollinators, and the patience required for a fruit to ripen. "This is not just about growing apples," she would explain, her voice soft but resonant. "This is about understanding cycles, about the resilience of nature, and about our role as temporary caretakers, entrusted with a precious gift."

Eli, meanwhile, found himself drawn to the young men who showed an aptitude for mechanics, construction, or land management. He would invite them to join him as he inspected the irrigation systems, explaining the principles of water flow and the importance of efficient distribution. He would involve them in the planning of new pathways or the reinforcement of existing structures, demonstrating the meticulous calculations and the careful consideration of materials required. He shared his own journey, from an outsider seeking knowledge to a partner invested in the land's future.

He emphasized the importance of observation and problem-solving, encouraging them to identify potential issues before they became significant problems. "Every beam, every stone, every drop of water has a purpose," he would often tell them, his hands gesturing towards the vast expanse of Havenridge. "Our task is to understand that purpose and to ensure it is fulfilled with integrity and foresight. We build not just for today, but for the resilience of tomorrow."

Their mentoring sessions were not confined to formal settings. They often involved hands-on learning. Mara would involve eager young women in her medicinal herb garden, teaching them about the healing properties of various plants, the careful harvesting techniques, and the art of preparing remedies. She would share her knowledge of textile arts, demonstrating the creation of dyes from natural sources and the weaving of intricate patterns that told stories of their heritage.

Eli would invite young men to assist him in the workshops, teaching them basic carpentry, the use of tools, and the principles of structural integrity. He would explain the mechanics of the watermill, the workings of the ploughs, and the importance of maintaining these vital pieces of equipment. These were not mere chores; they were opportunities for immersive learning, for fostering a deep, intuitive understanding of the skills and knowledge essential for stewarding Havenridge.

A particularly impactful initiative they began was a series of informal "Stewardship Circles." These gatherings, held on a rotating basis in different parts of the estate – under the shade of the ancient apple trees, by the bubbling stream, or within the quiet confines of the library – brought together a diverse group of individuals, from seasoned villagers to inquisitive youngsters. Mara and Eli would set the tone, often sharing personal anecdotes about challenges they had faced and the lessons they had learned. They encouraged open dialogue, creating a safe space for questions, concerns, and the sharing of different perspectives.

During one such circle, held near the burgeoning community garden, a young woman named Elara, known for her quiet disposition but keen observational skills, hesitantly voiced a concern about the over-reliance on certain crops. Mara listened attentively, her gaze warm and encouraging. "That is a very astute observation, Elara," Mara said. "Tell us more about your thoughts." Elara, emboldened, explained her worry that if a blight were to affect their primary grain, the community would be left vulnerable. Eli, who was also present, nodded thoughtfully.

"Elara raises a crucial point about diversification and risk management," he stated. "Mara and I have been discussing the importance of exploring heirloom varieties of vegetables and legumes that have historically thrived in this region and offer greater resilience. Perhaps, Elara, you would be interested in spearheading a small project to research and cultivate a few of these less common, but potentially vital, crops?" Elara's eyes lit up with a mixture of surprise and excitement, and a seed of responsibility was firmly planted.

In another instance, a young man named Kael, who possessed a natural talent for understanding the flow of water and a restless energy, found himself struggling with the structured approach Eli often demonstrated. During a session by the creek, Kael kept trying to dam sections of it to create deeper pools, his intentions being to improve fishing. Eli, observing Kael's enthusiasm but also the potential disruption to the downstream flow, gently intervened. "Kael," he said, his voice calm and measured, "your desire to improve the creek is commendable. However, every adjustment we make upstream has an impact further down.

Let's look at the flow patterns together. I can show you how to create smaller, strategically placed pools that won't impede the overall flow, but will still provide havens for fish. It's about working *with* the water, not against it." Eli then spent the next hour with Kael, not just demonstrating engineering principles, but teaching him the art of observation and the importance of understanding the broader ecosystem. Kael, initially frustrated by the slower, more deliberate approach, began to appreciate the wisdom behind it, his youthful exuberance now tempered with a growing understanding of sustainable stewardship.

Mara and Eli also recognized that leadership extended beyond practical skills and environmental management. They understood the importance of community building, conflict resolution, and fostering a spirit of cooperation. They would often facilitate discussions about fairness, equity, and the responsibilities that came with leadership. They encouraged their mentees to consider the needs of all members of the community, not just the loudest voices.

One evening, a dispute arose between two neighboring families over a shared access road to their farmlands. Both parties, steeped in their own perspectives, approached Mara and Eli for arbitration. Instead of immediately offering a solution, Mara invited representatives from both families, along with a few of the younger individuals they were mentoring, to a meeting. She guided the conversation, ensuring each party had a chance to speak without interruption. Eli, meanwhile, drew up a simple map of the area, illustrating the practical implications of different access points and land use. The young mentees, observing this process, were encouraged to offer their own thoughts, not as arbiters, but as observers of the dynamics of resolution.

One young man, Liam, who had been mentored by Eli in land surveying, suggested a slight re-routing of the road that would benefit both families, using his newly acquired knowledge to propose a practical compromise. Mara praised Liam's contribution, highlighting how his understanding of the land, combined with his willingness to listen to both sides, had helped foster a solution. This experience served as a powerful lesson for all involved, demonstrating that effective leadership involved not just decision-making, but also facilitation, empathy, and the skillful application of knowledge.

The legacy they were building was inherently tied to the concept of succession. Mara and Eli understood that their time at the helm, however long it might be, was finite. Therefore, actively identifying and nurturing potential leaders was not merely a good practice; it was a fundamental pillar of their legacy. They looked for individuals who possessed not only the necessary skills and knowledge but also the character – integrity, compassion, a deep commitment to Havenridge, and a willingness to learn and grow.

They actively sought out these individuals, engaging them in conversations, offering them opportunities to take on small leadership roles, and providing them with guidance and support. This might involve asking a promising young woman to organize a village festival, or tasking a capable young man with overseeing a small construction project. These were not tests to be failed, but opportunities to learn and to build confidence. Mara and Eli were always available for counsel, offering constructive feedback and encouragement, celebrating successes, and helping to navigate challenges.

Eli, in particular, found satisfaction in seeing the younger generation embrace his principles of sustainable engineering. He would spend hours with Kael and others like him, explaining the long-term benefits of using locally sourced, durable materials, the importance of minimizing waste, and the philosophy of building structures that could withstand the test of time and the elements.

He taught them that true strength lay not in brute force, but in thoughtful design and meticulous execution. He showed them how to read the landscape, to understand its contours and its limitations, and to build in harmony with it, rather than in opposition. He emphasized that a well-built structure was not just functional, but a testament to the care and foresight of its creators. "A building that endures," he would say, his gaze sweeping across the valley, "is a promise to the future. It speaks of our commitment to those who will come after us."

Mara's approach to nurturing future leaders was equally profound, focusing on the heart of community. She guided young women and men in the art of active listening, of understanding the unspoken needs of their neighbors, and of fostering a sense of belonging for everyone within Havenridge. She instilled in them the belief that true leadership was about service, about lifting others up, and about creating a community where everyone felt valued and respected.

She taught them that empathy was not a weakness, but a profound strength, and that understanding diverse perspectives was essential for creating a cohesive and resilient society. She often shared stories of past leaders of Havenridge, highlighting their triumphs and their failures, drawing lessons from their experiences that would guide the next generation. "The heart of Havenridge beats in its people," she would explain, her voice filled with a gentle passion. "Our responsibility is to ensure that heart beats strong, with compassion and with unity."

The impact of their mentorship was becoming increasingly visible. The Stewardship Circles grew in size and in the depth of their discussions. Young leaders were emerging, not with grand pronouncements, but with quiet confidence and a growing sense of purpose. Elara, who had once been hesitant to speak, was now actively involved in experimenting with new crop varieties, her enthusiasm infectious. Kael, his youthful energy now channeled with precision, was helping Eli plan more intricate irrigation upgrades, demonstrating a newfound understanding of the delicate balance of the ecosystem. Liam was becoming a trusted voice in community discussions, his practical insights often bridging divides.

Mara and Eli understood that this was not an endpoint, but a continuous process. Their legacy was not just in the fertile fields or the sturdy buildings of Havenridge, but in the minds and hearts of the individuals they were shaping. They were not simply passing down knowledge; they were cultivating a culture of stewardship, a commitment to the land, and a deep-seated understanding of community responsibility.

They were, in essence, planting seeds of leadership, carefully tending them with wisdom, patience, and unwavering belief, ensuring that the legacy of Havenridge would not only take root but would flourish for generations to come. Their own intertwined journey, having found such profound strength and purpose in their union, had illuminated the path for others, showing them that true legacy was built not just on individual achievement, but on shared commitment, nurtured growth, and the enduring power of collective care.

The gentle hum of Havenridge, once a symphony solely conducted by Mara and Eli's shared vision, began to resonate with new, youthful harmonies. Their personal sanctuary had been solidified, not just in the stone and timber of their home, but in the interwoven certainty of their souls. With this profound bedrock of their shared existence firmly established, their gaze naturally broadened, encompassing the future custodians of the land they so deeply cherished. The legacy they were meticulously cultivating was not solely for themselves, but for the generations who would walk these paths, tend these fields, and hold the well-being of Havenridge in their hands. This burgeoning sense of responsibility, a natural extension of their commitment to each other, led them to a profound and purposeful endeavor: mentoring the future stewards of their community.

Mara, with her inherent understanding of the land's subtle language and the people's quiet hopes, felt a particular pull towards the younger members of Havenridge. She observed the earnestness in the eyes of the farmhands who were beginning to take on more responsibility, the budding curiosity of the children who asked insightful questions about crop yields and weather patterns, and the quiet determination of those who expressed a desire to contribute more actively to the community's governance. Eli, with his keen intellect and practical approach to problem-solving, saw the immense value in imparting his knowledge of sustainable practices, infrastructure development, and the intricate balance of resource management. Together, they recognized that a thriving legacy was not merely about maintaining the present, but about actively cultivating the future.

Their initial approach was organic, woven into the fabric of their daily lives. During communal gatherings, Mara would often draw young women into conversations, not just about the harvest, but about the history of their land, the stories behind the ancient oaks, and the importance of preserving these traditions. She would share anecdotes from her own upbringing, lessons learned from her predecessors, and the profound satisfaction that came from nurturing something that would outlive her. She spoke of the land as a living entity, deserving of respect, care, and a deep, abiding love.

Her words were never lectures, but gentle invitations to understand the interconnectedness of all things within Havenridge. She encouraged them to observe, to question, and to feel the pulse of the earth beneath their feet. She would often take them on walks through the orchards, pointing out the subtle signs of a healthy tree, the delicate dance of pollinators, and the patience required for a fruit to ripen. "This is not just about growing apples," she would explain, her voice soft but resonant. "This is about understanding cycles, about the resilience of nature, and about our role as temporary caretakers, entrusted with a precious gift."

Eli, meanwhile, found himself drawn to the young men who showed an aptitude for mechanics, construction, or land management. He would invite them to join him as he inspected the irrigation systems, explaining the principles of water flow and the importance of efficient distribution. He would involve them in the planning of new pathways or the reinforcement of existing structures, demonstrating the meticulous calculations and the careful consideration of materials required. He shared his own journey, from an outsider seeking knowledge to a partner invested in the land's future.

He emphasized the importance of observation and problem-solving, encouraging them to identify potential issues before they became significant problems. "Every beam, every stone, every drop of water has a purpose," he would often tell them, his hands gesturing towards the vast expanse of Havenridge. "Our task is to understand that purpose and to ensure it is fulfilled with integrity and foresight. We build not just for today, but for the resilience of tomorrow."

Their mentoring sessions were not confined to formal settings. They often involved hands-on learning. Mara would involve eager young women in her medicinal herb garden, teaching them about the healing properties of various plants, the careful harvesting techniques, and the art of preparing remedies. She would share her knowledge of textile arts, demonstrating the creation of dyes from natural sources and the weaving of intricate patterns that told stories of their heritage.

Eli would invite young men to assist him in the workshops, teaching them basic carpentry, the use of tools, and the principles of structural integrity. He would explain the mechanics of the watermill, the workings of the ploughs, and the importance of maintaining these vital pieces of equipment. These were not mere chores; they were opportunities for immersive learning, for fostering a deep, intuitive understanding of the skills and knowledge essential for stewarding Havenridge.

A particularly impactful initiative they began was a series of informal "Stewardship Circles." These gatherings, held on a rotating basis in different parts of the estate – under the shade of the ancient apple trees, by the bubbling stream, or within the quiet confines of the library – brought together a diverse group of individuals, from seasoned villagers to inquisitive youngsters. Mara and Eli would set the tone, often sharing personal anecdotes about challenges they had faced and the lessons they had learned. They encouraged open dialogue, creating a safe space for questions, concerns, and the sharing of different perspectives.

During one such circle, held near the burgeoning community garden, a young woman named Elara, known for her quiet disposition but keen observational skills, hesitantly voiced a concern about the over-reliance on certain crops. Mara listened attentively, her gaze warm and encouraging. "That is a very astute observation, Elara," Mara said. "Tell us more about your thoughts." Elara, emboldened, explained her worry that if a blight were to affect their primary grain, the community would be left vulnerable. Eli, who was also present, nodded thoughtfully.

"Elara raises a crucial point about diversification and risk management," he stated. "Mara and I have been discussing the importance of exploring heirloom varieties of vegetables and legumes that have historically thrived in this region and offer greater resilience. Perhaps, Elara, you would be interested in spearheading a small project to research and cultivate a few of these less common, but potentially vital, crops?" Elara's eyes lit up with a mixture of surprise and excitement, and a seed of responsibility was firmly planted.

In another instance, a young man named Kael, who possessed a natural talent for understanding the flow of water and a restless energy, found himself struggling with the structured approach Eli often demonstrated. During a session by the creek, Kael kept trying to dam sections of it to create deeper pools, his intentions being to improve fishing. Eli, observing Kael's enthusiasm but also the potential disruption to the downstream flow, gently intervened.

"Kael," he said, his voice calm and measured, "your desire to improve the creek is commendable. However, every adjustment we make upstream has an impact further down. Let's look at the flow patterns together. I can show you how to create smaller, strategically placed pools that won't impede the overall flow, but will still provide havens for fish. It's about working *with* the water, not against it."

Eli then spent the next hour with Kael, not just demonstrating engineering principles, but teaching him the art of observation and the importance of understanding the broader ecosystem. Kael, initially frustrated by the slower, more deliberate approach, began to appreciate the wisdom behind it, his youthful exuberance now tempered with a growing understanding of sustainable stewardship.

Mara and Eli also recognized that leadership extended beyond practical skills and environmental management. They understood the importance of community building, conflict resolution, and fostering a spirit of cooperation. They would often facilitate discussions about fairness, equity, and the responsibilities that came with leadership. They encouraged their mentees to consider the needs of all members of the community, not just the loudest voices.

One evening, a dispute arose between two neighboring families over a shared access road to their farmlands. Both parties, steeped in their own perspectives, approached Mara and Eli for arbitration. Instead of immediately offering a solution, Mara invited representatives from both families, along with a few of the younger individuals they were mentoring, to a meeting. She guided the conversation, ensuring each party had a chance to speak without interruption. Eli, meanwhile, drew up a simple map of the area, illustrating the practical implications of different access points and land use.

The young mentees, observing this process, were encouraged to offer their own thoughts, not as arbiters, but as observers of the dynamics of resolution. One young man, Liam, who had been mentored by Eli in land surveying, suggested a slight re-routing of the road that would benefit both families, using his newly acquired knowledge to propose a practical compromise. Mara praised Liam's contribution, highlighting how his understanding of the land, combined with his willingness to listen to both sides, had helped foster a solution. This experience served as a powerful lesson for all involved, demonstrating that effective leadership involved not just decision-making, but also facilitation, empathy, and the skillful application of knowledge.

The legacy they were building was inherently tied to the concept of succession. Mara and Eli understood that their time at the helm, however long it might be, was finite. Therefore, actively identifying and nurturing potential leaders was not merely a good practice; it was a fundamental pillar of their legacy. They looked for individuals who possessed not only the necessary skills and knowledge but also the character – integrity, compassion, a deep commitment to Havenridge, and a willingness to learn and grow.

They actively sought out these individuals, engaging them in conversations, offering them opportunities to take on small leadership roles, and providing them with guidance and support. This might involve asking a promising young woman to organize a village festival, or tasking a capable young man with overseeing a small construction project. These were not tests to be failed, but opportunities to learn and to build confidence. Mara and Eli were always available for counsel, offering constructive feedback and encouragement, celebrating successes, and helping to navigate challenges.

Eli, in particular, found satisfaction in seeing the younger generation embrace his principles of sustainable engineering. He would spend hours with Kael and others like him, explaining the long-term benefits of using locally sourced, durable materials, the importance of minimizing waste, and the philosophy of building structures that could withstand the test of time and the elements. He taught them that true strength lay not in brute force, but in thoughtful design and meticulous execution. He showed them how to read the landscape, to understand its contours and its limitations, and to build in harmony with it, rather than in opposition. He emphasized that a well-built structure was not just functional, but a testament to the care and foresight of its creators. "A building that endures," he would say, his gaze sweeping across the valley, "is a promise to the future. It speaks of our commitment to those who will come after us."

Mara's approach to nurturing future leaders was equally profound, focusing on the heart of community. She guided young women and men in the art of active listening, of understanding the unspoken needs of their neighbors, and of fostering a sense of belonging for everyone within Havenridge. She instilled in them the belief that true leadership was about service, about lifting others up, and about creating a community where everyone felt valued and respected.

She taught them that empathy was not a weakness, but a profound strength, and that understanding diverse perspectives was essential for creating a cohesive and resilient society. She often shared stories of past leaders of Havenridge, highlighting their triumphs and their failures, drawing lessons from their experiences that would guide the next generation. "The heart of Havenridge beats in its people," she would explain, her voice filled with a gentle passion. "Our responsibility is to ensure that heart beats strong, with compassion and with unity."

The impact of their mentorship was becoming increasingly visible. The Stewardship Circles grew in size and in the depth of their discussions. Young leaders were emerging, not with grand pronouncements, but with quiet confidence and a growing sense of purpose. Elara, who had once been hesitant to speak, was now actively involved in experimenting with new crop varieties, her enthusiasm infectious. Kael, his youthful energy now channeled with precision, was helping Eli plan more intricate irrigation upgrades, demonstrating a newfound understanding of the delicate balance of the ecosystem. Liam was becoming a trusted voice in community discussions, his practical insights often bridging divides.

Mara and Eli understood that this was not an endpoint, but a continuous process. Their legacy was not just in the fertile fields or the sturdy buildings of Havenridge, but in the minds and hearts of the individuals they were shaping. They were not simply passing down knowledge; they were cultivating a culture of stewardship, a commitment to the land, and a deep-seated understanding of community responsibility.

They were, in essence, planting seeds of leadership, carefully tending them with wisdom, patience, and unwavering belief, ensuring that the legacy of Havenridge would not only take root but would flourish for generations to come. Their own intertwined journey, having found such profound strength and purpose in their union, had illuminated the path for others, showing them that true legacy was built not just on individual achievement, but on shared commitment, nurtured growth, and the enduring power of collective care.

This blossoming of responsibility had, in turn, nurtured an expansive flowering within Mara herself. She discovered that her commitment to Havenridge, to its people and its future, had indeed led to an undeniable expansion of her own self. It wasn't a shedding of her former identity, but a rich layering upon it, like the rings of a wise old oak, each new growth a testament to resilience and depth.

Her leadership, once so finely tuned to the nuances of Eli's partnership and the needs of their shared life, now possessed a new, robust independence, yet it remained intrinsically collaborative. She found herself initiating projects with a confidence that surprised even herself, not by dictating terms, but by inviting participation, by weaving her vision into the collective tapestry of Havenridge.

One such endeavor was the revitalization of the old weaver's guild. For years, the looms had stood silent, draped in dust sheets, a relic of a past era. Mara, remembering the vibrant stories woven into the very fabric of her childhood, felt a strong calling to revive this tradition. She approached the elders, not with demands, but with a proposal steeped in history and potential. She spoke of the medicinal herbs she cultivated, their vibrant colors that could be transformed into natural dyes, of the flax fields that, with a little care, could yield strong, lustrous threads.

She envisioned young women learning not just the craft of weaving, but the stories behind the patterns, the ancestral knowledge embedded in each knot and thread. She organized workshops, patiently demonstrating the intricate process of spinning flax, the careful mixing of dyes from berries and roots, and the rhythmic dance of the shuttle. Her hands, once primarily tending to delicate herbs or Eli's well-being, now moved with a practiced grace over the warp and weft, her eyes alight with a passion that was entirely her own, yet deeply connected to the soul of Havenridge. She wasn't merely teaching a skill; she was reigniting a heritage, a testament to her growing belief in her own capacity to initiate and sustain meaningful change.

Furthermore, she took on the management of the village market, transforming it from a place of simple trade into a vibrant hub of community interaction. She organized themed market days – a harvest festival, a spring bloom celebration – encouraging local artisans to showcase their crafts, farmers to share their bounty, and musicians to fill the air with lively tunes. She meticulously planned the layout, ensuring accessibility for all, and instituted a system for early notification of weather patterns, mitigating potential disruptions for vendors. She created a small communal space within the market, furnished with handcrafted benches, where people could gather, share news, and build connections.

This wasn't merely about logistics; it was about fostering a sense of belonging, about creating spaces where relationships could flourish alongside commerce. Her independent initiative in this regard was remarkable, a clear demonstration of her capacity to conceive, plan, and execute complex projects, drawing upon her understanding of community dynamics and her innate organizational skills.

Her partnership with Eli remained the steadfast anchor in this expanding sea of activity. The security of their bond allowed her to venture further, to embrace these new roles without apprehension. The permanence they had built together wasn't a cage, but a launchpad. When Eli would return from overseeing infrastructure projects, his hands dusted with soil and his mind brimming with schematics, he would find Mara not waiting passively, but actively engaged, her own hands stained with dye or flour, her eyes shining with the fulfillment of her own pursuits. He would listen, with genuine interest and pride, as she recounted the successes and challenges of her market initiatives or the progress of the revived weaver's guild. He saw not a competitor for his attention, but a partner whose own flourishing enriched their shared life immeasurably.

"The market was bustling today," Mara reported one evening, a contented smile gracing her lips as she served a fragrant stew. "Old Man Hemlock sold all his honey, and young Lyra's woven scarves were gone by noon. It's more than just trade, Eli. It's about seeing people connect, about feeling that pulse of life beating strong."

Eli, stirring his bowl, met her gaze, a warmth spreading through him. "And it's you, Mara, who is orchestrating that pulse. You've given them a space to breathe, to share, to thrive. It's a beautiful thing to witness." He paused, a thoughtful glint in his eyes. "You know, I was thinking about the old granary. It's structurally sound, but its potential is largely untapped. Perhaps, with your knack for community engagement, we could explore transforming a section into a proper workshop for the artisans? A shared space where they could work, store their materials, and even exhibit their finished pieces more formally."

Mara's eyes widened, a spark of excitement igniting within her. "Oh, Eli, that's a brilliant idea! We could... we could even hold small demonstrations there, perhaps even evening classes. Imagine, the weaver's guild having a dedicated space, a place where the old traditions can truly come alive again!"

This easy collaboration, this seamless intertwining of their individual passions and shared vision, underscored Mara's flourishing independence. She was no longer solely defined by her role as Eli's partner, though that remained a cornerstone of her identity. She was Mara, the skilled herbalist, the insightful community organizer, the revitalizer of forgotten crafts, and the unwavering steward of Havenridge's spirit.

Her confidence was not an outward show, but a deep, internal certainty that grew from the knowledge that she was contributing meaningfully, that her ideas were valued, and that her actions had a tangible, positive impact on the world around her. She had found that true independence was not about isolation, but about the freedom to grow and contribute, securely rooted in love and belonging.

The secure framework of her partnership with Eli had not stifled her; it had liberated her, allowing her to explore the full breadth of her capabilities and to discover a strength and creativity she might never have known otherwise. Havenridge was not just her home; it was her canvas, and she was painting it with bold, vibrant strokes, guided by her own evolving vision.

Eli's vision for enduring stability was less about erecting imposing structures and more about cultivating a robust, resilient ecosystem, both natural and societal. He recognized that the physical foundations of Havenridge – the wells, the irrigation channels, the solid timber of the communal hall – were only as strong as the principles that guided their upkeep and the community's commitment to their preservation.

His partnership with Mara had solidified this understanding; their shared life, built on mutual trust, open communication, and a deep respect for each other and their surroundings, was the blueprint for the kind of enduring stability he envisioned for Havenridge as a whole. It was a living testament to the fact that true strength lay not in solitary power, but in interwoven lives, dedicated to a common purpose.

He often found himself observing the younger generations, his gaze not just seeing their potential, but the foundational understanding they were beginning to grasp. He saw how Kael, once a whirlwind of untamed energy, now approached the creek with a surveyor's eye, understanding the delicate balance of water flow. He witnessed Elara's meticulous notes on heirloom seed viability, her quiet determination a harbinger of successful agricultural diversification.

These were not just individual successes; they were the threads of a more robust future, woven with foresight and a growing respect for the land's intricate systems. Eli understood that nurturing these individuals was paramount. He believed that a community's longevity was directly tied to its ability to adapt, to innovate, and to learn from both its successes and its setbacks. His commitment was to ensure that Havenridge possessed not only fertile soil and reliable infrastructure but also a deep-seated cultural wisdom that would guide it through the inevitable cycles of change.

His days were filled with a quiet but persistent dedication to the structural integrity of their shared life. This translated into practical endeavors. He would spend hours with the young men interested in construction, not just teaching them how to lay bricks or mend a roof, but imbuing them with a philosophy of building for permanence. He spoke of the importance of understanding the earth beneath the foundations, of choosing materials that were not only readily available but also sustainable and durable, able to withstand the changing seasons and the passage of time.

He would often take them to inspect the older buildings, pointing out the subtle signs of wear, the ingenious solutions of past builders, and the lessons that could be learned from both. "A structure that stands the test of centuries," he would explain, his voice resonating with quiet conviction, "is not built on haste or on convenience alone. It is built with respect for the materials, for the land, and for the people who will seek shelter within its walls long after we are gone."

He was particularly focused on the efficient management of resources, a principle he had learned through his own journey and now sought to instill in others. The irrigation systems, the water mill, the communal granary – these were not mere tools, but vital organs of Havenridge's body. He initiated a series of regular inspections, inviting those with an aptitude for mechanics or engineering to join him.

He taught them to listen to the hum of the mill, to understand the subtle groans of stressed timber, to recognize the signs of potential leaks in the irrigation channels. He would explain the mathematics of water distribution, the importance of minimizing waste, and the long-term implications of over-reliance on any single source. "Every drop of water is precious," he would tell them, "and every system we build must be designed with its conservation in mind. Our aim is not just to manage, but to steward, ensuring that these resources are available for generations to come."

The communal hall, the heart of Havenridge's social and civic life, was another area of his keen interest. He saw it not just as a meeting place, but as a symbol of their collective strength. He oversaw its maintenance with meticulous care, ensuring that the timbers were sound, the roof watertight, and the interior welcoming. He initiated discussions about its future needs, considering how it might need to adapt to accommodate a growing community or new forms of gathering.

He encouraged the younger members to contribute their ideas, fostering a sense of ownership and shared responsibility for this vital communal space. He believed that a well-maintained and functional communal hall was essential for fostering social cohesion and for providing a resilient hub for community life, capable of weathering both literal and metaphorical storms.

His vision extended beyond the physical realm to the structure of community governance. He understood that enduring stability required clear, fair, and adaptable systems of decision-making. He observed the informal ways in which Mara led, her ability to listen, to empathize, and to guide consensus, and saw in it a model for broader community leadership. He began to engage with the village elders, not to dictate terms, but to foster a dialogue about how their established traditions could be strengthened and adapted for the future.

He believed in the wisdom of experience, but also in the necessity of embracing new perspectives. He proposed the formalization of certain practices, such as regular community forums where issues could be openly discussed and resolved, and clear processes for electing representatives to oversee specific aspects of community life, such as resource management or dispute resolution. His aim was to create a framework that was both rooted in their history and flexible enough to accommodate the evolving needs of Havenridge.

"Our strength, Mara," he articulated one evening, as they sat by the hearth, the scent of woodsmoke and dried herbs filling the air, "lies not just in the land we tend or the homes we build, but in the way we relate to each other, and the systems we put in place to ensure that care continues. I see a future where Havenridge isn't just a place people live, but a community that actively thrives, that can face challenges with a unified spirit and a clear purpose. And that requires deliberate planning, a commitment to building robust structures, both visible and invisible."

He saw their personal union as a microcosm of this ideal. The trust they had built, the way they navigated disagreements with respect, the shared commitment to their vision – these were the bedrock principles that could, and should, be reflected in the wider community. He began to share these thoughts more openly during their Stewardship Circles and in conversations with individuals he felt were ready to consider these broader implications. He wasn't suggesting a rigid replication of their personal dynamic, but rather an inspiration drawn from its success.

"Look at us," he might say, gesturing between himself and Mara, "we don't always agree on every detail, but we share a fundamental understanding of what matters most. We listen to each other, we respect each other's strengths, and we are committed to building a life together that is stronger than either of us alone. That same spirit, that same commitment to thoughtful partnership, is what Havenridge needs to truly endure."

Eli's focus on enduring stability also manifested in his quiet but persistent encouragement of intergenerational knowledge transfer. He believed that the wisdom accumulated over years was as vital a resource as any fertile field. He would often seek out the older villagers, not just for their stories, but for their practical knowledge – the subtle signs of approaching frost that a younger farmer might miss, the medicinal properties of plants that were slowly being forgotten, the traditional methods of preserving food that were efficient and sustainable.

He would then facilitate opportunities for these elders to share their insights with the younger generations. He might arrange for an elder to demonstrate traditional basket weaving to a group of interested youths, or to share their experiences in managing livestock during harsh winters. He saw these exchanges as crucial for weaving a rich tapestry of knowledge that would sustain Havenridge for years to come.

He also recognized the importance of resilience in the face of uncertainty. His background had taught him the harsh lessons of scarcity and the importance of planning for the unexpected. He began to advocate for the establishment of a community resource reserve, a collection of essential supplies that could be drawn upon in times of hardship, whether due to natural disaster, crop failure, or other unforeseen circumstances.

This was not about fostering a culture of fear, but of preparedness. He envisioned a system managed collectively, with clear guidelines for contribution and access, ensuring that the community's ability to weather difficult times was not left to chance. He would often use analogies from nature, pointing to how a forest ecosystem was designed for resilience, with diverse species and interconnected root systems that allowed it to recover from disturbances. "Nature teaches us the value of diversification and preparedness," he would explain. "A single point of failure is a vulnerability. A well-prepared community is like a forest with deep roots; it can withstand the storm and regrow."

The integration of their personal lives with their public roles was a source of constant strength for Eli. Mara's intuitive understanding of people and her innate ability to foster connection complemented his more structured, pragmatic approach. He often found himself seeking her counsel, not just on matters of community governance, but on how to best communicate his ideas, how to ensure that his focus on structural integrity did not alienate those who valued a more organic approach. Her ability to weave his visions into the fabric of community life, to translate his blueprints into shared aspirations, was invaluable.

He saw their partnership as the living embodiment of the enduring stability he championed. It was a constant, evolving testament to the power of mutual support, shared purpose, and unwavering commitment, a quiet yet profound force that radiated outwards, shaping the very foundations of Havenridge's future. He knew that as long as their bond remained strong, as long as their shared vision continued to guide them, Havenridge would not only survive but flourish, a testament to a legacy built on love, resilience, and a profound understanding of what it truly meant to build for eternity.

The gentle hum of the water mill, a sound Eli had grown to associate with the steady heartbeat of Havenridge, was a familiar comfort. It was a sound that spoke of labor, yes, but also of sustenance, of the ceaseless turning of the world that provided for them. Beside him, Mara's hand found his, her fingers intertwining with his calloused ones. The touch was a silent language, a shared acknowledgment of the day's work and the quiet satisfaction that settled in its wake.

Their lives had settled into a rhythm, a cadence that felt both profoundly natural and deliberately cultivated. It wasn't a life without its demands, its inevitable pebbles in the stream, but they had learned to navigate those challenges not as individuals facing separate obstacles, but as two halves of a unified whole, their strengths complementing each other, their burdens lightened by the sharing.

He remembered the early days, the tentative steps they had taken towards building a life together, a life that extended beyond their own hearth to encompass the nascent community of Havenridge. There had been a nervous energy then, a blend of hope and trepidation. Now, years later, that energy had transformed into a deep, abiding peace. The anxieties had been replaced by a quiet confidence, a certainty that whatever lay ahead, they would face it together. This wasn't the boisterous joy of new love, but a richer, more profound contentment, the kind that bloomed from shared experiences, from weathered storms, and from the enduring strength of a bond forged in commitment.

"The new irrigation channels are holding beautifully," Mara murmured, her gaze drifting towards the emerald fields stretching out before them. "Kael and his team have done exemplary work. I saw him explaining the flow regulators to some of the younger boys earlier. He has such a natural way of teaching, Eli."

Eli squeezed her hand. "He's learned to see the land, Mara, truly see it. Just as Elara has learned to coax life from the most stubborn seeds. It's this kind of understanding, this deep connection, that will ensure Havenridge continues to thrive." He paused, a thoughtful smile touching his lips. "And it's in moments like these, watching them grow, that I feel the deepest sense of purpose. It's not just about building structures; it's about nurturing the spirit of this place."

The quiet joy that permeated their shared existence was not a passive gift, but an active creation. It was built, brick by careful brick, through countless conversations, through shared laughter that echoed through their modest home, and through the silent understanding that passed between them in the stillness of the night. It was in the way Mara would preemptively prepare his favorite tea when she saw the weariness etched on his brow after a long day of overseeing the timber harvest, or the way Eli would ensure the hearth was always well-stocked with dry wood before the first hint of autumn chill touched the air. These were small gestures, perhaps, but they were the threads that wove their lives into a tapestry of unwavering support and affection.

He recalled a recent discussion about the communal granary, a project that had demanded considerable effort and foresight. There had been differing opinions on the best approach to reinforcement, a minor disagreement that could have easily festered. Yet, Mara had listened patiently to his concerns about structural integrity, while he, in turn, had acknowledged her insights into the logistical challenges of storing such a large quantity of grain. They had spent an evening poring over the schematics, not as adversaries, but as partners, their combined perspectives leading them to a solution that was both robust and practical. The resulting granary stood as a silent testament to their collaborative spirit, a monument to the quiet strength that lay in their union.

"Do you remember," Mara began, her voice soft, "when we first decided to expand the orchards? There was so much skepticism. People wondered if we were overextending ourselves, if the soil could truly support so many new trees."

Eli chuckled, a warm, rumbling sound. "And yet, look at them now. The apple harvest was the most bountiful we've ever seen. And the new varieties Elara is cultivating... she has a gift, Mara. A genuine gift." He turned to face her fully, his eyes holding hers. "It's because we dared to believe, isn't it? Because we believed in the land, and we believed in each other's ability to bring that vision to fruition."

That was the essence of it, he realized. Their shared purpose wasn't a grand, sweeping declaration, but a quiet, persistent commitment to the well-being of Havenridge, a commitment that was mirrored in the deliberate cultivation of their own relationship. Every successful harvest, every mended fence, every child who learned a new skill – these were not isolated victories, but extensions of the life they were building together. The joy they found in these achievements was amplified by the knowledge that they were the product of a shared endeavor, a testament to the power of two hearts beating with the same rhythm, two minds working towards the same horizon.

He often found himself watching Mara as she moved through their home, her presence a source of calm and order. Whether she was tending to their small herb garden, her fingers stained with soil, or meticulously organizing the village records, her dedication was evident. There was a quiet competence about her that Eli deeply admired, a way she had of making even the most daunting tasks seem manageable. And she, in turn, seemed to draw strength from his unwavering presence, from his steady hand and his thoughtful consideration of every aspect of their shared life.

"The winter stores are looking good," Mara remarked, shifting her weight beside him. "Thanks to the efficiency of the new threshing machine. You know, when you first suggested investing in it, there were some who worried about the cost. But it's already paid for itself tenfold."

"It's about looking ahead, Mara," Eli replied, his gaze sweeping over the peaceful landscape. "It's about understanding that preparedness isn't a luxury, but a necessity. And it's about trusting that the decisions we make, when guided by a shared vision, will ultimately serve us well." He turned to her, a warmth spreading through him that had nothing to do with the setting sun. "We've built something special here, haven't we? Something that goes beyond mere survival. It's a community, yes, but it's also... a testament to what can happen when people choose to build together, with intention and with care."

The quiet joy was in the understanding that they were not merely coexisting, but actively co-creating. It was in the unspoken acknowledgment of each other's efforts, the seamless way they anticipated each other's needs. When Eli spent his days planning the expansion of the communal workshops, ensuring there were adequate tools and resources for the apprentices, Mara was often found coordinating the distribution of surplus produce to those families who needed it most, her empathy a guiding force. When a sudden storm threatened the newly planted seedlings, they had worked side-by-side, a shared urgency propelling them, their actions in perfect synchrony, to protect the fragile life.

"I saw Lyra today," Mara said, her voice carrying a note of gentle pride. "She was helping Old Man Hemlock with his bees. He said she has a remarkable patience for it, a gentleness with the creatures that he hasn't seen in years."

Eli smiled. "Another seed planted. That's what it all comes down to, doesn't it? Nurturing what will grow and flourish long after we're gone." He paused, then added, "And it's made easier, immeasurably easier, by having you by my side. Your ability to see the potential in people, to encourage their growth... it's a gift, Mara. A precious gift."

Their relationship was a cornerstone of Havenridge's burgeoning stability, a quiet testament to the power of a shared life built on deliberate choices. They had chosen to trust, to communicate, to support each other's dreams, and in doing so, they had created a sanctuary not just for themselves, but for the entire community. The contentment they felt was not the passive acceptance of fate, but the active, joyful embrace of a life they had intentionally shaped, a life where purpose and partnership intertwined, creating a legacy of quiet strength and enduring love that resonated through every corner of Havenridge. The setting sun painted the sky in hues of orange and rose, casting a warm glow over the land, a reflection of the quiet joy that filled their hearts.

CHAPTER NINE

FACING THE HORIZON

The fading light of the day cast long shadows across the fields, a familiar and comforting sight. Eli and Mara sat together on the worn wooden bench overlooking the valley, a quiet stillness settling between them. The day's work was done, the gentle rhythm of Havenridge softening into the evening's embrace. But their minds, ever active, were already turning towards what lay beyond the setting sun, towards the unfolding tapestry of days, months, and years yet to come. This wasn't a fleeting thought, but a deeply ingrained habit, a testament to the kind of partnership they had cultivated – one that looked not just at the immediate needs, but at the enduring legacy they wished to leave.

"The council meeting today was... productive," Mara began, her voice soft, yet carrying the weight of thoughtful consideration. "We finalized the proposal for the expanded water catchment system. It's a significant undertaking, but the projections for consistent water supply, even through prolonged dry spells, are promising." She turned to Eli, her eyes reflecting the warm glow of the lantern they had lit. "It feels good, doesn't it? To be making these plans, not just for us, but for generations who will walk these paths long after we are gone."

Eli reached for her hand, his thumb tracing the delicate veins on her skin. "It does, my love. It feels like a sacred trust. We've been given this land, this community, and the responsibility to steward it well. And that stewardship extends far beyond our own lifetimes."

He gazed out at the sprawling landscape, the neat rows of crops, the sturdy buildings of the village, the distant, verdant hills. "When we first envisioned Havenridge, it was about survival, about building a sanctuary. Now, it's about flourishing, about creating a place that will not only sustain but enrich the lives of all who call it home."

Their conversations had evolved over time, mirroring the growth of Havenridge itself. The early discussions had been about the immediate – clearing land, building shelter, ensuring there was enough food for the winter. Now, their dialogues delved into a much deeper, more intricate consideration of the future. They spoke of soil enrichment techniques that would ensure fertility for centuries, of crop rotation strategies that would prevent depletion, and of investing in hardy, resilient plant varieties that could withstand unpredictable weather patterns. It was a constant balancing act, a mindful approach to resource management that was as much about ecological respect as it was about practical planning.

"I've been studying the patterns of the river flow," Mara continued, pulling a small, worn notebook from her satchel. "The current system, while effective, relies heavily on predictable rainfall. If we are to truly secure Havenridge's future, we need to consider more robust methods of water management. The proposals for the underground cisterns, coupled with an expanded network of permeable surfaces to encourage groundwater replenishment, seem the most promising. It's a significant investment, both in terms of resources and labor, but the long-term security it offers is invaluable."

Eli nodded, his brow furrowed in thought. "And the ecological impact? We must ensure that these changes don't disrupt the natural balance. We've worked so hard to foster a healthy ecosystem here – the diverse flora and fauna are a testament to that. Any new infrastructure must be designed with minimal disruption in mind. Perhaps we can incorporate elements that double as habitat or filtration systems, a way of giving back to the land for what we take."

"Exactly," Mara agreed, her eyes alight with shared understanding. "I've been consulting with Elara on that very point. She has some fascinating ideas about creating bio-swales along the new channels, using specific native plants that will not only filter the water but also attract beneficial insects and provide forage for small wildlife. It's a beautiful synergy, isn't it? Where our practical needs align perfectly with the needs of the natural world."

Beyond the immediate concerns of agriculture and water, their vision extended to the economic resilience of Havenridge. They discussed diversification of their industries, not just relying on farming, but fostering artisan crafts, developing sustainable timber harvesting practices that ensured the forests would regenerate, and exploring potential for trade with neighboring communities, always with a focus on fair exchange and mutual benefit.

"The textiles workshop is producing some of our finest work," Eli observed, his gaze sweeping over the distant cluster of buildings. "The dyes are vibrant, the weave is strong. But we need to ensure we are not solely reliant on our own internal demand. What if we were to explore a partnership with the coastal settlements? They have a need for durable fabrics, and we have the means to produce them. It could open up new avenues of trade, bringing in resources we currently lack, and ensuring a steady income stream for our craftspeople."

Mara's fingers tapped a gentle rhythm on her notebook. "That's a sound idea. And it would also require us to think about production capacity. If we expand our textile output, we'll need to ensure a consistent supply of wool, flax, and other raw materials. That means looking at our livestock management and our crop planning with an even keener eye. It's a cascading effect, isn't it? Every decision has implications that ripple outwards."

"It does," Eli affirmed, his voice laced with a quiet satisfaction. "And that's the beauty of it. We are building a complex, interconnected system, much like the natural world we strive to protect. Each part supports the other, and the strength of the whole depends on the health of each individual component." He paused, a thoughtful expression crossing his face. "We also need to consider the human element, Mara. The social fabric of Havenridge. How do we ensure that as we grow, we maintain the sense of community that is so vital to our strength?"

This was a question that lay particularly close to Mara's heart. She had always possessed a deep empathy for the people of Havenridge, a keen understanding of their individual needs and aspirations. Their long-term visioning sessions often involved discussions about education, about ensuring that every child, regardless of their background, had the opportunity to learn and to contribute their unique talents. They spoke of mentorship programs, of apprenticeships that spanned generations, and of creating spaces for shared learning and cultural exchange.

"I've been thinking a great deal about the elders," Mara confided, her voice softening. "Their wisdom is invaluable, and yet, their voices sometimes get lost in the hustle of daily life. We need to create more formal avenues for them to share their knowledge, their histories, their experiences. Perhaps a dedicated archive, or regular storytelling sessions where they can pass on traditions and life lessons to the younger generations. It's not just about practical skills; it's about preserving our identity, our shared heritage."

Eli wrapped an arm around her, drawing her close. "You are so right. Our history, our stories, are the threads that bind us. And the future we build must be strong enough to carry those threads forward. We need to foster a sense of belonging, a deep-rooted connection to Havenridge that transcends individual ambition. It's about creating a culture where people feel valued, where their contributions are recognized, and where they have a stake in the collective well-being."

Their discussions often extended into the late hours, illuminated by the flickering lamplight. They would pore over maps, sketch out plans on scraps of parchment, and debate the merits of different approaches, always with a shared respect and a profound understanding that their combined perspectives were greater than the sum of their individual parts. There were no disagreements that could not be resolved, no challenges that felt insurmountable when they faced them together.

"What about governance?" Eli mused, gesturing with a piece of charcoal. "As Havenridge grows, and our interactions with the outside world increase, our current council structure might need to adapt. We need to think about how we make decisions, how we ensure representation, and how we maintain transparency. We want to remain true to our core values, but also be adaptable enough to navigate a changing world."

Mara picked up the charcoal, adding her own thoughts to the sketch. "A more formalized system of representation, perhaps. Rotating council members from different guilds or districts, ensuring that all voices are heard. And a clear process for dispute resolution, one that emphasizes mediation and understanding over punitive measures. We want to build a community that is not only resilient but also just and equitable."

They spoke of infrastructure, not just the roads and bridges that connected them physically, but the intangible infrastructure of shared knowledge and collective support. They envisioned a Havenridge where resources were pooled efficiently, where innovation was encouraged, and where the pursuit of individual well-being was intrinsically linked to the well-being of the community as a whole.

"We've talked about expanding the educational facilities," Mara recalled, her gaze distant. "Ensuring that we have enough skilled teachers to cater to the growing number of children. And what about specialized training? We have individuals with exceptional talents in fields like herbalism, masonry, and engineering. We need to create pathways for them to hone their skills and pass them on."

"And we must not forget the arts," Eli added, his voice warm with appreciation. "The music that fills our gatherings, the carvings that adorn our buildings, the stories that are passed down. These are not mere diversions; they are essential elements of a vibrant and fulfilling life. We need to ensure that our long-term vision supports and nurtures creativity in all its forms."

Their planning was not rigid or dogmatic; it was fluid and responsive, a continuous process of learning and adaptation. They understood that the future was not a fixed destination, but a landscape that would shift and change, presenting new challenges and new opportunities. Their role, as they saw it, was to lay a strong foundation, to cultivate a spirit of resilience and innovation, and to empower the people of Havenridge to shape their own destinies.

"It's about cultivating a mindset, I think," Mara said, her voice reflective. "A mindset of responsibility, of foresight, and of interconnectedness. Teaching our children to think not just about themselves, but about the impact of their actions on others, on the land, and on the future. That's the most valuable inheritance we can leave them."

Eli squeezed her hand, a deep sense of peace settling over him. He looked at Mara, at the passion and intelligence that shone in her eyes, and felt an overwhelming sense of gratitude. They were more than just partners; they were kindred spirits, bound by a shared vision and a profound love for the community they had helped to build.

"We've come so far, Mara," he murmured, his voice thick with emotion. "From those first hesitant steps, to this – a community looking towards a future with hope and purpose. And it's all because we dared to dream, and more importantly, we dared to build those dreams together."

The moon had risen, casting a soft, silvery light over the valley. The sounds of the village had quieted, replaced by the gentle chirping of crickets and the distant murmur of the river. Eli and Mara remained on the bench, their silhouettes etched against the starlit sky. Their conversation was winding down, but the thoughts, the plans, the shared vision, would continue to germinate, to grow, and to shape the future of Havenridge for generations to come.

They had faced the horizon, not with trepidation, but with a quiet confidence, a deep-seated belief in their ability to navigate whatever lay ahead, together. Their long-term vision was not a static blueprint, but a living, breathing testament to their enduring commitment – to each other, to the land, and to the promise of a brighter tomorrow. The seeds of their foresight, sown in these quiet moments of shared reflection, were already taking root, promising a harvest of prosperity and peace for all who would follow.

The lantern's glow, once a comforting beacon in the deepening twilight, now seemed to cast a more focused beam, illuminating the parchment spread between Mara and Eli. The plans they had meticulously drafted, the projections they had painstakingly calculated, felt both substantial and yet, somehow, incomplete. They had wrestled with the intricacies of water management, the nuances of economic diversification, and the foundational pillars of education and community. But as the moon climbed higher, a quiet understanding settled between them – there was a deeper wellspring of knowledge they needed to tap, a wisdom honed not by numbers and charts, but by seasons lived and lessons learned.

"We've considered the soil, the water, the trade routes," Eli murmured, his gaze drifting towards the clusters of homes that dotted the valley, each one a testament to years of hard work and shared endeavor. "But what of the heart of Havenridge? The continuity of our spirit, the transmission of our values?"

Mara nodded, her hand resting on Eli's. "The council meeting was productive, as you said. The proposals for the expanded water catchment and the new trade agreements were met with enthusiasm. Yet, I felt a familiar pull, a sense that we were missing a vital layer of understanding. Our plans are built on a foundation of what we know now, what we can predict. But the elders... they hold the echoes of times we haven't experienced, the resilience forged in trials we can only imagine."

It was a sentiment they had discussed before, a quiet acknowledgment of the profound respect they held for the elder members of their community. These were the individuals who had weathered the initial storms of Havenridge's founding, who had laid the very groundwork upon which their current prosperity was built. Their memories were living histories, their experiences invaluable guides.

"We need to speak with them," Mara stated, a resolve hardening her voice. "Not just to present our ideas, but to truly listen. To understand how our vision for the future resonates with the lessons of the past. Their perspective is a vital anchor, ensuring that our forward momentum doesn't detach us from the roots that sustain us."

The following morning, under a sky painted with the soft hues of dawn, they made their way to the communal hearth, the traditional gathering place for the village's most seasoned members. A gentle breeze rustled the leaves of the ancient oak that stood sentinel nearby, a silent witness to generations of counsel and camaraderie. Elder Maeve, her face a roadmap of life's journey, her eyes sharp with an enduring clarity, was the first to greet them. Beside her sat Silas, his hands gnarled like the roots of an old tree, and Elara, whose quiet demeanor belied a keen intellect and a deep understanding of the natural world.

"Eli, Mara," Maeve's voice was like the rustling of dry leaves, warm and imbued with a gentle wisdom. "You come with purpose, I sense it. The air around you hums with the energy of planning."

Eli offered a respectful bow. "Indeed, Elder Maeve. We have been working on comprehensive plans for Havenridge's future, focusing on expanding our water resources and diversifying our trade. We believe these initiatives will secure our prosperity for decades to come." He paused, then added, "But we also believe that true foresight requires the wisdom of experience. We have come to seek your counsel, to ensure our path forward honors the legacy you have so diligently built."

Silas grunted, a sound that was neither dismissive nor encouraging, simply... present. "Plans," he rumbled, his voice deep and gravelly. "We've seen many plans bloom in Havenridge. Some wither, some flourish. What makes these different?"

Mara stepped forward, unrolling a section of the parchment. "We are proposing the construction of a network of underground cisterns, coupled with a system of permeable pathways to encourage groundwater replenishment. We also envision expanding our textile production and exploring trade agreements with the coastal communities. The aim is to create a more resilient Havenridge, less susceptible to the whims of drought and market fluctuations."

Maeve leaned closer, her brow furrowed in concentration as she studied the diagrams. "The cisterns," she mused, tracing a line with a calloused finger. "A wise endeavor. We learned the hard way, many seasons ago, when the river dwindled to a trickle for three full years. We lost so much. But remember, the earth breathes. Do not seal it entirely. Allow it to exchange, to replenish, lest you create a void that is hard to fill."

Elara, who had been observing with quiet intensity, finally spoke. "The permeability is key, as you've noted. But also consider the source of the replenishment. Are you planning to reroute any natural streams, or disturb established drainage patterns? The smallest shift can have unforeseen consequences on the flora and fauna that rely on those flows. We've cultivated a delicate balance, and any intervention must be approached with the utmost care, ensuring new channels are designed to mimic natural contours where possible, and that native vegetation is prioritized for its role in filtration and soil stability."

Eli and Mara exchanged a glance. Elara's insights, particularly regarding the ecological integration, were invaluable. They had discussed these points with her in their preliminary stages, but hearing her reinforce their importance, and offer even finer detail, was precisely why they sought this council.

"You speak of trade," Silas interjected, his gaze fixed on the section detailing textile exports. "Fine fabrics are good. But do not forget the soil that grows the flax, the pastures that feed the sheep. A strong harvest ensures a strong community. If you send too much out, what will you have left for yourselves when the seasons turn sour?"

"That is a concern we have addressed, Silas," Eli replied, his voice steady. "Our plans include strategies for soil enrichment and crop rotation to ensure continued fertility. And the expansion of textile production is carefully calibrated. We are not looking to deplete our resources, but to create value from them in a sustainable manner. We believe the increased income from trade will allow us to invest further in our agricultural practices, to actually *enhance* our yields and soil health in the long run."

Maeve nodded slowly. "A fair point. The old ways taught us the rhythm of the land. Take too much, and it will eventually take from you. But wise husbandry can ensure abundance. We remember the lean years, yes, but we also remember the bountiful ones. The challenge is always to prepare for the lean, without sacrificing the present."

"And the diversity you speak of," Maeve continued, her gaze now sweeping across the faces gathered, "it is good. A single crop, a single craft, is a fragile thing. But how will you ensure that this diversity is accessible to all? That it doesn't create new divisions, new haves and have-nots?"

This was a question that resonated deeply with Mara. The social fabric of Havenridge was as crucial as its economic or ecological stability. "That is precisely why we are also proposing expanded mentorship programs and apprenticeships," she explained. "We want to ensure that knowledge and skills are shared across generations and across different disciplines. We envision a system where anyone with the aptitude and the desire can learn, whether it's advanced weaving techniques, water management, or sustainable farming practices. Our goal is not just to grow stronger, but to grow together."

Silas leaned back, his eyes closed for a moment. "Mentorship," he repeated softly. "That is the true legacy. The stories we tell, the hands that guide the young. We have seen too many talents wither because no one took the time to see them, to nurture them. If your plans truly foster that, then you are on solid ground."

Elara added, "And consider the knowledge held within the wild places. The medicinal properties of plants, the habits of animals that can inform our planting cycles, the subtle signs of changing weather. These are not things found on parchment. They are learned through observation, through patience, through a deep respect for the non-human inhabitants of our world. Integrating this observational knowledge into your educational programs would be a profound step towards true sustainability."

The conversation flowed, unhurried and rich. They spoke of the importance of communal decision-making, of ensuring that the voices of all, not just the elders, were heard and valued. The elders shared stories of past challenges – of near-starvation during a prolonged winter, of a devastating blight that had threatened their livestock, of disputes that had tested the community's resolve. Each anecdote was a lesson, a reminder of the fragility of their existence and the strength that came from unity.

"You plan for the future," Maeve said, her voice taking on a reflective tone, "but do not forget to honor the past. Our histories are not mere tales; they are the bedrock of our identity. When you build your new cisterns, do you remember the wells our ancestors dug with their bare hands? When you weave your new fabrics, do you recall the simple looms that first clothed us?"

Mara felt a pang of recognition. They had spoken of preserving history, but perhaps not with the same reverence Maeve conveyed. "We have been considering an archive," Mara admitted, "a place to store our records, our stories. But perhaps it needs to be more than just a repository. Perhaps it needs to be a living space, a place where the elders can share their memories, where the young can actively engage with our history."

Silas nodded, a flicker of approval in his eyes. "A place for the old to speak, and for the young to listen. That is a good start. But remember, history is not just written. It is sung. It is danced. It is woven into the very fabric of our lives. The songs we sing at harvest, the lullabies we sing to our children – they carry the weight of centuries. Ensure these traditions are not lost in the pursuit of novelty."

Eli looked at his hands, the hands that had worked the soil, built the shelters, and now, helped to shape the future. "We are charting a course for growth, for progress," he acknowledged. "But your words remind us that true progress is not about forgetting where we came from, but about carrying the best of it forward. The resilience you have demonstrated, the community you have fostered – that is the inheritance we must safeguard."

The elders spoke of the subtle signs of the land, the language of the birds, the patterns of the clouds, the scent of the earth after rain. They described how these observations, honed over a lifetime, offered a deeper understanding of the world than any written record. Elara elaborated on how these traditional ecological knowledge systems were vital for adapting to changing environmental conditions.

"The seasons are not as predictable as they once were," Elara observed. "The old timers would notice subtle shifts, a change in the wind's direction, a particular kind of insect appearing earlier than usual. These were not superstitions, but keen observations passed down through generations. Incorporating these intuitive understandings into our meteorological predictions, our agricultural planning... that could be a significant advantage."

Maeve added, "And the spirit of the community. It is not built on plans and projections alone. It is built on shared burdens, on laughter around the fire, on the helping hand offered without being asked. As you expand, as you connect with the world beyond Havenridge, remember the core of what makes us strong: our interconnectedness, our willingness to sacrifice for one another."

Silas, who had been particularly quiet for a while, spoke again, his voice carrying a weight of accumulated experience. "There will be challenges. New ideas often bring new conflicts. Do not shy away from them. Seek to understand, not to conquer. The strongest bonds are forged in the fires of disagreement, when faced with honesty and a shared commitment to the well-being of all."

He looked at Eli and Mara, his gaze steady. "You have vision. You have drive. But wisdom is a slow-growing tree. Do not be in too great a hurry to lop off the branches that seem old. They may yet bear the sweetest fruit, or offer the deepest shade when the sun burns too hot."

As the sun began its descent, painting the sky in hues of orange and gold, Eli and Mara gathered their parchments, their minds not burdened, but enriched. The counsel of the elders had not altered their plans so much as it had deepened their understanding of them. It had infused their projections with a sense of history, their innovations with a grounding in tradition, and their aspirations for growth with a profound respect for continuity.

"They are right," Mara said softly, as they walked back towards their home, the scent of woodsmoke and evening blossoms filling the air. "Our plans are good. They are necessary. But they are only the framework. The wisdom of the elders, the stories they carry, the spirit of community they embody – that is the heart and soul of

Havenridge. And that is what we must truly endeavor to preserve and nurture for the generations to come."

Eli squeezed her hand, a sense of quiet gratitude settling over him. "We are building not just for the future, but with the wisdom of the past. And with their guidance, I believe we can face whatever horizon lies before us, stronger and more connected than ever." The elders' council had offered more than just advice; it had offered a vital thread, weaving the past into the fabric of their future, ensuring that Havenridge would continue to be a place of enduring strength, rooted in tradition and reaching for the stars.

Mara's leadership in sustainable practices wasn't merely a professional pursuit; it was an intrinsic extension of her being, a calling that had only deepened since her partnership with Eli solidified. The gentle hum of their shared life now resonated with a profound purpose, allowing her to channel an energy she'd previously held in reserve.

The land, which had always whispered its needs to her, now seemed to sing, its song amplified by the security of knowing she wasn't alone in listening. Her vision for Havenridge was one of harmonious coexistence, where prosperity didn't come at the earth's expense, but rather, was nurtured by its bounty. This wasn't a radical overhaul, but a thoughtful, organic evolution, building upon the wisdom of generations and the innovative spirit of their present.

Her first major endeavor, born from countless hours spent with Eli poring over soil samples and rainfall charts, was the comprehensive "Havenridge Greening Initiative." This wasn't just about planting trees, though that was a vital component. It was a multi-faceted approach to ecological stewardship. Mara began by establishing a community-wide composting program. She personally oversaw the initial setup, converting a section of the old communal farmlands into a series of strategically placed composting bins. She organized workshops, drawing on the knowledge of the elders who remembered the intricate art of turning organic waste into rich, life-giving soil.

Elara, with her intimate understanding of fungi and microbial decomposition, was an invaluable consultant, guiding Mara on optimal moisture levels and aeration techniques. The workshops were lively affairs, filled with the scent of damp earth and the enthusiastic chatter of residents eager to contribute. Children, with their boundless energy, were tasked with collecting kitchen scraps from households, transforming a chore into an engaging lesson in resourcefulness. Mara, with her infectious enthusiasm, would often join them, her laughter mingling with theirs as they explained the magic of turning discarded peels and stems into the foundation of future harvests.

Parallel to the composting initiative, Mara spearheaded a significant reforestation project. She identified areas within Havenridge that had been heavily utilized in the past, some showing signs of erosion or depleted soil. Working with Silas, whose knowledge of native tree species and their ecological roles was unparalleled, she selected a diverse range of saplings: sturdy oaks for their longevity and timber potential, fast-growing poplars for shade and windbreak, and fruit-bearing trees like apple and pear, adding another layer of food security.

The community planting days became a cherished tradition. Families worked side-by-side, digging holes, carefully placing saplings, and tamping down the soil. Mara, often with Eli by her side, would move among them, offering encouragement, sharing stories of the trees' resilience, and explaining the vital role they played in maintaining water tables and preventing soil degradation. She emphasized that these trees were not just ornaments, but an investment in Havenridge's future, a living legacy for generations yet to come.

Mara's commitment to organic farming practices was equally unwavering. She recognized that Havenridge's agricultural heart was its strength, and that strength needed to be preserved and enhanced through methods that worked in harmony with nature, not against it. She worked closely with the farmers, encouraging the phasing out of chemical fertilizers and pesticides in favor of natural alternatives. This involved extensive research and collaboration with agricultural experts from neighboring communities.

She facilitated the exchange of knowledge, organizing visits to farms that had already successfully transitioned to organic methods. Mara herself experimented on a small plot adjacent to her home, showcasing the effectiveness of companion planting, crop rotation, and natural pest deterrents. She invited anyone to visit, to see firsthand how ladybugs could be a farmer's best friend, how marigolds could deter nematodes, and how a carefully planned rotation could replenish the soil's nutrients naturally. Her own garden became a vibrant testament to her beliefs, a riot of color and life, teeming with beneficial insects and thriving vegetables.

Water conservation was another area where Mara's leadership shone brightly. Having grown up with an acute awareness of water's preciousness, she championed the expansion and optimization of Havenridge's water catchment systems. Building on the elders' ancestral knowledge of natural water flows and the community's existing infrastructure, she designed a comprehensive plan.

This included the installation of more extensive rainwater harvesting systems on public buildings and private homes, the creation of swales and berms to slow and capture rainwater runoff on agricultural lands, and the careful monitoring and maintenance of the existing reservoir to ensure its longevity. She advocated for the use of greywater recycling systems for non-potable uses like irrigation, a concept that initially met with some skepticism but was soon embraced after Mara demonstrated its efficiency and water-saving potential on a pilot project at the community center.

Her presentations on water conservation were always filled with compelling data, illustrating the impact of even small changes on overall water security, but they were also infused with her personal passion, her belief that every drop saved was a testament to their respect for the natural world.

Responsible resource management extended beyond agriculture and water. Mara initiated a community-wide drive to reduce waste and promote recycling. She established clear guidelines for separating recyclable materials and organized regular collection points. She championed the repair and reuse of tools and equipment, fostering a culture of longevity and resourcefulness. She even explored the potential for renewable energy sources, initiating discussions about small-scale wind turbines and solar panels for public buildings, recognizing that Havenridge's future prosperity depended on weaning itself from less sustainable energy dependencies. This wasn't about drastic upheaval, but about incremental, thoughtful changes that, over time, would significantly reduce their ecological footprint.

What truly set Mara apart was her ability to inspire. She didn't just implement policies; she embodied them. Her days were filled with a tireless dedication to these initiatives. Whether she was overseeing the construction of a new composting bin, walking the fields with farmers, or explaining the intricacies of a greywater system to a group of curious villagers, her passion was palpable. She celebrated every success, no matter how small, and always framed setbacks as opportunities for learning and adaptation. She made a point of engaging with every member of the community, from the youngest children to the most seasoned elders, ensuring that everyone felt a part of the collective effort. She understood that true sustainability wasn't just about ecological balance, but about fostering a shared sense of responsibility and pride in their stewardship of Havenridge.

Her partnership with Eli provided her with a strong foundation of support and encouragement. In the quiet evenings, after long days spent advocating for the earth, they would discuss the progress, the challenges, and the dreams they held for Havenridge's future. Eli's steady presence, his belief in her vision, and his willingness to help wherever needed were invaluable. He often assisted with the more labor-intensive aspects of the projects, his strength and practical skills complementing Mara's organizational and inspirational talents. Their shared commitment to a sustainable Havenridge was a cornerstone of their relationship, a silent promise to protect and nurture the land that sustained them.

One of Mara's most impactful contributions was the establishment of the "Havenridge Seed Bank." Recognizing the importance of preserving genetic diversity and ensuring future food security, she worked with the elders to collect and store seeds from a wide variety of heirloom crops. This involved meticulous documentation, ensuring that each seed was labeled with its origin, its growing requirements, and any traditional knowledge associated with it.

The seed bank was housed in a cool, dry, and secure location within the community archives, a testament to the foresight and dedication of those who had cultivated these varieties for generations. Mara saw it as a living library, a vital insurance policy against unforeseen environmental changes or agricultural challenges. She organized annual "Seed Swaps," events that not only facilitated the exchange of seeds but also served as vibrant celebrations of Havenridge's agricultural heritage, bringing together farmers, gardeners, and enthusiasts to share their bounty and their knowledge.

Mara also recognized the crucial role of education in fostering a culture of sustainability. She developed and implemented educational programs for all ages. For the children, she created engaging workshops that taught them about the life cycle of plants, the importance of bees, and the magic of decomposition. These were often hands-on experiences, involving planting seeds, tending to a small garden at the school, and visiting the community compost site. For adults, she organized more in-depth seminars on topics such as permaculture design, water-wise gardening, and the economic benefits of sustainable practices.

She invited guest speakers, experts in their fields, to share their knowledge and inspire new approaches. She also championed the integration of ecological principles into the general curriculum, ensuring that future generations of Havenridge residents would grow up with a deep understanding and appreciation for the natural world.

Her leadership wasn't always met with immediate universal acclaim. Some were resistant to change, comfortable with the old ways, or skeptical of the long-term benefits. Mara approached these challenges with patience and understanding. She would listen intently to their concerns, acknowledge their perspectives, and then, with gentle persistence, present the evidence, share success stories, and highlight the tangible benefits for their families and the community as a whole. She understood that building trust and fostering genuine buy-in was as crucial as any policy or program.

Her genuine passion and unwavering commitment, coupled with the tangible positive outcomes of her initiatives, gradually won over even the most hesitant members of the community. The increased yields from the organic farms, the noticeable improvement in soil health, the reduced reliance on external resources – these were all testament to her vision.

Mara's efforts also extended to the conservation of Havenridge's natural beauty. She advocated for the protection of local wildlife habitats, working with the elders to identify and preserve areas of ecological significance. She initiated projects to restore and maintain walking trails, ensuring that the natural beauty of the valley was accessible to all while minimizing human impact. She organized regular clean-up drives along the riverbanks and in the surrounding forests, fostering a sense of shared responsibility for the environment.

Her belief was that by actively engaging with and protecting the natural world around them, the people of Havenridge would deepen their connection to their home and their commitment to its long-term well-being. She saw the vibrant wildflowers in the meadows, the clear water of the river, and the ancient trees in the forest not just as natural resources, but as integral parts of Havenridge's soul, deserving of reverence and protection.

The impact of Mara's leadership rippled through every aspect of Havenridge life. The "Havenridge Greening Initiative" became more than just a series of projects; it became a philosophy, a way of life. The community's commitment to sustainability fostered a renewed sense of unity and purpose. People worked together, shared knowledge, and celebrated their collective achievements.

Mara's dedication, fueled by her love for Eli and her deep reverence for the land, had transformed Havenridge into a beacon of ecological responsibility, a testament to what could be achieved when vision, passion, and a commitment to the earth converged. Her legacy was being written not just in the fertile soil and the thriving forests, but in the hearts and minds of every resident, who now understood that true prosperity lay in living in balance with the world that sustained them.

Eli's role in community resilience was a quiet but profoundly impactful counterpoint to Mara's more visible ecological initiatives. While Mara's passion ignited the spirit of Havenridge, Eli's pragmatism and foresight built the sturdy scaffolding that would support their shared vision through any storm. His was the meticulous planning, the behind-the-scenes strategizing that ensured Havenridge wasn't just beautiful and sustainable, but also robust and prepared. His contributions were less about the outward manifestation of growth and more about the inner strength and adaptability of the community, a testament to his belief that true prosperity was rooted in security and self-sufficiency.

He understood that even the most vibrant ecosystem could be vulnerable. A harsh winter, a prolonged drought beyond the scope of Mara's water conservation efforts, or an unforeseen external challenge could test the resilience of Havenridge in ways they hadn't yet fully experienced. This awareness spurred him to focus on developing tangible contingency plans. He didn't possess Mara's natural gift for inspiring grand gestures, but he had an uncanny ability to anticipate potential problems and devise practical solutions. His evenings, often spent with Mara discussing the day's events, were also filled with his own quiet contemplations on risk assessment and preparedness.

One of Eli's primary focuses was on resourcefulness. He believed that the greatest strength of Havenridge lay not just in its natural bounty, but in the ingenuity and collective spirit of its people. He began by systematically cataloging the skills and knowledge present within the community. This wasn't a formal survey, but a series of informal conversations, observations during community gatherings, and an astute understanding of who excelled at what. He noted the individuals with a deep understanding of mechanics, those skilled in first aid, the resourceful seamstresses, the carpenters, the experienced foragers, and those with a knack for communication. This mental inventory became the bedrock of his preparedness strategy.

He initiated a series of "Skill-Share" workshops, distinct from Mara's educational programs. While Mara's focused on sustainability and ecological practices, Eli's aimed at practical, survival-oriented skills. He organized sessions on basic home repairs, teaching residents how to address common issues before they became major problems. He facilitated workshops on preserving food beyond the usual canning methods, exploring techniques like drying, salting, and smoking that relied on minimal external resources. He encouraged the revival of traditional crafts that had fallen by the wayside, recognizing their inherent value in a situation where manufactured goods might become scarce. He even worked with the younger generation, teaching them knot-tying, fire-starting without matches, and basic navigation, skills that might seem archaic in their current comfortable existence but were essential for self-reliance.

Eli also turned his attention to Havenridge's infrastructure, ensuring it was as robust as possible. He worked with the community council to assess the state of their communal buildings, the integrity of their bridges, and the reliability of their energy systems. He wasn't afraid to advocate for necessary, albeit sometimes costly, upgrades. He meticulously planned for potential power outages, organizing the stockpiling of non-perishable fuel sources and exploring the feasibility of redundant backup power options, perhaps a small, community-managed generator that could be powered by biofuels developed through Mara's initiatives. He understood that a community's ability to withstand disruption was directly linked to the reliability of its fundamental services.

His work with the water system, in collaboration with Mara, extended beyond conservation to emergency preparedness. He ensured that the reservoir had multiple overflow points to prevent catastrophic failure and that the filtration systems were robust and easily maintainable. He explored the possibility of establishing smaller, decentralized water collection and purification points throughout Havenridge, providing redundancy in case the main system was compromised. This involved detailed hydrological surveys and a deep understanding of the local topography, an area where his innate sense of place served him well.

Eli also championed the concept of communal resource sharing. He recognized that in times of scarcity, pooling resources could be the difference between hardship and survival. He proposed the establishment of a community "reserve" – a carefully managed stockpile of essential goods: non-perishable food items, basic medical supplies, tools, and materials for repair. This wasn't about creating a free-for-all, but a structured system governed by clear protocols, ensuring equitable distribution in emergencies while also discouraging hoarding or misuse. He spent countless hours debating the logistics with the council, ensuring the reserve was accessible, secure, and replenished consistently.

His belief in the strength of Mara's vision was a constant source of motivation. He saw his role as strengthening the foundations upon which her ecological dream was built. He knew that a thriving environment was only truly sustainable if the community that stewarded it was resilient. He often used the analogy of a strong root system: Mara's initiatives were the leaves and branches, reaching out and drawing sustenance, while his work was to ensure the roots were deep, secure, and able to withstand drought and storm. He took pride in the fact that his pragmatic approach complemented her inspirational leadership, creating a balanced and formidable force for Havenridge's future.

Eli's contributions were often understated, manifesting not in grand pronouncements but in the quiet confidence that settled over the community. When a sudden, unseasonal frost threatened the early fruit blossoms, it was the community's preparedness for such eventualities, a network of protective coverings and shared knowledge he had helped foster, that minimized the damage. When a vital piece of agricultural machinery broke down during harvest, it was the readily available spare parts and the skilled mechanic he had identified and encouraged through his workshops who ensured the harvest continued. These were the quiet victories, the evidence of a community strengthened from within.

He understood that resilience wasn't just about surviving crises; it was also about fostering a mindset of proactive adaptation. He encouraged a culture where questions were welcomed, where potential problems were discussed openly, and where solutions were sought collaboratively. He was a constant advocate for learning from every experience, whether a minor inconvenience or a significant challenge. His own approach was one of continuous learning and refinement, always seeking to improve Havenridge's ability to navigate the unpredictable currents of life.

Eli's belief in the enduring strength of Havenridge was rooted in his deep appreciation for its people and their collective spirit. He saw how Mara's initiatives had brought them together, fostering a sense of shared purpose. His work was to ensure that this unity was not fragile, but forged in the fires of preparation and mutual reliance. He meticulously mapped out evacuation routes and contingency plans for different scenarios, working with the local leaders to establish clear communication channels and responsibilities. He understood that in a crisis, clear leadership and coordinated action were paramount.

His dedication was a steady flame, burning brightly in the background of Havenridge's burgeoning ecological renaissance. While Mara painted the vibrant future, Eli ensured the canvas was strong and the easel stable. His strategic thinking, his focus on practical skills, and his unwavering commitment to infrastructure and preparedness provided a vital layer of security, ensuring that Havenridge's horizon, however bright, was also a safe and stable one. He was the silent guardian, the pragmatic architect of their enduring stability, his belief in the power of a prepared community as strong as his love for Mara and their shared home.

The shared weight of their vision settled upon Mara and Eli not as a burden, but as a profound affirmation. As they walked hand-in-hand through the twilight-kissed pathways of Havenridge, the scent of blooming night jasmine a gentle caress, they spoke of the quiet understanding that had blossomed between them. It wasn't just the grand pronouncements of ecological stewardship or the meticulous planning for unforeseen challenges that defined their role. It was the subtle, yet powerful, fusion of their individual destinies into a singular, unwavering commitment to this place and its people.

Mara's heart swelled with a tenderness that was as vast as the star-dusted sky above. She had always been drawn to the outward expression of growth, the vibrant unfolding of life, and Eli's steady presence had anchored her, providing a grounding force that allowed her vision to take flight without fear of falling. His foresight, his ability to anticipate the shadows before they fell, had not diminished her passion; it had amplified it, giving her the confidence to dream bolder, to reach further. She saw how his pragmatic approach, his meticulous attention to detail, wove a protective tapestry around the delicate threads of her ecological initiatives. He was the sturdy trunk that supported the burgeoning branches, the deep roots that ensured sustenance even in the harshest seasons.

"Do you ever feel it, Eli?" Mara's voice was soft, almost a whisper, as they paused by the whispering stream that meandered through the heart of Havenridge. "This immense responsibility? It's more than just our lives now, isn't it? It's a thousand futures, a thousand stories waiting to be written."

Eli squeezed her hand, his thumb tracing slow, comforting circles on her skin. "I feel it, Mara. Every single day. But it doesn't weigh me down. It... it fuels me. It's a reminder of what we're building, of what truly matters." He looked out at the scattered lights of the homes, each one a testament to the lives they were helping to nurture. "Before Havenridge, my days were filled with charts and projections, calculating risks in a world that felt abstract. Now, every plan, every precaution, has a face. It has a name. It's Mrs. Gable tending her prize-winning roses, it's young Leo learning to identify edible berries, it's the laughter of children playing in the community garden."

Their partnership, born from a shared love for this land and a mutual respect for each other's strengths, had become the very bedrock of Havenridge's enduring resilience. They had learned, through countless discussions under the moon and shared endeavors under the sun, that true strength lay not in individual brilliance, but in the harmonious integration of diverse talents. Mara's ability to inspire, to paint vivid pictures of a thriving future, ignited the collective spirit. Eli's capacity to meticulously plan, to anticipate and mitigate risks, provided the framework for that inspiration to flourish, ensuring that the dreams they shared were built on a foundation of unshakeable security.

He remembered the initial workshops he had organized, the hesitant murmurs of residents unsure of the practical application of learning basic knot-tying or fire-starting. Mara, with her characteristic warmth, had been instrumental in encouraging participation, framing these seemingly rudimentary skills not as relics of the past, but as vital tools for self-reliance, empowering elements that would complement the broader ecological goals. She understood that a community's ability to thrive was intrinsically linked to its people's sense of agency and preparedness.

"It's funny, isn't it?" Mara mused, her gaze drifting towards the community greenhouse, its glass panes glowing softly under the porch lights. "I used to think that nurturing the earth was the ultimate act of creation. And it is, in so many ways. But seeing the way people here have embraced the skills you've taught them, the way they've started sharing them with each other... that feels like a different kind of growth, a more profound one." She turned back to Eli, her eyes shining. "It's the growth of independence, of quiet confidence. It's the realization that they, too, are stewards of their own well-being, and by extension, the well-being of Havenridge."

Eli nodded, a gentle smile touching his lips. He recalled the time a sudden storm had threatened to flood a low-lying section of the community, near the ancient oak grove. Mara had been focused on rallying everyone to reinforce the natural drainage channels, her voice a beacon of calm amidst the rising wind. But it was the swift, organized response of those he had trained in basic emergency preparedness – the immediate deployment of sandbags, the efficient routing of water away from homes, the calm communication between teams – that had prevented significant damage. It was a testament to their combined efforts, a practical demonstration of their shared responsibility bearing fruit.

"That's the beauty of it, Mara," he said, his voice resonating with quiet pride. "You inspire the 'why,' and I try to facilitate the 'how.' When we work together, the 'why' becomes actionable, and the 'how' becomes meaningful. It's not just about surviving a storm; it's about knowing, deep down, that we have the collective capacity to weather it, and even to learn from it." He paused, his thoughts drifting to the community reserve he had meticulously planned. "The reserve, for instance. It's more than just stockpiled supplies. It's a symbol of trust, of mutual reliance. It says that we believe in each other enough to pool our resources, to ensure that no one is left vulnerable."

Mara leaned her head against his shoulder, a contented sigh escaping her. "And we chose this, Eli. We chose this responsibility. It wasn't thrust upon us. We saw the potential, we felt the calling, and we committed ourselves to it. That choice, I think, is what makes all the difference. It infuses everything we do with a different kind of energy, a deeper purpose."

Her words echoed his own sentiments. Their love for each other had been the initial spark, a powerful force that had drawn them together. But it was the shared purpose, the deliberate choice to invest their lives in the well-being of Havenridge, that had transformed that love into something enduring and impactful. They were not merely inhabitants; they were architects of its future, weaving their lives into the very fabric of its existence.

"Every decision we make, every plan we implement," Eli continued, "it's a thread in the tapestry of Havenridge's legacy. We're not just building a sustainable community; we're building a tradition of care, of foresight, of collective strength. We're showing that love isn't just a feeling; it's an action. It's the commitment to ensuring that the ground beneath our feet remains fertile, and the hands that tend it are capable and united."

He thought of the community's response to the unexpected blight that had threatened the staple crops last season. Mara's knowledge of natural pest control had been crucial, but it was Eli's foresight in diversifying the crop types, a measure he had advocated for during a particularly lean planning session, that had prevented widespread food scarcity. And it was the rapid, coordinated response of the community members, many of whom had participated in the planting and harvesting strategies he'd helped them develop, that had allowed them to recover swiftly. Each challenge, faced together, had only solidified their bond and demonstrated the efficacy of their combined leadership.

"Remember when we first started discussing the decentralized water collection points?" Mara asked, a smile playing on her lips. "Some of the older council members were skeptical, worried about the added complexity. But you patiently explained the redundancy, the increased security it offered, and I painted a picture of how it would look, like little veins of lifeblood feeding into every corner of our community, even if the main artery was compromised."

"And you were right," Eli replied. "It was your vision that made them see the beauty in the practicality. It's that balance, isn't it? Your ability to see the soul of the project, and mine to ensure its bones are strong enough to carry it." He stopped, turning to face her fully, his gaze warm and unwavering. "This partnership, Mara, it's more than just a personal commitment. It's a vital component of Havenridge's enduring strength. We are a testament to what happens when love and purpose intertwine, when two individuals choose to build something larger than themselves, together."

Mara reached up, her fingers brushing a stray strand of hair from his forehead. "And I wouldn't trade it for anything, Eli. This shared responsibility, this life we've chosen to build here, it's the greatest gift. It's the legacy we are actively creating, not just for ourselves, but for every generation that will call Havenridge home." The air was thick with the unspoken understanding that their journey was far from over, but in this shared moment, under the watchful gaze of the stars, they found a profound peace, a quiet strength in the knowledge that together, they were facing the horizon, ready for whatever it might hold. Their love, once a personal flame, had become a beacon, illuminating the path forward for their cherished community.

Chapter Ten

ECHOES OF THE PAST, SEEDS OF THE FUTURE

The air, crisp with the early autumn chill, carried the faint, earthy scent of fallen leaves as Mara and Eli found themselves drawn back to the northern ridge. It wasn't a place of grand vistas or scenic overlooks; instead, it was a quiet, unassuming clearing, marked by a gnarled old oak that had stubbornly resisted the encroaching winds of time. This was where their journey had truly begun, not with a grand unveiling, but with a hesitant, almost fearful exploration of what Havenridge could become. The memory of their first days here, the skepticism they had faced, the sheer weight of doubt that had hung heavy in the air, was etched into the very soil beneath their feet.

Mara traced the rough bark of the oak, her fingers finding familiar grooves and imperfections. "Do you remember this tree?" she asked, her voice soft, tinged with a nostalgia that resonated deeply within Eli. "We sat here for hours that first week, just... talking. Trying to convince ourselves, more than anyone else, that this wasn't a fool's errand." The clearing was still much as it had been then, a testament to the deliberate decision to preserve the wildness of certain spaces, a reminder of the raw, untamed spirit that had first captured their imaginations. The only difference was the subtle presence of a few well-worn stones arranged in a circle, a silent testament to the gatherings they had held here, the tentative seeds of community sown under this very tree.

Eli leaned against the sturdy trunk, his gaze sweeping over the landscape. "I remember. You were sketching plans for the arboretum, drawing those intricate root systems and imagining them spreading beneath the earth. I was wrestling with the budget projections, trying to make them align with your boundless optimism." A faint smile touched his lips. "We were quite the pair, weren't we? The dreamer and the pragmatist, both equally convinced that Havenridge held a promise worth fighting for, even when others saw only challenges." He recalled the gnawing uncertainty that had accompanied those early days, the nights spent poring over maps and feasibility studies, the constant internal debate about whether they were truly equipped for the task ahead.

"And the wind," Mara added, a light laugh escaping her. "It felt like it was trying to blow our ideas away, didn't it? Every gust seemed to whisper doubts, to remind us of the immense effort it would take to coax life and order from this wilderness. We had to build not just structures and systems, but belief. We had to build a collective faith in what was possible." She remembered the arduous process of clearing the land, the initial resistance from some of the older residents who were wary of change, the sheer physical and emotional toll it had taken. Yet, even in the midst of those struggles, there had been moments of unexpected beauty, of shared purpose that had forged their resolve.

Eli reached out, his hand finding hers, their fingers intertwining. "It's funny how those moments of doubt, those initial struggles, have become the very foundations of our strength. We didn't just overcome obstacles; we learned from them. We learned how to listen, how to adapt, how to find solutions where none seemed to exist." He thought of the initial resistance to the idea of communal farming, the fear of relinquishing individual plots.

It had taken countless hours of patient explanation, of demonstrating the benefits of shared resources and collaborative effort, of Mara's ability to articulate the vision of abundance and shared harvest, and his own to break down the practical steps involved. The success of those first communal harvests, the bounty they had shared, had been a powerful turning point, silencing many of the lingering doubts.

"Remember the first workshop on rainwater harvesting?" Mara reminisced, her eyes sparkling with the memory. "We were so worried no one would show up. It was a sweltering day, and the concept felt... foreign to many. They were used to the old ways, to relying on the main reservoir. But then, young Leo, barely ten years old, started asking questions with such enthusiasm, and soon others were drawn in. He pointed out how the roof of his grandfather's shed could be a source, and suddenly, it wasn't just a technical lesson; it was about practical ingenuity, about harnessing what was already there." She saw in that moment the beginning of a shift, the awakening of a proactive spirit within the community.

Eli nodded, the memory vivid. "And you, Mara, you took his idea and wove it into a narrative. You spoke about the resilience of water, how it finds its own path, and how we could learn from that, create our own network of sustenance. You made it poetic, and I made sure the measurements and materials were sound." He remembered the careful calculations involved in designing the catchment systems, the consideration of different rainfall patterns, the meticulous planning to ensure the collected water was safe and accessible. "It was a perfect example of how our different approaches complement each other. Your vision inspires the heart, and my planning ensures the head is satisfied."

They walked further into the clearing, the silence between them comfortable, punctuated only by the rustling leaves. The gnarled oak stood as a silent sentinel, a marker of their shared history. This was not about dwelling on past hardships, but about acknowledging the crucible in which their partnership, and Havenridge itself, had been forged. The difficulties had been real, the anxieties palpable, but they had navigated them together, each challenge serving as a stepping stone, solidifying their resolve and deepening their understanding of each other.

"The biggest surprise, for me," Eli confessed, his voice thoughtful, "was how much I came to rely on your... intuition, Mara. There were times when the data was inconclusive, when the projections offered no clear path forward. And you would just *know*. You'd sense the right direction, the unspoken need of the land or the people. It was something I couldn't quantify, but it was always, invariably, correct."

He thought of the decision to shift from a solely solar-powered energy grid to incorporating wind turbines. The initial data had favored a pure solar approach, but Mara had felt an unease, a sense of vulnerability in relying on a single source. She had spoken of the ancient stories of the wind, of its power and its constancy, and it had prompted him to conduct a more thorough analysis of wind patterns, leading to the innovative hybrid system that now powered Havenridge with remarkable efficiency.

Mara squeezed his hand, a warm blush rising to her cheeks. "And I, Eli, learned to trust your meticulous nature, your unwavering commitment to detail. There were times when my enthusiasm might have overlooked a critical flaw, a potential pitfall. You were always there, the steady hand guiding us away from the precipice. You made sure that the dreams we chased were grounded in reality, that our aspirations had a solid framework to hold them."

She remembered the early days of the community's financial management, her tendency to focus on the grand vision rather than the nitty-gritty of bookkeeping. Eli's patient tutelage, his insistence on transparent accounting and responsible resource allocation, had been instrumental in establishing the financial stability that allowed Havenridge to thrive.

They reached a small, moss-covered stone bench nestled beneath the oak's sprawling branches. It was a simple structure, hand-built by Eli and a few early volunteers during a particularly gruelingly productive weekend. Sitting there, the familiar scent of damp earth and decaying leaves filling the air, they allowed themselves a moment of quiet contemplation. This was not a time for planning or for future-oriented discussions, but a pause, a breath, to honor the journey.

"It's like... looking back at old photographs," Mara mused, her gaze distant. "You see the younger versions of yourselves, the awkwardness, the uncertainty. But you also see the beginnings of who you were becoming, the nascent strengths that would later define you. This clearing, this tree, this bench – they are our photographs." She gestured to the landscape around them. "Every challenge we faced here, every disagreement we worked through, every small victory we celebrated, it all contributed to the resilience we have now. It's why we don't flinch at the unexpected, why we approach every new hurdle not with fear, but with a quiet confidence."

Eli sat beside her, his arm wrapping around her shoulders, drawing her close. "And it's why our bond is as strong as this old oak, Mara. We didn't just fall in love; we built a life together, brick by painstaking brick, decision by deliberate decision, here, on this land. We learned to navigate storms, both literal and metaphorical, side-by-side. We learned that true strength isn't about never falling, but about always getting back up, together."

He thought of the time a late-season frost had threatened to decimate the newly planted fruit trees. Mara's knowledge of frost protection techniques had been invaluable, but it was Eli's foresight in establishing a contingency fund, a small but crucial buffer, that had allowed them to purchase the necessary protective coverings and replace any trees that were lost.

"Remember that first community meeting after the initial land clearing?" Mara's voice was light, a hint of amusement coloring her tone. "Everyone was exhausted, covered in dirt, and a little grumpy. I was trying to rally them for the next phase, talking about soil enrichment and sustainable agriculture, and the energy was... low. Then you stood up, Eli, and you didn't talk about yields or budgets. You talked about the satisfaction of creating something with your own hands, the dignity of honest work, and the quiet pride of building a home that would last." She chuckled. "It was so fundamentally *you*, and it worked like magic. You reminded them of the 'why' behind all the 'hows.'"

Eli smiled, the warmth of the memory settling over him. "And you, Mara, you followed up by envisioning the future harvests, the shared meals, the children playing under the shade of the trees we were planting. You painted a picture so vivid, so full of life, that it made the hard work feel not just bearable, but deeply meaningful. We were planting not just trees, but a legacy."

He looked out at the sprawling valley below, dotted with the lights of Havenridge, each one a beacon of the life they had cultivated. "These reflections, they aren't about dwelling on the past, are they? They're about recognizing the path we've traveled, the lessons learned, and the strength we've gained. They're about appreciating the foundation upon which we continue to build."

As the sun began its slow descent, casting long shadows across the clearing, they remained on the bench, a quiet testament to their shared journey. The gnarled oak, the hand-built bench, the very earth beneath them, all whispered stories of their resilience, their growth, and their enduring love. These were not just memories; they were the bedrock of their present and the promise of their future, a continuous echo of the past that fueled the seeds of what was yet to come. Havenridge, they knew, was more than just a place; it was a testament to what two people, united by love and purpose, could build, starting with a dream in a quiet clearing and an unwavering belief in the potential of the land and its people.

The late afternoon sun cast long, ethereal shadows across the valley as Mara and Eli walked, their steps synchronized, their hands clasped loosely. The familiar paths of Havenridge, once trodden with the hesitant steps of pioneers, now felt like an extension of themselves, a landscape etched not just in the earth, but in their very beings. They had spent the morning in a flurry of activity, a blend of practical preparations and reflective conversations, and now, as the day began to wane, a new thread of purpose emerged, one that tugged at the very heart of their shared endeavor. It was the understanding that as Havenridge expanded, as new families arrived and new ideas bloomed, the essence of what had brought them all together needed not just to be remembered, but actively nurtured.

"It's more than just preserving buildings or documenting milestones," Mara mused, her gaze sweeping over the vibrant community gardens, now bursting with the late harvest. "It's about ensuring the spirit of Havenridge doesn't get diluted, doesn't get lost in the sheer momentum of growth." She paused, a thoughtful frown creasing her brow. "We built this place on a foundation of genuine connection, of mutual respect, and a deep appreciation for the natural world. Those weren't just buzzwords; they were the guiding principles that shaped every decision we made."

She remembered the fierce debates, the compromises, the sheer effort it had taken to weave these values into the fabric of their nascent community. It hadn't always been easy. There were moments when the practicalities of survival, the immediate needs of shelter and sustenance, threatened to overshadow the more abstract ideals. But Mara and Eli, and those early pioneers, had held firm, understanding that the intangible was as vital as the tangible.

Eli squeezed her hand, his thumb tracing absentminded circles on her skin. "You're right. Growth is inevitable, and it's a good thing. It means Havenridge is thriving. But a strong tree, even as it grows taller and wider, keeps its roots firmly anchored. We need to ensure our roots remain strong, nourished by the very ideals that inspired us in the beginning." He thought of the initial conversations, the brainstorming sessions held under the open sky, the shared vision that had ignited a spark in so many hearts.

They had dreamed of a place where people could live in harmony with nature, where collaboration was the norm, and where every individual felt valued and heard. This wasn't a utopian fantasy, but a tangible goal they had strived to manifest, day by painstaking day. "We need to be intentional about how we pass that on," he continued, "to the children born here, to the families who are choosing to make Havenridge their home."

"Exactly," Mara agreed, a renewed energy infusing her voice. "It can't just be a matter of osmosis. We need to actively celebrate and educate. Imagine creating a small, dedicated space—perhaps near the old oak—that tells our story. Not just the dates and the facts, but the *why*. Why did we choose this land? What were the challenges we faced, and how did we overcome them, not just as individuals, but as a community?" She envisioned a space that would be more than just a museum. It would be a living testament, perhaps with interactive elements that allowed visitors to understand the early agricultural techniques, the sustainable building practices, or the participatory decision-making processes that had been so integral to their founding.

Eli nodded, his mind already working through the logistics. "A 'Founders' Grove,' perhaps? Where we could have subtle markers, not just naming the trees, but explaining their significance in our early days. The resilience of the oak, the water-holding capacity of the willow, the medicinal properties of the elderberry. Each element a lesson in its own right, mirroring the lessons we learned about self-sufficiency and respect for the environment."

He pictured a gentle pathway winding through a curated section of the forest, leading to interpretive signs crafted from natural materials, perhaps incorporating some of the early tools or sketches that had been so vital in those formative years. "We could even include excerpts from those early journals, the ones filled with hopes and anxieties. It would humanize the story, make it relatable."

"And the community storytelling events," Mara added, her eyes shining. "We've always had them, loosely structured gatherings where people share their experiences. But we could formalize them, perhaps once a season, dedicated to a specific theme related to our founding values. One event could focus on 'The Spirit of Collaboration,' where people share stories of how they worked together to overcome a challenge. Another could be 'Harmony with Nature,' highlighting the innovative ways people have learned to live sustainably." She recalled the very first communal barn-raising, a project born out of necessity but which had become a powerful symbol of shared effort and mutual reliance. The laughter, the shared meals, the feeling of collective accomplishment – that was the spirit they wanted to bottle and share.

"Educational programs for the children are crucial," Eli stated, his tone firm. "We're already doing a wonderful job integrating environmental studies into their curriculum, but we can deepen it. Imagine a 'Havenridge Pioneers' club within the school, where older children learn about the history and values through hands-on activities. They could help maintain the historical markers, learn traditional crafts, or even participate in mock 'community council' meetings to understand our governance structure."

He thought of his own children, how they absorbed information like sponges, and how vital it was that they understood the lineage of their community, the sacrifices and triumphs that had paved the way for their comfortable lives. It wasn't just about historical facts; it was about instilling a sense of belonging and responsibility.

Mara walked over to a young sapling, its leaves a vibrant green, reaching towards the sky. She gently touched a leaf, a soft smile gracing her lips. "This sapling," she began, her voice filled with a gentle reverence, "represents not just future shade or fruit, but the continuation of a legacy. The founders, they planted seeds of hope, of a different way of living.

And now, it's our responsibility to ensure those seeds don't just survive, but *thrive*, and that future generations understand the soil from which they sprang." She looked back at Eli, her eyes conveying a deep understanding. "It's about creating a living history, not a static monument. A history that continues to inspire, to guide, and to remind us all of what makes Havenridge unique."

The idea began to take root, not just in their conversation, but in the very air around them. They envisioned a "Founders' Day" celebration, distinct from other community festivals, a day dedicated to honoring the early settlers and recommitting to the core values. This would involve more than just speeches; it would be an immersive experience. Perhaps a reenactment of a significant early event, or a series of workshops led by long-time residents who could share their personal stories and impart practical skills learned from the pioneers. The children could be tasked with creating artwork or short plays depicting key moments in Havenridge's history, fostering a sense of ownership and connection to their heritage.

"We could also establish a 'Legacy Fund'," Eli suggested, his practical mind already considering the practicalities. "A dedicated fund, supported by voluntary contributions, that would help maintain and develop these historical and educational initiatives. It would ensure that the preservation of our founding values is not dependent on the whims of the moment, but is a sustained, communal effort." He imagined a simple, transparent system for managing the fund, with clear guidelines on how the resources would be allocated – to the upkeep of historical sites, the development of new educational materials, or the support of community projects that directly embodied the founding principles.

Mara picked up a fallen acorn, turning it over in her palm. "And this acorn," she said softly, "holds the potential for a mighty oak. Just as our community holds the potential for continued growth and evolution, as long as we remember the strength of our beginnings. We need to ensure that the narrative of Havenridge is not just about progress, but about purposeful progress, guided by the wisdom of those who came before us." She thought of the quiet strength of the early settlers, their unwavering belief in a better future, their willingness to sacrifice for the common good. It was a legacy that deserved to be honored, not just with words, but with actions.

They discussed the possibility of creating a dedicated section on the community's digital platform, a "Havenridge Heritage" hub. This would house digital archives of historical documents, oral history recordings, photographs, and educational resources. It would be accessible to all residents, and even to those outside the community who were interested in learning about Havenridge's unique model.

This digital space would serve as a constant reminder of their roots, a readily available resource for anyone seeking to understand the principles that underpinned their society. It could also feature a "Ask a Pioneer" forum, where newer residents could pose questions to some of the elder members of the community, facilitating intergenerational learning and the transfer of knowledge.

"We must be careful not to romanticize the past, though," Eli cautioned, his gaze earnest. "The early days were undeniably challenging. There were struggles, hardships, moments of doubt. We need to present an honest account, one that acknowledges the difficulties but highlights the resilience and the solutions that were found. It's the human element that will resonate, the stories of perseverance and adaptation." He remembered the constant worry about the water supply in the first few years, the precariousness of the early crops, the isolation they had sometimes felt. These were not points of shame, but of pride in their ability to overcome.

"Absolutely," Mara agreed. "It's about learning from their journey, not just admiring it. Understanding the challenges they faced can equip us to better face our own. When we share the story of how they navigated a particularly harsh winter, or how they pooled their resources to build a much-needed bridge, it provides a blueprint for how we can approach similar situations today." She smiled, picturing the children's faces as they learned about the ingenuity of their ancestors, their eyes wide with wonder and a dawning sense of connection.

The conversation flowed naturally, weaving together threads of remembrance, education, and future planning. They spoke of integrating the founding values into community surveys and feedback mechanisms, ensuring that new initiatives aligned with the established principles. They discussed the possibility of mentorship programs, pairing newer residents with those who had lived in

Havenridge for longer, to facilitate the sharing of knowledge and the understanding of community traditions.

As the sun dipped below the horizon, painting the sky in hues of orange and purple, Mara and Eli found themselves standing on the small rise overlooking the valley, the lights of Havenridge twinkling like fallen stars. The air was cool and still, carrying the faint scent of pine and woodsmoke. It was a moment of profound peace, a quiet understanding that their work was far from over. The creation of Havenridge had been a monumental undertaking, but the ongoing task of nurturing its soul, of ensuring its enduring spirit, was equally vital.

"It's about creating a continuous dialogue between our past, our present, and our future," Mara said, her voice soft but resolute. "Ensuring that the echoes of the founders' vision continue to resonate, guiding us as we sow the seeds for what is yet to come." She turned to Eli, her eyes reflecting the deepening twilight, filled with a shared purpose that had always been their strongest bond. "We owe it to them, and to ourselves, and to all those who will call Havenridge home after us."

Eli wrapped an arm around her, drawing her close. "And we'll do it together," he murmured, his voice a low rumble of conviction. "Just as we always have." The lights of Havenridge below seemed to glow a little brighter, a testament to the enduring power of a shared vision, a vision that was being carefully preserved, nurtured, and passed on, ensuring that the heart of their community would beat strong for generations to come. The commitment to honoring the founders' vision was not an endpoint, but a vital, ongoing process, woven into the very fabric of their lives and the future of Havenridge. It was a promise they were making anew, under the vast, star-dusted canvas of the night sky, a promise to remember, to teach, and to live by the enduring principles that had brought them all together.

Mara's wisdom, once a quiet undercurrent, now flowed as a steady, guiding river through the dynamic landscape of Havenridge. The years had been a crucible, forging her not into a rigid idealist, but into a leader of remarkable resilience and insight. Her past struggles with control, those intensely personal battles fought within the quiet confines of her own heart, had not left scars, but rather a profound understanding of the delicate dance between guiding a community and allowing it to breathe and grow organically.

She had learned that true strength wasn't in holding the reins too tightly, but in knowing when to gently guide, when to offer support, and when to step back and trust the collective wisdom of Havenridge to chart its own course. This maturity was palpable in her interactions, a quiet confidence that emanated not from an assumption of infallibility, but from a deep-seated belief in the inherent goodness and capability of the people she led.

The current wave of change sweeping through Havenridge, while bringing with it immense opportunity, also presented its share of anxieties. New families, eager and full of fresh perspectives, were integrating into the established rhythm of the community. This influx was a testament to Havenridge's success, yet it also necessitated a re-evaluation of how their core values would be shared and embraced by those unfamiliar with their genesis. Mara approached these conversations with a seasoned grace. She understood that imposing the past on the present would stifle the future.

Instead, she facilitated dialogues, creating spaces where the "why" behind Havenridge's unique way of life could be explored, not as a historical lesson, but as a living, evolving philosophy. She would often start by acknowledging the very real benefits and innovations that the newcomers brought, validating their contributions before gently weaving in the threads of Havenridge's founding principles. "We are so fortunate to have you all here," she might say, her voice warm and inclusive, "and as we move forward, I'm eager to explore how your fresh perspectives can help us not just grow, but deepen our commitment to the values that have always been the bedrock of our community. Think of it as adding new, vibrant colors to a tapestry that is already rich and meaningful."

Her ability to balance vision with adaptability was a skill honed through experience. There were times in Havenridge's early days when Mara, like many of the pioneers, had clung fiercely to specific outcomes, sometimes to the point of hindering progress. She recalled the intense debates over farming techniques, where rigid adherence to certain methods had initially met resistance from those with different, yet equally valid, approaches.

Those moments of friction had taught her that the most fertile ground for innovation lay not in the unwavering pursuit of a single path, but in the willingness to explore multiple avenues, guided by a shared destination. Now, when faced with a challenge, Mara would first articulate the desired outcome – the preservation of sustainability, the fostering of community connection, the pursuit of equitable growth – but she would then open the floor to diverse solutions.

She actively solicited opinions, not just from the seasoned members of Havenridge, but from the newer residents as well, understanding that sometimes, the most obvious solutions were invisible to those too deeply embedded in the existing framework. This openness fostered an environment where innovation could flourish, where individuals felt empowered to propose ideas without fear of immediate dismissal.

This empowerment was a deliberate cornerstone of Mara's leadership. She had learned that true community development was not a top-down directive, but a collective endeavor. Her own journey, marked by the need to learn to trust – both herself and others – had made her acutely aware of the power of delegated responsibility and genuine encouragement. She saw the potential in every individual, the unique talents and insights they brought, and she actively worked to create opportunities for those skills to be utilized. This wasn't about assigning tasks; it was about cultivating ownership. When a new project arose, Mara would be instrumental in identifying individuals or groups who possessed the passion and aptitude to lead different facets of it.

She would offer guidance and support, but the ultimate responsibility would rest with them, fostering a profound sense of pride and commitment. She remembered, for instance, the initial apprehension some of the younger residents felt when tasked with organizing the seasonal harvest festival. Instead of dictating every detail, Mara had met with them, listened to their ideas, and offered her experience as a resource. The result was a festival that, while honoring tradition, also reflected the vibrant energy and creative flair of the younger generation, a testament to Mara's trust in their ability to bring their own unique contributions to the fore.

Her wisdom also manifested in her approach to conflict resolution. Years of navigating the inevitable disagreements that arise in any close-knit community had taught her that true resolution wasn't about declaring a winner and a loser, but about fostering understanding and finding common ground. She approached disputes not as adversaries, but as opportunities to clarify underlying needs and values.

Her calm demeanor and empathetic listening skills created a safe space for individuals to express their concerns, and her ability to reframe issues, to help people see the situation from different perspectives, was invaluable. She had a knack for identifying the root cause of a disagreement, often tracing it back to unspoken fears or misunderstandings, and then guiding the parties towards solutions that addressed these deeper issues. This process, while sometimes requiring patience, always resulted in stronger relationships and a more cohesive community, as individuals felt heard and respected, even in disagreement.

Mara's leadership style was, in essence, a living embodiment of Havenridge's core tenets. Her ability to embrace change, her commitment to fostering trust, and her skill in empowering others were not just strategies; they were intrinsic to her character, forged through a lifetime of experience and a deep-seated belief in the collective capacity for good. She understood that Havenridge was not a static entity, but a dynamic ecosystem, constantly evolving and adapting. Her role, as she saw it, was not to control this evolution, but to nurture it, to ensure that as the community grew and transformed, it remained anchored in the foundational principles of respect, sustainability, and mutual support.

This nuanced approach allowed her to navigate the complexities of growth with an unwavering sense of purpose, ensuring that Havenridge's future would be as vibrant and meaningful as its past. She was not just a leader; she was a gardener, tending to the soil, providing the right conditions for growth, and trusting the inherent strength of the seeds to reach towards the sun. This subtle, yet powerful, form of leadership allowed the community to blossom, not under the shadow of strict control, but in the warm, encouraging light of shared vision and collective empowerment.

Her presence during community meetings had a grounding effect. When discussions became heated, or when the weight of a decision seemed overwhelming, Mara would often interject with a simple, yet profound, question that refocused the group. "What outcome best serves the long-term health and harmony of Havenridge?" or "How can we approach this challenge in a way that honors our commitment to each other and to this land?" These questions acted as anchors, pulling the conversation back from the precipice of individual desires or short-term anxieties towards the collective good. She never presented these questions as pronouncements, but as invitations to shared reflection, encouraging everyone to engage with the core values that had, for so long, guided their path.

Furthermore, Mara actively promoted intergenerational learning, understanding that the wisdom of experience and the fresh perspective of youth were both vital components of a thriving community. She would often pair older, more established residents with newer members for specific projects, creating natural mentorship opportunities. This wasn't just about skill-sharing; it was about fostering empathy and understanding between different life stages and experiences. She recognized that the "old ways" held valuable lessons, but that the "new ways" often held innovative solutions.

By encouraging these connections, she ensured that the narrative of Havenridge wasn't a monologue of the past, but a rich dialogue between all who called it home. She would often highlight instances where a younger resident's innovative approach had solved a problem that had long puzzled older members, or where an elder's patient guidance had saved a new initiative from potential pitfalls. These anecdotes, shared openly, reinforced the value of every voice and every contribution, solidifying the sense of shared ownership and collective wisdom that was so central to Havenridge's enduring strength.

Her capacity for foresight was also remarkable. While deeply rooted in the present, Mara had a keen ability to anticipate future challenges and opportunities. This wasn't about predicting the unpredictable, but about understanding the underlying trends and the potential impact of various decisions. When discussions arose about expanding the community's infrastructure, for example, Mara would be the one to gently steer the conversation towards long-term sustainability, asking questions about resource management, ecological impact, and the potential for future growth.

Her perspective was always inclusive, considering not just the immediate needs of the current residents, but the legacy they were building for generations to come. This holistic view ensured that Havenridge's development was not haphazard, but thoughtful and deliberate, built on a foundation of enduring principles.

Mara's wisdom wasn't loud or boastful. It was a quiet strength, a steady hand, a listening ear. It was the accumulated understanding of a life lived with intention, a life that had weathered storms and celebrated triumphs. Her leadership during times of transition was a testament to her personal growth, her hard-won ability to trust, and her unwavering commitment to the principles that made Havenridge more than just a place, but a thriving, connected, and resilient community.

She had, through her own journey, become a living example of the very ideals she sought to nurture, a beacon of mature leadership guiding Havenridge not just towards a brighter future, but a future that was deeply rooted in the wisdom of its past. This nuanced approach allowed her to guide the community through the inevitable complexities of growth, not by imposing her will, but by fostering an environment where collective wisdom could flourish, ensuring that Havenridge would continue to be a place of belonging, purpose, and enduring connection for all who chose to call it home.

Eli's role in ensuring the tangible continuity of Havenridge was as crucial as Mara's stewardship of its spirit. While Mara navigated the ebb and flow of community ideals and interpersonal dynamics, Eli was the steady hand that kept the very foundations of their shared life from eroding. His focus was on the practical, the structural, the systems that allowed Havenridge to not merely exist, but to thrive and expand without succumbing to entropy.

He was less of a visionary and more of a steadfast builder, concerned with the integrity of the scaffolding that supported their collective aspirations. His commitment to stability was not a rigid adherence to the status quo, but a deep-seated understanding that true resilience lay in robust, adaptable infrastructure. He believed that a community's ability to evolve was directly tied to its capacity to house that evolution, to provision for it, and to ensure that the underlying mechanisms remained sound.

He approached his work with a quiet, methodical diligence, much like a master craftsman meticulously inspecting every joint and beam. Eli understood that Havenridge's growth, particularly with the influx of new families and their attendant needs, required a foresight that anticipated not just immediate demands, but the needs of generations yet unborn. This meant scrutinizing their current resource management – water systems, energy grids, waste disposal – not with an eye for mere efficiency, but for scalability. He envisioned a Havenridge that could accommodate twenty, fifty, even a hundred more households without straining its ecological balance or compromising the quality of life that drew people there in the first place.

This involved an ongoing dialogue with environmental scientists, engineers, and even historians who understood the long-term implications of infrastructure choices. He saw his task as weaving a resilient fabric, one that could stretch and adapt without tearing, a living testament to Havenridge's enduring commitment to sustainability.

One of Eli's primary preoccupations was the evolution of their energy systems. The solar arrays and wind turbines that had been revolutionary in Havenridge's early days were now a baseline. Eli, however, was constantly exploring the next frontier. He initiated studies into more advanced energy storage solutions, investigating geothermal possibilities that could provide a more consistent baseline power supply, and even researching localized micro-grid technologies that would enhance resilience against external grid failures. His approach was not to discard the old, but to integrate the new. He saw the existing solar farms not as an endpoint, but as a crucial component of a diversified energy portfolio.

He meticulously tracked the performance of each system, analyzing usage patterns, and forecasting future demand based on projected population growth and the increasing integration of smart home technologies. This data-driven approach allowed him to make informed recommendations, advocating for phased upgrades and strategic investments that ensured Havenridge remained at the forefront of sustainable energy practices, a practical legacy for future residents.

Water management was another critical area that occupied much of Eli's attention. Havenridge had always prided itself on its responsible stewardship of its water resources, but increasing demand necessitated a proactive approach. Eli spearheaded initiatives to upgrade their rainwater harvesting systems, implementing more sophisticated filtration and purification technologies. He also championed water conservation education programs, working with Mara to integrate these principles into the community's broader outreach efforts.

His vision extended beyond mere collection and conservation; he explored greywater recycling systems for irrigation and landscaping, and even investigated the feasibility of small-scale desalination plants, should future climate shifts make it a necessary, albeit last-resort, option. He understood that water was the lifeblood of any community, and his dedication to its preservation was a profound expression of his commitment to Havenridge's long-term viability. He would often walk the land, tracing the paths of the streams and reservoirs, a quiet reverence in his posture, ensuring that every drop was accounted for, every usage optimized.

Eli's work on housing and community infrastructure was equally vital. As Havenridge grew, the need for thoughtful, sustainable housing solutions became paramount. He established a community design review board, composed of architects, builders, and long-time residents, to ensure that any new construction adhered to Havenridge's aesthetic principles and ecological standards. This wasn't about stifling creativity, but about ensuring that growth was harmonious and integrated. He facilitated workshops on sustainable building materials, passive solar design, and energy-efficient construction techniques, empowering builders and residents alike to create homes that were not only beautiful but also environmentally responsible.

He also focused on the communal spaces, advocating for the expansion of walking trails, the creation of new green spaces, and the upgrading of community centers to accommodate larger gatherings. His vision was for a Havenridge where every structure, from the smallest dwelling to the largest public space, contributed to the overall well-being and sustainability of the community.

Furthermore, Eli understood the importance of creating systems that facilitated the seamless transition of knowledge and responsibility between generations. He developed comprehensive digital archives for community records, infrastructure plans, and historical documents, ensuring that vital information was accessible and preserved. He also instituted a mentorship program within the infrastructure departments, pairing seasoned technicians and administrators with younger apprentices. This ensured that the practical knowledge accumulated over years of experience was not lost but actively passed down.

Eli himself was a mentor to many, patiently explaining the intricacies of the water purification system or the maintenance schedules for the power grid. He saw this transfer of knowledge as an essential form of continuity, an investment in Havenridge's future resilience. He believed that a community's strength lay not just in its physical structures, but in the embedded knowledge and skills of its people, a living inheritance passed from one hand to another.

He was also instrumental in developing flexible zoning regulations and adaptable building codes. Eli recognized that Havenridge's needs would change, and rigid rules could become impediments to progress. Instead, he advocated for a framework that allowed for adaptation and innovation, while still upholding the core principles of sustainability and community character. This meant developing guidelines that could accommodate new technologies, changing family structures, and evolving economic activities, without compromising the essential values that defined Havenridge.

He was constantly engaged in forecasting these potential shifts, engaging in scenario planning to anticipate future needs and challenges. His approach was to build a framework that could bend without breaking, a testament to his understanding that true stability was not about immutability, but about dynamic equilibrium. He saw his role as ensuring that the ground upon which Havenridge stood was not only firm but also fertile, capable of supporting whatever future endeavors its inhabitants might dream up.

Eli's commitment to continuity extended to the realm of disaster preparedness. He spearheaded the development of comprehensive emergency response plans, coordinating with local emergency services and establishing a network of community volunteers trained in first aid, communication, and basic rescue operations. He ensured that essential supplies were strategically located, backup power systems were tested regularly, and communication channels remained robust even in the event of widespread disruption. This was not an act of pessimism, but a pragmatic recognition of the unpredictable nature of life. He believed that by preparing for the worst, Havenridge could better protect its residents and ensure its survival, reinforcing its inherent resilience. He saw this preparedness as another layer of structural integrity, a safeguard against unforeseen shocks that could threaten the community's very existence.

In his interactions, Eli was rarely one for grand pronouncements. His wisdom was in the meticulous detail, the thoughtful analysis, the quiet reassurance that the systems underpinning their lives were in capable hands. He understood that while Mara might inspire the heart, he had to provide the solid ground upon which those dreams could be built. He worked tirelessly behind the scenes, ensuring that the infrastructure of Havenridge was not just functional, but future-proof, capable of adapting to the ever-changing landscape of needs and challenges.

His dedication was a testament to a different kind of leadership, one that found its power in the unwavering commitment to the practical, the enduring, and the resilient. He was the quiet architect of Havenridge's enduring strength, ensuring that the echoes of the past would resonate not as limitations, but as foundations for an ever-evolving future. His work was a continuous dialogue with the land, with the resources, and with the generations to come, a silent promise of stability and adaptability in a world of constant flux.

The tapestry of Havenridge, woven with threads of innovation and deep-rooted tradition, was as much a product of deliberate choices as it was of serendipitous encounters. Mara and Eli, standing at the precipice of what felt like a new dawn, found themselves in constant, quiet communion about the weight and wonder of these choices. It wasn't just the monumental decision to pour their lives into this nascent community, nor the collective resolve of its early inhabitants to rise from the ashes of past failures. It was the ongoing, day-to-day act of choosing – choosing understanding over judgment, collaboration over conflict, and long-term vision over short-term gratification.

"Sometimes," Mara mused one evening, the setting sun casting long shadows across the community plaza, "I wonder if we truly grasp the power we wield. Not power in terms of control, but the power of intentionality. Every sapling planted, every design etched into the earth, every conversation we have – it's all a choice that ripples outwards."

Eli, ever the pragmatist, nodded, his gaze sweeping over the faces of children playing near the communal garden, their laughter a testament to the vibrant life they were cultivating. "And it's not just our choices, Mara. It's the choices we empower others to make. We can build the sturdiest homes, the most efficient systems, but if the people within them don't feel they have the agency to shape their own lives, to contribute their unique talents, then the foundation, no matter how strong, will eventually crack."

Their discussions often circled back to their own union, a profound affirmation of choice. It hadn't been a whirlwind, star-crossed romance, but a slow, steady unfolding of shared values and mutual respect. They had chosen each other, not out of obligation or convenience, but from a deep-seated recognition of a kindred spirit, a shared commitment to a life of purpose. This choice, so personal and intimate, had become a cornerstone of their shared vision for Havenridge. It was a living example that intentionality in relationships could foster a community built on trust and genuine connection.

"Think about it, Eli," Mara continued, her voice soft but resonant. "When we first arrived, so much was uncertain. We could have retreated, focused only on our own survival. But we, along with so many others, chose to see possibility. We chose to invest not just our labor, but our hope. That collective choice to rebuild, to reimagine, is what's allowed Havenridge to become what it is today. It wasn't a passive inheritance; it was an active creation."

Eli picked up a fallen leaf, turning it over in his fingers. "And that act of rebuilding has, in turn, created a legacy of choice for those who come after us. They inherit not just land and structures, but a philosophy. They can choose to maintain that spirit of active participation, or they can let it wane. Our responsibility, I believe, is to ensure the environment is such that the positive choice is the most natural, the most appealing one."

This was where their efforts converged, where Mara's focus on nurturing the community's spirit met Eli's dedication to building its robust framework. They understood that a thriving community wasn't merely about efficient resource management or well-designed public spaces, though those were undeniably crucial. It was about cultivating a culture where individuals felt empowered to make conscious, positive decisions, where their agency was not only recognized but actively encouraged.

Consider the design of the new community center. Mara had championed its open, fluid architecture, incorporating spaces for spontaneous gatherings alongside planned workshops. Eli, in turn, had ensured its construction utilized sustainable materials and incorporated advanced climate control, making it a comfortable and inviting space year-round, regardless of the weather. But it was the choices made *within* that space that truly mattered.

The decision to host a diverse range of events, from art exhibitions to skill-sharing sessions, from intergenerational storytelling circles to problem-solving forums, was a conscious choice by the community to foster connection and shared learning. The availability of these opportunities, facilitated by the thoughtful design and infrastructure, made it easier for individuals to choose engagement.

"It's about creating fertile ground for those future choices," Eli elaborated, his thoughts aligning seamlessly with Mara's. "We can't dictate what paths the next generation will forge, but we can ensure they have the tools, the knowledge, and the encouragement to make those paths meaningful. That means continuous education, not just in technical skills, but in critical thinking, in empathy, in understanding the long-term consequences of their actions. It means fostering a sense of responsibility that extends beyond the immediate."

Mara envisioned this not just in grand community projects, but in the very fabric of daily life. "Think of the choices families make about how they raise their children," she said. "We can provide excellent schooling and safe play areas, but the parents are the ones choosing to instill values of kindness, curiosity, and resilience. Our role is to support that, to create a community that reflects those values back to them, reinforcing their positive choices."

This was the essence of their legacy: not just the tangible infrastructure of Havenridge, but the intangible culture of intentionality they strived to cultivate. It was a legacy that acknowledged the inherent human need for autonomy and the profound satisfaction that comes from shaping one's own destiny, and by extension, the destiny of the community.

Eli's meticulous planning for the town's water management system, for instance, went beyond mere engineering. It was an act of choosing foresight, of ensuring that the fundamental resource of life was managed with an eye towards sustainability for generations. But the true legacy lay in how the community then *chose* to interact with that system.

Educational programs, developed collaboratively by Mara's outreach initiatives and Eli's technical teams, taught residents about water conservation not as a chore, but as a conscious act of stewardship. Families were encouraged to choose water-wise gardening, to opt for low-flow fixtures, to participate in community-wide water-saving challenges. These were small, seemingly insignificant choices, but when amplified across hundreds of households, they became a powerful testament to the community's collective commitment.

Similarly, Eli's commitment to diversifying Havenridge's energy sources, moving beyond simple solar and wind to explore geothermal and advanced energy storage, was a choice to secure the community's energy independence and environmental integrity. Mara's complementary efforts focused on educating residents about energy usage, encouraging them to choose mindful consumption patterns. Smart home technologies, integrated by Eli's infrastructure teams, provided data to empower these choices, allowing individuals to see the impact of their decisions in real-time. The choice to adopt these technologies, and to use the information they provided wisely, was a direct result of the culture of conscious decision-making that Mara and Eli championed.

They recognized that the path forward was rarely linear, and that the spirit of Havenridge would be tested. There would be disagreements, inevitable setbacks, and moments when the weight of responsibility felt immense. But in those moments, they held onto the profound understanding that their strength lay not in avoiding challenges, but in the ability of the community to collectively choose how to navigate them.

"The beauty of it, Eli," Mara reflected, "is that the more we empower people to make good choices, the more resilient we become. A community where individuals feel they have a voice, where their contributions are valued, is a community that will naturally rally when faced with adversity. They've already made the choice to be invested."

Eli's meticulous work on community governance and adaptable building codes also played a crucial role. By creating flexible frameworks that allowed for innovation while upholding core values, he was, in essence, choosing to future-proof the community. This gave future generations the freedom to adapt and evolve without being shackled by rigid past decisions. Mara, in parallel, focused on fostering the dialogue that informed these adaptations. She encouraged open forums where residents could voice their evolving needs and aspirations, ensuring that the community's future choices were rooted in genuine dialogue and shared understanding.

This sub-section of their lives, this ongoing conversation about choice, was not about grand pronouncements or sweeping mandates. It was about the quiet, persistent cultivation of an environment where intentionality could flourish. It was about the small, consistent acts of empowering individuals to be active participants in their own lives and in the life of Havenridge.

They understood that the legacy they were building was not a static monument, but a dynamic, evolving organism. Its vitality depended on the continuous infusion of conscious decision-making, on the courage of its inhabitants to choose growth, to choose connection, to choose a future that reflected their highest aspirations. It was a legacy built on the profound belief that the future of Havenridge would not be determined by what they had built, but by the countless, deliberate choices that its people would continue to make, generation after generation.

This principle of agency, of informed and empowered choice, was the very seed from which Havenridge's enduring future would sprout, a testament to the enduring power of human will and the collective pursuit of a better tomorrow.

CHAPTER ELEVEN

THE QUIET JOY OF ACCOMPLISHMENT

The landscape of Havenridge had transformed, not just in its physical manifestation but in the very atmosphere that permeated its streets and homes. The ambitious land stewardship plans, once a series of hopeful blueprints, had matured into thriving ecosystems. Vast swathes of once-dormant land now pulsed with life, a testament to the careful, intentional hands that had guided their regeneration. Fields of native grasses swayed in the gentle breeze, interspersed with carefully cultivated groves of fruit trees and nut-bearing saplings.

The air itself felt cleaner, imbued with the scent of rich soil and blooming wildflowers. This was no accident; it was the direct result of a community's collective commitment to working *with* the land, not against it. Every planting, every carefully managed burn, every conservation effort was a deliberate act of stewardship, a promise to the future. Mara found herself often pausing during her walks, simply absorbing the visual symphony of vibrant green, the hum of pollinators, the distant call of birds that had returned to inhabit these revitalized spaces. It was a quiet triumph, a visible manifestation of their shared vision.

Eli, too, found immense satisfaction in observing the tangible results of their long-term planning. He would often walk the perimeter of the community's managed forests, his hand tracing the bark of a young oak, a sense of deep connection resonating within him. He saw not just trees, but carbon sinks, sources of sustainable timber, and vital habitats. He recalled the initial debates, the cautious skepticism some had harbored about the extensive commitment required for ecological restoration. Now, those same individuals were among the most vocal proponents, actively participating in planting drives and conservation patrols.

The success of the land stewardship was a powerful affirmation of the community's ability to embrace long-term thinking and collective action, demonstrating that investing in the earth was, in fact, investing in their own enduring prosperity. The watercourses, once prone to unpredictable surges and dwindles, now flowed with a steady, reliable rhythm, thanks to the integrated watershed management systems Eli had meticulously designed and overseen. Reservoirs, carefully constructed to blend into the natural contours of the land, held their precious cargo, a lifeline for every garden, every home, and every flourishing ecosystem.

The irrigation channels, cleverly designed to minimize evaporation and maximize efficiency, snaked through the fields like silver ribbons, a testament to the marriage of ecological principle and engineering ingenuity. This wasn't just about water security; it was about re-establishing a natural balance, allowing the land to breathe and thrive once more.

Beyond the land, the infrastructure of leadership succession had also taken root, bearing a rich harvest of stability. The mentorship programs, initially an experiment in weaving the wisdom of experience with the fresh perspectives of emerging leaders, had blossomed. Younger members of Havenridge, those who had grown up within its embrace or joined in their formative years, were now stepping into crucial roles. They approached these responsibilities with a blend of innovation and respect for the established foundations, a balance Mara and Eli had consciously strived to foster.

There were fewer hurried, reactive decisions, and more thoughtful, deliberative processes. The council meetings, once a sometimes-contentious forum, now often hummed with a collaborative energy. Diverse viewpoints were not just tolerated but actively sought, creating a richer tapestry of ideas from which to draw solutions. Mara had witnessed several instances where younger council members, armed with fresh data and innovative approaches, had gently guided established protocols towards even greater efficiency or equity, always with the overarching well-being of Havenridge as their guiding principle. Eli, with his characteristic foresight, had ensured that the framework for this succession was robust, incorporating clear pathways for training, evaluation, and ongoing support, but the true success lay in the willingness of the community to embrace it.

This careful cultivation of leadership extended beyond formal governance. In the workshops and studios, in the educational initiatives and the caregiving networks, individuals were emerging as natural leaders, guiding their peers with competence and grace. The artisans were mentoring apprentices, the educators were sharing pedagogical insights, and the caregivers were establishing best practices that ensured the well-being of Havenridge's most vulnerable.

This decentralization of leadership, this organic growth of expertise and influence, was perhaps the most profound indicator of Havenridge's maturation. It meant that the community's vitality was no longer solely dependent on a few individuals, but distributed across a broad and engaged populace. Mara often felt a swell of pride watching these internal currents of leadership at play, seeing the seeds they had sown bearing such fruit. It was a testament to the trust and empowerment that had become hallmarks of their society.

The palpable sense of peace that now settled over Havenridge was not an absence of challenges, but a profound internal quietude, an assurance that the community possessed the collective wisdom and resilience to navigate whatever storms might come. It was the peace that arises from shared purpose, from mutual respect, and from the deep satisfaction of seeing one's efforts yield positive, lasting results.

Homes were no longer just shelters; they were extensions of the individuals and families who inhabited them, imbued with their unique personalities and a sense of belonging. The communal spaces, from the bustling marketplace to the serene contemplation gardens, were vibrant hubs of connection, places where laughter echoed and quiet conversations unfolded. Children played with an unburdened joy, their imaginations unfettered, knowing they were part of a secure and nurturing environment. The elderly, their faces etched with the wisdom of years, were deeply integrated into the community fabric, their stories cherished and their contributions valued.

Mara and Eli, standing together on the overlook that offered a panoramic view of their flourishing community, often found themselves in a profound, unspoken communion. They would watch the sun dip below the horizon, painting the sky in hues of orange and rose, casting a warm glow over the houses nestled amongst the verdant landscape. The lights beginning to twinkle on in the homes were like tiny stars, each representing a life, a family, a story unfolding. It was a scene of profound beauty and enduring accomplishment, a tangible realization of the dreams they had once nurtured in more uncertain times.

They had played a significant role, that was undeniable. Their dedication, their vision, their willingness to pour their lives into this endeavor had been foundational. But they also recognized that Havenridge was far more than just the sum of their contributions. It was a living entity, shaped by the collective spirit of every individual who called it home.

"Look at it, Eli," Mara whispered, her voice thick with emotion, gesturing towards the peaceful expanse below. "It's... more than we could have imagined."

Eli wrapped an arm around her shoulders, drawing her close. His gaze was steady, filled with a quiet satisfaction that mirrored her own. "We imagined it, Mara. We *chose* it. Every step of the way."

He was right, of course. It hadn't been a passive unfolding of destiny, but a deliberate, conscious creation. They had chosen to believe in the possibility of a better way of life, and they had, with the unwavering support of their community, brought that vision into being. The challenges they had faced, the moments of doubt, the sheer hard work – it had all been worth it. The harmony that now characterized Havenridge was not merely a fortunate coincidence; it was the carefully cultivated outcome of countless intentional choices, made by individuals and by the collective, all working towards a shared future.

The serene beauty of Havenridge was not a static picture, but a dynamic testament to ongoing effort. The land stewardship wasn't just about maintaining what had been achieved; it involved continuous monitoring, adaptive strategies for changing environmental conditions, and ongoing educational outreach to ensure that the next generation understood and embraced their role as custodians. Eli's infrastructure was designed for longevity and adaptability, but it required regular upkeep and upgrades to remain at peak efficiency.

The leadership succession wasn't a one-time event, but a continuous process of nurturing talent, fostering dialogue, and ensuring that the governance structures remained responsive to the evolving needs of the community. The sense of peace was not an end point, but a state of being that was actively maintained through open communication, conflict resolution, and a shared commitment to the community's core values.

Mara often reflected on the subtle nuances that contributed to this profound sense of harmony. It wasn't just the grand gestures, but the small, everyday interactions. The spontaneous offers of help between neighbors, the way people naturally looked out for one another, the genuine interest people took in each other's lives. These were the threads that wove the fabric of their community together, strengthening its resilience and deepening its sense of belonging.

She saw this in the way the local school integrated hands-on learning with community projects, where students weren't just learning about ecology, but actively participating in reforestation efforts alongside seasoned land stewards. She saw it in the shared meals that frequently gathered residents from different neighborhoods, breaking down any potential silos and fostering a sense of unified identity.

Eli's focus on creating accessible, intuitive systems for resource management had also played a crucial role. Simple online platforms allowed residents to track their energy consumption, monitor their water usage, and even participate in community-wide sustainability challenges. This data, presented in an easily understandable format, empowered individuals to make informed choices about their own impact, fostering a sense of agency and responsibility. The systems weren't designed to dictate behavior, but to inform and enable conscious decision-making. When residents saw the tangible benefits of their collective efforts – reduced energy bills, cleaner waterways, healthier ecosystems – it reinforced their commitment and encouraged further participation.

The joy they felt was not one of passive observation, but of active, ongoing engagement. They were still deeply invested in the well-being of Havenridge, still involved in its growth and evolution, albeit in ways that were now more about guidance and support than direct implementation. Their role had shifted from builders to gardeners, tending to the soil, ensuring the sunlight reached the tender shoots, and pruning where necessary to encourage robust growth. They found a particular fulfillment in seeing how their own relationship, a testament to intentional choice and mutual respect, had become a quiet example for others. The stability and trust that characterized Havenridge were, in many ways, a reflection of the stable and trusting foundation of their own partnership.

As they stood there, the fading light casting long shadows, Mara leaned her head against Eli's arm. The air was filled with the gentle chirping of crickets and the distant murmur of families gathered for the evening meal. It was a symphony of contentment, a testament to a dream realized. The quiet joy of accomplishment wasn't a fleeting emotion; it was a deep, abiding sense of peace, a profound gratitude for the harmonious haven they had helped to build, and a quiet anticipation for the continued flourishing of the community they loved.

They had sown the seeds of intention, nurtured them with dedication, and now, they were reaping the reward of a community that was not just functional, but truly alive, a vibrant testament to the power of shared purpose and the quiet strength of accomplishment. The harmonious haven of Havenridge was a living, breathing entity, a testament to the enduring power of collective will and the sweet reward of a dream diligently pursued.

The quiet hum of Havenridge had a new melody to it, a subtle harmony that resonated with personal triumphs woven into the collective narrative. Mara found herself frequently pausing, not just to admire the verdant landscape or the efficient flow of water systems, but to witness the unfolding of individual achievements, each a miniature echo of the larger success story they had all written together. It began with a simple acknowledgment, a small nod to a job well done, but it had blossomed into a rich tradition of shared celebration, a testament to the community's understanding that every individual's journey was intrinsically linked to the well-being of the whole.

One of the most cherished recent milestones was Elias Thorne's – Eli's younger brother – finally completing his apprenticeship as a master craftsman in woodworking. For years, Elias had apprenticed under the tutelage of old Silas, whose hands, gnarled with age, still possessed an uncanny ability to coax beauty from raw timber. Elias, with his youthful energy and Silas's seasoned wisdom, had embarked on a project that had captured the attention of the entire community: a new community pavilion for the central green.

It wasn't just any pavilion; it was to be a true masterpiece, a place where stories could be shared, where musicians could perform, and where the simple act of gathering could be elevated. The design itself was a collaborative effort, incorporating elements that reflected Havenridge's commitment to sustainability and its connection to nature. Eli had even contributed some of his engineering expertise, ensuring the structural integrity and the integration of a rainwater harvesting system for the surrounding planters.

The day of the unveiling was marked by a spontaneous gathering. There was no formal invitation list, no scheduled time – just the natural gravitational pull of shared anticipation. As the sun rose, casting a golden light on the polished wood of the pavilion, residents began to drift towards the green. Children chased each other around the newly erected structure, their laughter echoing, while adults milled about, admiring the intricate carvings on the support beams, the seamless joinery, and the way the roofline seemed to cradle the sky. Silas, beaming with a paternal pride that transcended his own accomplishment, stood beside Elias, his hand resting on his former apprentice's shoulder. Elias, looking a little overwhelmed but radiating a quiet confidence, accepted the congratulations with genuine humility.

Mara watched as Eli approached Elias, a genuine smile gracing his lips. There were no grand pronouncements, no elaborate speeches.

Eli simply clasped Elias's hand firmly, his eyes conveying a depth of brotherly pride. "You've done it, Eli. Truly remarkable."

Elias, his voice a little rough with emotion, replied, "Couldn't have done it without Silas, or without all of you. This... this is for Havenridge."

The ensuing celebration was a quintessential Havenridge affair. Neighbors brought out their best baked goods, musicians spontaneously formed an ensemble, and for hours, the green was alive with music, laughter, and the clinking of glasses filled with homemade cider. Mara felt a familiar warmth bloom in her chest, a feeling that was becoming increasingly synonymous with her life in Havenridge. This wasn't just Elias's triumph; it was a victory for their collective spirit, a tangible manifestation of their commitment to fostering talent and celebrating every individual's contribution. The pavilion, standing proud and sturdy, was more than just a structure; it was a symbol of shared purpose, a place where future memories would be forged, built by the hands of one of their own.

Another milestone, equally significant but far more personal, was Mara's own successful completion of the advanced herbalist certification. For years, she had dedicated herself to understanding the intricate language of plants, their healing properties, and their place in Havenridge's holistic approach to well-being. Her small apothecary, once a humble collection of dried herbs and tinctures, had grown into a vital resource, offering remedies and comfort to those in need. The certification was the culmination of countless hours of study, practical application, and a deep dive into the scientific underpinnings of traditional knowledge.

The day she received her official accreditation, she had intended to keep it quiet, perhaps sharing the news only with Eli. But Havenridge, in its inimitable way, had a knack for sensing such things. As she walked home from the post office, clutching the embossed certificate, she noticed a subtle shift in the atmosphere. People she passed on the street offered knowing smiles, their eyes twinkling with unspoken congratulations. By the time she reached her doorstep, a small gathering had formed. Old Mrs. Gable, her face a roadmap of smiles, held a bouquet of freshly picked lavender. Young Leo, who had benefited immensely from Mara's remedies for his persistent asthma, presented her with a drawing of a vibrant garden.

Eli met her at the door, his gaze full of adoration. He didn't need to ask. He simply pulled her into a warm embrace. "I'm so proud of you, Mara. You've always had a gift, and now the world knows it too."

The informal celebration that followed was intimate and heartfelt. Neighbors shared stories of how Mara's knowledge had helped them or their loved ones, weaving a tapestry of gratitude that underscored the profound impact of her work. She spoke about her journey, about the inspiration she drew from the natural world and the unwavering support she'd received from Eli and the community. It wasn't a formal acceptance speech, but a genuine outpouring of shared joy. The simple act of receiving her certificate had transformed into a communal affirmation, a beautiful illustration of how individual dedication could ripple outwards, touching and enriching so many lives.

These moments, the grand gestures like the pavilion and the intimate acknowledgments like Mara's certification, were not isolated events. They were woven into the fabric of daily life in

Havenridge, creating a continuous thread of positive reinforcement and shared accomplishment. Eli, too, had experienced his share of personal milestones, often intertwined with the community's progress. One such instance was the successful implementation of the new geothermal heating and cooling system he had designed for the community center. It was a complex undertaking, requiring meticulous planning, extensive collaboration with external specialists, and a significant investment from the community.

The day the system was officially switched on, a quiet buzz of anticipation filled the community center. Eli, along with the lead engineers and several community representatives, stood by the control panel, their breaths held. When the temperature gauge began to register a steady, comfortable warmth, a collective sigh of relief and satisfaction swept through the room. It was a testament to years of research, countless hours of intricate work, and the community's unwavering faith in Eli's vision.

The celebration that followed was understated but deeply meaningful. It wasn't a raucous party, but a gathering of shared accomplishment. Eli, in his typically humble manner, deflected much of the praise, emphasizing the collaborative effort and the dedication of the entire team. He spoke about the long-term benefits of the system – the reduced reliance on fossil fuels, the significant cost savings for the community, and the creation of a more sustainable and comfortable environment for everyone. Mara, standing beside him, felt a swell of pride not just for his technical prowess, but for his unwavering commitment to the collective good. His personal achievement was inextricably linked to the well-being and future prosperity of Havenridge.

What made these celebrations so profound was their inherent authenticity. They weren't driven by a need for external validation or a desire for recognition. Instead, they stemmed from a deep-seated appreciation for progress, for growth, and for the interconnectedness of their lives. When Elias completed the pavilion, it wasn't just about his skill; it was about creating a beautiful, functional space for everyone to enjoy. When Mara received her herbalist certification, it was a celebration of her dedication to the health and well-being of her neighbors. And when Eli's geothermal system was activated, it was a triumph of collective investment in a sustainable future.

The ripple effect of these celebrated milestones was far-reaching. They served as powerful motivators, inspiring others to pursue their own passions and develop their unique talents. Young children, witnessing Elias's dedication to his craft, might be inspired to explore their own creative inclinations. Teenagers, seeing Mara's commitment to healing and her earned expertise, might consider careers in healthcare or environmental science. Adults, observing Eli's innovative solutions for sustainability, might be encouraged to think more critically about their own impact and explore new ways of contributing to the community's well-being.

The beauty of Havenridge's approach to celebration lay in its inclusivity. There was no hierarchy of achievement. Whether it was a grand project like the pavilion or a deeply personal accomplishment like mastering a new skill, each milestone was met with genuine appreciation and shared joy. Small, everyday successes were also acknowledged. A neighbor helping another with a difficult task, a child achieving a personal best in their studies, an elder sharing a valuable piece of wisdom – all these were threads in the rich tapestry of Havenridge's communal life, and they were recognized and cherished.

Mara often found herself reflecting on how this culture of shared celebration had evolved organically. It wasn't dictated by rules or regulations, but by the underlying values that had shaped Havenridge: mutual respect, genuine care for one another, and a deep understanding that their collective strength lay in the individual contributions of every member. This was more than just community spirit; it was a lived philosophy, a constant affirmation of their shared commitment to building a life together that was both meaningful and fulfilling.

The quiet joy of accomplishment, therefore, was not a singular emotion experienced in isolation, but a collective resonance, a harmonious chorus that sang the praises of individual growth and communal progress. It was the sound of lives being lived to their fullest, of dreams being realized, and of a community thriving in the quiet, profound beauty of shared success. Each celebration, whether grand or intimate, served as a powerful reminder that in Havenridge, no accomplishment was truly solitary. Every victory, no matter how small, was a testament to the strength and resilience of their interconnected lives, a beacon of light that illuminated the path forward for all. The pavilion stood not just as a structure, but as a monument to Elias's dedication; Mara's apothecary hummed with the quiet confidence of her earned wisdom; Eli's geothermal system pulsed with the promise of a sustainable future. And around them, the people of Havenridge moved, inspired, connected, and deeply satisfied by the quiet joy of a life well-lived, together.

Mara's contentment wasn't a sudden revelation, but a gentle dawn that had slowly, irrevocably, illuminated her world. The gnawing fear of losing herself, a shadow that had once clung to her heels like a persistent echo, had finally retreated, dissolving into the warm embrace of a life fully lived. It was a profound realization, one that settled deep within her bones, a quiet hum of peace that underscored her days. She looked at Eli, at their shared life in Havenridge, and saw not a surrender of self, but an expansion. Her identity, far from being diminished, had been enriched, broadened by the very love and commitment she had once feared would erase her.

This wasn't about merging into a singular entity; it was about two distinct souls finding a harmonious rhythm, a dance where each step celebrated the individuality of the other. The vibrant tapestry of her life now included threads of shared dreams, intertwined passions, and the quiet understanding that came from building a future together. Yet, within this partnership, she found an even greater freedom to explore her own landscape, to nurture the curiosities that sparked within her.

Her days were no longer dictated by the anxieties of what *might* be, but by the quiet satisfaction of what *was*. The herbalist's path, which had once been a solitary pursuit of knowledge, now felt like a vital contribution to the vibrant ecosystem of Havenridge. The certification was more than just a piece of paper; it was a validation, a testament to her dedication, and a springboard for even greater exploration. She found herself drawn to new areas of study, her mind like a fertile field eager to absorb every new seed of knowledge.

Recently, she had become fascinated by the intricate world of fungi, not just for their medicinal properties, but for their role in the delicate balance of the forest floor. She spent hours poring over botanical texts, venturing into the woods with Eli, learning to identify species, to understand their symbiotic relationships, and to appreciate their silent, essential work. Eli, ever supportive, would often accompany her, his practical mind finding marvel in the unseen networks that sustained life. He'd listen with rapt attention as she explained the complex mycelial structures, his hand finding hers as they navigated the dappled sunlight filtering through the ancient trees. It was in these shared moments, these quiet explorations of the natural world, that Mara felt the deepest connection, both to herself and to the man who walked beside her.

This desire for growth wasn't limited to the realm of plants. Mara found herself increasingly drawn to the community's burgeoning artistic endeavors. She had always appreciated beauty, but now, with her own sense of security firmly established, she felt a burgeoning desire to participate, to create. She attended pottery classes, her hands, accustomed to the delicate work of harvesting herbs, now learning to coax form from clay. The initial results were, admittedly, rudimentary – lopsided bowls and misshapen vases.

But the process itself was deeply therapeutic, a mindful engagement that quieted the lingering remnants of old anxieties. She discovered a quiet joy in the tactile sensation of the spinning wheel, the earthy scent of the clay, and the transformation that occurred under her touch. Eli, who had a surprising knack for recognizing artistic potential, had gifted her a set of professional sculpting tools for her birthday, a gesture that had brought tears to her eyes. He understood, with an uncanny prescience, that her contentment wasn't about stillness, but about a dynamic, evolving engagement with life.

Her leadership within the community also felt different now, imbued with a seasoned wisdom and a quiet confidence. When the council sought her input on the expansion of the community garden, for instance, her suggestions were no longer tentative questions but clear, well-reasoned proposals. She spoke with a newfound authority, drawing not just from her herbalist knowledge but from her broader understanding of sustainability, community needs, and the interconnectedness of their efforts.

She advocated for a more diverse planting strategy, incorporating native species that would support local pollinators and require less intensive watering. She also proposed workshops on seed saving and natural pest control, empowering residents to take a more active role in their food security. Her insights were met with the respect she had earned, and her vision for a more resilient and biodiverse garden was enthusiastically embraced. This felt like a profound accomplishment, not just for the garden, but for her own journey of self-discovery and her ability to contribute meaningfully to the collective good.

The fear of loss, once a constant companion, had been replaced by an enduring appreciation for presence. She savored the everyday moments with Eli – the quiet mornings sharing coffee on their porch, the comfortable silence that often settled between them during their evening walks, the way he would instinctively reach for her hand. These weren't grand gestures, but the small, consistent affirmations of their shared life, and they filled her with a profound sense of gratitude.

She recognized that this contentment wasn't a passive state but an active cultivation, a conscious choice to embrace the joy and beauty that surrounded her. Her fear of losing herself in a relationship had, paradoxically, led her to discover a stronger, more vibrant version of herself within the secure framework of their partnership. She was no longer a hesitant shadow; she was a woman grounded in her own strengths, enriched by her love, and empowered to continue exploring the boundless possibilities of her life in Havenridge.

She continued to find immense satisfaction in her work at the apothecary, her role evolving beyond simply dispensing remedies. She became a confidante, a source of comfort, and a gentle guide. She saw how her knowledge, rooted in both ancient wisdom and modern understanding, provided not just physical healing but emotional solace. When young Lily, whose chronic cough had plagued her for years, finally found relief through Mara's carefully crafted herbal syrups, the child's infectious laughter became a melody that echoed in Mara's heart.

When old Mr. Abernathy, struggling with the aches and pains of age, found solace in a liniment Mara had prepared, his grateful smile was a reward far richer than any material compensation. These were the moments that solidified her purpose, reminding her of the profound impact of her chosen path. Her apothecary was more than just a business; it was a sanctuary, a place where healing bloomed in myriad forms, nurtured by her expertise and the inherent resilience of the natural world.

Her ongoing explorations led her to experiment with new formulations, pushing the boundaries of her knowledge. She delved into the study of aromatherapy, discovering how the subtle scents of essential oils could uplift moods, ease anxieties, and promote a sense of well-being. She began offering bespoke blends, tailoring each one to the specific needs of her clients. She even started a small herb garden at the community center, a vibrant space where residents could learn about the plants, their uses, and the simple joy of nurturing life from seed to bloom.

This garden became a living extension of her apothecary, a place for education and connection, fostering a deeper appreciation for nature's bounty within the community. Eli, with his practical skills, helped her design an efficient irrigation system for the garden, ensuring its sustainability and ease of maintenance. Their collaboration, whether in the workshop or in the garden, was a testament to their shared commitment to enriching Havenridge.

Mara's growth was also evident in her interactions with the younger generation. She had become a mentor to several aspiring herbalists, sharing her knowledge and encouraging them to forge their own paths. She saw in their eager faces the reflection of her own younger self, the same spark of curiosity and the same desire to understand the world around them. She guided them not just in the science of herbs but in the art of listening – to their patients, to nature, and to their own intuition. She encouraged them to be bold in their research, to question established practices, and to find their unique voices in the field. Witnessing their progress, their blossoming confidence, brought her a profound sense of fulfillment, a realization that her own journey had paved the way for others to follow.

The fear that had once held her captive had not simply vanished; it had been transmuted. It had been transformed into a deep wellspring of strength, a quiet resilience that allowed her to embrace vulnerability and to love fiercely, without reservation. She understood that true contentment wasn't the absence of challenges, but the inner capacity to navigate them with grace and courage. Her partnership with Eli was the anchor that provided this stability, but her individual growth was the sail that propelled her forward, allowing her to explore the vast expanse of her own potential. She was no longer defined by what she feared, but by what she embraced – a life of purpose, of love, and of continuous, joyous becoming. The quiet joy of accomplishment was not a destination, but a continuous journey, and Mara, with Eli by her side and Havenridge as her home, was embracing every step of it.

Eli's steadfast devotion was not a sudden blaze, but a deep, enduring ember that warmed the very foundations of Havenridge and, more importantly, Mara's heart. He watched with a quiet pride that swelled his chest, a feeling that had grown steadily since their shared dream began to take root and blossom. The community, once a collection of scattered intentions, was now a thriving entity, a testament to the collective will and the countless hours of sweat and dedication that had been poured into its creation. He saw the sturdy new homes, the bustling marketplace, the children's laughter echoing from the newly built schoolhouse – each a tangible piece of the vision he and Mara had painstakingly nurtured. And at the center of it all, a beacon of unwavering strength and quiet capability, was Mara.

His satisfaction was intrinsically linked to hers. When Mara's face lit up with the accomplishment of a new herbal formulation, or the successful planting of a rare medicinal herb in their community garden, Eli felt a profound sense of fulfillment. Her triumphs were his triumphs, her contentment a reflection of his own. He found a deep resonance in their shared endeavors, a mirroring of purpose that amplified the joy in each small victory. He recalled the early days, the uncertainty that had tinged even their most optimistic plans. Now, looking around at the stable, prosperous Havenridge, he knew they had built something lasting, something that would stand as a testament to their shared belief in a different way of life. This wasn't just about survival; it was about flourishing, about creating a sanctuary where lives could be lived with intention, with kindness, and with a deep connection to the land and to each other.

Mara's own journey of self-discovery had, in turn, illuminated his path. He had always been a man of action, of building and providing, but Mara had shown him the profound beauty in cultivating something more intangible: a sense of belonging, a shared purpose, and the quiet strength that came from vulnerability. He saw how her fear of losing herself in their partnership had, paradoxically, led her to discover an even richer, more vibrant version of herself. This evolution, this blossoming of her spirit, was a source of constant wonder and deep love for him. He found himself inspired by her courage, her unwavering dedication to her craft, and her innate ability to bring comfort and healing to others. Her apothecary was more than a business; it was a haven, a place where people came not just for remedies, but for solace, and Mara was the heart of it all.

He often found himself simply observing her, a silent sentinel of his affection. He'd watch her tending to her herb garden, her fingers moving with an practiced grace as she coaxed life from the soil, or listen to her explain the intricate properties of a rare plant to a curious newcomer. In these moments, he felt an overwhelming gratitude for the life they had built, a life rich in shared purpose and quiet devotion. His commitment to her, to their life together, was not a burden, but a profound privilege. He would readily take on any task, no matter how mundane, if it meant contributing to the stability and happiness of their home. Whether it was reinforcing the barn after a storm, spending long hours meticulously planning the expansion of their water catchment system, or simply ensuring their home was always a warm and welcoming refuge, his actions were always guided by this unwavering devotion.

His own work, too, had found a new depth of meaning within the context of Havenridge. As he continued to refine his woodworking skills, he found immense satisfaction in creating pieces that were not just functional but imbued with a sense of place and purpose. He built sturdy furniture that would serve generations, crafted intricate carvings that adorned their community buildings, and fashioned tools that made the lives of his neighbors just a little bit easier. Each piece was a silent promise, a physical manifestation of his commitment to the community they had poured their lives into. He found a particular joy in collaborating with Mara on projects, their different skill sets weaving together seamlessly. When he helped her build sturdy shelves for her expanding collection of botanical texts or designed a more efficient drying rack for her harvested herbs, their shared work became a tangible representation of their partnership.

Eli understood that true accomplishment wasn't just about grand gestures or public recognition; it was about the quiet, consistent effort that built a life of substance. It was in the shared meals, the comfortable silences, the unspoken understanding that passed between them. It was in the knowledge that they were building something meaningful, not just for themselves, but for the future. He found a deep contentment in knowing that his love for Mara was a steady, unwavering force, a constant in their ever-evolving lives.

He saw their shared vision not as a destination, but as a continuous journey, and he was content to walk that path with her, his hand in hers, his heart full of quiet joy. He would often reflect on how their initial hopes for a simpler life had blossomed into something so much richer, so much more profound. It was a testament to their resilience, their adaptability, and the enduring power of their love. The quiet hum of accomplishment resonated not just in Mara's world, but deeply and resonatingly within his own. He was a builder, yes, but he was also a nurturer, a protector, and a partner in the truest sense of the word, and that was a foundation upon which he could build anything.

The tapestry of Havenridge, vibrant and rich with the colors of a life deliberately woven, was not a gift of chance, but a testament to the enduring spirit of choice. Mara and Eli, looking out over the thriving community, understood this deeply. Their quiet joy wasn't a passive inheritance, but a hard-won prize, meticulously cultivated through countless decisions, both grand and minute, that reaffirmed their commitment to each other and to the vision they had dared to dream.

The stability that now permeated their lives, the palpable sense of belonging that drew newcomers in and held their own residents steadfast, was not an accidental byproduct of their efforts, but the direct consequence of a conscious, unwavering dedication to building something meaningful. They had chosen, from the very outset, to imbue their lives and their endeavor with a profound intentionality, and the results were now a source of deep, resonant satisfaction.

This wasn't simply about the physical structures that housed their lives – the sturdy homes, the functional workshops, the welcoming communal spaces. It extended far beyond the tangible, permeating the very fabric of their relationships, the way they interacted, the way they supported one another. Eli often reflected on the early days, on the sheer audacity of their undertaking. They had set out to create a haven, a place where lives could be lived with purpose and connection, and in doing so, they had also, by necessity, forged a new path for their own relationship.

Every challenge overcome, every setback weathered, had been met with a deliberate choice to lean into their partnership, to communicate, to trust, and to reaffirm their shared commitment. This active engagement with their bond, this constant tending to the flame of their love, was what had prevented it from flickering out under the pressures of building a community from the ground up.

Mara, in her own quiet way, was acutely aware of this too. She saw how their individual pursuits, her dedication to healing and his to crafting, were not separate entities but threads woven together to strengthen the overall design of their lives. When she meticulously documented the properties of a new herb, or perfected a complex tincture, it was a choice to dedicate herself to her passion, a passion that Eli had always encouraged and supported. And when Eli spent hours sketching out the plans for a new irrigation system or painstakingly carved the intricate details onto the doors of the community hall, he was making a choice to invest his skills, his time, and his energy into the collective good, a good that directly benefited their shared life. These weren't acts of obligation, but expressions of a deeper commitment, a conscious decision to contribute to the world they were building together.

The concept of "choice" wasn't merely an abstract notion for them; it was a lived reality, an ongoing practice. It was in the decision to extend a hand of friendship to a newcomer, even when resources were stretched thin. It was in the choice to listen patiently to a neighbor's concerns, even after a long day of labor. It was in the deliberate act of carving out time for each other amidst the demanding rhythm of community life, a quiet dinner by candlelight, a shared walk under the stars, simply to reconnect and remind themselves of the personal foundation upon which their collective endeavors rested. These moments, often overlooked in the grand narrative of building a community, were, in fact, the very mortar that held everything together. They were the affirmations of a love that refused to be complacent, a love that understood its own strength lay in its continuous, active engagement.

Mara remembered the initial anxieties that had sometimes gnawed at her – the fear of being subsumed by Eli's vision, or of their shared dreams diverging. But with each passing season, she had learned that true partnership wasn't about the surrender of individuality, but about the conscious cultivation of shared space. Eli had never once tried to mold her into something she wasn't; instead, he had created an environment where she could blossom, where her unique talents were not just accepted, but celebrated. This, too, was a choice. It was Eli's choice to see her not as an extension of himself, but as a vital, independent force whose contributions were essential to their mutual flourishing. And it was Mara's choice to embrace that space, to trust his support, and to invest her own spirit into their shared enterprise.

The quiet joy they experienced was, therefore, a direct reflection of this ongoing commitment to conscious choice. It wasn't a fleeting happiness that evaporated with the first hint of difficulty. Instead, it was a deep, abiding contentment, born from the knowledge that they were actively shaping their lives, not merely reacting to them. They had chosen to prioritize kindness over quick judgment, collaboration over competition, and long-term vision over immediate gratification. These weren't always the easiest choices, but they were the ones that had led them to the profound sense of accomplishment they now felt. Their relationship, like Havenridge itself, was a living, breathing entity, sustained by the consistent, deliberate acts of love, respect, and mutual dedication. It was a constant reaffirmation of their belief in the power of intention, and the profound beauty of a life built, choice by deliberate choice, together.

Eli's perspective on this was particularly insightful. He saw himself as a craftsman, and in many ways, his approach to building Havenridge mirrored his approach to his woodworking. Each beam was placed with care, each joint secured with precision, not because it was easy, but because it was necessary for the integrity of the structure. He applied this same philosophy to his relationship with Mara and to the community itself. He understood that true strength wasn't found in brute force or hasty construction, but in meticulous attention to detail and a consistent adherence to sound principles. This meant making the deliberate choice to communicate openly, even when it was difficult, to offer support without being asked, and to celebrate the small victories that often went unnoticed in the grander scheme of things. He recognized that the foundation of their happiness, much like the foundation of their homes, was built not on a single grand gesture, but on a multitude of small, consistent efforts.

He would often sit by the hearth in the evenings, watching Mara as she prepared her remedies or read from one of her many botanical texts. In those quiet moments, a profound sense of peace would settle over him. It wasn't the peace of idleness, but the deeply satisfying peace of knowing that the life they shared was a testament to their combined will. He saw their journey not as a destination, but as an ongoing process of creation. They had chosen to build a life that was rich in meaning, a life that extended beyond their own immediate needs and aspirations. This had required them to make choices that sometimes went against the grain of conventional wisdom, to forgo immediate comforts for the sake of future stability, and to invest their energy in nurturing relationships rather than simply accumulating possessions.

The laughter of children playing in the newly established schoolyard was a particularly potent reminder of the choices they had made. They had chosen to create a place where families could thrive, where the next generation would have the opportunity to grow up with a strong sense of community and a deep connection to the land. This required a commitment to education, to providing resources, and to fostering an environment where learning was not just an academic pursuit, but a way of life. Mara's dedication to teaching the younger ones about the natural world, her patient explanations of plant cycles and the interconnectedness of all living things, was a direct manifestation of this choice. Eli's involvement in building and maintaining the schoolhouse, ensuring it was a safe and welcoming space, was another tangible expression of their shared vision.

Their commitment to sustainability was another area where their choices were paramount. They had consciously decided to live in harmony with the environment, to minimize their impact, and to embrace practices that would ensure the long-term health of their land. This meant making difficult choices about resource allocation, about embracing new technologies that aligned with their values, and about educating themselves and others on the principles of ecological stewardship. Mara's herbalism was intrinsically linked to this; her deep understanding of the plants and their medicinal properties was not just a skill, but a philosophy, a belief in the inherent wisdom of the natural world. Eli's practical approach, in designing efficient water collection systems and building structures that were both durable and energy-conscious, complemented her efforts perfectly.

The very essence of their happiness was intertwined with this concept of active participation. They had chosen not to be passive observers of their own lives, but active participants, shaping their destiny with intention and purpose. This meant embracing challenges as opportunities for growth, learning from mistakes, and consistently striving to be better, both as individuals and as a couple. The "quiet joy" they experienced was, in essence, the earned peace that came from knowing they had faced life's complexities with courage and conviction, always choosing the path that led them closer to their shared ideals. It was a testament to the power of love as an action, a verb, a constant, unfolding narrative of commitment and dedication. Their story was a living embodiment of the truth that a fulfilling life is not found, but built, through the enduring spirit of choice.

Chapter Twelve
A Legacy of Love, Rooted and Resilient

Havenridge, a testament to Eli and Mara's unwavering vision, pulsed with a life all its own. It was more than just a collection of homes and workshops; it was a living, breathing entity, a thriving ecosystem where every individual played a vital role. The principles they had painstakingly laid down in those formative years – a deep reverence for the land, a commitment to mutual support, and an unwavering belief in the power of collective effort – had not only endured but had blossomed into something truly extraordinary. The air itself seemed to hum with a quiet energy, a palpable sense of purpose that drew people in and fostered a profound sense of belonging.

The land, once a wild and untamed expanse, was now a meticulously managed tapestry of vibrant farms, flourishing orchards, and carefully preserved woodlands. The lessons Mara had so diligently imparted about the delicate balance of nature, about understanding the rhythms of the earth and working in harmony with them, had taken root in the hearts and minds of every Havenridge resident.

This wasn't merely about survival; it was about flourishing. Generations of careful stewardship had ensured that the soil remained rich, the water pure, and the biodiversity abundant. From the smallest herb garden to the sprawling communal fields, every patch of earth was tended with a profound respect, a recognition that they were not masters of the land, but its caretakers, entrusted with its well-being for those who would come after. The practice of crop rotation, the mindful use of natural fertilizers, and the dedication to preserving native flora were not just agricultural techniques; they were deeply ingrained cultural values, passed down from the elders to the eager young apprentices.

Eli's influence, too, was etched into the very architecture and infrastructure of Havenridge. His understanding of sustainable building, his knack for creating systems that worked in concert with nature, had shaped the community's physical form. The passive solar designs of the homes, the ingenious water catchment systems that ensured a steady supply even in drier seasons, and the network of well-maintained paths and bridges that facilitated easy movement throughout the settlement all spoke of his foresight and practical wisdom.

He had always believed that true progress lay not in dominating the environment, but in understanding and adapting to its strengths, and Havenridge was a living embodiment of that philosophy. Even the materials used in construction were sourced responsibly, with an emphasis on local timber, quarried stone, and reclaimed resources, minimizing their environmental footprint and further embedding the community's identity within its natural surroundings. The workshops, buzzing with activity, were not only centers of production but also places of innovation, where traditional crafts were honed and new techniques explored, all with an eye towards sustainability and efficiency.

Mara and Eli, though no longer at the forefront of the daily grind, remained the quiet anchors of this flourishing community. Their presence, a blend of gentle wisdom and steadfast encouragement, was a constant source of strength. They had deliberately cultivated a leadership model that was both inclusive and effective, ensuring that the transition of responsibility to the next generation was seamless and deeply rooted.

Young leaders, mentored by the seasoned residents, had emerged with fresh perspectives and a keen understanding of the founding principles, ready to guide Havenridge into its future. There were formal councils for addressing larger community matters, but just as importantly, there were informal networks of guidance and mentorship, where the accumulated wisdom of years was shared freely and generously. Eli, with his calm demeanor and logical approach, often found himself advising on larger infrastructure projects, while Mara's intuitive understanding of community dynamics and her deep empathy made her a sought-after confidante for personal challenges.

The innovation that characterized Havenridge was a delicate dance between honoring tradition and embracing the future. While the core values remained steadfast, the community was not afraid to adapt and evolve. New technologies that aligned with their principles of sustainability and community well-being were explored and, if found beneficial, integrated. There was a vibrant exchange of ideas, a constant flow of learning and adaptation that kept Havenridge dynamic and relevant.

For instance, the introduction of more efficient solar-powered tools in the workshops, or the exploration of advanced natural farming techniques, were met with open minds and rigorous evaluation, ensuring that progress did not come at the expense of their deeply held values. This forward-thinking approach was crucial, recognizing that a truly resilient community was one that could not only withstand change but actively shape it.

The educational systems within Havenridge were a source of particular pride. The children were not only taught the practical skills necessary for community life but were also instilled with a profound understanding of their heritage, their connection to the land, and their responsibilities as citizens of Havenridge. Mara, in her role as a revered elder, often led sessions on botany and natural healing, sharing her encyclopedic knowledge with an infectious passion.

Eli, meanwhile, often spoke to the young ones about the importance of craftsmanship, the satisfaction of building something with your own hands, and the ethical considerations that went into every project. The integration of apprenticeships within the various workshops and farms ensured that practical knowledge was passed down directly, creating a seamless flow of expertise across generations. They believed that education was not just about acquiring knowledge but about cultivating character, fostering a deep sense of interconnectedness, and nurturing a lifelong commitment to the well-being of the community and its environment.

The economic model of Havenridge was another testament to its unique philosophy. It was a system built on cooperation rather than cutthroat competition, on shared prosperity rather than individual accumulation. While individual initiative was encouraged and rewarded, the emphasis was always on how that initiative contributed to the collective good. Bartering, communal resource sharing, and cooperative ventures were common, ensuring that everyone had access to the necessities of life and the opportunities to contribute their talents.

This created a sense of security and stability that was the envy of many outside communities, where economic anxieties often ran rampant. The artisans and craftspeople of Havenridge produced goods of exceptional quality, sought after for their integrity and their connection to the natural world, and these exports not only supported the community's economy but also served as ambassadors for their unique way of life.

The social fabric of Havenridge was woven with threads of deep connection and mutual respect. Celebrations and festivals were not mere social gatherings but opportunities to reaffirm their shared values, to celebrate their successes, and to strengthen the bonds that held them together. The Harvest Festival, a grand affair that marked the culmination of the growing season, was a vibrant display of communal spirit, with shared meals, music, and storytelling.

The Solstice celebrations, held with reverence for the turning of the seasons, offered moments of reflection and gratitude. Even the smaller, more intimate gatherings, like the weekly communal suppers held in rotating households, fostered a sense of belonging and encouraged open communication. Mara and Eli, as the elder figures, were often at the heart of these gatherings, their quiet presence a calming influence, their words of wisdom a gentle guide.

The challenges that Havenridge had faced in its early days had forged an unbreakable resilience within the community. They had learned to weather storms, both literal and metaphorical, by leaning on each other, by trusting in their shared values, and by demonstrating an unwavering commitment to their collective future. This resilience was not about avoiding hardship, but about facing it with courage, adaptability, and a profound sense of unity. They had learned that true strength lay not in the absence of problems, but in the ability to overcome them together. This collective memory of past struggles and triumphs served as a powerful reminder of their shared journey and a potent source of inspiration for future endeavors.

Looking out over the vibrant expanse of Havenridge, Mara and Eli often found themselves lost in a quiet contemplation of the journey they had undertaken. The laughter of children echoing from the schoolhouse, the steady rhythm of hammers from the workshops, the gentle rustle of leaves in the wind-swept orchards – all these sounds and sights were a symphony of their shared dream realized. It was a dream that had begun with a simple belief in the possibility of a different way of life, a life rooted in connection, purpose, and a profound respect for the natural world.

And now, that dream was a thriving reality, a legacy of love, hard-won and deeply cherished, that would continue to inspire and nurture generations to come. They saw not an endpoint, but a continuous unfolding, a testament to the enduring power of intention, dedication, and the unwavering strength of a love that had dared to build a world. The future of Havenridge, illuminated by the principles they had so carefully cultivated, was as bright and promising as the dawn breaking over the rolling hills, a testament to the enduring power of a legacy built on love and resilience. Their quiet satisfaction wasn't a passive observation, but an active appreciation for the life they had consciously created, a life that resonated with purpose and promised a future as rich and fulfilling as the land they tended.

The quiet hum of Havenridge was more than just the symphony of its daily life; it was the steady pulse of Mara and Eli's enduring partnership. Years had softened their youthful fire into a more profound, incandescent glow, a testament to a love that had not merely survived but had thrived, deepening with each shared sunrise and sunset over their beloved valley. Their connection was no longer a passionate wildfire, but a deeply rooted oak, its branches reaching out to shelter and its roots anchoring them both, and by extension, their community, firmly to the earth. This was not a love that demanded constant declarations, but one that was spoken in the quiet language of knowing glances, the comfortable silence shared across a meal, and the instinctive way their hands found each other's.

Mara often watched Eli from their porch, the late afternoon sun casting a warm benediction on his silver-streaked hair as he worked in his woodworking shed. The familiar scent of sawdust and aged timber was as comforting to her as the scent of rain on dry earth. He moved with a grace that belied his years, his hands, once capable of so much, now etched with the stories of countless projects, each one a reflection of his dedication and skill.

She saw not just the man, but the boy who had dared to dream, the young man who had poured his heart and soul into building not just structures, but a way of life. His dedication to sustainability, to creating beauty and utility in equal measure, was a quiet testament to the values they had woven into the very fabric of Havenridge. He still took immense pride in his craft, and watching him, Mara felt a surge of profound gratitude for the life they had built, brick by brick, beam by beam, dream by dream. His quiet focus was a meditation in itself, a reminder of the power of presence, of being fully engaged in the task at hand, a principle he had always championed.

Eli, in turn, would often pause, wiping his brow with the back of his hand, and his gaze would inevitably find Mara. Her presence, even in her stillness, was a vibrant force, a splash of colour against the verdant backdrop of Havenridge. She was the keeper of their collective memory, the gentle guide who reminded them all of the deeper currents that flowed beneath the surface of daily life. He saw the wisdom etched in the lines around her eyes, the unwavering strength in her posture, and he knew, with a certainty that settled deep within his soul, that he was the luckiest man alive. Their journey had been a tapestry woven with threads of challenge and triumph, and through it all, their bond had been the golden thread that held it all together. He remembered their early days, the sheer audacity of their vision, and the countless moments of doubt that had threatened to unravel them. But Mara, with her unwavering faith and her ability to see the possibility in every setback, had always been his anchor.

Their shared life in Havenridge was a masterclass in chosen commitment. They had not stumbled into this partnership; they had consciously chosen it, nurtured it, and continued to choose it every single day. It was a commitment that went beyond romantic love, extending to a deep-seated respect for each other's individuality and a shared vision for their community. They understood that true partnership wasn't about sameness, but about complementing each other, about recognizing and celebrating their differences. Eli's grounded practicality, his methodical approach to problem-solving, was beautifully balanced by Mara's intuitive understanding, her ability to connect with people on an emotional level, and her visionary foresight. They were two halves of a whole, each making the other stronger, more complete.

One crisp autumn evening, as the scent of woodsmoke mingled with the sweet aroma of ripening apples, Mara and Eli sat on their porch swing, a worn wool blanket draped over their laps. The stars were beginning to prick the darkening sky, mirroring the countless small lights that twinkled across Havenridge. Children's laughter, faint but clear, drifted up from the communal gathering space where a storytelling session was underway.

"Remember when we first imagined this?" Mara murmured, her voice soft as she leaned her head against Eli's shoulder. "A place where people could truly belong, where life had meaning beyond the hustle and bustle."

Eli's arm tightened around her. "I remember. It felt like a whisper of a dream then. So fragile, so easily crushed by the weight of the world." He paused, his gaze sweeping across the landscape that had been their life's work. "But you, Mara. You always saw the solidity of it, even when it was just an idea sketched on a napkin. You breathed life into it."

"And you built the foundations, my love," she replied, her hand finding his. "You gave our dream a tangible form. Without your hands, your vision for how things could *be*, it would have remained just that – a dream." She traced the lines on the back of his hand with her fingertip. "Look at them now, Eli. Our children, our grandchildren, and the many others who have found their home here. They are the bloom of that seed we planted."

He squeezed her hand. "And they are resilient, Mara. They have faced their own challenges, their own storms. But they have learned, just as we did, to weather them together." He spoke of the recent drought, how the community had rallied, sharing water resources, adapting their planting schedules, and innovating with new water-saving techniques. He spoke of young Liam, who had stepped up to lead the irrigation committee with a maturity that had surprised and impressed them all. Liam, who had learned so much from Eli's early lessons in hydrology and sustainable water management.

"That's the legacy, isn't it?" Mara said, her voice filled with quiet pride. "Not just the land, or the buildings, but the spirit of it all. The understanding that we are all connected, that the well-being of one is the well-being of all." She thought of the recent dispute over resource allocation between the orchard keepers and the grain farmers. It had been a tense few weeks, but the mediation council, comprised of representatives from both groups and guided by the wisdom of elder members like Mara and Eli, had found a solution that honored everyone's needs. It was a testament to the established processes and the ingrained culture of compromise and mutual respect.

"It's the partnerships, Mara," Eli said, his voice resonating with conviction. "The countless small partnerships that happen every day. The way Elara and Ben work together on the apiary, the way the weavers and the dyers collaborate on new textile designs, the way the healers share their knowledge with the apprentices." He smiled, a genuine, heartfelt smile that lit up his face. "And of course," he added, his eyes twinkling as he met hers, "our partnership. The one that started it all."

Mara's heart swelled. Their partnership was a living testament to the power of conscious choice, to the beauty of a love that deepened and evolved. It wasn't a passive state; it was an active, ongoing process of nurturing, of choosing to see the best in each other, of offering unwavering support. They had learned to navigate the inevitable rough patches, not by ignoring them, but by facing them with open communication and a shared commitment to their union. They had learned to forgive, to adapt, and to grow, individually and together.

Their leadership style, too, had become a natural extension of their partnership. They had moved from hands-on management to a more advisory role, guiding and inspiring rather than dictating. They were the quiet anchors, the steady presence that reminded everyone of the core values that Havenridge was built upon. When new challenges arose, when the community faced decisions that required deep consideration, it was often Mara and Eli who were sought out for their wisdom. They would listen intently, offer their perspectives, and then step back, allowing the community's own leaders, whom they had so carefully mentored, to make the final decisions. This was the true measure of their success: the creation of a community that could thrive and govern itself, a living organism that had absorbed their principles and was now pulsing with its own vibrant life.

Eli often recalled a conversation he'd had with young Anya, one of the aspiring architects. She had come to him with a complex design for a new community hall, one that incorporated innovative passive heating systems. He had seen in her eyes the same spark of vision he'd once had, the same drive to create something enduring and beautiful. He had spent hours with her, not telling her what to do, but asking questions, prompting her to consider different approaches, to think about the long-term impact of her design on the community and the environment. He saw her grow in confidence with each discussion, her design evolving from a clever concept to a truly integrated, sustainable structure. It was moments like these that filled him with a profound sense of fulfillment.

Mara, too, found joy in mentoring. She had been guiding a group of younger herbalists, sharing her extensive knowledge of medicinal plants and their properties. She watched with delight as they discovered new remedies, as they developed a deeper understanding of the delicate balance of the ecosystem and the interconnectedness of all living things. She remembered how she had once been the eager student, absorbing every word from her own elders, and now, she was the one passing on that legacy, ensuring that the knowledge would not be lost. She saw in their bright, eager faces the continuation of their vision, the promise of a future where the wisdom of the past would continue to inform and enrich the present.

Their days were now filled with a gentler rhythm, a more reflective pace. They still rose with the sun, but their mornings were often spent in quiet contemplation, in reading, or in gentle walks through the orchards, observing the changing seasons. Their evenings were often dedicated to the community, attending gatherings, sharing meals, or simply being present. They had cultivated a life of balance, a testament to their understanding that true fulfillment lay not in constant striving, but in mindful appreciation, in the cultivation of inner peace, and in the deep, unwavering connection they shared.

One evening, during the Harvest Festival, as the community gathered for the grand feast, Mara and Eli stood hand-in-hand, watching the vibrant scene unfold. The air was alive with music, laughter, and the aroma of freshly baked bread and roasted vegetables. Children, faces smeared with berry juice, chased each other around the bonfire, their joy infectious. Couples danced, their movements reflecting the easy grace that had become characteristic of Havenridge.

"It's all here, isn't it?" Mara whispered, her eyes shining with unshed tears. "Everything we ever hoped for."

Eli turned to her, his gaze filled with an adoration that had not dimmed in all their years together. "It is. And it's more beautiful than we could have ever imagined. Because it's not just ours, Mara. It's theirs. It's a living thing, born of our love, but sustained by the love of everyone here."

He raised his hand, not to draw attention, but in a silent gesture that encompassed the entire valley. It was a gesture of profound gratitude, of deep contentment, and of an enduring love that had not only built a home, but had sown the seeds for a perpetual legacy of connection, resilience, and boundless affection. They were partners, not just in life, but in perpetuity, their love a quiet, steady beacon guiding Havenridge toward an ever-brighter future. The shared glances they exchanged spoke volumes of a lifetime of shared dreams, of challenges overcome, and of a love that had found its truest expression in the vibrant, thriving community they had so lovingly brought into being. It was a love that had become a part of the very soil, the very air, the very soul of Havenridge, a testament to the enduring power of two hearts beating as one, dedicated to a shared vision of a life lived with purpose, integrity, and unwavering devotion.

Hope, a fragile seedling in the early days of Havenridge, had blossomed into a majestic, towering tree, its roots anchoring the community, its branches reaching towards an ever-brightening future. Mara often felt it, a palpable presence in the air, a quiet hum that resonated with the collective heartbeats of the valley. It was in the laughter of children chasing fireflies on a summer evening, in the earnest discussions at the community council meetings, in the shared meals that punctuated their days. This wasn't a forced optimism, a desperate clinging to positivity, but a deep-seated certainty, hard-won and deeply cherished, that life, in its truest form, was good.

Eli saw it too, especially when he watched the younger generation navigate their own burgeoning relationships. He saw echoes of their own journey in their tentative steps, their shared anxieties, and their unwavering commitment to each other. There was young Anya, who had found her voice and her stride as an architect, designing not just buildings, but spaces that nurtured connection and sustainability. He remembered her youthful trepidation, the way she had sought his counsel, her designs sometimes faltering under the weight of self-doubt.

But Mara, with her gentle encouragement and her belief in Anya's innate talent, had helped her unfurl. Now, Anya's designs were a testament to a future built on thoughtful integration, where human needs and ecological harmony danced in perfect step. Eli saw in her a reflection of the resilience they had strived to instill, the quiet strength that allowed dreams to take root and flourish.

"She reminds me of us, doesn't she?" Eli said to Mara one evening, as they watched Anya present her latest proposal for the new aquaponics farm. Her voice, once soft and hesitant, now carried a clear, confident tone, her ideas articulated with passion and precision. "That spark. That unwavering belief that something better is possible."

Mara smiled, her gaze fixed on Anya. "She has a beautiful spirit, Eli. And she carries the lessons of our valley within her. The understanding that true progress isn't about conquering nature, but about working with it, in partnership." She recalled how Anya had come to her, distressed about a seemingly insurmountable challenge in her design – a delicate balance of water flow and nutrient distribution. Mara had listened, her mind sifting through years of experience with the valley's natural systems, and then, instead of offering a solution, she had asked Anya to simply sit with her by the river, to observe its flow, its rhythms, its inherent wisdom. It was in that shared quietude, amidst the murmurs of the water, that Anya had found her breakthrough, a solution born not of engineering alone, but of a deeper attunement to the natural world.

This was the embodiment of hope, Mara mused. It wasn't just in grand gestures or sweeping pronouncements, but in these countless small moments of learning, of growth, of shared understanding. It was in the quiet confidence of Liam, who had spearheaded the water conservation efforts during the drought, his youthful leadership a beacon of practical innovation and community spirit. He had approached Eli, not with demands, but with thoughtful proposals, backed by meticulous research and a genuine desire to serve the collective good. Eli had seen in Liam not just a follower, but a natural leader, someone who had absorbed the principles of sustainable resource management and was now applying them with fresh insight and an unyielding sense of responsibility.

"It's the understanding that we are all interconnected," Mara continued, her voice a soft melody against the evening breeze. "That the health of the soil affects the health of the crops, which affects the health of our bodies, which affects the health of our community. It's a web, Eli, and each thread, no matter how fine, is vital." She thought of the storytellers, who continued the tradition of passing down the valley's history and wisdom, weaving new tales that incorporated the triumphs and challenges of the present. Young Leo, in particular, had a gift for making ancient parables resonate with the contemporary lives of the villagers, his interpretations bridging the gap between generations and ensuring that the core values of Havenridge remained vibrant and relevant.

Eli nodded, his hand finding hers. "And that web is strengthened by love, Mara. Not just the romantic love between partners, but the love that binds families, the love that fuels friendships, the love that inspires us to care for our neighbors, for the land, for the future." He remembered the early days, the gnawing fear that had sometimes threatened to paralyze them, the uncertainty that had loomed like a shadow. They had faced whispers of doubt, anxieties about the unknown, and the sheer, overwhelming task of building something from nothing. But through it all, their love, their shared vision, had acted as a compass, guiding them through the fog, their hands always reaching for each other, a silent promise of steadfast support.

This hope wasn't a naive denial of hardship; it was an informed optimism, a profound understanding that even in the face of adversity, love, when rooted in conscious choice and a shared purpose, could illuminate the path forward. It was the knowledge that the storms would come, that challenges would arise, but that the foundations they had laid, both tangible and intangible, were strong enough to weather any tempest. They had learned that fear, while a natural human emotion, did not have to be the architect of their lives. Instead, they had chosen courage, resilience, and an unwavering faith in each other and in the community they had nurtured.

"Think of Elara and Ben," Mara said, a fond smile gracing her lips. "Their decision to dedicate their lives to the bees, to the vital work of pollination. It wasn't an easy choice. It meant long hours, a deep understanding of nature's delicate balance, and a willingness to embrace the unexpected." She recalled their initial hesitations, the questions they had posed to Mara and Eli about the long-term viability of such a specialized pursuit. But Mara had seen the passion in their eyes, the genuine reverence they held for the intricate lives of the bees, and she had encouraged them, reminding them that every contribution, no matter how seemingly small, was essential to the larger ecosystem of Havenridge. Their success in cultivating not only a thriving apiary but also a vital educational program for the children had become a testament to the power of following one's calling, even when it led down an unconventional path.

"And they are not alone," Eli added. "They have the support of the entire valley. When pests threatened their hives, the entire community rallied. Farmers shared their knowledge of natural pest control, gardeners offered their skills in creating protective plant barriers, and even the children contributed by learning about the importance of beneficial insects. That, Mara, is the embodiment of hope – the collective spirit that says, 'We will not let this endeavor fail. We will support each other.'"

This collective spirit, this interwoven tapestry of mutual reliance and affection, was the very essence of Havenridge's enduring strength. It was a legacy not just of buildings and sustainable practices, but of a deeply ingrained understanding of interdependence. Mara and Eli had planted the seeds, but the community, with their guidance and unwavering support, had tended the garden, ensuring that it continued to grow, to bloom, and to provide sustenance for generations to come.

The fear that had once been a whisper in the wind had been replaced by a resounding chorus of hope, a testament to the enduring power of love, shared purpose, and the conscious choice to build a future not just for themselves, but for all. They had dared to dream of a place where love could thrive, unburdened by the specter of fear, and in Havenridge, that dream had taken flight, a vibrant, resilient testament to the boundless possibilities that unfolded when hearts and hands worked together, guided by an unwavering beacon of hope.

The sun, a gentle painter, cast long, warm strokes across the worn wooden floorboards of their sunroom. Mara traced the grain with a fingertip, a faint smile gracing her lips. It was a simple gesture, an unconscious act of connection with the quiet life they had woven together, thread by patient thread, here in Havenridge. The vibrant hum of the community, once a vibrant symphony of building and overcoming, had softened into a harmonious melody, a reassuring constant in their days. Their 'happily ever after' wasn't a grand, dramatic pronouncement etched in stone, but a gentle, persistent rhythm, found in the ordinary, the understated, the profoundly peaceful.

Eli, engrossed in a well-loved book, a mug of steaming herbal tea warming his hands, offered a soft sigh of contentment. It wasn't the sigh of someone settling, but of someone deeply, fully present. He glanced up, his eyes meeting Mara's across the sun-drenched space, and the unspoken understanding that flowed between them was as palpable as the afternoon light. It was a language built on shared glances, on the comfortable cadence of their breathing, on the knowledge that beneath the surface of their calm existence, a profound and abiding love pulsed steadily.

Their home, a testament to years of shared dreams and diligent work, was more than just a dwelling; it was a sanctuary. The scent of drying herbs mingled with the faint, sweet aroma of Mara's latest baking experiment, creating an olfactory tapestry that spoke of comfort and care. Each object, from the hand-carved wooden bowls on the shelves to the worn, comfortable armchair where Eli often found solace, held a story, a memory of their journey. These were not relics of a past they sought to escape, but anchors, reminders of the resilience that had brought them to this tranquil harbor.

Mara remembered the early days, the whirlwind of activity, the constant need for vigilance and decisive action. There had been a certain exhilaration in that, a potent energy that fueled their efforts. But this quietude, this earned peace, held a different kind of power. It was a deeper, more resonant joy, one that didn't require constant outward validation. It resided within the shared silence, the easy companionship, the simple act of being together.

Eli closed his book, marking his page with a gentle precision. He watched Mara for a moment, her profile etched against the golden light, and a wave of tenderness washed over him. He saw in her the same quiet strength that had guided them through every challenge. It was in the way she still tended her garden with meticulous care, in the thoughtful way she listened to the concerns of others, in the unwavering warmth she extended to everyone who crossed their threshold.

"What are you thinking about?" he asked, his voice a low rumble that didn't disturb the quiet.

Mara turned, her eyes crinkling at the corners. "Just... this," she gestured vaguely around the room. "Us. Havenridge. It's all so... settled. In the best possible way."

He rose and walked over to her, his hand resting lightly on her shoulder. "It is," he agreed, his thumb stroking her arm. "We built something, Mara. Something good."

"We did," she murmured, leaning into his touch. "But it wasn't just us, was it? It was everyone. All the little threads woven together."

He nodded, his gaze drifting to the window, where children's laughter, faint but clear, drifted on the breeze. "And those threads are stronger now than ever. Look at how they've grown. Anya's designs, Liam's initiatives, Elara and Ben's dedication to the bees... They've taken what we started and made it their own, infused it with their own unique vision."

Mara's heart swelled. She recalled Anya's early anxieties, her self-doubt a palpable presence in their shared conversations. Now, Anya's voice, confident and clear, resonated through the community, her architectural innovations breathing new life into Havenridge's landscape. It was a testament to the valley's philosophy – that true progress was born from harmony, not dominance, from integration, not imposition. Eli had always seen the potential in people, a gift he'd honed over years of careful observation and genuine belief. He'd seen Liam's quiet determination, his inherent sense of responsibility, and had encouraged his leadership in water conservation, a crucial effort that had seen Havenridge through lean times.

"It's the continuity, Eli," Mara said softly. "That's what brings me such a deep sense of peace. Knowing that the values we hold dear – community, sustainability, compassion – are not just being preserved, but are actively thriving, evolving. It's not about us holding onto power, or dictating what happens. It's about nurturing a spirit that can carry on long after we are gone."

Eli squeezed her shoulder. "And that spirit is a reflection of the love that underpins it all. The love we share, the love that binds this community. It's the quiet kindnesses, the shared burdens, the spontaneous acts of generosity. It's in Mrs. Gable still leaving fresh-baked bread on her neighbors' doorsteps, even though her own joints ache. It's in young Leo, who spends hours with the elders, not just listening to their stories, but weaving them into new narratives for the younger generations. That's not just preservation; that's vibrant, living history."

Mara smiled, picturing Leo's earnest face, his ability to connect the ancient wisdom of the valley with the immediate realities of their lives. It was a skill that had been honed by Mara's own gentle guidance, her understanding that the past was not a static entity but a dynamic force that could inform and enrich the present. "And the way they all rallied around Elara and Ben when those pests threatened the hives," she added, her voice filled with pride. "That was Havenridge at its best. Not just individual effort, but collective strength. A shared commitment to a vital part of our ecosystem."

Eli's gaze softened as he looked at Mara. Their journey had been marked by moments of profound challenge, by fear that had sometimes felt like an insurmountable wall. But their love, a steadfast beacon, had always guided them through. It was a love that had been tested, refined, and ultimately, made stronger by the very trials it had faced. It wasn't the passionate, fiery love of their youth, but a deeper, more intricate tapestry of shared understanding, unwavering trust, and profound companionship.

"Remember how we used to worry?" he mused, a hint of a smile playing on his lips. "Whether we were doing enough, whether we were strong enough. Whether this dream of ours could truly take root and flourish."

"And look at it now," Mara said, her hand finding his. "It's not perfect, of course. No life ever is. There will always be new challenges, new adjustments to be made. But the foundations are so strong. The sense of belonging, the shared purpose... it's a quiet joy, isn't it? A deep, abiding contentment that settles in your bones."

He brought her hand to his lips, pressing a tender kiss to her knuckles. "It's more than contentment, Mara. It's fulfillment. It's knowing that we poured our hearts and souls into this place, and that it's responded in kind. It's seeing the ripple effect of every decision, every act of kindness, every moment of shared vulnerability." He thought of their own home, filled with the gentle echoes of their life together, the quiet rhythm of their days a testament to years of shared experiences. The comfort wasn't just in the physical surroundings, but in the intangible atmosphere of peace and security they had cultivated.

"It's the everyday miracles," Mara agreed, her eyes shining. "The way the sun rises each morning, promising a new beginning. The way the rain nourishes the earth, ensuring life's continuation. The way a simple conversation can mend a rift, or spark a new idea. These are the things that sustain us, Eli. These are the quiet celebrations of a life well-lived."

He pulled her gently into his embrace, resting his chin on the top of her head. The scent of her hair, familiar and comforting, filled his senses. "And it's knowing that we're not alone in appreciating them," he murmured. "That this whole valley shares in that appreciation. We've created a place where joy isn't a fleeting emotion, but a sustained state of being. A horizon that is always quietly, joyfully bright."

Mara sighed, a sound of pure peace. She nestled closer, her hand resting on his chest, feeling the steady beat of his heart beneath her palm. It was a rhythm that had echoed her own for so many years, a silent testament to their enduring connection. The grand adventures of their past had shaped them, had forged them into the people they had become, but it was in these quiet moments, in the gentle unfolding of their shared life, that their truest, most profound happiness resided.

It was a joy rooted in gratitude, in acceptance, and in the unwavering certainty that they had found their home, not just in a place, but in each other. The legacy they had built was not just in the tangible structures of Havenridge, but in the intangible spirit that permeated every corner of the valley, a spirit of resilience, of interconnectedness, and most importantly, of enduring, quietly joyful love.

The setting sun painted the sky in hues of apricot and rose, a fitting celestial flourish to a day that had been as rich and layered as the lives Mara and Eli had meticulously crafted. They stood on their porch, hand in hand, overlooking the valley that had become their heart and soul. The air, still warm from the afternoon's embrace, carried the faint scent of pine and the distant murmur of evening activity – children playing their final games, the lowing of cattle settling down for the night, the gentle hum of conversations drifting from open windows. It was a symphony of a life lived fully, of a community that had bloomed from the seeds of their shared vision.

Mara squeezed Eli's hand, her gaze sweeping across the familiar landscape. The sturdy, sun-weathered houses, the thriving orchards, the carefully tended fields, and the winding paths that connected them all – each element was a testament to years of collective effort, of countless individual contributions that had woven together to form the intricate tapestry of Havenridge. It wasn't just a collection of buildings and land; it was a living, breathing entity, a testament to what could be achieved when people committed themselves not just to a place, but to each other.

"It's... everything," Mara murmured, the word catching in her throat, laden with the weight of years and the depth of her gratitude. "More than we ever dreamed."

Eli's arm tightened around her waist, drawing her closer. He understood the unspoken emotion that surged through her, the quiet awe that settled upon them as they witnessed the fruition of their labor. He'd seen the initial skepticism, the whispers of doubt, the sheer enormity of the task they had set for themselves all those years ago. And he'd seen, with unwavering clarity, the slow, persistent blossoming of something truly extraordinary.

"It's the commitment, Mara," Eli said, his voice a low, resonant hum that vibrated through her. "That's what's endured. Not just our commitment, but theirs. The willingness to invest, to nurture, to believe in something bigger than themselves."

He gestured towards the community center, a beacon of warm light now as twilight deepened. It was a place that had witnessed countless celebrations, debates, and moments of quiet solace. It stood as a physical manifestation of their shared purpose, a hub where ideas were exchanged, where friendships were forged, and where the spirit of Havenridge was continually rekindled. Anya, their spirited granddaughter, now led the design and ongoing development of the community's shared spaces, her innovative vision seamlessly blending with the established aesthetic, ensuring that Havenridge remained both timeless and relevant. She spoke with such passion about sustainable architecture and community integration, lessons she had absorbed not just from books, but from observing the very foundations Mara and Eli had laid.

"Remember Liam's efforts with the water management system?" Eli continued, a fond smile playing on his lips. "How he meticulously mapped out every stream, every reservoir, ensuring our water security even through the driest summers? That wasn't just a job; it was a sacred trust. He understood the delicate balance, the responsibility we all shared for this precious resource. And now, young Leo is shadowing him, absorbing every detail, ready to carry that torch forward. It's that passing of knowledge, that unwavering dedication to continuity, that truly makes this legacy."

Mara nodded, picturing Leo, his eyes bright with curiosity, his hands already calloused from tending the community gardens. He was a testament to the generational investment they had fostered, a young soul already deeply connected to the valley's rhythms and needs. The spirit of Ubuntu, the African philosophy of interconnectedness, which had been a guiding principle for them, had truly taken root and blossomed here. It was evident in the way people looked out for one another, in the shared meals, in the collective effort to support anyone facing hardship.

"And Elara and Ben and their bees," Mara added, her heart swelling with pride. "When that blight threatened their hives, the entire community mobilized. People from all walks of life, dropping everything to help them rebuild, to find solutions. It wasn't just about saving the bees; it was about safeguarding a vital part of our ecosystem, about preserving the delicate web of life that sustains us all. That instinct to protect, to support, to act as one – that's the enduring echo of our commitment."

Eli's gaze met hers, a deep, quiet understanding passing between them. Their love, once a fierce, all-consuming flame, had evolved into a steady, radiant warmth, a constant source of strength and comfort. It was a love that had weathered storms, that had been tested by fire, and had emerged, not unscathed, but profoundly enriched. It was in the shared silences, the knowing glances, the comfortable companionship that had become the bedrock of their lives.

"It's the choices we made, isn't it?" Eli mused. "The conscious decision, again and again, to choose permanence over fleeting satisfaction. To build, not just for ourselves, but for the generations that would follow. It wasn't always easy. There were times when compromise felt like surrender, when the allure of a simpler, less demanding path was tempting."

Mara reached up, her fingers tracing the lines etched around his eyes, lines that spoke of laughter, worry, and a lifetime of shared experiences. "But we knew, didn't we? Deep down, we knew that this was worth fighting for. That a life built on intention, on shared values, on genuine connection, would ultimately be the most fulfilling. And look at what we've created. It's not just a beautiful place; it's a way of life. A conscious cultivation of happiness, not as a destination, but as a continuous journey."

He leaned his forehead against hers, the familiar scent of her hair a comforting balm. "It's in the everyday miracles, too, Mara," he whispered. "The way Mrs. Gable still leaves her legendary apple pies on the doorsteps of anyone feeling under the weather. The way young families are now bringing their own children to the valley, eager to share this legacy. It's in the quiet determination of the farmers to preserve our traditional methods while embracing innovation. It's in the way every individual's contribution, no matter how small it may seem, is recognized and valued."

The valley below was now bathed in the soft glow of a thousand lights, each one a tiny testament to a life lived with purpose. It was a panorama of interconnectedness, of a community that had learned to thrive through shared effort and unwavering support. Their story, intertwined with the very fabric of Havenridge, was no longer just their own. It was a narrative that had been absorbed, embraced, and carried forward by every soul who had found a home within its embrace.

"We gave them a foundation," Mara said, her voice filled with a quiet satisfaction. "A blueprint for a life lived with meaning. But they are the ones who have breathed true life into it, who have made it their own, in ways we could never have imagined."

Eli looked out at the stars beginning to prick the darkening sky, each one a distant promise. "And that's the truest measure of success, isn't it? Not in the monuments we build, or the accolades we receive, but in the enduring spirit we inspire. The knowledge that the love, the resilience, the commitment we poured into this place will continue to echo, long after we are gone. It's a legacy of belonging, of purpose, and of a profound, quiet joy that will forever be woven into the heart of Havenridge."

He turned her to face him fully, his eyes reflecting the starlight, and Mara saw in their depths the same unwavering love that had guided them through every step of their journey. It was a love that had built a home, nurtured a community, and created a legacy that would continue to shine, a gentle, enduring beacon for generations to come. The peace that settled over them wasn't just a fleeting moment; it was the quiet hum of a life well-lived, a testament to the power of commitment, and the enduring echo of a love that had chosen permanence, and in doing so, had created something truly eternal.

GLOSSARY

Ubuntu: An African philosophical concept emphasizing interconnectedness, humanity, and the belief that one's existence is tied to the existence of others.

Havenridge: The name of the community founded by Mara and Eli, a place built on shared values, sustainability, and strong community bonds.

Community Center: A central hub in Havenridge, serving as a gathering place for events, discussions, and the fostering of community spirit.

Sustainable Architecture: Design and construction practices that minimize environmental impact and promote long-term ecological balance.

ACKNOWLEDGEMENTS

The development and philosophy of Havenridge draw inspiration from various sources, including:

- The concept of Ubuntu as articulated by Desmond Tutu and other African scholars.

- Principles of sustainable community development and permaculture design.

- Works on intentional communities and their impact on societal well-being.

- Studies on intergenerational knowledge transfer and legacy building.

9 781971 356464